Mary Higgins Clark

✳ AND ✳

Carol Higgins Clark

He Sees You
When
You're Sleeping

SCRIBNER / SIMON & SCHUSTER

New York   London   Toronto   Sydney   Singapore

SCRIBNER / SIMON & SCHUSTER
1230 Avenue of the Americas
New York, NY 10020

This book is a work of fiction. Names, characters,
places, and incidents either are products of the
author's imagination or are used fictitiously. Any
resemblance to actual events or locales or persons,
living or dead, is entirely coincidental.

Copyright © 2001 by Mary Higgins Clark and Carol Higgins Clark
All rights reserved,
including the right of reproduction
in whole or in part in any form.

SCRIBNER and design are trademarks of Macmillan Library Reference USA, Inc.
used under license by Simon & Schuster, the publisher of this work.

For information about special discounts for bulk purchases,
please contact Simon & Schuster Special Sales:
1-800-456-6798 or business@simonandschuster.com

Designed by Kyoko Watanabe
Set in Baskerville

Manufactured in the United States of America

1   3   5   7   9   10   8   6   4   2

Library of Congress Cataloging-in-Publication Data is available.

ISBN 0-7432-3005-1

Acknowledgments

It is with gratitude we acknowledge:

Our editors, Michael Korda, Chuck Adams, and Roz Lippel.

Our publicist, Lisl Cade.

Our agents, Gene Winick, Sam Pinkus, and Nick Ellison.

Our copyeditors, Associate Director of Copyediting Gypsy da Silva and copy editor Carol Catt.

Our home backup support, John Conheeney, Irene Clark, Agnes Newton, and Nadine Petry.

And, of course you, our readers.

Blessings one and all.

We dedicate this book to the victims of the September 11, 2001, tragedy,
to the families and friends who loved them,
and to the rescuers who risked their own lives to help them.

He Sees You

When

You're Sleeping

*T*here's nothing worse than listening to the sounds of preparations for a great party, knowing that you're not invited. It's even worse when the party is located in heaven, Sterling Brooks thought to himself. He had been detained in the celestial waiting room, located right outside the heavenly gates, for forty-six years by earthly count. Now he could hear the heavenly choir doing a run-through of the songs that would commence the upcoming Christmas Eve celebration.

"Hark, the herald angels sing . . . "

Sterling sighed. He'd always loved that song. He shifted in his seat and looked around. Rows of pews were filled with people who were waiting to be called before the Heavenly Council. People who had to answer for certain things they'd done—or not done—in life, before they received admission to heaven.

Sterling had been there longer than anyone. He felt like the kid whose mother forget to pick him up from school. He usually was able to keep up a cheerful front, but lately he'd been feeling more and more forlorn. From his seat by the window, he had watched over the years as so many people he had known on earth whizzed past, on a nonstop trip to heaven. Occasionally he was shocked and a little irritated when some of them were not made to do time in the celestial waiting room. Even the guy who had cheated on his income tax and lied about his golf score soared blissfully over the bridge that separated the celestial waiting room from the heavenly gates.

But it had been the sight of Annie that tore his heart. A couple of weeks ago, the woman he'd loved but hadn't married, the woman he'd kept dangling had wafted past, looking as pretty and young as the first day they'd met. He ran to the information desk and inquired about Annie Mansfield, the soul who had just flown by the observation window. The angel checked his computer, then raised his eyebrows. "She died a few minutes ago, on her eighty-seventh birthday. While blowing out the candles, she had a dizzy spell. What an exemplary life she led. Generous. Giving. Caring. Loving."

"Did she ever marry?" Sterling asked.

The angel pressed some keys and moved the cursor, much like a ticket agent at the airport, trying to find confirmation of a reservation. He frowned. "She was engaged for a long time to some jerk who strung her along, then was heartbroken when he died unexpectedly. He was beaned in the head by a golfball." The angel pressed the cursor again and looked up at Sterling. "Oh, sorry. That's you."

Sterling slunk back to his seat. Since then he'd done a lot of thinking. He admitted to himself that he had sailed through his fifty-one years on earth, never taking on any responsibility and always managing to stay away from the unpleasant and the worrisome. I adopted Scarlett O'Hara's motto, "I'll think about it tomorrow," he acknowledged to himself.

The only time Sterling remembered experiencing prolonged anxiety was when he was on the waiting list for Brown University. All his friends from prep school had received thick envelopes from the colleges of their choice, welcoming them into the fold and strongly encouraging them to send in their checks immediately. It was only a few days before school started that he got the call from an official in the admissions office at Brown confirming that there was room for him in the freshman class. It put an end to the longest four and a half months of his life.

He knew that the reason he had only squeaked into Brown was that, although he was blessed with a keen intelligence and excellent all-around athletic skills, he had simply coasted through high school.

A chill that was pure fear engulfed him. He'd finally gotten into the college he wanted, but maybe up here he wouldn't be so fortunate. Until right now he had been absolutely sure that he'd make it to heaven. Sterling had reminded the angel at the door to the Heavenly Council that some of the people who came in behind him had been called and suggested that perhaps he had been inadvertently overlooked. He had been told politely but firmly to return to his seat.

He so much wanted to be in heaven this Christmas Eve. The expression on the faces of the people who soared past the window, seeing the open gates ahead of them, had filled him with wonder. And now Annie was there.

The angel at the door signaled for everyone's attention. "I have glad tidings. Christmas amnesty has been granted to the following. You will not have to appear before the Heavenly Council. You will go straight through the exit door on the right that leads directly to the heavenly bridge. Stand and file through in an orderly fashion as your name is called . . . Walter Cummings . . ."

A few pews over, Walter, a sprightly ninety-year-old, jumped up and clicked his heels together. "Hallelujah!" he shouted as he ran to the front of the room.

"I said in an orderly fashion," the angel chided in a somewhat resigned voice. "Though I can't much blame you," he murmured as he called the next name. "Tito Ortiz . . ."

Tito whooped with joy and raced down the aisle, hot on Walter's heels.

"Jackie Mills, Dennis Pines, Veronica Murphy, Charlotte Green, Pasquale D'Amato, Winthrop Lloyd III, Charlie Potters, Jacob Weiss, Ten Eyck Elmendorf . . ."

Name after name after name was called as the pews emptied out.

The angel finished reading from the list and folded the paper. Sterling was the only one left. A tear formed in his eye. The celestial waiting room felt cavernous and lonely. I must have been a terrible person, he thought. I'm not going to make it to heaven after all.

The angel laid down the list and began to walk toward him. Oh no, Sterling thought frantically, don't tell me he's sending me to the other place. For the first time, he realized what it was like to feel completely helpless and hopeless.

"Sterling Brooks," the angel said. "You have been summoned to an extraordinary meeting of the Heavenly Council. Follow me, please."

A tiny whisper of hope flickered in Sterling's being. Maybe, just maybe, he still had a chance. Bracing himself, he stood up and followed the angel to the door of the chamber. The angel, his face and voice full of sympathy, whispered, "Good luck," as he opened the door and pushed Sterling inside.

The room was not large. It was bathed in a soft, exquisite light, the likes of which Sterling had never experienced. The floor-to-ceiling window gave an awesome view of the heavenly gates and he realized the light was reflecting off them.

Four men and four women were seated at a long table, facing him. From the halos shining around their heads, he realized immediately that they were all saints, even though he didn't recognize them from the stained-glass windows in cathedrals he had visited while on vacation. The outfits they were wearing varied from biblical robes to twentieth-century dress. With the instinctive knowledge that was now part of him, Sterling understood that they were wearing the typical garb of the periods in which they had lived. The man at the far end, a grave-faced monk, opened the proceedings.

"Sit down, Sterling. We've got a bone to pick with you."

Sterling took the seat, acutely aware that all eyes were fixed on him.

One of the women, dressed in an elegant red velvet gown

and wearing a tiara, said in a cultured voice, "You had an easy life, didn't you, Sterling?"

Looks like you did too, Sterling thought, but held his tongue. He nodded meekly. "Yes, ma'am."

The monk looked at him sternly. "Uneasy lies the head that wears a crown. Her majesty did great good for her subjects."

My God, they can read my thoughts, Sterling realized, and he began to tremble.

"But you never went out of your way for anybody," the queen continued.

"You were a fair-weather friend," said a man in shepherd's garb, seated second from the right.

"Passive-aggressive," declared a young matador, who was picking a thread off the end of his red cape.

"What does that mean?" Sterling asked, frightened.

"Oh, sorry. That earthly expression came into use after your time. It's a very popular one now, believe me."

"Covers a multitude of sins," muttered a beautiful woman who reminded Sterling of the pictures he'd seen of Pocahontas.

"Aggressive?" Sterling said. "I never lost my temper. Ever."

"Passive-aggressive is something different. You hurt people by *not* doing things. And by making promises you have no intention of keeping."

"You were self-absorbed," a sweet-faced nun on the end said. "You were a good estate lawyer, tidying up little problems for the ultrarich, but you never lent your expertise to the poor unfortunate who was unfairly losing his home or the lease on his store. What's worse, you actually considered helping out once in a while and then decided not to get involved." She shook her head. "You were too much of a good-time Charlie."

"The kind who jumped into the first lifeboat when the ship was going down," a saint in the uniform of a British admiral snapped. "A cad, by George. Why, you never once helped an old lady cross the street."

"I never once spotted an old lady who needed help!"

"That's it in a nutshell," they said in unison. "You were too smug and self-absorbed to really notice what was going on around you."

"I'm sorry," Sterling said humbly. "I thought I was a pretty nice guy. I never meant to hurt anybody. Is there anything I can do now to make it up?"

The members of the council looked at each other.

"How bad could I have been?" Sterling cried. He pointed toward the waiting room. "In all this time I've talked to a lot of the souls who have passed through there. None of them were saints! And by the way, I saw someone who cheated on his income tax go straight to heaven. You must have missed him!"

They all laughed. "You're absolutely right. We were on a coffee break. But on the other hand, he donated a lot of that money to charity."

"What about his golf game?" Sterling asked eagerly. "I never once cheated the way he did. And I got hit in the head by a golf ball. As I was dying, I forgave the guy who did it. Not everyone would be that nice."

They stared at him as his mind filled with images of all the times in his life when he'd let people down. Annie. He was too selfish to marry her, but he always let her keep hoping because he didn't want to lose her. After he died, it was too late for her to have the family she always wanted. And now she was in heaven. He had to see her again.

Sterling felt wretched. He had to know his fate. "What are you telling me?" he asked. "Will I ever get to heaven?"

"Funny you should ask," the monk replied. "We've discussed your case, and we've decided that you seem to be the appropriate candidate for an experiment we've been weighing for some time."

Sterling's ears pricked up. All was not lost.

"I love experiments," he said enthusiastically. "I'm your boy. Try me. When do we start?" He realized he was starting to sound like a jerk.

"Sterling, be quiet and listen. You are being sent back to earth. It is your job to recognize someone with a problem and help that person solve it."

"Sent back to earth!" Sterling was dumbfounded.

The eight heads nodded in unison.

"How long will I stay?"

"As long as it takes to solve the problem."

"Does that mean if I do a good job I'll be allowed to enter heaven? I'd love to be there for Christmas."

They all looked amused. "Not so fast," the monk said. "In the jargon of the day, you have a lot of frequent flier miles to earn before you achieve permanent residence inside those holy gates. However, if you complete your first mission to our satisfaction by Christmas Eve, you will be entitled to a visitor's pass for twenty-four hours."

Sterling's heart sank a little. Oh well, he thought. Every long journey begins with one small step.

"You'd do well to remember that," the queen cautioned.

Sterling blinked. He'd have to remember they were mind readers. "How will I know the person I'm supposed to help?" he asked.

"That's part of the point of this experiment. You have to learn to recognize people's needs and do something about them," a young black woman wearing a nurse's uniform told him.

"Will I have any help? I mean, anyone I can talk to if I'm not sure what to do? I'll do anything to get the job done properly, you understand."

I'm babbling again, he thought.

"You are free at any time to request a consultation with us," the admiral assured him.

"When do I start?"

The monk pressed a button on the council table. "Right now."

Sterling felt a trap door open beneath him. In an instant he was hurtling past the stars, around the moon, through the clouds, and then suddenly whisking past a tall, brilliantly lit Christmas tree. His feet touched the earth.

"My God," Sterling breathed. "I'm in Rockefeller Center."

arissa's dark hair cascaded around her shoulders as she twirled around the rink in Rockefeller Center. She had started taking ice-skating lessons when she was three. Now that she was seven, skating was as natural to her as breathing, and lately it had been the only thing that eased the hurt that filled her chest and throat.

The music changed, and without thinking she adjusted to the new, softer rhythm, a waltz. For a moment she pretended she was with Daddy. She could almost feel his hand linked with hers, could almost see NorNor, her grandmother, smiling at her.

Then she remembered that she really didn't want to skate with Daddy or even talk to him, or to NorNor. They had gone away, hardly saying good-bye to her. The first bunch of times they phoned she had pleaded with them to come back or to let her come visit them, but they had said that was impossible. Now when they called, she wouldn't talk to them.

She didn't care, she told herself.

But still, she closed her eyes whenever a car she was in happened to drive past NorNor's restaurant; it hurt to remember how much fun it had been to go there with Daddy. The place was always crowded, sometimes NorNor played the piano, and people always asked Daddy to sing. Sometimes they'd bring over his CD and ask him to sign the cover.

Now she never went there. She had heard Mommy tell Roy—he was Mommy's husband now—that without NorNor, the restaurant was really struggling and would probably have to close soon.

What did Daddy and NorNor expect when they went away? Marissa wondered. NorNor always said that unless she was there every night the place would fall on its face. "It's my living room," she used to tell Marissa. "You don't invite people over to your house and not be there."

If NorNor loved her restaurant so much, why did she go away? And if Daddy and NorNor loved *her* like they said, why did they leave her behind?

She hadn't seen them in almost a whole year. Christmas Eve was her birthday. She would be eight years old, and even though she still was very angry with them, she had promised God that if the bell rang on Christmas Eve and they were standing at the door, she would never be mean to anyone as long as she lived and would help Mommy with the babies and stop acting bored when Roy told the same stupid stories over and over. If it would help, she'd even promise never to skate again as long as she lived, but she knew that was a promise Daddy wouldn't want her to make, because if he ever *did* come back, he'd want to take her skating.

The music stopped and the skating teacher, Miss Carr, who had brought twelve students to Rockefeller Center as a special treat, motioned that it was time to go. Marissa did one final pirouette before she coasted to the exit. The minute she started to untie her laces the hurt came back. She could feel it growing around her heart and filling her chest and then rising like a tide into her throat. But though it was a struggle, she managed to keep it from pressing against her eyes.

"You're a terrific skater," one of the attendants said. "You'll be a star like Tara Lipinsky when you grow up."

NorNor used to tell her that all the time. Before she could help herself, Marissa's eyes began to blur. Turning her head so that the attendant wouldn't see that she was almost crying, she looked straight into the eyes of a man who was standing at the fence around the rink. He was wearing a funny-looking hat and coat, but he had a nice face and he was sort of smiling at her.

"Come along, Marissa," Miss Carr called, and Marissa, hearing the slightly grouchy tone in her teacher's voice, began to run to catch up with the other kids.

"It seems familiar and yet so different," Sterling murmured to himself as he glanced around Rockefeller Center. For one thing it was far more crowded than the last time he was here. Every inch of space seemed to be filled with people. Some were carrying shopping bags laden with gifts, hurrying about, while others stood gazing up at the big tree.

This tree seemed taller than the last one he had seen here—forty-six years ago—and it had more lights on it than he remembered. It was magnificent, but so different from the otherworldly light he had experienced in the celestial conference room.

Even though he'd grown up on Seventieth Street off Fifth Avenue, and lived most of his life in Manhattan, a sudden wave of homesickness for the celestial life swept over him. He needed to find the person he was supposed to help so he could complete his mission.

Two young children came racing toward him. He stepped aside before they ran into him, then realized he had bumped into a woman who was admiring the tree.

"I beg your pardon," he said. "I hope I didn't hurt you?" She did not look at him or indicate that she had heard a single word he said, or even that she'd felt the bump.

She doesn't know I'm here, he realized. He had a moment of total dismay. How can I help someone if that person can't see or hear me? he wondered. The council really left me to sink or swim on my own.

Sterling looked into the faces of the passersby. They were talking to each other, laughing, carrying packages, pointing to the tree. No one seemed to be in any special distress. He thought of how the admiral said he never helped an old lady cross the street. Maybe he should try to find one now.

He walked quickly toward Fifth Avenue and was appalled at the volume of traffic he saw. He passed a shop window, then stopped, astonished when he saw his reflection gazing back at him. Other people couldn't see him, but he could see himself. He studied his image in the window. Not bad, old boy, he thought admiringly. It was the first time he'd seen his reflection since that fateful morning when he left for the golf course. He noted his salt-and-pepper hair, in the early stages of recession, his somewhat angular features, his lean, muscular body. He was wearing his winter outerwear: a dark blue chesterfield coat with a velvet collar, his favorite hat, a gray felt homburg, and gray kidskin gloves. Noticing the way other people were dressed, he realized that his clothing must have gone out of style.

If people could see me, they'd think I was heading for a costume party, he decided.

At Fifth Avenue, he looked uptown. His best friend used to

work at American President Lines. The office was gone. He was aware that many of the shops and firms that he remembered had been replaced. Well, it *has* been forty-six years, he thought. Now, where is the sweet old lady who requires assistance?

It was almost as though the council had heard him. An elderly woman with a cane began crossing the street as the light was turning red. That's too dangerous, he thought, even though the traffic was barely crawling.

Taking long strides, he rushed to assist her, but was chagrined to see that a young man had recognized her plight and was already grabbing her elbow.

"Leave me alone," she screamed. "I've gotten by for a long time without the likes of you trying to grab my pocketbook."

The young man muttered something under his breath, dropped her arm, and left her in the middle of the street. Horns blared, but the traffic stopped as, without any indication of haste, the old lady made her way to the curb.

Clearly the council didn't send me back to earth for her, Sterling decided.

There was a long line in front of the Saks Fifth Avenue windows. He wondered what they were looking at that was so special. Nothing but clothes was ever displayed in those windows, he thought. From the corner of his eye he could see the spires of Saint Patrick's Cathedral, and he felt his sense of urgency deepen.

Let's reason this out, he thought. I was sent to help someone, and I was placed in Rockefeller Center. That certainly suggests that I'm supposed to begin my task there. Sterling turned and retraced his steps.

With ever-increasing care he studied the faces of the people he was passing. A couple walked by, both wearing skintight, black leather outfits, both also appearing to have been scalped. Pierced noses and eyebrows completed the fashion statement. He tried not to stare. Times sure have changed, he thought.

As he moved through the crowd, he sensed he was being drawn back toward the majestic Christmas tree that was the heart of the holiday season at Rockefeller Center.

He found himself standing next to a more traditional looking young couple, holding hands and appearing to be very much in love. He felt like an eavesdropper, but he had to hear what they were saying. Something made him certain the young man was about to propose. Go for it, he thought. Before it's too late.

"I've decided it's time," the young man said.

"I'm ready too." The girl's eyes were shining.

Where's the ring? Sterling wondered.

"We'll move in together for six months and see how it works out."

The young woman looked blissful. "I'm so happy," she whispered.

Shaking his head, Sterling turned away. That was never an option in my time, he told himself. Somewhat discouraged, he walked to the railing overlooking the ice-skating rink and looked down. The music was just ending, and skaters were heading for the exit. He saw one little girl give a final twirl. She's very good, he thought admiringly.

A moment later she looked up, and he could see that she was trying to blink back tears. Their eyes locked. Does she see me? Sterling wondered. He couldn't be sure, but he was certain that she had sensed his presence, and that she needed him. As he watched her slowly skate off the ice, her shoulders drooping noticeably, he knew with certainty that she was the one he had been sent to help.

He watched as she changed into her shoes and then headed up the stairs from the rink. He momentarily lost her in the crowd, but then caught up with her just as she was boarding a van marked MADISON VILLAGE SCHOOLS that was waiting on Forty-ninth Street. So that's where they were going, he thought—Long Island. He heard the teacher call his new little charge Marissa. Obviously the youngest student in the group, she went straight to the back and sat alone in the last seat. Quickly becoming comfortable in the knowledge that no one could see him, he followed the little girl onto the van and slid into the seat across the aisle from her. She glanced in his direction several times, as if she somehow were aware that he was there.

Sterling settled back. He was on his way. He looked over at Marissa, who had leaned against the window and closed her eyes. What was weighing so heavily on that little girl's heart? Who was she thinking about?

He couldn't wait to see what was going on in her home.

"I can't believe it. Another Christmas with Mama so many miles away." Eddie Badgett was close to tears. "I miss my homeland. I miss my mama. I want to see her."

His ruddy face dissolved in grief. He ran his thick fingers through his plentiful grizzled hair.

The Yuletide season had thrown Eddie into a blue funk that all his worldly wealth, accumulated through loan-sharking and pyramid schemes, could not erase.

He was speaking to his brother Junior, who, at fifty-four, was three years younger. Junior had been named for their father, who had spent most of his sons' lives incarcerated in a dank prison cell in Wallonia, a tiny country bordering Albania.

The brothers were in the room their pricey decorator had grandly dubbed the library, and which he had filled with books that neither one of them had any intention of reading.

The Badgetts' mansion, set on twelve acres on Long Island's North Shore gold coast, was a tribute to the ability of the brothers to separate other human beings from their hard-earned assets.

Their lawyer, Charlie Santoli, was with them in the library, seated at the ornate marble table, his briefcase beside him, an open file in front of him.

Santoli, a small, neat, sixtyish man with the unfortunate tendency to complete his daily toilette with a substantial quantity of Manly Elegance cologne, eyed the brothers with his usual combination of disdain and fear.

It frequently occurred to him that in appearance the pair resembled a bowling ball and a baseball bat. Eddie was short, squat, rounded, hard. Junior was tall, lean, powerful. And sinister—he could chill a room with his smile or even the grin he considered ingratiating.

Charlie's mouth was dry. It was his unhappy duty to tell the brothers that he'd been unable to get another postponement of their trial for racketeering, loan-sharking, arson, and attempted murder. Which meant that Billy Campbell, the handsome, thirty-year-old, climbing-the-charts rock singer, and his glamorous mother, aging cabaret singer and popular restaurant owner Nor Kelly, would be whisked out of hiding and brought to federal court. Their testimony would put Eddie and Junior in prison cells that they could cover with pictures of Mama, because they'd never lay eyes on her again. But Santoli knew that, even from prison, they would manage to make sure that Billy Campbell never sang another note, and that his mother, Nor Kelly, never welcomed another patron to her restaurant.

"You're too scared to talk to us," Junior barked. "But you'd better start. We're all ears."

"Yeah," Eddie echoed, as he dabbed his eyes and blew his nose, "we're all ears."

*M*adison Village was a few exits past Syosset on the Long Island Expressway.

At the school parking lot, Sterling followed Marissa off the van. Wet snowflakes swirled around them. A guy in his late thirties, with thinning sandy hair—tall, lanky, the kind Sterling's mother would describe as "a long drink of water"—called to Marissa and waved vigorously.

"Over here, honey pie. Hurry. No hat on? You'll catch a cold."

Sterling heard Marissa groan as she ran toward a beige sedan parked in the midst of a half-dozen vehicles that looked to Sterling more like trucks than cars. He had noticed a lot of this kind of vehicle on the highway. He shrugged. Just another change in the last forty-six years.

Marissa said, "Hi, Roy," as she hopped into the front seat. Sterling squeezed himself into the back between two tiny seats that were obviously for very small children. What will they think of next? Sterling wondered. When I was a toddler, my mother used to drive with me in her lap and let me help her steer.

"How's our little Olympic skater?" Roy asked Marissa. Sterling could tell he was trying his best to be pleasant, but Marissa wasn't having any of it.

"Good," she replied without a trace of enthusiasm.

Who is this guy? Sterling wondered. It can't be her father. Maybe an uncle? The mother's boyfriend?

"Fasten your seat belt, princess," Roy cautioned in a too-cheery voice.

Honey pie? Princess? Olympic skater? This guy is embarrassing, Sterling thought.

Give me a break, Marissa sighed.

Startled, Sterling looked for Roy's reaction. There was none. Roy was staring straight ahead, paying rapt attention to the road. His hands were wrapped tightly around the steering wheel, and he was driving ten miles below the speed limit.

I could skate home faster, Marissa moaned.

Sterling was inordinately pleased to realize that he not only had the power to make himself visible to her on demand, but when he tuned in, he could read her thoughts as well. The Heavenly Council was obviously making certain tools and powers available to him, but leaving it up to him to discover their extent. They certainly weren't going to make it easy for him.

He leaned back, aware that even though he was not there in the flesh, he nonetheless felt crowded and uncomfortable. He had had much the same reaction when he'd bumped into the woman at the skating rink.

The rest of the seven-minute ride home was spent mostly

in silence, except for the radio, which was tuned to a station playing particularly bland music.

Marissa remembered the time she had switched the station in Daddy's car to the one that played this stuff. He had said, "You're kidding! Haven't I given you any taste in music?"

"This is the station Roy listens to!" Marissa had cried triumphantly. They had laughed together.

"How your mother went from me to him I'll never know," Daddy had marveled.

So that's it, Sterling thought. Roy is her stepfather. But where's her father, and why, now that she's thought about him, is she both sad and angry?

"Roy went to pick her up. They should be here any minute, but I don't think she'll want to talk to you, Billy. I've tried to explain that it isn't your fault that you and Nor have to stay away for a while, but she isn't buying it." Denise Ward was on her cordless phone, talking to Marissa's father, her ex-husband, and trying to keep her two-year-old twin boys from pulling down the Christmas tree.

"I understand, but it's killing me that—"

"Roy Junior, let go of that tinsel!" Denise interrupted, her voice rising. "Robert, leave the baby Jesus alone. I said . . . Hold on, Billy."

Two thousand miles away, Billy Campbell's concerned expression cleared for a moment. He was holding up the receiver so that his mother, Nor Kelly, could hear the conversation. Now he raised his eyebrows. "I think the baby Jesus just went flying across the room," he whispered.

"Sorry, Billy," Denise said, back on the phone. "Look, it's pretty hectic here. The munchkins are all excited about Christmas. Maybe you'd better call back in fifteen minutes, even though it's going to be a waste of time. Marissa just doesn't want to talk to either you or Nor."

"Denise, I know you've got your hands full," Billy Campbell said quietly. "You have the packages we sent, but is there anything Marissa really needs? Maybe she's talked about something special I could still get for her."

He heard a loud crash and the sound of a wailing two-year-old.

"Oh my God, the Waterford angel," Denise Ward nearly sobbed. "Don't go near it, Robert. Do you hear me? You'll get cut." Her voice taut with anger, she snapped, "You want to know what Marissa needs, Billy? She needs you and Nor, and she needs both of you soon. I'm worried sick about her. Roy is too. He tries so hard with her, and she simply won't respond."

"How do you think I feel, Denise?" Billy asked, his voice rising. "I'd give my right arm to be with Marissa. My guts are torn out every day that I'm not with her. I'm grateful that Roy is there for her, but she's my kid and I miss her."

"I think of how lucky I am to have met a dependable man who has a nice steady job, who isn't out till all hours playing with a rock group, and doesn't get himself into situations where he has to hightail it out of town." Denise did not pause for breath. "Marissa is hurting. Have you got that, Billy? Her birthday is in four days. Christmas Eve. I don't know what she'll be like when you're not here for that. The child feels abandoned."

Nor Kelly saw the expression of pain that came over her son's face and watched as he clasped his hand over his forehead. Her ex-daughter-in-law was a good mother, but was nearing the end of her rope out of frustration with the situation. She wanted them back for Marissa's sake, but would be frantic with worry that Marissa might be in danger if they were around.

"So, Billy, I'll tell her you called. I've got to hang up. Oh, wait a minute. The car just pulled into the driveway. I'll see if she'll talk to you."

A nice house, Sterling thought as he followed Marissa and Roy up the steps. Tudor style. Evergreens covered with blue lights. A small sleigh with Santa and the eight reindeer on the lawn. Everything pristine. He was sure Roy was a neatnik.

Roy unlocked the door and flung it open. "Where are my munchkins?" he called playfully. "Roy Junior, Robert, your daddy's back."

Sterling jumped aside as two identical sandy-haired toddlers raced toward them. He could see into the living room where a pretty blond woman, looking extremely harried, was holding a phone with no cord (obviously another innovation since Sterling's departure). She gestured to Marissa. "Your dad and NorNor want to talk to you very, very much," she said.

Marissa walked into the living room, took the phone from her mother, and to Sterling's astonishment, replaced the receiver on the cradle, and, her eyes brimming with tears, ran upstairs.

Wow! Sterling thought.

He didn't yet know what the problem was, but he empathized with the helpless glance Marissa's mother exchanged with her husband. It looks as though I've got my work cut out for me, he decided. Marissa needs help *now*.

He followed Marissa up the stairs and knocked on the door of her room.

"Please leave me alone, Mom. I'm not hungry, and I don't want to eat."

"It's not Mom, Marissa," Sterling said.

He heard the lock turn, and the door opened slowly. Marissa's eyes widened, and her woebegone expression changed to one of astonishment. "I saw you when I was skating and then when I got in the van," she whispered. "But then I didn't see you anymore. Are you a ghost?"

Sterling smiled at her. "Not really a ghost. I'm more on the order of an angel, but I'm not really an angel. In fact that's why I'm here."

"You want to help me, don't you?"

Sterling felt a wrench of tenderness as he looked into Marissa's troubled blue eyes. "I want to help you more than anything in the world. For my sake as well as yours."

"Are you in trouble with God?"

"Let's just say he's not thrilled with me at the moment. He doesn't think I'm ready for heaven yet."

Marissa rolled her eyes. "I know lots of people who are never going to get to heaven."

Sterling laughed. "There were some people I was sure wouldn't make it, and now they're right up there with the best of them."

"Go figure," Marissa said. "Do you want to come in? I have a chair that was big enough for my dad when he came over to help me with my homework."

She's charming, Sterling thought as he followed her into the spacious room. What a little personality. He was glad that Marissa knew instinctively that he was a kindred spirit, one she could trust. She already looked a little happier.

He settled himself in the armchair she indicated and realized he was still wearing his hat. "Oh, sorry," he murmured, took it off, and placed it neatly on his lap.

Marissa pulled out her desk chair and sat down with the air of a polite hostess. "I wish I could offer you a soda and some cookies or something, but if I go downstairs they'll want me to eat dinner." She wrinkled her nose. "I just thought about something. Do you get hungry? Can you eat? Because it looks like you're there, but not really."

"I'm just trying to figure all that out myself," Sterling admitted. "This is my first shot at this sort of thing. Now tell me, why won't you talk to your dad?"

Marissa looked down as a shadow fell over her face. "He won't come and see me and he won't let me go and visit him and neither will NorNor—she's my grandmother. And if they don't want to see me, I don't want to see them."

"Where do they live?"

"I don't know," Marissa burst out. "They won't tell me, and Mom doesn't know. She said they're hiding out from bad people who want to hurt them and they can't come back until it's safe, but at school kids say they think Daddy and NorNor got in trouble and had to run away."

Which is it? Sterling wondered. "When was the last time you saw them?"

"Two days after Christmas last year was when I *really* saw them. Daddy and I went ice skating. Then we went back to NorNor's restaurant for lunch. We were supposed to go to Radio City Music Hall on New Year's Eve morning, but he and NorNor had to go away. They rushed in when I was hardly even awake and said good-bye. They didn't tell me when they were coming back, and it's been almost a whole year." She paused. "I have to see Daddy, I have to see NorNor."

Her heart is broken, Sterling thought. He understood that kind of ache. It was like the yearning he felt when he saw Annie go past the window to heaven.

"Marissa . . ." There was a knock at the bedroom door.

"Oh, I knew it," Marissa said. "Mom is going to make me go down and have dinner. I'm not hungry and I don't want you to leave."

"Marissa, I'm going to get to work on your problem. I'll be back to say good night."

"Promise?"

"Marissa." There was another knock at the door.

"Yes, but you promise me something in return," Sterling said hastily. "Your mom is really worried about you. Give her a break."

"Okay. I'll even give Roy a break, and anyhow, I like chicken. Mom, I'm coming," she called. She turned back to Sterling. "Give me a high five."

"What's that?" Sterling asked.

Marissa was incredulous. "You must be pretty old. Everybody knows what a high five is."

"I've been out of touch," Sterling admitted as, following her example, he raised his hand, palm flat, and held it open as she gave it an enthusiastic slap.

Precocious, he thought, smiling. "See you later," he whispered.

"Great. Don't forget your hat. I don't want to be mean, but it really looks dumb."

"Marissa, dinner's getting cold," her mother called.

"Dinner's always cold," Marissa whispered to Sterling as he walked her to the door. "Roy takes forever to say grace. Daddy says Mommy should stick to cold cuts."

Her hand was on the knob. "Mommy can't see you, can she?"

Sterling shook his head and disappeared.

$\mathcal{I}$n the celestial conference room, the board had been following Sterling's movements with interest. "He's made contact immediately. Using the old noggin, I call it," the admiral said approvingly.

"That little girl is so unhappy," the nun said softly.

"And quite outspoken," the monk observed. "However, I do realize it was different in my day. Sterling is about to request a conference with us. I believe we should grant it."

"So be it," they chorused.

Deep in thought, Sterling stood for a brief time in the breezeway of Marissa's home, sheltered from the slowly falling snow. I could snoop around town and find out about her father and grandmother, he thought, but there's an easier way to get the full picture, one that would involve requesting permission from the council.

He closed his eyes. Before he even had time to make the request, he found himself in the conference room. Relieved, he saw from their faces that his saintly mentors seemed to be observing him with guarded favor.

"I see you tried to find an old lady in distress," the admiral chuckled. "The young fellow who beat you to her got quite a surprise. I say, she was a prickly one."

"At least Sterling didn't waste a minute when he reached earth," the nurse said approvingly.

Sterling glowed to hear the praise. "Thank you, thank you. As you can understand, I don't want to waste a minute now. I believe I can best help Marissa when I fully understand the cause of her problem.

"Marissa's father and grandmother were planning to take her to Radio City Music Hall last New Year's Eve morning. But something went wrong just before that. They came to see her very early that day and told her they had to go away for a while."

The monk nodded. "To get to the root of most problems you have to do some digging in the past."

The shepherd, who had been very quiet, suddenly spoke up. "Most people's problems go way back. You should have met my family. Why do you think I became a shepherd? The only place I got a little peace was out on the hill."

They all laughed. "Don't get me started," the queen said. "My family's problems were the talk of the kingdom."

The monk cleared his throat. "I think we all understand you, Sterling. We know why you're here. You are requesting permission to go back in time to learn why Marissa's father and grandmother needed to leave town."

"That's it, sir," Sterling said humbly. "Perhaps you feel

that by granting permission you'll make my job too easy, and of course, if that's the case, I don't expect special favors."

"When you see what this is all about you may need a few special favors," the matador said wryly. "Personally, it's my opinion that you'll be stepping in the ring with two bulls, not one, and—"

The monk shushed the matador. "It is Sterling's job to figure this out for himself." His hand reached for the button.

That was fast, Sterling thought as he felt himself once again hurtling through the solar system. They're sending me a different way. I guess because I'm going back in time.

The next thing he knew he was standing in the parking lot of an inviting-looking restaurant. Seems to be pretty popular, he observed. Through the windows he could see that there was a bustle of activity inside. To get his bearings, he walked to the end of the driveway and read the sign: NOR'S PLACE.

Very good, he thought. Marissa's grandmother's restaurant. He didn't need to be Sherlock Holmes to figure out that the next step would be to go inside and take a look around. He hurried back up the driveway, climbed the steps, crossed the porch, and started to open the door.

I can just go through it, he chided himself. No use wasting heat. A sharp breeze accompanied him inside, where a shapely woman of about sixty, with blond hair held up in a loose twist by a jeweled comb, was standing at a small desk, studying the reservations book.

She looked up. Tendrils of blond hair brushed her forehead.

A most attractive woman in a showy kind of way, Sterling thought.

"I'd swear I shut that door tight," Nor Kelly murmured as with two quick strides she was beside him, giving the door a decisive pull.

"NorNor, sit down. Your coffee's here," a child's voice called.

A familiar voice. Sterling whirled around to face the dining room. Mahogany paneled walls, tables covered with crisp white cloths and topped with wide red candles created a cheery and welcoming atmosphere. A piano was at a right angle to the bar. Strings of Christmas lights twinkled on the walls and windows, and holiday music was playing softly in the background.

"NorNor," the child called again.

His eyes roamed the crowded room. A little girl was standing at a corner table just to the right of the door. She was looking in his direction. It was Marissa! She was slightly younger looking, her hair a little shorter, but the most noticeable difference was how happy she looked. Her eyes were sparkling, her lips were curved in a smile, she had on a bright red skating outfit. With her was a strikingly handsome, blue-eyed, dark-haired man in his late twenties.

Billy Campbell, Sterling thought. He's got movie-star looks. I wish I'd looked like that when I was alive, he reflected. Not that I had anything to complain about.

Nor looked up. "I'll be right there, Rissa."

It was obvious Marissa had not seen him. Of course, Sterling thought. We're not due to meet until next year.

He strolled over to the table and took a seat opposite Marissa. What a difference in her, he thought tenderly.

She and her father were finishing lunch. The crusts of a grilled cheese sandwich were on Marissa's plate. I never liked crusts either, Sterling remembered.

"Daddy, can't I please go to the party with you?" Marissa asked as she played with the straw in her soda. "I love to hear you and NorNor sing, and I promise I won't be a pest."

"You're never a pest, Rissa," Billy said, giving her hair a tug. "But this party is not for kids, believe me."

"I want to see what that big house looks like inside."

"A lot of people do," Billy murmured, raising one eyebrow. "Listen, we're going to Radio City on New Year's Eve. That will be a lot more fun. Trust me."

"A kid at school said that the men who own that house are like the people in *The Sopranos*."

Billy laughed. "That's another reason not to bring you there, kiddo."

Sopranos? Sterling thought.

Nor Kelly slipped into the chair next to Marissa. "Don't forget your other grandma is coming to your mom's house in time for dinner tonight. You were looking forward to seeing her."

"She's staying for three days. I can see her tomorrow. I don't want to miss the chance to hear you two sing."

Billy's eyes twinkled. "You're too young to be a groupie."

Groupie? So many new words, Sterling thought.

"Daddy, everybody loves your new song. You're going to be so famous."

"You bet he is, Rissa," Nor confirmed.

I can see why Marissa has missed them so much, Sterling thought. She's in her element with them. Already, he thoroughly liked Nor Kelly and Billy Campbell. You could not mistake that they were mother and son, and that Marissa had inherited those blue eyes, fair skin, and good looks from them. Nor and Billy had the natural charisma of born performers, and Marissa was already showing signs of possessing that same quality.

The restaurant was beginning to empty, and people were stopping by the table to say good-bye. "See you on New Year's Eve," a number of them said. "We'd never miss your party, Nor."

"That party I'm coming to," Marissa said decisively, pointing her finger for emphasis.

"Until ten o'clock," Billy agreed, "then you're out of here."

"Don't try last year's trick of hiding behind the bar when it's time to go home," Nor warned, laughing. "And speaking of going home, your mother should be here any minute, and Daddy and I have to get moving. We're due at our job in an hour."

Billy stood up. "Here's Mom, Rissa."

Denise Ward was crossing the room to them. "Hi, Billy. Hi, Nor. I'm sorry I'm late," she apologized. "I had to pick up some groceries, and the line at the checkout counter practically went around the store. But I bought what we need to make cookies, Marissa."

Neither Denise nor Billy could be thirty yet, Sterling thought. They obviously had married young, and although divorced, seemed to have stayed friendly. Just looking at the two of them, she in her somewhat prim winter pantsuit and he in his black jeans and boots, you could tell they weren't on the same wavelength.

And God knows Billy Campbell hadn't followed the adage that every man marries his mother. No one would ever accuse Nor Kelly of looking prim. She was wearing a striking white cashmere pantsuit with a colorful print silk scarf, complemented by eye-catching costume jewelry.

"How are the babies?" Nor asked.

"Just starting to walk," Denise announced proudly. "When Roy Junior took his first step, Roy Senior stayed up half the night, installing gates all over the house."

Sterling thought he detected a slight roll of Billy's eyes. She's letting Billy know how helpful Roy is, Sterling decided. I bet he hears about some new accomplishment of Roy's every time he sees her.

Marissa stood up and hugged her father and grandmother. "Have fun with the Sopranos," she said.

Denise looked surprised. "The Sopranos?"

"She's joking," Nor said hastily. "Our job this evening is at the party the Badgett brothers are giving to benefit the senior citizens center."

"Don't they live in that big house—?" Denise began.

"Yes, they do," Marissa blurted, "and I hear they have an indoor pool and a bowling alley."

"We'll let you know every sorry detail," Billy promised. "Come on. Let's get your jacket."

As they started walking toward the coat check, Sterling took a moment to look at the framed photos along the walls. Many of them showed Nor posing with diners at the tables. Some were autographed by people who were probably present-day celebrities, he decided. There were pictures of a glamorous Nor onstage, singing with a band; Billy, guitar in hand, performing with a group; Nor and Billy together onstage; Billy and Nor with Marissa.

Sterling could see from the older pictures that Nor once must have been a cabaret singer. He came upon a number of photographs in which she was performing with a partner. The sign on the bandstand read NOR KELLY AND BILL CAMPBELL. Billy's father, Sterling thought. I wonder what happened to him, and how long has she had the restaurant? Then a poster for a New Year's Eve celebration at Nor's Place dating back twenty years made him realize that she had been in this business a long time.

Marissa left after a final kiss from Billy and Nor. Even though Sterling knew that Marissa couldn't see him, he felt left out that she hadn't somehow sensed his presence and maybe given him a high five.

You're being ridiculous, he chided himself. But when he saw Marissa with Billy it made him think of the child he might have had if he and Annie had married.

Agreeing to be ready to leave in fifteen minutes, Billy and Nor rushed to change. To kill time, Sterling wandered over to the bar, where a single patron was chatting with the bartender. He sat on a nearby stool. If I were still alive, I'd order a scotch, he thought. It's certainly been a long time since I had one. Next year Marissa will ask me if I get hungry or thirsty. Actually, I don't have any desire to eat or drink, he realized, even though I get cold when I'm outside and feel crowded in cars. As Marissa would say, "Go figure."

"Christmas was nice, Dennis," the patron was saying. "I never thought I'd get through it, the first one without Peggy. Honest to God, when I went downstairs that morning I was ready to shoot myself, but then when I came here it was like being with family."

Well, I'll be darned, Sterling thought. That's Chet Armstrong, the sportscaster. He was just starting out on Channel 11 when I got beaned. He was a skinny kid then, but the way he delivered the sports news, you'd think every play was crucial. Now he's broad shouldered, white haired, and has the craggy face of a man who spent a great deal of time outdoors.

"I felt almost guilty that Christmas Day turned out to be so pleasant," Armstrong continued, "but I knew Peggy was probably smiling down on me."

I wonder if Peggy ever did time in the celestial waiting room, Sterling thought. He wished Chet would open his wallet. Maybe he was carrying her picture.

"Peggy was a terrific gal," Dennis, a beefy redhead with large, agile hands, agreed as he polished beer glasses and filled orders from the slips of paper the waiters dropped in front of him. Sterling noticed that Armstrong's eyes darted to one of the framed pictures over the bar. He leaned forward to get a good look at it. It was a picture of Nor with Chet, whose arm was around the shoulders of a petite woman who had to be Peggy.

I *did* see her, Sterling thought. She was a couple of rows behind me in the waiting room. But she didn't stay there long enough to really settle in.

"Peggy was a lot of fun, but don't get on her bad side," Chet reminisced with a chuckle.

Oh, that's what delayed her, Sterling thought. She had a bit of a temper.

"Listen," Dennis said in the tone of a father confessor, "I know it seems impossible, but I bet that someday down the line you'll meet someone. You've still got plenty of time."

Just watch who you play golf with, Sterling reflected.

"Turned seventy last March, Dennis."

"Today that's young."

Sterling shook his head. I'd be ninety-six. No one would accuse me of being a spring chicken.

"How long have you been here anyhow, Dennis?" Chet asked.

Thank you, Chet, Sterling thought, hoping that Dennis's reply would be a big help in his getting the lay of the land.

"Nor opened this place twenty-three years ago. Bill died just when Billy was starting school. She didn't want to be on the road anymore. I knew her from one of the clubs in New York. After six months, she gave me a call. She'd caught her bartender with his hand in the till. Our kids were almost school age, and my wife wanted to get out of the city. I've been here ever since."

Out of the corner of his eye, Sterling saw that Billy and Nor were on the way out. I'm falling down on the job, he thought, hurrying to catch up with them as they walked across the parking lot.

He was not surprised to see that they had one of those little trucks. Must be the style these days. He smiled at the thought of Marissa getting into Roy's staid vehicle. Like any kid, she probably hated her friends to see her associated with anything boring.

He hoisted himself into the backseat as Billy was turning the key in the ignition, then glanced over his shoulder at the boxes of what appeared to be musical equipment. If only they knew they had a "groupie" in the backseat, Sterling chuckled to himself.

Settled in, he stretched his legs. I don't miss being crowded by baby seats, he thought. He realized he was looking forward to the party. At the party the night before his final golf game, they had been playing Buddy Holly and Doris Day records. It would be fun if Nor and Billy sang like them, he mused.

The car drove through the snow-covered streets of Madison Village. Reminds me of Currier and Ives, Sterling thought, looking at the well-kept houses, many of them tastefully adorned with holiday lights. Evergreen wreaths with holly berries graced front doors. Festive Christmas trees sparkled through parlor windows.

On one lawn, the sight of a beautiful crèche with exquisitely carved figures provoked a wistful smile.

Then they passed a house with a dozen lifesized plastic angels cavorting on the lawn. That bossy angel at the door of the Heavenly Council room should get a load of that monstrosity, he thought.

He caught a glimpse of Long Island Sound. I always liked the North Shore of the Island, he reflected, as he craned his neck for a better look at the water, but it's a lot more built up than it used to be.

In the front seat, Nor and Billy were chuckling about Marissa's attempts to be with them so she could see for herself the inside of the big house.

"She's some piece of goods," Billy said proudly. "She takes after you, Mom. Always with her ear to the ground, afraid she'll miss something."

Agreeing, Nor laughed. "I prefer to call it a healthy interest in her surroundings. Shows how smart she is."

As Sterling listened, his spirits fell. He knew that their lives were about to change and that they were soon to be separated from this child who was the center of their lives.

He only wished he had the power to prevent it.

henever Junior and Eddie Badgett held an event in their mansion, Junior had an attack of nerves. Here we go, Charlie Santoli thought as he followed the baseball bat and the bowling ball brothers. Junior, the baseball bat, had small, cold eyes. Eddie, the bowling ball, was always in tears when he talked about Mama, hard as nails about everything else.

The usual flurry of activity before a party was going on. The florists were scurrying around, placing holiday arrangements throughout the house. The caterer's team was setting up the buffet. Jewel, Junior's airheaded twenty-two-year-old girlfriend, was tripping back and forth in stiletto heels, getting in everyone's way. Junior and Eddie's special confidential assistants, uneasy in jackets and ties, were standing together, looking like the thugs they were.

Before he left home, Charlie had been forced to listen to yet another sermon from his wife about the Badgett brothers.

"Charlie, those two are crooks," she told him. Everybody knows it. You should tell them you don't want to be their lawyer anymore. So what if they put a wing on the senior citizens home? It wasn't their money that did it. Listen, I told you not to get involved with them fifteen years ago. Did you listen? No. You'll be lucky if you don't end up in the trunk of a car, and I don't mean a rumble seat. Quit. You've got enough money. You're sixty-two years old, and you're so nervous you twitch in your sleep. I want the grandchildren to know you in the flesh and not have to kiss your picture good night."

It was no use trying to explain to Marge that he couldn't get out. He had intended to handle only the various legitimate businesses of the Badgett brothers. To his regret, however, he had learned that when you lie down with dogs, you get up with fleas, and a number of times he'd been coerced into suggesting to potential government witnesses that it would be worth their while financially—and physically—to forget about certain events. In that way he had managed to prevent the brothers from being indicted for a number of criminal activities, including loan-sharking, fixing basketball games, and illegal bookmaking. So to refuse to do anything they requested of him, or to try to quit working for them, was tantamount to committing suicide.

Today, because of the magnitude of their donation to the senior citizens center, a two million dollar wing given in honor of their mother, they'd managed to get an A-list of guests to come to celebrate their absent mother's eighty-fifth birthday. Both U.S. Senators from New York, the Commissioner of Health and Human Services, various mayors and dignitaries, and the entire board of governors of the senior citizens center would be there. The board alone included some of the most prominent names on Long Island.

In all, a total of about seventy-five people would be present, the kind of people who would give the brothers the aura of respectability they craved.

It was essential that the party go well.

The main event would be held in the grand salon, a room that combined various aspects of a French royal palace. Bright gold walls, spindly gilt chairs, ornate rosewood tables, satin draperies, tapestries, and hovering over all, the reproduction of a two-story-high fifteenth-century marble fireplace, replete with sculpted cherubs, unicorns, and pineapples. Junior had explained that pineapples "symbolized lots of good luck," and he'd instructed the decorator to make sure there were lots of pineapples on the reproduction and to forget about some of those other doohickeys.

The result was a room that was a monument to bad taste, Charlie thought, and he could only imagine the reaction of the social set.

The party was scheduled to begin at five and last until eight. Cocktails, hors d'oeuvres, and a sumptuous buffet would be served. The entertainment would be provided by Billy Campbell, the up-and-coming rock singer, and his mother, Nor Kelly, the former cabaret singer. They were very popular throughout the North Shore. The highlight of the evening would occur at 7:30 P.M. when, via satellite hookup from Wallonia, the mother of the Badgett brothers would be present to hear the assemblage sing "Happy Birthday Heddy-Anna."

"You sure you got enough food?" Junior was asking the caterer.

"Relax, Mr. Badgett, you've ordered enough food to feed an army." Conrad Vogel, the caterer, smiled dismissively.

"I didn't ask you to feed an army. I wanna know if you've got enough fancy food so that if somebody likes one thing and eats a ton of it, you won't be telling him there's none left."

Charlie Santoli watched as the caterer withered under Junior's icy glare. You don't dis Junior, pal, he thought.

The caterer got the message. "Mr. Badgett, I assure you that the food is extraordinary and your guests will be very pleased."

"They better be."

"How about Mama's cake?" Eddie asked. "It better be perfect."

A tiny bead of perspiration was forming over Conrad Vogel's upper lip. "It was specially made by the finest bakery in New York. Their cakes are so good that one of our most demanding clients used them for all four of her weddings. The pastry chef himself is here, just in case the cake requires any slight touch-up after it's unboxed."

Junior brushed past the caterer and went to study Mama Heddy-Anna's portrait, which would be formally presented to the senior center's trustees to be hung in the reception area of the center's new wing. It had been painted by a Wallonian artist and ornately framed by a New York gallery. Junior's phoned instructions to the artist had been precise: "Show Mama to be the beautiful lady she is."

Charlie had seen snapshots of Mama. The portrait of a

handsome matriarch in black velvet and pearls bore not the slightest resemblance to any of them, thank God. The artist had been handsomely rewarded for his services.

"She looks real nice," Junior conceded. Immediately his moment of satisfaction evaporated. "Where are those people I'm paying to sing? They're supposed to be here by now."

Jewel had come up behind him. Slipping an arm through his, she said, "I just saw them turn in to the driveway, sweetie pie. Don't worry about them. They're good, really good."

"They better be. You recommended them."

"You heard them sing, lovey. Remember I took you to Nor's Place for dinner?"

"Yeah, I forgot. They're okay. Good restaurant, good food. Good location. Wouldn't mind owning it myself. Let's take a look at the cake."

With Jewel still on his arm, her flaming red hair dancing around her shoulders, her microminiskirt barely reaching her thighs, Junior led the inspection tour into the kitchen. The pastry chef, his towering white hat regally settled on his head, was standing beside the five-layered birthday cake.

As he saw them approach, he beamed with pride. "Is it not magnificent?" he asked, kissing his fingertips. "A spun-sugar masterpiece. My finest, finest effort. A worthy tribute to your beloved mother. And the taste. The divine taste. Your guests will cherish every bite."

Junior and Eddie walked reverently to view the masterpiece. Then, as one, they began shouting.

"Stupid!"

"Jerk!"

"Dope!"

"It's HEDDY-ANNA, not BETTY-ANNA," Eddie snarled. "My mama's name is *Heddy*-Anna!"

The pastry chef looked incredulous as he wrinkled his nose and frowned. "*Heddy*-Anna???"

"Don't you dare make fun of my mama's name!" Eddie shouted as his eyes welled with tears.

Don't let anything else go wrong, Charlie Santoli prayed. They'll both lose it if anything else goes wrong.

$\mathcal{I}$t was a supreme effort for Hans Kramer even to begin the fifteen-minute drive from his home in Syosset to the Badgett brothers' mansion on Long Island Sound. Why did I ever borrow from them? he asked himself for the thousandth time as he turned onto the Long Island Expressway. Why didn't I just declare bankruptcy and have done with it?

An electronics executive, forty-six-year-old Hans had quit his job two years earlier, taken his retirement fund and all his savings and mortgaged his home to open a dot-com company to sell software he had designed. After a promising start, with orders rushing in and the warehouse filled with inventory, the technology industry had crashed. Then the cancellations began. In desperate need of immediate cash, and in an effort to keep the business afloat, he had borrowed from the Badgett brothers. Unfortunately, his efforts so far hadn't paid off.

There's no way on God's earth I can raise the two hundred thousand dollars I borrowed from them, not to mention the fifty percent interest they've added, he despaired.

I must have been out of my mind to go near them. But I've

got a great line of products, he reasoned. If I can just hang in there, things will turn around. Only now I've got to convince the Badgetts to let me renew the note.

In the year since his financial troubles began, Hans had lost twenty pounds. His light brown hair had become streaked with gray. He knew his wife, Lee, was worried sick about him, although she had no idea how bad the situation was. He hadn't told her about the loan, opting instead to tell her only that they needed to cut back on their spending. Why, they'd even practically given up going out for dinner.

The next exit off the expressway led to the Badgett mansion. Hans felt his palms begin to sweat. I was so cocky, he thought as he flicked on the turn signal. Came over here from Switzerland when I was twelve years old and didn't speak a word of English. Graduated from M.I.T. with high honors and thought I'd set the world on fire. And I did for a while. I thought I was immune to failure.

Five minutes later he was approaching the Badgett estate. The gates were open. Cars were lined up, waiting to be admitted by a guard at the foot of the long and winding driveway. Obviously the Badgetts were having a party.

Hans was both relieved and disappointed. I'll phone and leave a message, he thought. Maybe, just maybe, they'll give me an extension.

As he made a U-turn, he tried to ignore the voice inside him that warned that people like the Badgetts never give extensions.

$\mathcal{S}$terling, Nor, and Billy entered the rear door of the Badgett mansion just in time to hear the insults being heaped on the hapless pastry chef. Sterling hastened into the kitchen to see what was going on and found the chef frantically adjusting something in the lettering on the cake.

Wrong age? Sterling wondered. He'd been at a party once where the twelve-year-old daughter had baked a birthday cake as a surprise for her mother. When she proudly carried out the cake, candles blazing, the mother had nearly fainted. The age she had so carefully concealed was starkly revealed in hot-pink lettering on the vanilla cake. I remember thinking that anyone who couldn't read could always count, Sterling thought. That wasn't too charitable of me.

Fortunately this chef's mistake was small. With a few twirls of his pastry tube, he changed Betty-Anna to Heddy-Anna. Nor and Billy had been drawn to the kitchen by the uproar. "Just make sure not to sing 'Happy Birthday, Betty-Anna,' " Nor whispered to Billy.

"I'm tempted, but I want to get out of here alive."

Sterling tagged along as they went into the salon. Nor ran her fingers over the piano; Billy took his guitar out of the case, and they tested the microphones and sound system.

Charlie Santoli had the responsibility of giving them a list of songs that were favorites of the brothers. "They don't want you blasting your music so loud that people can't think," he said nervously.

"We're musicians. We don't blast," Nor snapped.

"But when Mama is hooked up via satellite, you'll be leading the 'Happy Birthday' song, and then they want you to really project."

The bell rang and the first wave of guests were admitted.

Sterling had always liked being around people. He studied the guests as they came in, and as he listened, realized that there were some pretty important people present.

His general impression was that they were here purely because of the largesse of the donation to the senior citizens center, and that after the party they would be happy to forget the Badgett brothers. But a number of the guests stopped to admire the portrait that would be hanging in the new wing.

"Your mother is a beautiful woman," the president of the center's board of governors said sincerely, nodding at the portrait. "So elegant, so dignified. Does she come to visit you often?"

"My precious mother isn't a good traveler," Junior told her.

"Mama gets airsick and seasick," Eddie mourned.

"Then of course you visit her in Wallonia," she suggested.

Charlie Santoli had joined them. "Of course they do, as frequently as possible," he said smoothly.

Sterling shook his head. He's not telling the truth.

Billy and Nor started their first song and were immediately surrounded by an appreciative audience. Nor was a fine musician with an attractive, husky voice. Billy, however, was exceptional. Standing in the crowd, Sterling listened to the murmured comments.

"He's a young Billy Joel . . ."

"He's going to be a star . . ."

"And he's gorgeous," the daughter of one of the board members cooed.

"Billy, let's hear 'Be There When I Awake.' "

The request brought spontaneous applause.

His fingers moving lightly on the strings of the guitar, Billy began to sing, "I know what I want . . . I know what I need."

That must be his hit record, Sterling thought. Even to my out-of-date ears, it's great.

Thanks to the music, the atmosphere at the party loosened up. The guests began interacting, allowing their glasses to be refilled with the excellent wines, and piling their plates with the truly spectacular food.

By 7:15 the Badgett brothers were beaming. Their party was a success. They were a success.

At that point, Junior picked up the microphone and cleared his throat. "I wanna welcome all of you, and my brother and me hope you're enjoying yourselves very much. It is our pleasure to have you as our guests, and we are very, very happy to have given you the money, I mean donated the money, for the wing of the senior citizens center to be known as the Mama Heddy-Anna wing in honor of our saintly mother's eighty-fifth birthday. And now, by the miracle of satellite, from the historic village of Kizkek where my brother and me were raised, our mama will appear. Mama stayed up way past her bedtime to be with us 'cause she's so honored. Now I ask all of you to join in singing 'Happy Birthday' to her. Our wonderful Billy Campbell and his mother, that doll Nor Kelly, will lead us in song."

There was a faint smattering of applause. The birthday cake was rolled out, ablaze with eighty-six candles, one to grow on. The ten-foot screen dropped down from the ceiling, and Mama Heddy-Anna's dour face emerged to fill it.

She was seated in her rocking chair, sipping grappa.

Eddie's eyes streamed with tears, and Junior blew kisses at the screen as the guests dutifully sang "Happy Birthday, Heddy-Anna" in Wallonian, working from phonetically marked song sheets.

Her cheeks puffed like twin red balloons, Mama blew out the candles on the cake her sons had sent by chartered plane to Wallonia. That was when it became all too clear that she'd filled the hours past her usual bedtime by drinking more than her share of grappa. In broken English she started cursing and complaining loudly that her sons never came to see her and she wasn't feeling so hot.

Junior quickly turned down the volume but not before she had screamed, "How much bad things you two do, you can't come see your mama before she die? Not once you come in all these years."

Billy and Nor immediately started another vigorous round of "Happy Birthday, Heddy-Anna." This time no one joined in, however, and the telecast closed on the unforgettable sight of Mama thumbing her nose at her offspring and their guests, as she came down with a case of the hiccups.

Jewel's laugh was a high-pitched trill. "Doesn't Mama have a wonderful sense of humor? I just love her."

Junior brushed Jewel aside and stalked out of the room. Eddie followed close behind.

Nor quickly whispered to Billy, "This is a disaster. What should we do? He told us to sing 'For She's a Jolly Good Fellow' while people ate the cake.

"And then the medley of songs about mothers, starting with 'I always loved my mama, she's my favorite girl . . . ' "

How about "Little old lady, time for tea," Sterling thought. That was a hit in my day.

"We'd better check on what they want us to do now. I'm not taking any chances on second-guessing them," Nor said, glancing around the room at the stunned expressions on the faces of the guests.

As Sterling trotted after Nor and Billy, he sensed imminent disaster. Junior and Eddie were disappearing into a room at the end of the hall.

Billy and Nor raced to catch up with them, and Billy tapped on the now-closed door. When there was no response, he and Nor looked at each other. "Let's take a chance," Nor whispered.

Just go home, Sterling urged, but knew it was a year too late to even think that.

Billy turned the handle and cautiously opened the door. He and Nor stepped into what appeared to be a small reception room. It was empty.

"They're in there," Nor whispered, pointing to an inner room that could be seen through a partially open door. "Maybe we'd better . . ."

"Wait a minute. They're checking the answering machine."

An electronic voice was announcing, "You have one new message."

Nor and Billy hesitated, not sure whether to wait or to leave, but then the message they were overhearing froze them to the spot.

It was a plea from a man who sounded desperate, begging for "wery little extra time" to pay back a loan.

The answering machine clicked off, and they heard Junior shout, "Your time just ran out, buddy. Eddie, get on it. Tell the guys to burn his stinking warehouse down and do it now. I don't wanna hear that it's still standing tomorrow."

"There won't be nuthin' left," Eddie assured him, sounding much cheerier, his mind off Mama for the moment.

Billy put his finger to his lips. Silently he and Nor tiptoed from the room and hurried back to the salon. "Let's get our stuff," Billy whispered. "We're out of here."

What they did not notice, but Sterling did, was that Charlie Santoli, at the other end of the hall, had seen them come out of the office.

$\mathcal{T}$he celestial waiting room was filled with newcomers gazing around and trying to adjust to their surroundings. The angel in charge had been ordered to hang a large DO NOT DISTURB sign on the door of the conference room. There had been several instances of former top executives, not used to being kept waiting, who had rushed in demanding a meeting when the angel's back was turned.

Inside the conference room, the Heavenly Council was following Sterling's activities with keen interest.

"Did you notice how chagrined he was when Marissa didn't even sense that he was present in the restaurant?" the nun asked. "He was truly taken aback."

"That was one of the first lessons we wanted him to learn," the monk stated. "During his lifetime, too many people were invisible to him. He'd look right past them."

"Do you think Mama Heddy-Anna will turn up in our waiting room soon?" the shepherd asked. "She told her sons she's dying."

The nurse smiled. "She used the oldest trick in the book to get her sons to visit her. She's as strong as a bull."

"I wouldn't want her in the ring with me," the matador commented wryly.

"That lawyer is in real trouble," said the saint who had reminded Sterling of Pocahontas. "Unless he does something drastic very soon, when his time comes, he won't be dealing with us."

"Poor Hans Kramer is desperate," the nun observed. "The Badgett brothers have absolutely no mercy."

"They belong in the brig," the admiral proclaimed sternly.

"Did you hear that?" the queen's tone was shocked. "They're going to set that poor man's warehouse on fire."

Shaking their heads, the saints fell silent, reflecting sadly on man's inhumanity to man.

$\mathcal{V}$alets frantically rushed to deliver the cars of the guests pouring out of the house. Sterling leaned against a column on the porch, bent on hearing the reactions of the departing merrymakers.

"Bizarre!"

"Give them their money back. *I'll* donate two million for that wing," a dowager snapped.

"Reminded me of the movie 'Throw Momma From the Train.' I bet that's what those two characters feel like doing now," a board member's husband snickered.

"At least the food was good," someone said charitably.

"I hope you caught that they haven't set foot in Wallonia since they left. Figure out why."

"You got a load of Mama, didn't you?"

Sterling noticed that the two U.S. Senators were screaming at their top aides as they were whisked away. They're probably worrying that they'll be written up in the tabloids for partying with mobsters, Sterling thought. They should know what Junior is going to do to some poor guy's warehouse. He couldn't wait to slip into Nor and Billy's car and hear what they had to say about everything that had happened.

A guest, who clearly had slurped as much vodka as Mama had grappa began to sing, "Happy Birthday, Heddy-Anna" in Wallonian, but didn't have his phonetically marked song sheet to consult. He switched to English and was joined by several other guests, who were also feeling no pain.

Sterling heard a valet ask one of the guests if his vehicle was an SUV. What's that? Sterling wondered. A moment later the valet pulled up in one of those little trucks. So that's what it is, Sterling thought. I wonder what SUV stands for.

Billy's SUV was parked in the back. Don't want to miss them, Sterling thought. Two minutes later, when Nor and Billy appeared, lugging their equipment, he was in the backseat.

It was obvious from the nervous expressions on both their faces that they were deeply worried.

Wordlessly, they loaded the car, jumped in, and joined the line of vehicles exiting the long driveway. They did not speak until they were out on the main road. Then Nor asked, the words rushing out, "Billy, do you think they were serious about burning down someone's warehouse?"

"Absolutely, and we're damn lucky they don't know we overheard them."

Uh-oh, Sterling thought. Their lawyer—what's his name? Charlie Santoli—saw you come out of the office. If he tells the Badgetts, your goose is cooked.

"I can't help thinking that I've heard that voice before, the one on the phone message," Nor said slowly. "Did you notice he said 'wery,' not 'very,' when he asked for more time?"

"Now that you say it, I guess I did," Billy agreed. "I just figured the poor guy was so nervous he was practically stuttering."

"No, it wasn't that. Maybe he has a slight lisp. I think he's had dinner at the restaurant. The thing is, if I could only remember who it was, then we could warn him."

"When we get to the restaurant, I'm going to call the police," Billy said. "I don't want to use the cell phone."

They rode the rest of the way in silence. In the backseat, Sterling shared their anxiety.

It was nearly nine o'clock when they entered Nor's Place. The holiday diners were in full force. Nor tried to greet people quickly. At the same moment, she and Billy spotted one of their old friends, Sean O'Brien, a retired detective, sitting at the bar.

They looked at each other. "I'll ask him to sit with us. He'll know what we should do," Billy said.

A smile plastered on her face, Nor went to her usual table at the front of the restaurant. From this vantage point she could oversee the operation, hold court, and easily greet her patrons. Sterling joined her, taking the seat he'd been occupying a few hours earlier.

Billy came to the table followed by Sean O'Brien, a solid-looking man of about fifty-five, with a full head of graying brown hair, alert brown eyes, and a genial smile.

"Season's greetings, Nor," he began, then immediately sensed something was wrong. "What's up?" he asked abruptly, as he and Billy sat down.

"We were hired for a party the Badgett brothers gave this afternoon," Nor began.

"The Badgett brothers?" O'Brien raised one eyebrow, then listened intently as they told him of the message on the answering machine and Junior Badgett's response to it.

"I know the voice," Nor finished. "I'm sure that man has been a customer here."

"Nor, the feds have been trying to pin something on those two for years. They're as slippery as fish in olive oil. They're crooks and they're vicious. If that was a local call, I wouldn't be surprised to be reading tomorrow about a warehouse that burned down overnight."

"Is there anything we can do to try to stop them?" Billy asked.

"I can alert the feds, but those guys have interests all over. We know for sure they have a presence in Vegas and Los Angeles. That message could have come from anywhere, but no matter where it came from, it doesn't mean the warehouse is in that vicinity."

"I never knew the Badgetts were that bad," Billy said. "You hear rumors, but they have those car and boat dealerships . . ."

"They've got a dozen legitimate businesses," O'Brien said.

"That's the way they launder their money. I'll make some calls. The feds will at least want to keep them under surveillance, but those guys never dirty their own hands."

Nor rubbed her forehead, her face troubled. "There's a reason I remember that voice. Wait a minute." She beckoned a waiter. "Sam, ask Dennis to join us. You cover the bar."

O'Brien looked at her. "It's better if nobody else knows you overheard that conversation."

"I trust Dennis with my life," Nor said.

The table is getting crowded, Sterling thought. I'll have to stand. He felt the chair being pulled out and jumped up quickly. He had no desire to have Dennis sitting on his lap.

" . . . and, Dennis, I'm sure I've heard that voice in this restaurant," Nor concluded a few minutes later. "He pronounced 'very' as 'wery.' Granted that could have been just nerves, but I thought maybe it's a guy who sits at the bar and talks with you sometimes."

Dennis shook his head. "I can't think of a soul, Nor. But I do know this—if that Badgett guy was on the level when he talked about burning down a warehouse, the fellow who called him will be 'wery upset.' "

"Wery, wery upset," Billy agreed.

They all laughed nervously.

They're trying to use humor to cover their very real anxieties, Sterling thought. If the Badgett brothers are as bad as Sean O'Brien believes they are, and if Nor and Billy have to testify about that call . . . Poor Marissa. She was so happy today.

O'Brien got up. "I've got to make some phone calls," he said. "Nor, can I use your office?"

"Of course."

"You and Billy come with me. I want to put you on the phone and have you repeat exactly what you heard."

"I'll be at the bar." Dennis pushed his chair back.

If I were still alive, that chair would have smashed my big toe, Sterling thought.

"Nor, I thought you and Billy were doing a holiday performance here at the restaurant tonight," a patron at a nearby table called. "We came specially to hear you two sing."

"You're going to." Nor smiled. "We'll be back in fifteen minutes."

In the office, O'Brien phoned his contact at the FBI, and Nor and Billy recounted what they had overheard. When the call ended, Nor shrugged her shoulders. "It is what it is. Unless I can remember whose voice that is, I'm no use to them."

Billy's cell phone rang. "It's Rissa," he said as he looked at the Caller ID. His troubled expression cleared. "Hi, baby . . . We just got back . . . No, we didn't see the swimming pool or the bowling alley . . . Well, I wouldn't say they were like the Sopranos."

"I would," Nor murmured.

"Uh-huh, we did our usual bit . . ." He laughed. ". . . Of course we were sensational. They couldn't get enough of us.

Listen, baby, NorNor will say a quick hello, then you get to bed. I'll see you tomorrow. Love you."

He handed the phone to Nor, then turned to O'Brien. "You've met my daughter, Marissa, haven't you?"

"Sure. I thought she owned this place."

"She thinks she does."

Nor said good night to Marissa and smiled ruefully as she snapped the phone closed and handed it to Billy. She looked at O'Brien. "I can't help wondering if that poor guy who was begging for more time to pay off a loan is supporting a family."

Billy put his arm around her shoulders and gave her a quick hug. "You look tired, Mom, so I hate to say it, but your public awaits . . ."

"I know. We've got to get out there. Give me a minute to do my face."

O'Brien reached in his pocket. "Here's my card. If you get a brainstorm, call me at any time. I'll give one to Dennis too."

By 9:30, when Nor and Billy began to perform, every table in the restaurant was filled. They did two half-hour shows, one at 9:30, then another at 11, for the late-night crowd.

They're troupers, Sterling thought. You'd never know they have a care in the world. The minute Nor finished the first show she slipped into her office, carrying the reservations books for the last two years under her arm. Sterling sat with her as she went through them, saying each name aloud as she went down the list.

Several times she stopped and repeated a name, then shook her head and continued to read. She's trying to see if the name of the guy whose voice they heard jumps out at her, Sterling thought.

The concern in Nor's face deepened as she spoke name after name. But then she glanced at her watch and jumped up, opened her bag and pulled out her compact. In seconds she had lightly powdered her face, touched up her eyes and lips. She pulled the jeweled comb out of her hair and shook her head. Sterling was amazed at how deftly she twisted the long tresses in her fingers, swept them up, and anchored them once again.

"I feel like Minnie off the pickle boat," she said aloud, "but I guess the show must go on."

You look wonderful, Sterling wanted to protest. You're a really beautiful woman. And who the heck is Minnie off the pickle boat?

At the door of the office, Nor let out a quick sigh, but a moment later she was wreathed in smiles as she stopped at table after table to exchange a few words with her patrons.

This place is full, Sterling noticed, and it's obvious from the way Nor talks to everyone that they're all regulars. They seem so glad to have a word with her. Well, she's good. He listened as she inquired about someone's mother, someone's son, another's planned vacation, then congratulated a couple who had just become engaged.

The Heavenly Council will never tell her that she didn't pay attention to other people, Sterling thought. That's for sure. Too bad I wasn't more like her.

Billy was deep in conversation with a man and woman at a corner table. Sterling decided to tune in. I hope nobody else joins us, he thought as he took the one empty chair. Then as he caught the gist of the conversation, he raised his eyebrows. These people were executives from Empire Recording Company, and they wanted to sign Billy to a contract.

The man was saying, "I don't have to tell you the kind of people we've launched. We've been scouting you for a while, and you've got it, Billy. We're offering you a two-album contract."

"I'm very flattered and it sounds great, but you'll have to talk to my agent," Billy said, smiling.

He's trying to hide that he's thrilled, Sterling realized. It's every young singer's dream to be signed up by a record company. What a crazy day.

The last stragglers left the restaurant at 12:30. Nor and Billy sat at the bar with Dennis as he finished cleaning up. Nor held up a glass. "I've heard it's bad luck to toast with water, but I'm going to take a chance. Here's to Billy and the new contract."

"Your dad would be so proud," Dennis said.

"You bet he would." Nor looked up. "Here's to you, Bill, wherever you are up there. Your kid's done good."

I definitely have to meet him, Sterling told himself. He saw the suspicious touch of moisture in the eyes of all three.

Billy was just about the age Marissa is now when he lost his dad. It must have been awfully tough on him and Nor.

"Let's keep our fingers crossed that it all goes through," Billy told them. "I don't want to get too excited yet. That'll wait until I have the offer in writing."

"You will," Nor assured him. "But you're still singing with me here at Christmastime next year."

"I know, Mom, and for free," Billy laughed.

"You'll have to hire a bouncer for crowd control," Dennis declared. He folded a towel. "Okay, that's it. Nor, you look awfully tired. Let me drive you home."

"Listen, if I lived fifteen minutes away, the way I feel now, I'd take you up on it. But for the three minutes it'll take me to get there, I'd rather have the car at the door in the morning. You can carry those reservations books out for me. I'm going to keep at them for a while."

She kissed Billy lightly on the cheek. "See you tomorrow."

"Okay. I'm heading upstairs. Don't try to go over those books tonight, Mom. Leave it for the morning."

They looked at each other. "I know," Billy said. "By then it may be too late."

So that's where Billy lives, Sterling thought. He must have an apartment up there. It would be interesting to see what Nor's home is like. She said it's only a three-minute drive away. That can't be too far for me to walk back. Once again he found himself hurrying across the parking lot, this time following Nor and Dennis.

The temperature has really dropped in these few hours, he

thought. He looked up. Clouds were forming and beginning to obscure the moon and stars. He sniffed. There was a hint of snow in the air. I was one of those people who preferred winter to summer, he thought. Annie thought I was crazy. If there was anything she loved, it was a day at the seashore. I remember her family had a place in Spring Lake.

Nor's car was a handsome Mercedes sedan. I used to drive one of these, Sterling thought, and in a lot of ways this one doesn't look that much different from the one I had. As Dennis laid the reservations books on the floor in the back and held the driver's door open for Nor, Sterling got in the front seat. I never liked to ride in the back of the car, he thought. My legs always felt cramped.

Nor locked the door and fastened her seat belt. Everybody does that these days, Sterling mused. I wonder if there's a law about it.

He readjusted his homburg, smiling as he remembered that next year Marissa would poke fun at it.

As they pulled out of the driveway, he jumped when Nor muttered aloud, "Mama Heddy-Anna. God help us!"

Sterling felt a little guilty. Nor thinks she's alone, and she's one of those people who talks to herself. I used to do that too, and I'd have died if I learned that someone was eavesdropping on me.

But it's okay because I'm here to help them, he comforted himself. Fortunately she turned on the radio and listened to the news the rest of the way.

Nor's house was at the end of a cul-de-sac, situated on a generous piece of property. The minute he saw it he sensed that it was the perfect home for her. It looked to him like a renovated farmhouse. The exterior was white clapboard with black shutters. The porch light was on, casting a warm glow around the front door.

"Thank God to be home," Nor sighed.

I know what you mean, Sterling said aloud, then rolled his eyes. Thank God she can't hear me. I might have given her a heart attack.

I'm not going to stay long, he promised himself as Nor fished through her purse for her house key, got out of the car, and gathered the reservations books in her arms.

Sterling walked to the front door, admiring the attractive shrubbery that was lightly coated with snow.

As soon as Nor opened the door, shut off the alarm, and switched on the light, he realized that she also had great taste. The ground floor was a single, very large room with white walls and wooden floors. A raised-hearth fireplace defined the living room area. At a right angle to it stood a floor to-ceiling-Christmas tree, decorated with strings of candle-shaped bulbs. The bottom three tiers clearly bore Marissa's touch. Handmade paper ornaments, a quantity of tinsel, and a dozen candy canes demonstrated her idea of how a Christmas tree should look.

Overstuffed couches, Persian area rugs, fine antique furnishings, and first-class paintings filled the rest of the room. The effect was that of vivid serenity—if there is such a thing, Sterling thought.

"Cup of cocoa," Nor murmured as she kicked off her shoes. She walked to the kitchen area, dropped the reservations books on the table, and opened the refrigerator. Hating to rush, Sterling scurried from painting to painting. These are valuable, he thought. I wish I had a chance to really study them. An English hunting scene particularly intrigued him.

As the attorney for a number of family trusts when he was alive, he'd developed an eye for good art. They used to tell me I could have been an appraiser, he remembered.

A staircase to the second floor beckoned him. One quick look and then I'm off, he promised himself.

Nor's bedroom was the largest. Framed pictures were on the bureau, the dressing table, and the night tables. These were all personal and many of them were of a much younger Nor with Billy's father. There were at least a half-dozen of Billy with his parents, starting from the time he was an infant. He seemed to be about six years old in the last one that showed the three of them together.

Sterling poked his head into the first of the other two bedrooms. It was small but cozy, with the uncluttered look of a guest room.

The third door was closed. The small porcelain tile on it said MARISSA'S PLACE. As he opened the door, Sterling felt a lump in his throat. This child is about to lose out on so much in this upcoming year, he thought.

The room was enchanting. White wicker furniture. Blue-and-white wallpaper. White eyelet bedspread and curtains. Shelves of books on one wall. A desk with a bulletin board against another.

He heard Nor's footsteps on the stairs. It was time to go. Remembering the door had been closed, he quietly pulled it shut, then watched as Nor went into her room. A moment later, with the collar of his chesterfield turned up, his homburg pulled down as far as he could get it, Sterling walked briskly down the road.

I've got several hours to kill, he thought. Billy's probably asleep. Maybe I'll just drop by and look in on Marissa. But where exactly does she live? I never was too good at directions.

Until now there'd been plenty of activity to keep him occupied, but with everyone going to bed, he felt a little lonely as he trudged through the quiet streets.

Should I try to contact the Heavenly Council? he wondered. Or will they decide I can't do the job? And if so, what then?

Suddenly something caught his eye.

What's that?

A piece of paper was fluttering from the sky. It stopped falling when it was directly in front of him. Sterling plucked it out of the air, unfolded it, and walked to the next street lamp to read it.

It was a map of the village. Marissa's home and Nor's Place were clearly indicated. A dotted line started at a point marked "you are here" and gave specific directions—"four blocks east . . . turn left one block, then right"—showing him the way to Marissa's house. A second dotted line illustrated the way from there back to the restaurant.

Sterling looked up, past the moon, past the stars, into eternity. Thank you. I am very grateful, he whispered.

$\mathcal{N}$o matter how late the hour, Dennis Madigan always read the *New York Post* before settling down to sleep. His wife, Joan, had long ago learned to sleep with his light on.

Tonight, however, he could not concentrate on the paper. He knew neither Nor nor Billy realized that their lives could be in serious danger. If the Badgetts were as bad as Sean O'Brien portrayed them . . . Dennis shook his head. When he worked in bars in Manhattan, he'd seen and heard a lot about their kind. None of it good.

Very. "Wery." What is this reminding me of? he asked himself as he irritably flipped through the pages of the newspaper. Nor thinks the man might be someone who comes into the restaurant. He can't be a regular, though, or I'd know him.

"Wery," he said aloud.

Joan opened her eyes and blinked. "What?"

"Nothing. Sorry, honey. Go back to sleep."

"Easy for you to say," she muttered as she turned her back to him.

Dennis skipped to the *Post*'s television section and smiled as he read Linda Stasi's funny review of a corny holiday special.

Still not remotely sleepy even though it was 3:30, he began to skim the restaurant pages. The write-up on a new midtown restaurant caught his eye. "We started with vichyssoise . . . ," the columnist began.

Sounds like a good joint, Dennis thought. Have to check it out. He and Joan enjoyed going into the city occasionally and trying new places.

He stared at the paper. Vichyssoise. He remembered a smart aleck waiter at Nor's—one who didn't last long—joking that a customer who ordered "wichyssoise" last time, now would like a cup of "wegetable" soup.

What's the customer's name? Dennis thought. I can see him. He and his wife always had a cocktail at the bar. Nice people. I didn't think of him right away because that's the only hint of an accent he had, and he hasn't been around in a long time . . .

In his mind, he could see a face. He's local, Dennis thought. And his name . . . his name . . . it sounds European . . .

Hans Kramer!

That's it! That's his name!

Dennis grabbed the phone. Nor answered on the first ring. "Nor, I've got it. The guy on the answering machine. Could it be Hans Kramer?"

"Hans Kramer," she said, slowly. "That doesn't ring a bell with me. I don't remember . . ."

"Think, Nor. He ordered 'wichyssoise' and 'wegetable' soup."

"Oh my God, of course . . . you're right." Nor leaned on one elbow and pulled herself up. Sean O'Brien's card was propped against the lamp on her night table. As she reached for it she could feel adrenaline surging through her body.

"I know Kramer has something to do with computers, Dennis. Maybe he has a warehouse. I'll call Sean O'Brien this minute. I just hope we're not too late."

s Sterling approached Marissa's house, everything looked quiet and peaceful. All was dark inside except for a faint light shining through an upstairs window.

My mother used to leave the hall light on for me, he remembered. And she'd leave my bedroom door open a crack so I could see it. I was chicken, he thought with a smile. Never mind the light, I slept with my teddy bear till I was ten.

Noting a small sign that indicated the house was wired against intruders, he slipped inside, not bothering to open the door just in case the alarm was on. He had the feeling that the Heavenly Council wanted him to move around like everybody else except when it prevented him from doing his job, but he was very sure they didn't want him setting off alarms.

He tiptoed up the stairs and stepped over Roy's safety gate, hoisting his leg high to clear it. How big does he think those kids are anyhow? Sterling wondered as he felt a tug on the cuff of his trousers. The next thing he knew he was tumbling onto the hallway floor.

Thank God I don't make any noise, he thought as he stared up at the ceiling. His hat had gone flying. He got up slowly, aware of a faint twinge in his back. Retrieving the homburg, he resumed his attempt to visit Marissa.

Her bedroom was the last one at the end of the hallway. All the bedroom doors were slightly ajar. A light snore was coming from inside the master bedroom. As he passed the munchkins' room, he could hear the sound of one of the boys stirring. Sterling hesitated and listened closely, but then the child seemed to settle down again.

Even though the night was beginning to cloud over, there was enough light from the heavens for him to see Marissa's face clearly. She was curled up in bed, her hair soft on her cheek, the covers tucked around her.

A pile of boxes in the corner were testimony to the fact that she had received an abundance of presents for Christmas and her birthday. Not surprising, Sterling thought. I'd love to be able to give her something myself.

He sat in the same chair he would sit in next year, when he would talk to Marissa for the first time. From there he could study her face. She looks like an angel, he thought tenderly. If only she didn't have to go through the change that is coming. If only I had the power to keep her world the way it is now. But I can't, so next year I'll do everything I can to put her world back together again. By hook or by crook, he resolved.

And not just because I want to go to heaven. I truly want to help her. She looks so small and vulnerable. Hard to believe she's the same kid who was trying to call the shots at the restaurant today, and who didn't waste any time phoning her father to get the lowdown on the party.

With a smile that ended in a sigh, Sterling got up and left the room. As he went down the hallway he heard one of the munchkins start to cry. Then the other one joined in.

Luckily, they don't need me, Sterling thought. An instant later Roy staggered out of the bedroom and into the nursery. "Daddy's here," he crooned. "Roy Junior, Robert, Daddy's here."

Denise has him well trained, Sterling thought. My friends used to turn a deaf ear when their kids started howling in the middle of the night. But times have changed.

I was an only child, he thought as he descended the stairs. My parents were in their forties when I was born. I became the center of their universe. They were in heaven long before I arrived in the celestial waiting room.

It will be so good to see Mother and Dad again, he thought, once more glancing skyward.

Sterling consulted the map before he left the house, then made his way to Nor's restaurant. As he walked through the quiet streets, he suddenly felt an acute sense of urgency. Even though it absolutely was not coming from anyplace nearby, he was beginning to smell smoke.

They did it! he thought. The warehouse fire has just been set.

$\mathcal{S}$ean O'Brien had put in twenty years with the Nassau County Police Department. During that time he had learned to expect predawn phone calls if there was an important development in a case he was working on.

When his phone rang at 3:40, Sean woke up immediately and grabbed it. As he hoped, it was Nor.

"Sean, I just heard from Dennis. He came up with the name of the guy on the answering machine, and he's right. I'm absolutely positive that he's right."

"Who is it?"

"His name is Hans Kramer. He lives in Syosset and has some kind of computer software company. He comes into the restaurant occasionally."

"Okay, Nor. I'll get right on it."

Thoroughly awake now, Sean sat on the side of the bed. He was alone in the room. His wife, Kate, a nurse, was working the night shift on the pediatrics floor of North Shore hospital.

His first call was to police headquarters in Syosset. There was a chance Kramer was known to them.

It proved to be a good bet. Nick Amaretto, the lieutenant

in charge, knew exactly who Kramer was. "Nice guy. He's lived in town twenty years. Was on the zoning board for a while. Ran the Red Cross drive a couple of years ago. Has his own software company."

"Does he have a warehouse?"

"Yeah. He bought property in the area off the expressway that had that string of crummy motels. He built a nice little complex with an office and warehouse."

"I have a tip that it may be torched. A matter of an overdue loan from the Badgett brothers."

"Oh, boy. We'll get over there right away. I'll contact the bomb squad and the fire department."

"I'm calling the feds. Talk to you later."

"Wait a minute, Sean," the lieutenant snapped. "Something big is coming in on the radio."

Sean O'Brien knew even before Amaretto got back on the phone that he was too late. The Kramer complex was already in flames.

*H*ans Kramer received the call from his security service at 3:43 A.M. The smoke detectors in the warehouse had been activated. The fire department was on the way.

In silent desperation, Hans and his wife, Lee, threw on clothes, stuffed their bare feet into sneakers, grabbed jackets, and ran to the car.

I dropped a lot of the insurance coverage, Hans thought desperately. I couldn't afford the premiums. If the fire department can't save the warehouse, what will I do?

He felt a tightening in his chest. Even though the car had not yet warmed up, he was dripping perspiration.

"Hans, you're trembling," Lee said, her voice sick with worry. "No matter how bad it is, we can handle it. I promise, we can handle it."

"Lee, you don't understand. I borrowed money, a lot of money. I thought I could pay it back. I was sure business would pick up." The road was almost empty. He pressed the accelerator and the car raced ahead.

"Hans, the doctor has been warning you. That last stress test you took wasn't good. Please calm down."

I owe them three hundred thousand dollars, Hans thought. The warehouse is worth three million, but I'm only insured enough to cover the mortgage. I won't have enough to pay off the loan.

As they turned onto the street that led to the complex, both Hans and Lee gasped. In the distance they could see flames shooting through the darkness, fierce angry flames surrounded by thick billowing smoke.

"Oh, dear God," Lee breathed.

Hans, in shock, said nothing. *They* did this, Hans thought. The Badgetts. This is their answer to my request for an extension on the loan.

When Hans and Lee reached the warehouse, it was surrounded by fire trucks. Gallons of water from high-powered hoses were pouring into the inferno, but it was obvious the blaze could not be contained.

As Hans pushed open the door of the car, a gigantic wave of pain washed over him, and he toppled onto the driveway.

Moments later he could feel something being clamped over his nostrils, a jolting in his chest, and strong hands lifting him. In a crazy way he felt relieved.

It was all beyond his control.

$\mathcal{S}$terling arrived back at the restaurant and was not surprised to see Nor getting out of her car in the parking lot. They must know about the fire already, he thought as he broke into a trot.

He followed Nor inside and up to Billy's apartment, which encompassed the entire second floor of the building. Dennis was already there, and Billy had made coffee.

"Sean is on his way over," Nor told Billy. She had no make-up on. Her hair was loosely caught up in a comb, but long tendrils were slipping around her neck and face. She was wearing a light blue sweat suit and a pair of sneakers.

Billy had on rumpled blue jeans, a wrinkled denim shirt, and old moccasins. His eyes looked tired, and he needed a shave.

Dennis was wearing a gray Madison Village sweatshirt over well-worn corduroy pants.

"Sean said it's important that he talk to us right away," Nor said as Billy poured coffee into mugs, and the three of them went to the table in the dining room.

From the chair he selected, Sterling could see into the living room. Billy's place was a comfortable bachelor pad, slightly untidy, with sneakers under the coffee table and a pile of newspapers on top of it. The couch and chairs were basically nondescript but looked inviting.

It was clear that Billy worked on his music in the living room. There were a couple of guitars propped up against the piano, and sheet music was scattered on the couch.

As at Nor's home, many of the homemade ornaments on the Christmas tree looked as though they had Marissa's touch.

The ringing of the doorbell indicated that Sean O'Brien had arrived. Billy buzzed him in and waited as he climbed the stairs.

O'Brien's expression was grave. He nodded when Billy offered coffee, joined them at the table, and told them about the fire.

"How bad is it?" Nor asked.

"About as bad as it gets," O'Brien said. "Hans Kramer is in the hospital. He's had a pretty severe heart attack, but he should make it."

Nor inhaled sharply. "Oh, no."

"His place burned to the ground," O'Brien continued. "There's absolutely nothing left. It was one expert job."

"It was definitely set?" Nor asked flatly, already knowing the answer.

"Yes, it was."

"What happens now?" Billy asked.

"The FBI will be here soon. They need to take statements from you. Your testimony directly implicates the Badgetts.

When Kramer is well enough, we'll get his statement. Then the feds will go for an indictment. Since you overheard Junior's order to torch the warehouse, it looks like this time there will finally be a solid case against them. But I warn you, it's absolutely imperative that no one knows you two are witnesses."

Billy and Nor exchanged glances. "I think we both understand," Billy said.

"I certainly do," Dennis said grimly.

Sterling shook his head. The lawyer, he thought. The Badgetts' lawyer, Charlie Santoli. He saw Billy and Nor coming out of the office. Do the Badgetts know that yet?

n Monday morning at 7:30, Charlie Santoli went downstairs to the kitchen of his home in Little Neck, Long Island. His wife, Marge, was already there preparing breakfast.

Hands on her hips, a worried frown on her face, she took a good look at him. "You look like you've been up for a week, Charlie," she said bluntly.

Charlie raised his hand. "Marge, don't start. I'm okay."

Marge was an attractive, generously sized woman with short brown hair, a shade she preserved by regular visits to the local beauty salon. For years she had kept a standing appointment every Saturday for a wash, set, and manicure. Every fourth Saturday she had a seaweed facial and a color job.

Marge never allowed circumstances to quiet her lively tongue. She had a reputation for conducting conversations with fellow patrons of the salon while sitting under the dryer. Of course this meant that she had to shout to be heard, but, as Charlie had learned, Marge was born with her Irish ancestors' gift of gab. Nothing stood in the way of her having both the first *and* the last word.

Now she continued to scrutinize her husband, studying his face, taking in the lines of fatigue around his eyes, the tightness of his lips, the faint quiver of a muscle in his cheek, and then began a familiar refrain. "You look terrible, and it's all because those two are driving you crazy."

A buzzer went off. Marge turned, and with her mittened hand, removed a tray of freshly baked corn muffins from the oven. "Did you get any sleep at all last night?"

Did I? Charlie wondered. His head was aching, his stomach was knotted and churning. He shrugged his answer.

Yesterday evening, when he arrived home at nine o'clock, Marge had pounced on him for details about the party, but he had begged off. "Marge, give me time to get over it."

Mercifully she had done just that, helped by the fact that a vintage Christmas movie she'd always loved was about to start on an obscure cable station. A box of tissues next to the couch, a cup of tea on the table in front of her, Marge had cheerfully prepared herself for a good cry.

Immensely relieved to have a reprieve, Charlie fixed a strong scotch and buried himself in the Sunday papers.

It had nearly killed Marge to miss the Badgett party, especially with the delicious prospect of seeing Mama Badgett on satellite television. What kept her away was a long-planned, late-afternoon, holiday reunion of her classmates from St. Mary's Academy. As chairperson of the event, she had chosen the date for it and therefore simply could not miss it. As Charlie had pointed out, she was hoist on her own petard.

Now Marge put a muffin on a plate and placed it in front of

him. "Don't stand there," she said. "Sit down and eat like a normal human being."

It was useless to protest. Charlie dutifully pulled out the chair as she poured him a cup of coffee. His vitamins were already lined up next to a glass of freshly squeezed orange juice.

If only he could call up the Badgetts and tell them he wasn't ever going to walk into their home or office again. If only he could just sit here in this cozy kitchen with Marge and have a peaceful breakfast without ever having to think about the brothers again.

Marge poured her own coffee and slathered jam on a muffin. "Now tell me," she ordered. "What happened at the party? The way you dragged yourself in last night, it must have been awful. Didn't the satellite hookup work?"

"Unfortunately, it came through loud and clear."

Her eyes widened. "What do you mean, 'unfortunately?' "

"Mama Heddy-Anna was plastered." Charlie relayed the rest of the story, omitting nothing and finishing with a vivid description of Mama Heddy-Anna thumbing her nose at the North Shore social set.

Frustrated, Marge thumped the table with her clenched fist. "I can't believe I missed that. Why do I only go with you to the boring parties? And to think I was the one who said Thanksgiving weekend was a bad time to have our reunion. What did I ever do to deserve this?"

Charlie sipped the last of his coffee. "I wish I *had* missed it! Those two are going to be in one foul mood today." It was on the tip of his tongue to tell her that it was now obvious to everyone present at the party that the Badgett brothers had not been back to Wallonia since they left it, and to relate to her Mama's own words, "How much bad you do, you can't come visit your mama?"

Charlie had never had the courage to tell Marge that it was only after he was in too deep to get out that he had learned the full extent of the situation in Wallonia. Junior and Eddie had been sentenced, in absentia, to life imprisonment there, for a host of crimes Charlie didn't even want to think about. They could never go back, and he could never get away from them.

With something akin to despair, he got up, kissed the top of Marge's head, went to the closet, put on his overcoat, picked up his briefcase, and left.

The Badgett office building where Charlie worked was in Rosewood, about fifteen minutes away from the estate. Junior and Eddie were already there when Charlie arrived. They were in Junior's private office, and to Charlie's surprise both men were in remarkably good spirits. He had expected them to be in foul moods and to somehow manage to blame at least part of the Mama fiasco on him.

On the drive there from Little Neck he had been preparing his defense: "I suggested you make the donation for the wing, give the party, and present the portrait. The satellite hookup was your idea."

But, of course, Charlie knew that was the last thing he could say. Any hint that Mama's appearance had been less than a delight would be unforgivable. By now the brothers would have figured out another reason why the party had been a colossal flop.

The entertainment, Charlie thought. They'll decide that Nor Kelly and Billy Campbell didn't cut the mustard. They'll blame Jewel for suggesting them and me for hiring them. As he turned into the reserved parking area, he suddenly remembered how upset Kelly and Campbell had been when they came out of Junior's office yesterday.

The brothers must have found fault with the way they sang "Happy Birthday" in Wallonian, Charlie decided. Reluctantly he turned off the ignition, got out of the car, and pressed the "lock" symbol on his key ring. Dragging his feet, he walked to the building and took the elevator to the fourth floor, which was entirely dedicated to the Badgett brothers' quasi-legitimate enterprises.

The reason for the early meeting was that Junior was interested in purchasing a new car dealership in Syosset that was beginning to cut into the profits of his own operation. Junior's secretary was not yet in. As Charlie murmured a greeting to a receptionist and waited to be announced, he wondered how long it would be before the deal closed, before the new dealer got the message that he didn't have a choice not to sell to the Badgetts.

"Tell him to come on in," Junior's genial voice boomed on the intercom.

The office had been done by the same decorator who had lavished his excesses on the mansion. An ornately carved partner desk with a shiny finish, gold-striped wallpaper, a dark brown carpet emblazoned with the brothers' initials in gold, heavy brown satin draperies, and a glass-enclosed miniature village with a plaque inscribed OUR BOYHOOD HOME were only some of the points of interest.

To the left of the door, a couch and chairs upholstered in a zebra pattern were grouped around a forty-inch television screen hung on the wall.

The brothers were drinking coffee and watching the local station. Junior waved Charlie in, pointing to a chair. "The news is coming on, I wanna see it."

"After six hours, the warehouse fire in Syosset is still burning fiercely," the reporter at the news desk began. "Two firemen have been treated for smoke inhalation. The owner of the warehouse, Hans Kramer, suffered a heart attack at the site, and has been removed to St. Francis hospital, where he is now in intensive care . . ."

Vivid images of the blazing building appeared. On a split screen, a tape was rerun of a fireman administering CPR to Hans Kramer, who was stretched on the ground, an oxygen mask clamped over his face.

"That's enough, Eddie. Turn it off." Junior got up. "Still burning, huh? Must be some heck of a fire."

"Faulty wiring, I bet." Eddie shook his head. "Happens, huh, Junior?"

Hans Kramer. Charlie knew that name. He'd been to see

Junior at the mansion. He was one of the people who received "private loans" from the brothers. They did this to him. He didn't pay on time, Charlie thought with absolute certainty, so they burned down his business.

This scenario had been played out before. If the cops can prove Junior and Eddie had anything to do with this fire, they'll be facing another arson charge, Charlie thought, quickly assessing the situation. If Kramer dies, they could be facing a murder rap.

But of course, none of this would ever be traced back to the Badgetts. They were too careful. The loan Kramer signed with them probably had a normal interest rate on the face of the note. No one would know that the fifty percent interest rate had already been built into the principal. And of course the guy who actually set the fire would not be one of the thugs on their payroll. For that they would have contracted a free-lancer.

But if anything comes up to tie this fire to Junior and Eddie, I get the job of helping people to forget what they know or think they know, Charlie thought despairingly.

"Hey, Charlie, why so glum?" Junior asked. "It's a beautiful morning."

"Yeah, a really great morning," Eddie echoed, as he got up.

"And, like Jewel said, Mama was cute as a button on the satellite," Junior added. "She always loved her grappa. Like Jewel said, after Eddie and I went into the office yesterday, everyone kept saying that Mama was adorable."

"Yeah," Eddie agreed, his smile becoming nostalgic.

"And those entertainers were something else. Good. I mean really good."

Charlie had not seen Junior bubbling over with such fervent good humor in months. Jewel isn't the airhead I thought she was, he decided. If she managed to convince those two that everybody loved Mama, she ought to be made ambassador to Wallonia.

"I'm glad you liked Nor Kelly and Billy Campbell," he said. "They looked so upset when they came out of your office that I thought maybe you'd told them you weren't satisfied with their music."

Charlie was immediately aware of a drastic change in the atmosphere. Junior looked at him, his eyes cold slits, his cheekbones flushed, the muscles in his neck suddenly prominent. "What did you say?" he asked, his voice chips of ice.

Nervously, Charlie glanced at Eddie, whose bovine cheeks were now rigid. The sweet sentiment evoked by Mama's name had vanished from his eyes. His lips had become a thin, grayish-red gash across his face.

"I simply said that . . ." his voice trailed off . . . "that Nor Kelly and Billy Campbell seemed a little upset when they came out of your office after your mother's satellite visit."

"Why didn't you tell us they were there?"

"Junior, there was no reason. Why would I have told you? I thought you knew."

"Eddie, the door was open from the reception room, wasn't it?" Junior asked.

"Yeah."

"All right, Charlie. You should have told us they followed us in. You should have known it would be important for us to know. Now you're going to have to make a few calls to the songbirds." He paused deliberately. "I think you know what I'm talking about."

I guess that's the end of the questions and the depositions, Sterling thought as he watched the FBI personnel shaking hands with Nor, Billy, Dennis, and Sean. It was now eleven o'clock. For the past two hours, the FBI had been taking sworn statements from the four. They even had Nor and Billy draw a floor plan to show where they were standing when they heard Hans Kramer's voice on the answering machine and Junior's order to burn the warehouse.

"Ms. Kelly, you're sure the Badgetts didn't suspect that you were in the room right outside their office?" Rich Meyers, the head investigator, asked again as he picked up his briefcase. "As I explained, if they knew you overheard them, you'd need to be protected immediately."

"I don't think they knew. From what I understand about the brothers, if they had seen us they probably would have called off their plans for the fire." Nor readjusted the comb that was holding her hair in place. "There's an old expression, 'I feel like something the cat dragged in.' . . .

My mother used to say that, Sterling thought.

". . . and that's exactly the way I feel now. If you're done with me, I'm going to go home, climb in the Jacuzzi, and then get a couple of hours' sleep."

"A very good idea," Meyers said sympathetically. "All right. We'll be in touch with you. In the meantime go about your business as usual."

Sounds easy, Sterling thought. Unfortunately it's not going to work like that.

Sean O'Brien lingered only a minute after the federal officers left. "I'll keep you posted," he promised.

"Dennis, why don't you take the day off?" Nor suggested. "Pete can handle the bar."

"And lose all those holiday tips? I don't think so." Dennis yawned. "I better start setting up. We've got another holiday lunch group, Nor."

"I haven't forgotten. But they'll have to do without me. See you later."

When the door closed behind Dennis, Billy said, "Holiday tips? Forget it. He just wants to make sure that he's around if any trouble starts."

"I know. Are you going to try to get some sleep, Billy? Don't forget, we've got two more shows tonight."

"Right now I have to check my messages. I talked to a couple of the guys about getting together for lunch sometime this week." .

Nor slipped her arm into her coat. "Hearing Hans Kramer's message was the reason we're in this mess. It would have been one thing if we could have stopped the fire, but now the prospect of being witnesses against those two scares me."

"Just remember they have no idea we overheard them." Billy pressed the playback button on the answering machine.

Sterling shook his head as he thought of Charlie Santoli. Maybe he won't mention that he saw Nor and Billy, he thought hopefully. But given the future events he already knew about, he was sure that wasn't the way things played out.

"You have two new messages," the electronic voice began.

The first was from a friend who was organizing a lunch for the next day. "You don't have to call back unless tomorrow doesn't work for you." The second was from the recording company executive who'd offered him the contract last night.

"Billy, this is short notice but Chip Holmes, one of our top guys, is coming into town unexpectedly. He would really like to meet with you today. He's staying at the St. Regis. Can you join us for a drink around 5:30? Let me know."

"Why do I think you can make it?" Nor asked when the message clicked off. "Chip Holmes. Billy, that's great. If Holmes likes you, the sky's the limit with that company. You won't just be another singer with potential. He'll put big money into building you up."

"Which is exactly what I need," Billy said, as he did a quick drumroll on the tabletop with his fingers. "I don't want to be a one-hit wonder. You know better than I do how many guys had a little success early on, and then ended up job hunting when they were thirty-five. Let's face it. In this business I'm already no kid."

"I know what you're talking about, but you're going to make it," Nor assured him. "Now I really will get out of here. Break a leg. I'll see you tonight."

At the door, she looked over her shoulder. "I always swear I won't give you advice, but I can't help myself. You'd better leave plenty of time to get into New York. The holiday traffic is still pretty heavy."

"I'll take the train," Billy said absently, as he picked up his guitar.

"That's smart."

When Nor left, Sterling settled back in the club chair, his legs stretched over the hassock. He listened as Billy began plucking at the strings and softly singing words he'd written on a crumpled sheet of paper.

He's trying out new lyrics, Sterling thought. Upbeat, but with a nice plaintive touch. Billy really is good. I always did have an ear for music, he recalled.

Forty-five minutes later, the phone rang. Billy picked it up, said, "Hello," listened, then said, nervously, "You're calling from Badgett Enterprises? What can I do for you?"

Sterling hoisted himself from the chair and in two quick strides was at Billy's side, his ear to the receiver.

At the other end of the line, Charlie Santoli stood in his office, hating himself more and more with every word he uttered. "I am a representative of the company. The reason I am calling is that, as you may know, the Badgett brothers are philanthropists who have a large scholarship program for children in the local area. They thoroughly enjoyed your performance last night, and they know you have a young daughter."

Sterling saw Billy's forehead tighten. "What has my daughter got to do with this?"

"Her future has a great deal to do with it. The Badgetts understand how uncertain your future as a performer may be. They would like to set up a trust fund to ensure that Marissa will be able to go to a fine college in another ten years."

"Why would they want to do that?" Billy asked, restrained anger in his voice.

"Because sometimes remarks made in jest are overheard and, if repeated, take on a life of their own. The Badgetts would be very upset if that happened."

"Are you threatening me?"

Of course I am, Charlie thought. It's my job. He cleared his throat. "What I am offering is to make your daughter one of the selected recipients of a one hundred thousand dollar trust fund. It would please Junior and Eddie Badgett very much if you'd accept. On the other hand, they would find it dismaying if you were to repeat lighthearted remarks that might be misconstrued."

Billy stood up. The receiver hit Sterling in the jaw, causing him to blink.

"Listen, you representative of Badgett Enterprises, whoever you are, you tell those two that my daughter doesn't need their trust fund. I'll take care of her education myself without any help from them . . . And as for their 'joking' or 'lighthearted' remarks, I don't have a clue what you're talking about."

He slammed down the phone, sank onto the couch, and clenched his hands into fists. "They know we heard them," he said aloud. "What are we going to do?"

$\mathcal{T}$he Heavenly Council was watching the developments on Earth with rapt attention. Charlie Santoli's phone call to Billy Campbell brought instant response.

"Charlie Santoli had better watch out," the monk said sternly.

"He'd better not come crying to us when his time is up." The shepherd's eyes flashed fire.

"It wasn't what the sisters taught him at St. Francis Xavier," the nun said sadly.

The queen's expression was grave. "He'd better wake up before it's too late."

"He wants to be good," the nurse volunteered.

"Well then, madam, for goodness sake, Charles Santoli must mend his ways and get on with it," the admiral thundered.

"I think Sterling will be looking to confer with us again," the Native American saint reflected. "He has great humility. He wants to do his job, and he's not afraid to ask for help."

"He was always capable of deep caring and love," the shepherd observed, his tone now mollified. "I was pleased by the expression in his eyes as he sat watching Marissa when she was sleeping."

$\mathcal{S}$terling caught up with Marissa just as she was putting her ice skates in her carrying case and rushing out to the car. When he had realized that Billy was going to catch a few hours' sleep, he had trotted over to Marissa's house to see how she was doing.

He arrived in time to join Roy as he drove Marissa to the rink, bringing the munchkins along for the ride. Squashed between the twins, Sterling ducked flailing arms that attacked him from both sides. His jaw was still a little sore from being bopped with the receiver when he'd been listening in on Santoli's conversation with Billy, and, at one year of age, Roy Junior had a mean right cross.

But they are cute babies, he conceded with only a shade of reluctance. It's kind of fascinating to see how they're taking in everything they see. My problem was that I didn't have any brothers or sisters. Maybe I wouldn't have been so anxious to stay away from kids all my life if I'd had some experience with them.

He remembered the time he was godfather at a christening and the baby had drooled all over his pin-striped suit. It was the first time I wore it, too.

In the front seat, Roy was saying to Marissa, "I understand Grandma is going to teach you how to make apple strudel today."

What a thrill, Sterling thought, and realized Marissa was having exactly the same reaction. However, she said politely, "I know. Grandma's so nice."

Roy smiled benignly. "I want to have at least *two* pieces."

"Okay, but don't forget I have to save a piece for Daddy and one for NorNor."

It's not easy to be a stepparent, Sterling thought sympathetically. Marissa always keeps him at arm's length. If I'd known Roy better before I met him next year, I wouldn't have been so quick to dismiss him as a bore.

But he does drive like a snail with a bad back. Sterling concurred totally with Marissa's impatient thought, "Step on it. Practice will be over before I get there."

She's Nor to a tee, Sterling decided.

When they arrived at the rink, Marissa thanked Roy for driving her, kissed him on the cheek, and waved to the twins before rushing out of the car.

Sterling climbed over Roy Junior's car seat and saw the surprised expression on the baby's face. He senses me, he thought. They both are beginning to sense me. Babies have so much awareness of the metaphysical. Too bad it gets lost along the way.

He caught up with Marissa and listened as she chatted animatedly with her friends at the side of the rink.

Miss Carr was the teacher he would see next year at the skating rink in Rockefeller Center. She blew a whistle and ten children, all the others a couple of years older than Marissa, skated onto the ice.

Some of the children were very good, but Marissa was simply outstanding. What a little trouper, Sterling thought as he watched her take a couple of hard spills. She just gets up, shakes herself off, and tries the spin or jump again.

Later, when the children had changed back into their shoes or boots, one of the girls came over to Marissa. "My sister got your dad's single for Christmas. She wondered if he would mind signing it for her."

Marissa's beaming with pride, Sterling thought as he watched and noted with amusement that she tried to sound oh-so-casual when she said, "Oh, sure. My dad likes to sign autographs for my friends."

"Is he writing a new song now?" the girl asked.

"He's always writing a new song."

"Tell him to write a song about us!"

"He's writing one about me first!" Marissa giggled.

Seven going on twenty-five, and bursting with love for her dad. Sterling sighed. And so near to being separated from him for a long time. Well, I've got to be off. He took one last look at Marissa's glowing smile, then left the rink.

Adjusting his homburg, he started walking back to Billy's apartment. He was planning to accompany him to his meeting, and was looking forward to being in Manhattan again.

But I'm really getting to know my way around Madison Village, he thought, as his feet crunched in the snow, making a sound only he could hear. I must say it's a very nice place to live.

o howd'ya make out when you talked to Johnny one note?" Eddie asked. He was standing behind Junior, who, like a judge about to pass sentence, was sitting upright at his desk.

"Not very well." Charlie's hands were drenched in perspiration. He wanted to keep his voice calm but could not. "I spoke to Billy Campbell and offered him the scholarship for his daughter and explained that you would be dismayed if any remarks made in jest were misconstrued."

"All right, all right, we know what you were gonna say," Eddie said impatiently. "So what did he say?"

There was no staving off the answer. "He said for me to tell you that he'd pay for his daughter's education himself, and that he doesn't know what you mean by joking or lighthearted remarks. Then he slammed down the phone."

Charlie knew he could not soften Billy's reaction to the call, that if he tried, the brothers would see through him. The fact that Eddie was asking the questions was a frightening sign that now the next step would be taken. Coercion. And if that didn't work . . .

117

"Get out of here, Charlie," Junior ordered. "You sicken me. You let this happen." He looked up at his brother and nodded.

Charlie slunk out of the office. By tonight, Billy Campbell and Nor Kelly would have a warning that might frighten them into silence. Please let them take that warning seriously, he prayed, then shook his head in misery.

Once again he cursed the day fifteen years ago that the Badgett brothers had come to his one-man law office in Queens and asked him to represent them in their purchase of a dry-cleaning chain. I needed the business, so I didn't ask enough questions about them, he thought. Truthfully, I didn't want to know the answers. Well, I know them now.

hen she reached home, Nor relaxed in the Jacuzzi, washed and blow-dried her hair, and, planning on a nap, dressed in lounging pajamas. Then Billy's phone call destroyed all thought of sleep.

Her throat closing, she listened as Billy related his conversation with "a representative of Badgett Enterprises."

"I called that FBI agent, Rich Meyers, and left a message for him. Then I called Sean, but he's out too. I waited to call you, Mom, because I hate to upset you, but you have to know what's going on."

"Of course I have to know about it. Billy, somehow those people found out that we were in that outer office. Maybe they have hidden cameras."

"Maybe. Or maybe someone spotted us coming out of there."

Nor realized she was trembling. "Do you know who it was on the phone?"

"He didn't give his name, but I think it might have been that guy who told us what to sing when we got there yesterday."

"I remember him. Kind of nervous and weasely-looking."

"That's the one. Look, I'd better get moving. I'm taking the three o'clock train into Manhattan."

"Billy, be careful."

"You're supposed to say, 'Break a leg.' "

"I already did."

"That's right, you did. See you later, Mom."

Mechanically, Nor replaced the receiver on the cradle. Break a leg. She had worked in a nightclub where the owner was behind in his payments to someone like the Badgetts. A broken leg had been his first warning to pay up.

And what didn't seem to have occurred to Billy yet was that the caller had talked about Marissa. Will the Badgetts try to get to Billy and me through Marissa? Nor agonized.

She dialed Sean O'Brien's number, hoping against hope that she'd reach him. He knew a lot about the Badgetts. Maybe he could tell her what they were likely to do next. We've already given statements, she thought. Even if we wanted to, how could we possibly take them back?

She knew the answer. It wasn't that they *couldn't* take them back. It was that they *wouldn't*.

always used to dress in a suit when I had a business meeting, Sterling thought as he followed Billy onto the three o'clock train to Manhattan.

For his appointment with the recording company executives, Billy had chosen vintage jeans, a loose-fitting dark blue shirt, boots, and a leather jacket.

I'll never get used to these new styles. But then again, in the 1880s, when Mother was a young woman, she wore laced corsets, high-button shoes, bonnets, and floor-length dresses. Sterling sighed, suddenly nostalgic for the serenity of the afterlife, where concerns about clothing simply didn't exist.

He took the aisle seat next to Billy, who had found a vacant window seat. I always wanted the window seat too when I traveled by train, Sterling remembered. When Annie and I went to visit our friends in Westport, I always grabbed the window seat, and Annie never complained. I wonder if that's what the Heavenly Council meant when they called me "passive-aggressive"?

He could see how deeply worried Billy was just by looking at the troubled expression in his eyes and on his face. He was glad when Billy closed his eyes. Maybe he can relax a little, Sterling hoped. He's going to need to be "on" when he meets that guy Chip Holmes.

The train was a local and took forty-five minutes to get to Jamaica, in Queens. From there they took the subway to Fifty-ninth Street in Manhattan.

We're an hour early, Sterling noted as they climbed the steps to the street. Darkness was just setting in. The traffic was heavy, and there were Christmas decorations in all the windows. I hope Billy kills the time by taking a walk. I haven't been in this part of Manhattan in forty-six years.

It looks the same and yet different. Bloomingdale's will never change. But I don't see Alexander's. I loved living here, he remembered as he took it all in. There's no place like it in the world.

He trailed behind Billy to Park Avenue. The trees on the center island were glowing with white lights. The air was cold but clear. Sterling inhaled appreciatively even though it wasn't necessary for him to breathe. The hint of evergreen in the air made his mind drift back to other Christmases.

They started downtown and passed the building at 475 Park Avenue. My boss used to live there, Sterling recalled. He always invited Annie and me to his New Year's Day open-house party. Whatever happened to him? I never noticed him in the celestial waiting room and I never saw him whizzing by the celestial window.

Just then, a very old man, cane in hand, hobbled out of the building and spoke to the doorman. "My driver's late. Get me a cab, sonny."

Sterling gasped. It's him, my boss. Josh Gaspero. He must be a hundred years old! I'd love to be able to say hello, but from the looks of things, I suspect I'll be seeing him soon enough.

Billy was half a block ahead of him, and Sterling hurried to catch up, glancing over his shoulder several times as he watched his boss impatiently tapping his cane on the sidewalk. He hasn't changed, Sterling thought fondly.

The St. Regis was on Fifty-fifth Street, but Billy kept going south on Park Avenue. At Fiftieth Street he turned right and walked a few blocks west to Rockefeller Center.

Here I am again, Sterling thought. It's such a great place to be at Christmastime. I bet I know just where Billy's headed. Five minutes later they were in front of the magnificent evergreen with its thousands of colorful lights, looking down at the skating rink.

This is where it all started. Sterling smiled to himself. Started next year. Together they watched the skaters and listened to the music floating up from the rink. I'll bet Billy has skated here with Marissa. Sterling looked at the expression on Billy's face. I can tell she's in his thoughts right now.

Billy turned to leave. Sterling tailed him across Fifth Avenue and up the steps of St. Patrick's Cathedral. He's stopping to say a prayer, Sterling thought. The moment they walked through the door and experienced the majestic beauty of the cathedral, Sterling felt an intense sense of longing. His mind became filled with the image of the joy and peace he had seen on the faces of the people approaching the open gates of heaven. Head bowed, he knelt beside Billy, who had lit a candle at a side altar.

He's praying for his future on earth. I'm praying for mine in eternity. To be in heaven even for an hour on Christmas Day . . . Sterling felt tears in his eyes and whispered, "Please, help me complete my mission on earth so that I may begin to be worthy of You."

When they left St. Patrick's a few minutes later, Sterling was filled with both gratitude and regret. He knew that at last he was beginning to truly appreciate the gift of life and the gift of life everlasting.

At the St. Regis Hotel, Billy went into the King Cole bar, sat at a small table, and ordered a Perrier.

Oh, they've changed it here, Sterling thought as he looked around. But the Maxfield Parrish mural behind the bar is the same. I always loved it.

It was almost five o'clock. The bar was suddenly filling up. I remember meeting friends here for a glass of wine after work, Sterling mused. Just as people are doing now, getting together with friends, enjoying each other's company—that at least is timeless.

A couple of young women at a nearby table cast smiling glances at Billy, who was too absorbed in his own concerns to even notice them.

At five-twenty, Sterling could see that Billy was gearing up for the meeting. He straightened his shoulders, began sipping the Perrier, and kept his eye on the door. Ten minutes later, when the recording executive who had been at Nor's

Place appeared with a fast-moving, balding man in tow, Billy was the picture of easy charm.

They moved to a bigger table. But there's always room for one more, Sterling thought as he took the unoccupied seat and began to sort out his companions. It only took a moment to figure out that Chip Holmes was the top executive of the recording company, while Eli Green headed the New York office.

Holmes was a no-nonsense, say-it-and-be-finished-with-it type. "You're good, Billy, you're very good. You've got a special quality to your singing that makes me confident you'll catch on big time."

That's what I said, Sterling thought.

"You've got good looks, too, which is a rarity among the male performers in this business . . ."

Sterling silently applauded Billy's demeanor throughout the half-hour meeting. He looked and sounded confident, and, while appreciative, he did not grovel when Holmes offered a substantial contract and promised that he would have the kind of backup support he needed.

"We're teaming you with one of our top producers. He wants to get to work with you as soon as possible. By this time next year you could be a star, Billy."

The meeting ended with handshakes and a fervent expression of gratitude from Billy.

Good move, Sterling thought. During the discussion, you impressed him with your composure, but it was time to let him know how happy you are. I know his type. He loves having the role of kingmaker.

In the lobby, Billy consulted his train schedule and looked at his watch. Looking over his shoulder Sterling could see that he was going to try to make the 6:50 from Jamaica. A little tight, Sterling worried, but it's an express train, and the next one is a local.

They covered the seven blocks back to Fifty-ninth Street in half the time it had taken them to get to the hotel. Billy must be walking on air, Sterling thought. For the moment, at least. I'm sure that instead of thinking about the Badgetts, he's reveling in what the recording contract means to his future.

They hurried down the subway steps and onto the crowded platform. Consulting his watch again, Billy made his way to the edge and leaned forward, hoping to see a headlight emerging from the tunnel.

It happened in an instant. Sterling saw a burly man suddenly materialize, and with a slam of his shoulder send Billy teetering over the tracks. Anguished, Sterling tried to grab Billy, knowing that he could not regain his balance on his own, but his arms went right through Billy's body.

The train was rushing into the station. He's going to fall, Sterling thought helplessly. A woman screamed as the same burly man suddenly pulled Billy back to safety, then disappeared into the crowd, headed toward the exit.

The doors of the train opened. Numbly, Billy stepped aside as exiting passengers rushed past him.

"Are you all right?" someone asked him anxiously as he boarded the train.

"Yes, I'm all right." Billy grabbed the center pole near the door and held on tight.

An elderly woman admonished him. "Do you know how lucky you are? You should never stand that close to the edge of the platform."

"I know. It was stupid," Billy agreed, then turned away, struggling quietly to normalize his rapid breathing.

It wasn't stupid, Sterling wanted to shout, dismayed that he could not warn Billy. Billy doesn't realize he was pushed. The platform was so filled with people, he must think that the press of the crowd caused him to lose his balance, and that somebody grabbed him in time.

Sterling hung onto the center post with Billy as the subway bounced and swayed down the tracks. They arrived in Jamaica just in time to make the 6:50 to Syosset.

All the way home, chilling thoughts kept running through Sterling's mind: What happened on the subway platform was no accident, and what will the Badgett brothers do next?

*L*ee Kramer sat alone in the small hospital waiting room reserved for the families of people in intensive care. Except for the few minutes at a time that she had been able to stand at the foot of Hans's bed, this was where she had been since before dawn, when she had followed the ambulance to the hospital.

A massive heart attack. The words echoed dully in her mind. Hans, who in the twenty-two years of their marriage had hardly ever had a cold.

She tried to remind herself that the doctor had said that Hans was stabilizing. He said that Hans had been lucky. The fact that the fire department was at the scene and had the equipment to shock his heart and start it beating again had saved his life.

He's been under too much stress, Lee thought. The sight of the fire put him over the edge.

She glanced up when the door opened, then turned away. A number of her friends had stopped in and sat with her during the day, but she did not know this sober-faced, dark-haired man.

FBI agent Rich Meyers had come to the hospital hoping that he would be allowed to speak to Hans Kramer for a few minutes. That was out of the question, the nurse had told him firmly, but then added that Mrs. Kramer was in the waiting room.

"Mrs. Kramer?"

Lee whirled around. "Yes. Is anything . . . ? "

The strain on Lee Kramer's face was obvious. She looked as though she'd been punched in the stomach. Her short, ash-blond hair, blue eyes, and fresh complexion told Meyers that, like her husband, she was probably of Swiss extraction.

Rich introduced himself and handed her his card. A look of alarm came over her face. "FBI?" she asked.

"We're investigating the possibility that the fire at your husband's warehouse was deliberately set."

"Deliberately set? Who would do that?" Her eyes widened.

Meyers sat down in the vinyl chair opposite her. "Do you know anything about loans your husband may have taken out?"

Lee put her hand to her mouth, and the thoughts that had tormented her all day tumbled out. "When everything turned and the business started to go bad, we took a second mort-gage on the house for every cent the bank would lend us. There's a mortgage on the warehouse, but only as much as we could borrow on it. I know it's underinsured. Hans was so sure that if he could tough it through a little longer, the business would take off. He really is brilliant. The software program he designed can't miss." Her voice faltered. "And now what does all that matter? If only he makes it . . ."

"Mrs. Kramer, in addition to the mortgages, were there any other loans your husband may have taken?"

"I didn't know about any, but this morning, after we got the call about the fire, he said something like, 'I borrowed a lot of money . . . ' "

Meyers's face remained impassive. "Did he tell you who it was borrowed from?"

"No, that was all he said."

"Then you probably wouldn't have known if he made a phone call yesterday evening and left a message for someone about repaying a loan?"

"No, I don't know anything about that. But he was very agitated last night."

"Mrs. Kramer, does your husband have a cell phone?"

"Yes."

"We'd like to have your permission to check his cell phone account and home phone records to see if he made a call last night."

"Who would he have been calling?"

"People who don't give extensions on loans."

Her insides churning, Lee was afraid to ask the next question. "Is Hans in any trouble?"

"With the law? No. We just want to talk to him about that loan. The doctor will tell us when it's possible to see him."

"*If* it's possible," Lee whispered.

Charlie Santoli had left the Badgetts' office as quickly as possible after he'd been excoriated for not succeeding in his mission to buy Billy Campbell's silence, but at four o'clock Junior sent for him again.

He hastened down the corridor and around the corner to the executive suite shared by Junior and Eddie. Their long-time secretary was at her desk. Years ago, Charlie had decided that even as a baby, Lil must have had pugnacious features. Now that she had passed the fifty mark, they had settled into a permanent scowl. Still, he liked Lil, and she was probably the only person in the building who was not afraid of Junior.

She looked up, her eyes magnified by her oversized glasses, and jerked her thumb over her shoulder, always the sign to go right in. Then in a voice made hoarse by years of chain-smoking, she rasped, "The mood is slightly better." She paused. "Ask me if I care."

Charlie knew he didn't have to respond. He took a deep breath and pushed open the door.

Junior and Eddie were sitting on the zebra chairs, glasses

in their hands. Toward the end of the business day they often had a drink together before getting into their limo and heading home. If Charlie happened to be there, he was usually told to help himself from the bar.

Today was not one of those days. He was neither offered a drink, nor was he asked to sit down.

Junior looked over at him. "Just in case Campbell smartens up, we need to have this scholarship program on the level. Everyone knows we just gave big bucks to the old folks. Now we gotta take care of the little ones. You figure out the details. Find nine other outstanding kids from the area, all of 'em the age of Campbell's kid. We think it would be very nice of us to give them scholarships too."

They've got to be kidding, Charlie thought. Hesitantly, he suggested, "I think it would be wise if at least some of the children are older. How can you explain to the media that you want to give ten college scholarships to first-graders when there are high school boys and girls who need them now?"

"We don't wanna do that," Eddie barked. "We wanna build for the future. And if Campbell is smart enough to fall in line, we slide his kid's name in with the others."

"Marissa's marks are good and she's a nifty little ice-skater," Junior remarked offhandedly as he bit the end off a cigar. "Go find us other talented kiddies like her."

Charlie felt one more turn of the winch that twisted his digestive system. *Nifty little ice-skater.* How does Junior know so much about Marissa Campbell? he wondered bleakly.

"Of course, if you can't persuade Billy Campbell to retract anything he might have said about our little joke, there won't be any need for a fund," Junior said quietly. "Don't let us keep you, Charlie. I know how busy you are."

Back in his own office, Charlie tried to reassure himself that, bad as they were, people like Junior and Eddie never went after the children of their enemies.

But those two . . . He could not pursue the thought. Instead he found himself praying that Billy Campbell would wise up and accept the scholarship.

Shaking his head, he reached for a folder with the information about the car dealership the Badgetts wanted to buy. He had intended to spend his whole day on it, but had been too distracted to concentrate.

At 6:30 he closed the file and got up. He had his coat on and his briefcase in his hand when the phone rang. Reluctantly he picked it up.

A low, husky voice that he did not recognize said, "Charlie, the boss told me to pass the word that Billy Campbell almost took a dive in front of a subway train, but I managed to save him."

Before Charlie could answer, the connection was broken.

He replaced the receiver and stood at his desk for a long minute. In all the years he'd worked for the Badgetts, the worst he'd done was to speak to potential witnesses as he had spoken to Billy Campbell, and later arrange laundered payments to them. It had never gone beyond that. He could get the book thrown at him for tampering with witnesses, but this was different, and much more serious. They want me to be involved in whatever happens to Billy Campbell and Nor Kelly if I can't convince them to keep their mouths shut, he thought. I've never seen Junior and Eddie as foul tempered as they were today, and I know it's because they're worried.

He closed the door to his office and walked to the elevator. Even if Billy Campbell and Nor Kelly agreed to forget what they had overheard, would that be enough to ensure their safety?

Charlie doubted it.

*N*or's Place was bustling when Billy and Sterling returned at eight o'clock. The dinner hour was in full swing and the bar was busy. Nor was talking to people at a table near the bar, but as though she had eyes in the back of her head, she turned around the instant Billy walked into the dining room. Her face brightened, and she hurried over to him.

"How did it go?"

Billy grinned. "Chip Holmes is crazy about the 'special quality to my singing.' "

He does a pretty good imitation of Chip Holmes, Sterling thought. He captures that nasal quality.

Nor threw her arms around him. "Oh, Billy, that's fantastic." She signaled to a nearby waiter. "Nick, we're celebrating. Bring us a bottle of Dom Perignon."

I wouldn't mind a glass of that, Sterling thought. As he took his usual seat at Nor's table, a host of memories rushed through his mind.

His mother and father opening a bottle of "Dom" on his twenty-first birthday . . .

Another "bit of the bubbly" shared with them when he passed the bar exam . . .

That wonderful crisp October day when he and Annie had driven with another couple to visit the Roosevelt home in Hyde Park. On the way back they stopped for a picnic lunch on the Palisades, and Annie had surprised everyone when she trotted out a chilled bottle of champagne and four glasses.

After I finished mine, I drank half of hers, he thought. Oh, Annie!

Sterling swallowed over a lump in his throat and realized he hadn't been paying attention to Billy and Nor. Obviously Billy had told her about the meeting, because she was saying, "Billy, that's wonderful! You're on your way."

None of them noticed that Sean O'Brien had come into the restaurant. They all looked up, surprised, when he joined them.

"Sorry I didn't get back to you earlier, Nor," he apologized. "Next time call me on my cell phone. Has anything else happened?"

"Tell Sean about the call from Badgett Enterprises, Billy," Nor said.

Sterling watched Sean O'Brien's expression darken as Billy related the scholarship offer.

When Billy shrugged his shoulders and said, "So that's it," Sean's first question was to ask if he had told the FBI about the call.

Billy nodded. "Rich Meyers wasn't in his office. I left a message."

"He called back here at about five o'clock," Nor said quietly. "My impression is that he thinks it was an iron fist in a velvet glove kind of warning."

O'Brien looked grim. "Listen, after being a detective for nearly thirty years, I know too much about these people. The iron fist will be front and center if you don't fall in line."

Billy, tell O'Brien about what happened in the subway, Sterling pleaded silently. You need protection.

"I guess we have no choice but to wait it out," Nor said. "Look, here's the champagne. On a happier note, we're drinking to Billy's future." She turned to him. "You'd better sip that fast. We have to go on pretty soon."

Billy got up. "I'll take it upstairs with me. I have to change, and I want to give Marissa a call. You know her. She wanted me to give her the scoop as soon as I got back."

I'll just wait here and keep Nor company, Sterling decided, when Dennis appeared from the bar.

"I wanted to congratulate Billy, but he's disappeared already."

"He went upstairs to change," Nor said.

Sterling listened as Nor happily filled the men in on Billy's meeting with the recording executives. Then she said, "The news about the contract is wonderful, but I can't tell you guys how tense I've been all day. Ever since Billy got that phone call, I've been so afraid of what the Badgetts might do next. . . . And right now I'd better get ready myself," Nor concluded. "We're on in fifteen minutes. Can you stay, Sean?"

"For a while. Kate's on duty tonight."

Dennis turned to Sean. "I've got to get back to work. Why don't you sit at the bar?"

As the group broke up, they all spotted Billy running down the stairs, a fire extinguisher under his arm.

"Mom, your car is on fire," he snapped. "I called 911."

Word of the fire spread through the dining room. Dennis grabbed a fire extinguisher from the bar. O'Brien and Sterling one step behind him, he raced outside to the blazing vehicle and, with Billy, tried to extinguish the flames.

Nor came out of the restaurant, surrounded by several diners whom she had been trying to calm.

Fire trucks came roaring into the parking lot, and immediately the firefighters ordered people to stand back.

It took only a few minutes for the fire to be extinguished. Nor's car had been in its usual spot near the kitchen entrance, well away from the general parking area.

Then Nor called, "Come on, everybody." She stood at the door, ushering people back into the restaurant.

When the hoses were turned off, the fire chief, Randy Coyne, accompanied by a Madison Village police officer, spoke to Nor, Billy, Sean, and Dennis privately in Nor's office.

"Nor, your car's a loss, but it could have been a lot worse. At least the fire didn't spread to any other vehicles, and I can tell you right now you're lucky it didn't spread to the restaurant."

"How did it start?" Nor asked quietly.

"We think it was doused with gasoline."

For a moment there was complete silence in the room, then Sean O'Brien said, "Randy, we have some idea of who's behind this, but it's a matter for the FBI. They're already investigating a telephoned threat Billy got this morning."

"Then call them immediately," the police officer said. "I'm going to make sure that we have a patrol car stationed here overnight."

"And one at Nor's house," Sean O'Brien said firmly.

"I'll be glad to know someone's keeping an eye out," Nor admitted.

Sean turned to Nor and Billy. "Nor, a piece of advice. The best thing you can do right now is for you and Billy to go out there and conduct business as usual."

"Wish I could stay for your show," the fire chief said with a half smile.

"I'll be outside until I can get someone posted here and at your home, Mrs. Kelly," the cop promised.

Billy waited until they were gone, then said slowly, "Something happened to me in the subway today. I really thought it was my own stupidity, but . . ."

Sterling watched the expressions on the faces of Nor, Dennis, and O'Brien become increasingly grave as Billy told them what had happened on the way home.

"The same guy who jostled you at the edge pulled you back," Sean said flatly. "That's an old trick with these people."

The phone rang. Billy answered it. He listened for an instant as the color drained from his face. Then, the receiver still in his hand, he said, "Someone just told me he's sorry he bumped into me on the platform, and maybe next time I should borrow my mother's car when I come in to New York."

$\mathcal{A}$n instant later in eternity, but one week later by the earthly calendar, Sterling requested and received a meeting with the Heavenly Council.

He sat in the chair facing them.

"You look as though you have the weight of the world on your shoulders, Sterling," the monk observed.

"I feel as though I do, sir," Sterling agreed. "As you know, the events of the past week moved rapidly after the car fire. The police and FBI convinced Nor and Billy that it was necessary to go into protective custody until the Badgett brothers' trial. The expectation was that the trial would take place in a relatively short time."

"We all know *that* won't happen," the shepherd said.

"Do you have a battle plan?" the admiral asked imperiously.

"I do, sir. I'd like to move through this earthly year quickly. I'm most anxious to get to the point where I meet Marissa and can start doing something to help her. My hands are tied until then. I'd just like to have glimpses along the way of what

I will need to know to assist me in safely reuniting Marissa with her father and grandmother."

"So you don't want to spend another full year on earth?" The queen sounded amused.

"No, I do not," Sterling told her, his voice solemn. "My earthly time is behind me. I'm impatient to help Marissa. She said good-bye to Nor and Billy only a few days ago, and already she's desolate."

"We're aware of that," the nurse said softly.

"Tell us your plan," the Native American saint suggested.

"Give me the freedom and the power to move through the year as quickly as I feel necessary, plus the ability to transfer myself from location to location by a simple request to you."

"Who are you planning to visit?" the matador asked.

"Mama Heddy-Anna, for one."

The Heavenly Council stared at him in shock.

"Better you than me," the monk muttered.

"Mama Heddy-Anna has put up with a lot," the nun said.

"I dread the day she shows up here," the admiral said. "I commanded ships in battle, but a woman like that, I must say, might just turn me into a coward."

They all laughed. The monk raised his hand, palm outward. "Go forward, Sterling. Do what needs to be done. You have our support."

"Thank you, sir." Sterling looked into the face of each of the eight saints and then he turned his head toward the window. The gates of heaven were so close he felt as though he could reach out and touch them.

"It's time to go, Sterling," the monk said, kindly. "Where do you want to be placed?"

"Wallonia."

"To each his own," the monk said and pushed the button.

A light snow was falling, the wind was cold, and the village of Kizkek looked as though it had been unchanged for a thousand years. It was in a little valley, nestled at the foot of snow-covered mountains that seemed to form a protective shield against the outside world.

Sterling found himself on a narrow street at the edge of the village. A wagon drawn by a donkey was approaching, and he stepped aside. Then he got a good look at the face of the driver. It was Mama Heddy-Anna herself, and she was hauling a load of logs!

He followed the wagon around the side of the house to the backyard. She stopped there, jumped down, tied the donkey to a post, and began to unload the logs, chucking them vigorously against the house.

When the wagon was empty, she unhitched the donkey and pushed it into a fenced-off section of the yard.

Stunned, Sterling followed Mama into the stone cottage. It appeared to be one fair-sized room built around a central fireplace. A large pot hanging over the fire was sending out the delicious smell of beef stew.

The kitchen area had a wooden table and benches. Mama's rocking chair was facing a television set, which stuck out like a sore thumb in its surroundings. A couple of other well-worn chairs, a hooked rug, and a scarred wooden cabinet completed the decor.

The walls were covered with photographs of Heddy-Anna's two offspring and her incarcerated husband. The mantel over the fireplace held framed pictures of several saints, obviously Mama's favorites.

While Mama pulled off her heavy parka and scarf, Sterling climbed the narrow staircase to the second floor. It contained two small bedrooms and a tiny bathroom. One room was clearly Mama's. The other had two side-by-side cots—obviously where Junior and Eddie laid their innocent heads during their formative years, Sterling decided. A far cry from the gaudy mansion on the north shore of Long Island they now inhabited.

The cots were piled with women's designer clothes, all with the tags still on. Clearly these were gifts from the missing sons, all items that their mother found absolutely useless.

Sterling could hear the faint sound of a phone ringing and hurried downstairs, immediately realizing that the Heavenly Council had given him a gift he hadn't thought to request. *I never thought I'd see the day I could understand Wallonian,* he reflected, as he heard Mama tell a friend to pick up some extra wine. Apparently there'd be ten of them for lunch and she didn't want to run short.

Oh good, Sterling thought. *Company's coming. It's a great way to find out what Mama Heddy-Anna is all about.* Then his eyes widened. She was speaking on a wall phone in the kitchen area. Next to the phone, where most people keep emergency numbers, there was a blackboard with a numbered list.

Probably a shopping list, he decided until he saw the words written in bold lettering across the top of the board:

ACHES AND PAINS

Sterling's eyes raced down the list:

1. Bad feet
2. Pains around heart
3. Gas
4. Dizzy spell
5. Threw up twice
6. Can't taste food no more
7. Need operation
8. Broken heart
9. Never close an eye
10. Bad back
11. Swollen gums

Now, I've seen it all, Sterling thought, as he noticed checks after each complaint, with dates of the brothers' phone calls from America. She's got this down to a science, he thought. She doesn't use the same complaint twice in a row.

Mama Heddy-Anna had hung up the phone and was standing next to him, examining the list with a satisfied smile.

Then, moving with the decisiveness of a drill sergeant, she began slinging dishes, glasses, and cutlery onto the table.

A few minutes later, her friends started to arrive. Wreathed in a smile, she greeted them with bear hugs.

She had said there would be ten of them. They're all very prompt, Sterling observed. The tenth guest was the one carrying the wine.

He guessed that they were all in their seventies and eighties and looked as if they had spent many years working outdoors. Their leathery complexions and callused hands were testimony to a lifetime of hard physical labor, but their ready laughter and joy in socializing was not different from that of the groups of friends Sterling had observed gathered at the King Cole bar in Manhattan, or at Nor's Place on Long Island.

Mama Heddy-Anna produced a steaming loaf of fresh-baked bread from the oven and dished out the stew. The wine glasses were filled, and everyone gathered at the table. Frequent bursts of laughter followed the exchanges of stories about their fellow villagers, or about outings they had enjoyed together. There had been a dance at the church hall the week before, and Heddy-Anna had done the Wallonian national folk dance on a tabletop.

"Now I want to dance on a tabletop at the monastery when they have their grand opening as a hotel on New Year's Day," Heddy-Anna announced.

"I skied over and took a look," the baby of the crowd, a sturdy seventy-year-old, said. "Can't believe how nice it is. It's been closed for twenty years, since the last monk left. It's nice to see it all fixed up."

"My boys used to ski over there all the time." Heddy-Anna helped herself to more beef stew. "Too bad the monastery is over the border. We could use the tourists' money here."

The peal of the telephone made them all giggle. Heddy-Anna wiped her mouth with her napkin, winked at her friends, put her finger to her lips, and waited for the fifth ring before answering feebly. "Ha . . . lllo."

She stood up to get a better look at the blackboard. "I can't hear. Talk louder. Wait, I gotta sit down. My foot's so bad today. It came out from under me. I laid on the floor all night. Finally managed to get up."

Her expression changed. "What'd'ye mean, 'Wrong number,' isn't this my Eddie?"

She slammed down the phone. "False alarm," she told her friends as she sat down and picked up her fork.

"It was good practice," the woman next to her said admiringly. "Heddy-Anna, believe me, you get better every time."

The phone rang again. This time Heddy-Anna made sure who she was talking to before she began to recite her list of complaints. She repeated almost verbatim the story she had told to the first caller. "And besides that . . ." she continued, tears in her voice.

The friend nearest the phone jumped up and pointed to item six on the list.

Heddy-Anna nodded. ". . . I can't taste a single bite of what I eat. The weight is dropping off me."

I guess I have the picture of what's going on in Wallonia,

Sterling thought wryly. *Now I'd like to jump ahead to the next season and look in on Marissa.*

He left the stone cottage, looked up at the mountains, then stared into the heavens.

May I please go back to Marissa's house? And let it be April, he requested, and then closed his eyes.

$\mathcal{S}$pring comes first to the willows, Sterling thought as he looked at the slender and graceful clump of willow trees on the lawn outside Marissa's home in Madison Village. There was a pinkish haze about them, a promise of the blossoms that would soon be visible.

It was early evening, and dusk was just beginning to settle as the lingering rays of the sun disappeared. He went inside and found the family at the dinner table.

He took a chair in the dining room as far away as possible from Roy Junior and Robert, who were vigorously thumping their high chairs with spoons.

Marissa was sitting opposite them, silently picking at a small slice of chicken.

Denise and Roy were at the ends of the table, each one with the chair pushed close enough to the side so that they could easily feed a twin.

"How was school today?" Roy asked Marissa, as he managed to get a spoonful of mashed potatoes into Robert's mouth.

"It was okay, I guess," Marissa said listlessly.

"Marissa, you're just pushing the food around on your plate. You've simply got to eat something," Denise pleaded, then abruptly closed her lips after receiving a warning glance from Roy.

Marissa put down her fork. "I'm really not hungry. May I be excused?"

Denise hesitated, then nodded. "Daddy and NorNor should be phoning in an hour."

"I know."

"I'll call up to you, and you can go into our room and talk to them there."

Sterling was tempted to follow her but decided he wanted to hear what Denise would say to Billy when he called.

Denise waited until Marissa had disappeared up the stairs before speaking. "Roy, I couldn't bring myself to talk to her about the progress reports. She just can't seem to focus on her classes. The teacher said that she believes Marissa is blaming herself for Billy and Nor leaving, that Marissa thinks that somehow she did something wrong."

"A lot of kids feel like that when something happens to their parents, whether it's death, or divorce, or separation," Roy said. "We just have to be understanding."

Roy's a good soul, Sterling thought. He's trying very hard.

"Down, down, down." Roy Junior had had enough of sitting at the table.

"Down, down," Robert echoed, bouncing in his high chair.

Roy took a final bite of salad and got up. "Coffee later. I'll get these two upstairs and their baths started."

Denise began to clear the table. The phone rang a few minutes later. "Oh, Billy, you're early," she began. "No, of course, Marissa isn't out. If she knows you're going to call, she doesn't budge from the house for fear of missing you. Any new developments?"

She listened, then said, "Well, when you talk to her, tell her how proud you are that she's always been such a good student. We both know she'd do anything to please you. All right, I'll put her on. Give my best to Nor."

She laid the receiver on the table and walked to the staircase. "Marissa," she called.

Marissa was already at the head of the stairs. "Is that Daddy on the phone?"

"Yes."

Sterling hurried up the steps and followed Marissa's flying feet to the master bedroom. She closed the door tightly behind her.

For the next few minutes, Sterling listened as Marissa pleaded with Billy to come back. She promised she wouldn't *ever* pester to go to the movies, or try to make him stay on the phone and talk to her when she knew he was busy, or . . .

Sterling went over and bent down to listen to what Billy was saying. "Baby, don't even *think* like that! This has nothing to do with anything *you* did. I loved it when you phoned me . . ."

"Then why won't you tell me your phone number right now?" Marissa asked tearfully.

"Rissa, it's just that I can't. I have to borrow a phone when

I talk to you. NorNor and I want nothing more than to get home to you as soon as possible. Once I'm back, I'll make this all up to you, I promise . . ."

After she had finally said a tearful good-bye, Marissa went back to her room, sat at her desk, and turned on her CD player.

The sound of Billy's hit single filled the room. "I know what I want . . . I know what I need . . ."

Sterling watched as she put her head down on her arms and began to sob. I'm going to get you what you want and need, Marissa, Sterling vowed. And I'll do it if I have to move heaven and earth. No, with the *help* of heaven, he corrected himself.

He closed his eyes and addressed the Heavenly Council. Would you please deliver me to wherever the Badgett brothers are at the moment?

hen Sterling opened his eyes, he found himself inside a large, bustling, noisy restaurant on the water.

Unless the brothers are traveling, I guess that's Long Island Sound, he thought. He looked over at a woman studying the menu. The cover read SAL'S ON THE SOUND.

It was a steak-and-seafood place. People with bibs were happily breaking lobster claws; sirloin steak on sizzling platters was obviously popular. And, he noticed, many diners had chosen his favorite appetizer, crabmeat cocktail.

But where were Junior and Eddie? He was on his second tour of the tables when he noticed a secluded semicircular corner booth with a prime water view. Upon closer inspection he saw the three occupants were none other than Junior, Eddie, and a scantily clad Jewel.

Junior and Eddie had just had one of their telephone visits with Mama Heddy-Anna, and as usual both of them were in a tailspin worrying about her. Jewel had suggested they'd all feel much, much better if they went out for a nice, relaxing dinner.

They were already sipping cocktails, and the waiter was in the process of collecting the menus.

Sterling took a seat on the windowsill at a right angle to them. I wonder what they ordered? he thought.

"I don't think I can eat a bite," Eddie lamented. "When I think of how sick Mama is, I'm crying inside."

"You've been crying outside too, Eddie," Jewel said. "Your nose is all red." She patted Junior's hand. "Yours is red too, lambie."

Junior pushed her hand away. "I have a cold."

Jewel realized her mistake. "And your allergies, honey. The allergy season is terrible right now. This is the worst it's been in years."

"Yeah, yeah." Junior picked up his glass.

"She fell again," Eddie mourned. "Our poor mama's foot gave way again, and on top of that, her gums are swollen. She can hardly chew."

I guess she didn't use that one last time, Sterling thought.

"And her friends keep begging her to eat. Nothing tastes good to her anymore."

"She's been saying that ever since I met you guys three years ago," Jewel said earnestly. "She must be eating *something*."

Beef stew, Sterling thought. Lots of beef stew.

"She hasn't fallen since January," Eddie continued. "I was hoping her legs were getting better." He turned to Junior. "We gotta go see our mama. I'm telling you we gotta go see her."

"We can't and you know it," Junior snapped. "We sent her some nice new clothes to cheer her up."

"She's gonna love them," Jewel enthused. "I picked them out special. Two pairs of satin lounging pajamas, a cocktail dress, and a hat with lots of flowers to wear to church on Easter Sunday."

Eddie's expression soured. "Mama says the clothes we send her stink."

"That hurts my feelings," Jewel said, pouting. "If I met her, I'd be able to shop for her better. Every woman has figure problems. I mean it could be her hips, it could be her waist, her behind might have a funny shape—"

"Shut up, Jewel," Junior thundered. "I don't want no more anatomy lessons."

I was enjoying it, Sterling thought.

Obviously offended, Jewel got up. "Please, excuse me," she said with exaggerated emphasis.

"Where yuh goin'?" Eddie asked.

"To the lala." She flounced away.

"Is she mad because I said Mama don't like the clothes she picked out?"

"Forget the clothes," Junior barked. "Listen, I got a call when *you* were in the lala."

"When was I in the lala?"

"You're always in the lala."

"No, I'm not."

"Yes, you are. Every time I go look for you, you're in the lala. Now listen to me. Our guys can't track down Nor Kelly and Billy Campbell."

"They're a bunch of dopes," Eddie said.

"It takes one to know one. Keep your mouth shut and listen to me. The whole case against us falls apart if Kelly and Campbell don't take the stand. We gotta get rid of them."

"It's a big country. How do we get rid of them when we can't find them?"

"We gotta find them. I took the next step. I called a certain hit man."

Eddie looked at Junior. "Not Igor?"

"Yes, Igor," Junior said. "He's very good at what he does. I told him the only lead we have so far is that they're somewhere out West."

"Here I am," Jewel chirped as she slid into the banquette and kissed Junior's cheek. "I've forgiven you both for not appreciating all I do to make Mama Heddy-Anna happy and comfortable, and I have to tell you something. I think you should figure out a way to go visit your mama in person, and you should do it before it's too late."

Junior glared at her. "Drop it."

The waiter appeared with a tray of appetizers.

I've learned what I needed to know, Sterling thought. The Badgett brothers are determined to track down Nor and Billy and make sure they don't live to testify against them.

Sterling decided to take a long walk before he made a request to be transported somewhere else. An hour later, he had made his decision. He closed his eyes and whispered, I'd like it to be midsummer, and may I please get together with Nor and Billy?

$\mathcal{S}$urely they're not staying *here*, Sterling thought, dismayed. He was standing on the second-floor balcony of a rundown motel directly off a busy highway. Although it was blazing hot, the area was beautiful. Like Mama Heddy-Anna's village, the landscape boasted magnificent mountain views.

Of the six vehicles parked outside the motel, four had Colorado plates.

He noticed a heavyset man with dark glasses sitting in an SUV. It seemed to Sterling that the man was staring at his rearview mirror, watching the door directly behind him.

Sterling turned and peeked in the window. Billy was standing inside the shabby room, hands in pockets. He was looking at Nor, who was sitting on the edge of the bed, a phone in her hand.

They looked different. Nor's blond hair was medium brown, and she wore it in a prim knot at the nape of her neck. Billy had a beard, and his dark hair was cut much shorter.

Maybe this is where they make their calls home, Sterling thought. If they're in the Witness Protection Program, they can only phone from secured lines. They both look worried sick.

He went inside, and taking off his homburg, put his ear to the receiver. I'm getting good at eavesdropping, he thought. He heard a familiar voice at the other end of the line and realized that Nor was talking to Dennis.

"Nor, I don't have to tell you that this place is all about you," Dennis was saying. "Sure, I can do drinks, and the guys are good waiters, and Al is the best chef we've ever had, but that's not good enough. When the customers come in, they want to see you at your table."

"I know. How big a loss this month?"

"Very big. We're not a quarter full for dinners, even on Saturdays."

"Which means, of course, that the waiters' tips are way down," Nor said, "Look, Dennis, this can't last much longer. The minute the trial is over and the Badgetts are in prison, we'll be able to come home. Figure out how much in tips the guys are losing, and let's make up half of it to them in their paychecks."

"Nor, maybe you didn't hear me. You're losing money hand over fist as it is."

"And maybe you didn't hear me," Nor flared. "I know the restaurant needs me to be there. But you and Al and the waiters and the kitchen help and the cleanup crew are all part of what make it work. It took me years to put together such a good team, and I'm not going to lose it now."

"Take it easy, Nor, I'm just trying to help you keep your head above water with this place."

"I'm sorry, Dennis," Nor said contritely. "This whole business is grinding me down."

"How's Billy?"

"How do you think? He just called Marissa and the recording company. Marissa absolutely refuses to talk to him—or to me either for that matter—and the recording company told him that unless this is over soon, they'll have to cancel his contract."

There was silence, then Nor said, "Dennis, you know that impressionist painting near the fireplace in my living room?"

"The pain-by-numbers one?"

It was an old joke between them.

"Yes. You have power of attorney. Go to my safe-deposit box and get the papers on it. Take everything to the Reuben Gallery. I know they'll make an offer on it. It should be worth at least sixty thousand dollars. That will help."

"You love that painting, Nor."

"Not as much as I love my restaurant. Okay, Dennis, I guess that's all the good news I can handle at one time. I'll talk to you in about two weeks."

"Sure, Nor. Hang in there."

Her next call was to Sean O'Brien to see if there was any word about the trial date. There wasn't.

They left the motel room in silence, went down the steps to the parking area, and got into the SUV in which the man in dark glasses was sitting. He's got to be the federal marshal who looks out for them, Sterling decided.

He rode in the backseat with Nor. Not a word was exchanged on the twenty-minute drive. He spotted a road sign that indicated Denver was thirty miles away. I know exactly where we are, he thought. The Air Force Academy is near here.

Billy and Nor were living in a run-of-the-mill bi-level house, the sole virtue of which, at least as far as Sterling could tell, was its location. It was set on a large piece of property, shaded by tall trees that afforded privacy.

When the car stopped, Billy turned to the marshal. "Frank, come inside please. I've got to talk to you."

"Sure."

The living room furniture looked as if it had been purchased at the auction of a bankrupt motel: Naugahyde sofa and chairs, mismatched Formica coffee and end tables, burnt-orange wall-to-wall carpeting. A groaning air conditioner labored to pump in cool air.

Sterling could pick out Nor's attempts to make the room livable. Tasteful framed prints drew the eye away from the hideous furnishings. A vase of black-eyed susans and several large green plants helped alleviate the depressing atmosphere.

The living room opened into what was meant to be a dining area. Billy had turned it into a music room, furnishing it with a scarred upright piano piled with sheet music, a CD player, and shelves of CDs. His guitar rested on a club chair near the piano.

"What can I do for you, Billy?" the marshal asked.

"You can help us pack. I'm not staying here another night. I've had it."

"Billy, this is not Frank's fault," Nor said, hoping to placate him.

"For all we know, this trial will never happen. Am I supposed to spend the rest of my life rotting in this house? Frank, let me explain something to you. I turned thirty years old last week. In the music business that's old, you understand? It's *old*. The ones who make it these days, start at seventeen, even younger."

"Billy, calm down," Nor begged.

"I can't calm down, Mom. Marissa is growing up without us. She's growing up *hating* me. Every time I talk to Denise she tells me how worried she is about Rissa, and she's right. I'm taking my chances. If anything happens to me, at least it will happen while I'm living my own life."

"Listen, Billy," the marshal interrupted. "I know how frustrating this is for you and for your mother. You're not the first one in this program who's gone crazy. But you *are* in real danger. We have ways of finding out things. There was no reason to tell you this before, but there's been a contract on you and your mother since January. And when the Badgetts' personal goons couldn't find you, they hired a hitman."

Nor paled. "When did they hire him?"

"Three months ago. We know who he is and our men are looking for him. Now, do you still want me to help you pack?"

The fire went out of Billy. "I guess not." He walked over and sat at the piano. "I guess I'll just keep writing music that somebody else will have the chance to sing."

The marshal nodded to Nor and left. After a few moments,

Nor went over to Billy and put her hands on his shoulders. "This really won't last forever, you know."

"It's hell on earth."

"I agree."

I do too, Sterling thought. But what do I do about it? The more he learned about the problem, the less he felt able to solve it.

With a sympathetic glance at Nor and Billy, he went outside. I'm used to the altitude in the heavens, but not in Colorado, he thought, feeling a little light-headed.

It's hard to believe that Nor and Billy will still be here in December. I can only imagine the emotional state they'll be in by then. Where else can I go? What can I do? Everything hinges on the trial. Maybe I should drop in on the Badgetts' legal counselor. After all, he was the one who saw Billy and Nor coming out of Junior's office.

I'll be glad to get out of this heat, Sterling decided as he closed his eyes. Summer was always my least favorite season.

Once more he addressed the Heavenly Council. May I please be transported into the presence of Charlie Santoli, and may it please be in early December? Amen, he added.

"We should have put the lights up at least a week ago," Marge commented as she unrolled another string of bulbs and handed them to Charlie, who was standing on a ladder outside their living room window.

"I've been too busy, Marge. I just couldn't get to it." Charlie managed to loop the string over the top of the evergreen, which had grown considerably taller since last year. "You know, there are people we can pay to do this. They have higher ladders, they're younger, they're stronger, and they could do a better job."

"Oh, but then we'd miss out on all the fun, Charlie. We've been doing this together for forty years. The time will come when you really can't do it, and then you'll wish you could. Admit it. You love this ritual."

Charlie smiled reluctantly. "If you say so."

Sterling sat on the steps observing the couple. He really is enjoying himself. He's a family man, he thought.

An hour later, chilled but pleased with themselves, Marge and Charlie went into the house, shed their coats and gloves, and gravitated to the kitchen for a cup of tea. When the teapot and freshly baked Christmas cookies were in front of them, Marge dropped her bombshell.

"I want you to quit that job with the Badgett brothers, Charlie, and I want you to quit it tomorrow morning."

"Marge, are you out of your mind? I can't do that."

"Yes, you can. We're not rich, God knows, but we've got enough to live on. If you want to keep working, put out your shingle again and do house closings and wills. But I'm not putting up with watching you build to a heart attack working for the Badgetts for another day."

"Marge, you don't understand—I can't quit," Charlie said desperately.

"Why not? If you drop dead, they'll get a new lawyer, won't they?"

"Marge, it's not that. It's . . . please, let's just forget it."

Marge stood up and placed both hands firmly on the table. "Then what is it?" she asked, her voice rising with every word. "Charlie, I want the truth. What's going on?"

Sterling listened as Charlie, at first hesitantly, then in a rush of words, confessed to his wife that over the years he had been sucked into making threats to people who stood in the way of the Badgetts. He watched Marge's reaction change from horrified shock to deep concern as she came to realize how emotionally tortured her husband had been for years.

"The trial I've been getting postponed has to do with the warehouse fire near Syosset last year. The singers hired for that Mama Heddy-Anna birthday party overheard Junior giving the order to have it torched. The word on the street is that the entertainers are working in Europe, but the truth is they're in protective custody."

So that's the story that's been circulated about Nor and Billy, Sterling thought.

"Why do you want the trial postponed?"

"We bribed experts who will swear the fire was caused by exposed wires. Hans Kramer, the guy who owned the warehouse, disappeared, but the brothers found out last month that he and his wife are living in Switzerland. They've got family there, and after what happened, Kramer doesn't want to tangle with the Badgetts."

"You haven't answered my question, Charlie."

"Marge, I'm not the one who wants the postponements. The Badgetts want them."

"Why?" She looked straight into his eyes.

"Because they don't want the trial to start until Nor Kelly and Billy Campbell are silenced for good."

"And you're going along with that?" she asked incredulously.

"They may not find them."

"And they *may* find them. Charlie, you can't let that happen!"

"I know I can't," he burst out. "But I don't know what to do. You must realize that the minute I go to the feds, the Badgetts will know it. They have a way of finding out those things."

Marge began to cry. "How did this happen? Charlie, no matter what the consequences for us, you have to do the right thing. Just wait a few more days until Christmas is over. Let's

have one more Christmas when we know we'll all be together." She wiped her eyes with the back of her hand. "I'll
pray for a miracle."

Charlie stood up and wrapped his wife in his arms. "Well,
when you say your prayers, be more specific," he said with a
tired smile. "Pray for a way to make Junior and Eddie visit
Mama Heddy-Anna in the old country. I can have the cops
ready to nab them the minute they set foot on Wallonian soil.
Then we'd all be in the clear."

Marge looked at him. "What are you talking about?"

"They've been tried in absentia for the crimes they committed over there and both got life sentences. That's why
they can never go back."

Life sentences! Sterling thought. At last he understood what
he had to get done. The only question was how to do it.

Sterling went outside. Marge had turned on the Christmas lights as soon as Charlie finished hanging them. The
weather was changing, and the late afternoon sun had disappeared behind heavy clouds. The multicolored bulbs on the
evergreen twinkled cheerily, helping to dispel the growing
gloom of the winter day.

Suddenly, like a gift, Sterling remembered something he
had overheard at Mama Heddy-Anna's lunch table. It's possible, he thought, it's possible. A plan to get the brothers back
to the old country began forming in his mind.

It was a long shot, but it just might work!

"*S*terling, it looks as if you've been doing your homework," the nun said approvingly.

"You're quite the world traveler," the admiral boomed.

"We were surprised that you went back to Wallonia," the monk told him, "but then we got an inkling of what you were up to. That was my old monastery, you know. I lived there fourteen hundred years ago. Hard to believe it's being turned into a hotel. I can't imagine that place having room service."

"I can understand that, sir," Sterling agreed, "but for our purposes it may be most fortuitous. I think I have at last found a way to help Marissa and Nor and Billy, and maybe even Charlie. He needs my help as much as Marissa does, but in a different way."

He squared his shoulders and looked into one face after the other. "I request permission to appear to Charlie so that he can work with me on solving the problems."

"Do you mean to appear as you did to Marissa, who understood you were not of her world?" the shepherd inquired.

"Yes. I think that's necessary."

"Perhaps you'd better plan to become visible to Marge as

well," the queen suggested. "Something tells me she rules the roost in that family."

"I was afraid to push the envelope and ask to meet her," Sterling admitted with a smile. "It would be wonderful if I could communicate with both of them."

"Push the envelope?" The matador's eyebrows raised. "That expression wasn't in vogue when you were alive."

"I know. But I heard it somewhere. Maybe in Nor's restaurant. I kind of like it." He stood up. "According to the earthly calendar, tomorrow will be the day when I first met Marissa. I've come full circle."

"Don't forget, it was also the day you first appeared before us," the Native American saint teased.

"That, I assure you, I'll never forget."

"Go forward with our blessing," the monk told him. "But remember—Christmas Day, which you hope to celebrate in heaven, is drawing very near."

*M*arissa opened the door of her room and was delighted to see Sterling sitting in the big chair by the desk. "I thought you were going away and would come back to say good night," she said.

"I did go away," he explained. "I took a look at the whole last year of your life when you were down at dinner and understand now why Daddy and NorNor had to leave."

"But I've only been downstairs for an hour!"

"Time is different for me," Sterling said.

"I kept thinking about you. I ate fast, then got stuck listening to Roy tell his boring story about Christmas when he was a little boy and was one of the shepherds in the school play. I got away as fast as I could. I'm so glad you're here."

"Well, I learned a lot while you were at dinner. I'm going to have to leave now because I'm going to be very busy trying to get your daddy and NorNor back for your birthday."

"That's Christmas Eve," she reminded him quickly. "I'll be eight years old."

"Yes, I know."

"That's only four days from now."

Sterling saw skepticism mixed with hope in Marissa's eyes. "You can help me," he told her.

"How?"

"Say a few prayers."

"I will. I promise."

"And be nice to Roy."

"It isn't easy." Her whole personna changed, and her voice deepened. " 'I remember the time when . . . blah, blah, blah.' "

"Marissa," Sterling cautioned, with a twinkle in his eye.

"I knowwwwww . . ." she said. "Roy's all right, I suppose."

Sterling stood, relishing the momentary lightheartedness he saw in Marissa's eyes. It was an instant reminder of the first time he had seen her with Billy and Nor. *I cannot fail her,* he thought. It was both a prayer and a vow.

"It's time for me to go now, Marissa."

"Christmas Eve—you promised!" she said.

*C*harlie and Marge always piled the presents under the tree a few days before Christmas. Their three children all lived nearby on Long Island, a blessing for which Marge gave daily thanks.

"How many people's kids are scattered to the ends of the earth?" she would ask rhetorically from under the dryer. "We're so lucky."

Their six grandchildren were a source of joy, from the seventeen-year-old about to start college to the six-year-old in the first grade. "All good kids. Not a lemon in the lot," Marge often boasted.

But tonight, after she and Charlie had arranged the gifts, they did not feel their usual sense of satisfaction and anticipation. Dread of the inevitable outcome of Charlie going to the FBI had settled over them, and at 8:30 they were sitting quietly side by side in the living room, Charlie aimlessly flipping the channels on the television.

Marge stared at the Christmas tree, a sight that usually brought her great comfort and joy. Tonight it didn't have that effect on her. Not even the homemade ornaments her grandchildren had made over the years could bring a smile to her face.

Then, as she watched, one of the ornaments slid to the carpet, the paper-mâché angel with one wing shorter than the other, and wearing a hat instead of a halo. She got up to retrieve the angel, but before she could reach it, the ornament started to glow.

Her eyes widened. Her jaw dropped. For once, not a word came from her lips. In ten seconds the angel had been transformed into a pleasant-faced man, neatly dressed in a dark blue chesterfield coat and wearing a homburg, which he promptly removed.

"AAAAAAAAAHHHHHHHHHH," Marge screamed.

Charlie had started to doze on the couch. He jumped up, saw Sterling, and cried, "Junior sent you, I know he did."

"Jesus, Mary, and Joseph," Marge cried prayerfully. "The Badgetts didn't send him, Charlie. He's a ghost."

"Please don't be alarmed. I'm here to help solve your problems with the Badgetts," Sterling said calmly. "Do sit down."

They looked at each other and then obeyed. Marge blessed herself.

Sterling smiled. For a moment he said nothing, wanting them to get used to him and lose any lingering fear that he might do them harm.

"Mind if I sit down?" he asked.

Marge's eyes were still like saucers. "Please do, and help yourself to the Christmas cookies," she said, pointing to the dish on the coffee table.

"No, thank you." He smiled. "I don't eat anymore."

"I wish I had that problem," Charlie said, staring at Sterling, the remote control still in his hand.

"Turn off the TV, Charlie," Marge ordered.

Click. Sterling was amused, remembering the queen's remark that in this house, Marge ruled the roost. He could see them both begin to relax. They understand that I'm not here to harm them, he thought. It's time to explain myself to them.

"You know Nor Kelly and Billy Campbell, Charlie," he began. "And you know they are in the Witness Protection Program."

Charlie nodded.

"I was sent here to help Billy's little girl, Marissa, who longs to be with her father and grandmother. In order to accomplish that, it is necessary to remove the threat that hovers over them."

"Junior and Eddie," Charlie said flatly.

"Those two!" Marge said contemptuously.

"As I began investigating the best way to ensure Nor and Billy's safety, I realized that you are in grave danger from the Badgetts as well."

Marge reached for Charlie's hand.

"Understanding all the circumstances, I have come to the conclusion that the best and most effective way to solve the problem is to get the Badgetts to go back to Wallonia, where they will be incarcerated for the remainder of their lives."

"And I hope they throw away the key," Marge pronounced. "Those two are bad, bad, bad."

Ever the lawyer, Charlie said, "I assure you, there is no way that those two will ever willingly set a foot on Wallonian soil."

"Even for Mama Heddy-Anna?" Sterling asked.

"They've been crying in their beer for nearly fifteen years about not seeing her, but they still haven't paid her a visit," Charlie said.

"I have a plan that just might take them back to their mother's side," Sterling explained.

Their expressions suddenly hopeful, Charlie and Marge listened raptly.

$\mathcal{T}$he next morning, FBI agent Rich Meyers, accompanied by his top assistant, agent Hank Schell, arrived at the home of Charlie and Marge Santoli. Dressed as repairmen, they carried in tool kits that held recording equipment.

They sat at the kitchen table with the Santolis while Schell set up and tested the microphone.

When Charlie had phoned Meyers the previous night, Meyers warned him that he might want to have legal counsel before going on the record with potentially self-incriminating disclosures.

Charlie had dismissed the suggestion. I've got something far better than a lawyer, he thought. I've got Sterling in my corner.

"Ready, Mr. Santoli?" Meyers asked.

"Yes, I am. For the record, my name is Charles Santoli . . ."

For the next hour, Charlie described his connection with the Badgetts, starting with their legitimate enterprises, then detailing his growing knowledge of their criminal activities. He concluded by saying that in his opinion the government would never be able to convict Junior and Eddie Badgett of arson in the Kramer warehouse fire, and that Nor Kelly and Billy Campbell would always be in grave danger, whether or not they were in protective custody.

Meyers listened impassively.

Charlie took a deep breath. "With what I'm going to suggest to you, you may decide I need medication, not legal help, but at least hear me out."

Sterling made a face at Charlie and winked.

With a slight smile, Charlie calmly laid out the plan Sterling had outlined to him the night before. Every once in a while he glanced over at Sterling for approval and was rewarded with an encouraging nod.

Meyers' first reaction—"You want to do *what*?"—gradually changed to a grudging "It's not impossible," to an eventual "We've spent thousands of hours trying to get these guys and haven't been able to make anything stick. But if they're in prison for good, in Wallonia, their whole rotten operation will fall apart."

"That's my point," Charlie said eagerly. "It may take years to get a conviction here, and even in prison, they'd still be dangerous. But put them in prison halfway around the world, and those dopey goons of theirs would just disappear."

When the recorder was turned off, the two agents stood up, and Meyers said, "Obviously I've got to talk to the big guys at the office about this. I'll get back to you in a couple of hours."

"I'll be here," Charlie said. "My office is closed through Christmas."

When Meyers and Schell left, Marge commented, "Waiting is always the hardest part, isn't it?"

Sterling thought of his forty-six years in the celestial waiting room. "I absolutely agree," he said. "Hopefully the waiting will be over very soon for all of us."

At one o'clock, Rich Meyers phoned back. "It's a go. If you can do your part, we'll take care of the rest."

$\mathcal{T}$he stores are always so busy at Christmastime," Jewel sighed as the limo pulled through the gates of the Badgett estate at three o'clock. "But doesn't it get you into the spirit, going to the mall and seeing everybody rushing around, doing their last-minute shopping?"

"It gets on my nerves," Junior said sourly. "I don't know how you talked me into going."

"Me too," Eddie echoed. "I'm not the type to eat lunch in the food court. That place was so noisy, I couldn't hear myself think."

"You never think anyway," Junior muttered.

"Very funny," Eddie growled. "Everybody says I take after you."

"But we got some good stuff," Jewel said brightly. "Those ski sweaters I treated you to look so nice. The trouble is we never go away, and there's not much skiing on Long Island." She shrugged her shoulders. "Oh, well. What're you gonna do?"

Inside the house, Jewel went straight to the salon to plug in the Christmas tree. "I can't say I'm crazy about all these purple lights," she murmured as she squatted, cord in hand, fishing for the outlet.

Junior was at the window. "You invite one of your ditzy friends over here, Jewel? There's a car down at the gate."

"My friends aren't ditzy, and no, they're all out shopping."

The intercom rang. Eddie went to the security panel on the wall and pushed the button. "Who is it?"

"It's Charlie, and I have my wife with me. Mind if we come up for a few minutes?"

Eddie rolled his eyes. "Sure, I guess it's okay."

"What the heck is Charlie bringing Marge over here for?" Junior asked irritably.

"It's the holidays," Jewel reminded them. "People drop in and visit each other. No big deal. Just nice and friendly. And caring."

"The holidays stink," Eddie said. "They make me feel bad."

"That's a very natural reaction," Jewel told him earnestly. "I was just reading an article written by a very smart psychologist. According to him, people get depressed because—"

"Because people like you drive them crazy," Eddie interrupted.

"Watch it, Eddie. Jewel is only trying to cheer us up."

"Oh, lambie pie, you're so right. That's all I want to do."

Eddie went to the door to admit the Santolis.

As the handle turned, Sterling whispered, "Don't be nervous, Marge."

Eddie's lame greeting, "Hi yah, come on in," made both Santolis know exactly how welcome they really were.

Marge braced herself and followed Eddie into the salon, trailed by Charlie and the ever-present Sterling.

"Welcome," Jewel trilled. "Happy holidays. What a nice surprise. We were thrilled to see your car drive in."

Oh my God, look at that tree, Marge thought. The few times she'd been in this house around Christmas, the trees had been reasonably traditional. Not this year.

She was holding a tin of cookies and handed it to Jewel. "I make these for all my friends every Christmas," she said.

"A sign of love," Jewel cooed.

"Sit down for a minute," Junior said. "We were on our way out."

"Sit, sit, sit," Jewel encouraged.

"We won't stay," Charlie promised as he and Marge sat together on a couch. "It's just that Marge had a dream last night that was so powerful, she felt she had to alert you."

"Alert us about what?" Junior asked, his tone measured.

"I had the most disturbing dream last night—about your mother," Marge began.

"MAMA!" Eddie bellowed. "Did something happen to her?"

Marge shook her head. "No, but does she suffer from dizzy spells?"

"Yeah," Junior's eyes bored into Marge's face.

"Pains around the heart?"

"Yeah."

"Gas?"

"Yeah."

"She can't taste her food?"

"Yeah."

"Never closes an eye?"

"Yeah."

"Throws up occasionally?"

"Yeah."

"Swollen gums?"

"I can't take it no more," Eddie shouted, his face crumbling into tears. "I gotta call her."

He ran to the phone.

Mama Heddy-Anna's annual Christmas party was in full swing. The wine and grappa were flowing. Everybody had brought a favorite dish, and the table was groaning with food. An old phonograph was scratching out Christmas carols, and a sing-along was in full swing.

When the phone rang, the person nearest to the phonograph yanked the needle from the record and screamed, "Pipe down, everybody!"

A few additions to Mama's list of ailments had been added by a couple of the partygoers, and someone obligingly pointed them out, as after waiting for the fifth ring, Mama Heddy-Anna picked up the phone.

"Ha . . . Ha . . . lllo."

"Mama, how are you? Someone had a dream you weren't feeling so good . . ."

"They dreamed right." Heddy-Anna winked at her friends

and motioned for her eyeglasses as she squinted at the new writing on the board.

"Mama, talk louder, I can't hear you. You sound so sick . . ."

Heddy-Anna read from the blackboard. "I think this is my last Christmas." She sighed, then improvised: "Did the person with the dream warn you that I'm a dying woman?"

"Mama, don't say that. It's not true. Grandmama lived to be one hundred and three, remember."

"She was a strong woman . . . not like me."

Junior picked up the extension. "Mama, is something worse?"

"I threw up this morning . . . because my gums are so swollen . . . dizzy, you should know how dizzy I am . . . can't see straight . . . wait a minute . . . I got the heart pain again . . . somedays it won't stop . . ."

Heddy-Anna's friends, impatient to resume partying, began to signal her to hang up the phone.

She nodded. "I can't talk anymore," she whined, "I'm short of breath. I need my rest. I can't believe you're calling so late. But what do I expect from sons who never come to see their mama?"

"Mama, you *know* how much we love you," Eddie sobbed.

A click in his ear was her response.

Jewel handed Eddie a fresh handkerchief. Junior blew his nose vigorously.

Marge and Charlie looked appropriately grave. Marge stood up. "I'm so sorry I said anything. I just thought it might be better to let you know, in case you wanted to go spend the holidays with her."

Charlie looked embarrassed. "Marge, would you wait in the car please? There's a little business I have to discuss with Junior and Eddie."

"Of course." Marge grabbed Junior's hand and pressed it. "I'm so sorry," she mouthed.

As she passed Eddie, she kissed him comfortingly on the cheek.

"Walk Marge to the car, Jewel, and then give us a few minutes," Junior ordered.

Jewel linked her arm with Marge. "Come on, honey. You were just trying to help."

When they were out of earshot, Charlie said hesitantly, "Of course, you understand that Marge is under the impression that you've visited Mama Heddy-Anna regularly over the years."

"It's a good thing she understands that," Junior snapped.

Charlie let it pass. "I felt so upset when Marge told me about her dream. Knowing the circumstances, something occurred to me. It may be a wild idea, but . . ." He paused and shrugged. "Well, at least I want you to know about it. It's a way that just might make it possible for you to safely visit your mother on Christmas Eve."

"What are you talking about?" Junior demanded.

"What does the St. Stephen of the Mountains monastery mean to you?"

"St. Stephen of the Mountains monastery? That was in the next town from us, just over the border. We used to ski there all the time when we were kids. It's been shut down since before we left."

"I thought you might have heard about it. They're reopening the monastery as a hotel on New Year's Day."

"No kidding." Eddie blinked. "Nobody was ever allowed in there. But what about it anyhow?"

"My cousin, who is a nun, usually joins us for Christmas dinner. She won't be with us this year because she's going on a pilgrimage. Sixty nuns and brothers and priests from all over the country will be staying at St. Stephen's during Christmas week, before it opens to the public."

They're getting the message, Charlie thought, as he saw the brothers exchange thoughtful glances. "They've chartered a plane that is leaving tomorrow evening from Teterboro Airport in New Jersey. They'll land at the new airstrip near the hotel, which, of course, is just over the border from your mother's home."

Charlie hesitated, wishing he could mop his brow, but he didn't want to seem nervous.

"I asked my cousin if there were any seats left on the charter, and as of this morning there still were four or five."

Junior and Eddie looked at each other. "We could ski from the monastery to Mama's house in no time at all," Eddie said.

Charlie swallowed, aware he either was about to hit a home run, or strike out. "I was thinking that if you two dressed as monks who had taken the vow of silence, there'd be no danger of anyone finding out who you are. I imagine you could easily arrange for the proper documentation."

"No problem," Junior said brusquely. There was a pause. He looked at his brother. "It always seemed too risky to go back home, but this could work."

"I'm going back," Eddie said, determination in his voice. "I'd never close an eye if anything happened to Mama before I got to see her again."

Charlie frowned. "We're going to have to act fast. The seats may already be gone."

"They better not be." Junior glowered. "When you heard about them, you shudda told us right away."

Charlie took out his cell phone.

"No, call from our phone. Put it on the speaker," Junior ordered.

"Of course."

"St. Mary's Convent," a woman's voice answered softly. "Sister Joseph speaking."

"Sister Joseph, this is Charles Santoli, Sister Margaret's cousin."

"Yes, how are you Mr. Santoli?"

"I'm well. Is Sister Margaret there?"

"No, I'm sorry, she's doing some last-minute shopping for her trip. We were advised to bring extra sweaters or wraps."

The brothers looked at Charlie. "Ask her," Junior said impatiently.

"Sister, do you happen to know if the flight to St. Stephen's is full?"

"I think it is, but let me take a look."

"There's *gotta* be room," Eddie whispered, clenching and unclenching his hands.

"I'm back, Mr. Santoli. I was right. We were full, but we just had two cancellations. One of our elderly sisters isn't well enough to make the long flight, so she and her companion are staying home."

"She better not have a quick recovery," Junior growled. "Book us those two seats."

On the other end of the phone, FBI agent Susan White, who had been sitting in the convent for several hours, waiting for the call, gave a thumbs-up to Rich Meyers.

Then she began to write, "Brother Stanislas and Brother Casper . . ."

Marge and Charlie were marvelous, Sterling thought, smiling from ear to ear as he realized that the first phase of the plan had worked perfectly.

Marissa, we're getting there, he thought.

"Good night, Marissa," Denise said, as she tucked her daughter in and bent down to give her a kiss.

"Good night, Mommy. I can't wait to wake up tomorrow. It's my birthday *and* it's Christmas Eve."

"We're going to have *lots* of fun," Denise promised as she turned out the light.

Downstairs, she joined Roy, who was drying the pots. "Everybody bedded down?" he asked cheerfully.

"Yes, but it's strange. I thought Marissa would be upset tonight, but she seems to be excited and happy, as though she's expecting a miracle, as though Billy and Nor will be here tomorrow."

"Then she's in for a terrible letdown," Roy said mournfully as he folded the dish towel.

"I got them everything they need," Charlie fretted. "The monks' habits, the sandals, the prayer books, the suitcases—real beat-up ones, like the brothers took the vow of poverty and meant it."

He and Marge and Sterling were sitting in the Santolis' living room, all of them tense with concern that the Badgett brothers would smell a rat before the pilgrimage charter plane took off.

"How about their passports?" Marge asked. "Any chance of a glitch with them?"

"First-rate forgeries," Charlie said. "They took care of that themselves."

"How were they getting to Teterboro?" Marge asked nervously. "I hope they didn't go in that showy limo."

"They were having the limo drive them to New York to one of their dry-cleaning shops that was closed. They were going to change there and take one of those cheap car services to the airport."

It was 11:55. The plane was due to take off at midnight.

"I don't know. Those two have a sixth sense," Charlie

moaned. "If at the last minute they figure out this was a setup, and don't get on that plane, I'm dead."

"Did you pick up any indication that they were suspicious when you saw them earlier today?" Marge asked, nervously shredding a cocktail napkin.

"None. I'm their new best friend. Don't forget, I'm the one who's getting them home to see Mama."

If this doesn't work, I'm the one who gets blamed for suggesting it, Sterling thought with a pang of guilt.

The ring of the phone made everyone jump.

Charlie grabbed the receiver. "Hello."

"Mr. Santoli?"

"Yes."

"This is Rich Meyers. You'll be glad to hear that a certain charter plane has just taken off, with Brothers Stanislas and Casper on board."

Charlie's relieved smile told Marge and Sterling what they needed to know.

"They should be landing in Wallonia in eight hours. The police there are waiting to arrest them. Our agents on board will shed their clerical robes and ride back home as soon as the plane refuels."

Charlie felt as though a two-ton weight had been lifted from his shoulders. "I imagine you'll want to be taking further statements from me."

"Next week. Enjoy your holiday. I know you'll cooperate with us." Meyers paused. "Don't worry too much, Mr. Santoli. I think you know what I mean."

"Thank you," Charlie said quietly.

Sterling stood up. "It's going to be okay," he said. "You're going to be fine, Charlie. You're a good man. And now I must leave you."

"Sterling, how can we ever thank you?" Marge asked.

"Don't even think about thanking me. Just use your time on earth wisely. Believe me, it goes very quickly."

Marge and Charlie entwined their hands. "We'll never forget you," Marge whispered.

"Never," Charlie echoed fervently.

"We'll meet again. I'm very sure of that," Sterling said as he disappeared.

"How much longer? This robe is making me itch," Eddie hissed, and was rewarded by an elbow in the ribs from Junior.

Junior fished a pad from his pocket and wrote, "Vow of silence. Shut up. Almost there."

At that moment the voice of the flight attendant came over the loudspeaker. "We are due to land at Monastery Airport in twenty minutes . . ." The usual instructions followed.

Eddie was twitching with excitement and beside himself with joy. Mama Heddy-Anna! I'm coming, Mama! he thought.

Junior didn't know the exact moment when the sinking feeling started. He looked out the window and narrowed his eyes. It was cloudy and, as the plane began to descend, light snow drifted against the windows.

He craned his neck and narrowed his eyes then spotted the monastery and the landing strip next to it. It's okay, he thought. For a minute I had a feeling that Santoli mighta skunked us.

191

Then the voice of the flight attendant came on again. "We have just been advised that due to extremely icy conditions, we will be unable to land at Monastery airport. Instead we will be landing at Wallonia City airport thirty miles away."

Junior and Eddie looked at each other. Eddie pushed back the hood of his robe. "Whaddaya think?"

SHUT UP, Junior scribbled furiously.

"You will be bussed immediately to St. Stephen's Monastery," the flight attendant chirped happily. "We do regret this inconvenience, but your safety is our first concern."

"How do we go through customs?" Eddie was trying unsuccessfully to whisper. "Are the passports okay if they really look at them under a special light or something?"

SHUT UP, Junior scrawled. Maybe it's okay, he thought. Maybe it's on the level. He looked around, searching out the faces of his fellow passengers. Most of them were deep in their prayer books.

THE PASSPORTS ARE OKAY, he wrote. IT'S YOUR BIG MOUTH I'M WORRYING ABOUT.

Eddie leaned over him to look out the window. "We're over the mountain. Look! There's the village. Look! I bet I can pick out Mama's house."

His voice was rising. To cover the sound, Junior began to cough violently. Immediately the hostess was at his side offering water.

I need a drink, he thought wildly. If we get back to Long Island, I'll tear Charlie Santoli apart limb from limb.

The plane landed, taxiing to a halt a good distance from

the terminal. What Junior and Eddie saw out on the tarmac rendered them both more speechless than any vow of silence could ever have accomplished.

In the midst of dozens of uniformed Wallonian policemen, a lone figure was jumping up and down and waving vigorously.

Mama Heddy-Anna.

Junior shook his head. "She don't look like she's dying to me."

Eddie's face was puzzled. "She looks so healthy. I can't believe it."

"We took this trip for nuthin', and now we're gonna spend the rest of our lives in jail."

The door of the plane opened and four policemen raced down the aisle. Junior and Eddie were encouraged to get out of their seats and put their hands behind their backs. As they were led away, their fellow passengers began removing roman collars and nun's veils, and burst into spontaneous applause.

At the foot of the stairs, they were enveloped in one of Mama Heddy-Anna's bear hugs.

"The nice policemen came for me. They said you were coming home as a surprise. I know you're in trouble, but good news! Papa was just made head trustee at the prison where you'll be staying from now on." She beamed, "All three of my boys together, nice and safe, where I can visit every week."

"Mama," Eddie sobbed as he laid his head on her shoulder. "I been so worried about you the whole time I was gone. How do you feel?"

Heddy-Anna patted him. "Never better."

Junior thought of the estate on Long Island, the limo, the money, the power, and Jewel, whom he knew would have a new boyfriend in two weeks. As Eddie's shoulders shook with emotion, all Junior could think was, How could I have been so stupid?

On Christmas Eve morning, Billy and Nor were lingering over the breakfast neither one of them had any interest in touching. The distracting reality that it was both Christmas Eve and Marissa's eighth birthday hung over them, a dense, oppressive blanket of pain.

The sudden steady ring of the doorbell startled both of them. Billy ran to answer it.

A beaming Marshall Frank Smith boomed, "Grab only what you need. You're booked on the 12:40 flight to New York, and if you want to catch it, you haven't got a minute to spare."

On Christmas Eve, Nor's Place usually enjoyed a pleasant flow of lunch customers. Some were last-minute shoppers, stopping for a quick bite. Others, more organized, came in for a quiet lunch before the religious and family celebrations began.

Today this place feels downright eerie, Dennis thought, as he surveyed the room from behind the bar. He shook his head. At least Nor had agreed that it was pointless to stay open on Christmas Day.

"I guess you're right, Dennis," she had admitted. "Only ten reservations! Those people would be better off at a place with a little life in it."

We're pretty much at the end of the line here, Dennis thought, as he was handed an order for a single beer.

Just then the bar phone rang. He picked it up.

"Dennis!" It was Nor's voice, buoyant and energetic. "We're at the airport, on our way home. We're in the clear. The Badgett brothers are gone, locked up for good," she exulted. "Get a birthday cake for Marissa for tonight, and phone our usual Christmas people. Tell them Nor's Place will be open for Christmas dinner and it's on the house. But don't let Marissa know! We want to surprise her."

$\mathscr{F}$rom the moment she opened her eyes on Christmas Eve and whispered to herself, "Today I am eight years old," Marissa began to lose faith that Sterling would be able to bring Daddy and NorNor home. She had been sure they would be there when she woke up, but now she realized it was going to be like all the other times.

She had promised herself they would be back for Easter, but they weren't. Then she had been sure they'd be home when school closed for the summer . . . Then when it opened in September . . . Then for Thanksgiving . . .

It's going to be just like that again today, she thought, as she got up and put on her bathrobe. Tears kept trying to flow from her eyes, but she pressed them back with her hands. Trying to put a smile on her face, she went downstairs.

Her mother and Roy and the twins were already at the kitchen table. They all began to sing "Happy Birthday" when they saw her. There were presents next to her cereal bowl: a new watch; books and CDs from Mommy and Roy and the twins; a sweater from Grandma. Then she opened the last two boxes: ice skates from Daddy and a new skating outfit from NorNor.

Now she was absolutely, positively sure they wouldn't be

coming home today. If they were, wouldn't they wait to give her the presents when she saw them?

After breakfast Marissa carried all her gifts upstairs. When she reached her room, she dragged the chair from her desk over to the closet and stood up on it. She lifted the boxes with the new ice skates and the skating outfit and put them on the top shelf. Then, with the tips of her fingers, she pushed them back as far as she could, until they were out of sight.

She never wanted to look at them again.

At eleven o'clock she was in the living room, reading one of her new books, when the phone rang. Even though her heart stopped when she heard Mommy say, "Hello, Billy," she still didn't look up.

But then Mommy came rushing over to her. She didn't give her a chance to say, "I don't want to talk to Daddy," before the phone was at her ear and Daddy was shouting, "Rissa, want to go to Nor's Place for your birthday dinner? We're on the way home!"

Marissa whispered, "Oh, Daddy." She was bursting with so much happiness that she couldn't say anything more. And then she felt someone pat the top of her head. She looked up and there he was—her friend who wore the funny hat and who was not quite an angel, and he was smiling at her.

"Good-bye, Marissa," he said, and then he was gone.

In a daze, Marissa climbed the stairs to her room, closed the door, pulled over her chair, and stood on her tiptoes to retrieve the presents she had pushed away. But when she pulled the boxes down, something fell from the shelf and landed at her feet.

She sank to the floor and stared at the tiny Christmas ornament that she had never seen before. It was an angel dressed just like her friend.

"You've got the same funny hat," she whispered as she picked it up and kissed it. Holding it to her cheek, she looked out the window and up at the sky.

"You told me you weren't quite an angel," she said softly. "But I know that you are. Thank you for keeping your promise to help me. I love you."

hen Sterling entered the celestial conference room of the Heavenly Council and saw the approving looks on the faces of the saints, he knew he had completed his task to their satisfaction.

"I say, that was most touching," the admiral said with uncharacteristic tenderness.

"Did you see that child's face?" The nun sighed. "It shone with as perfect happiness as is possible on earth."

"I couldn't help staying until I saw Marissa in her father's arms," Sterling explained to the council. "Then I went back to Nor's Place with them. What a wonderful birthday party it was. As you know, the word that they'd returned flashed all over town, and everyone came in to welcome them home."

"I had tears in my eyes when Billy sang the song he wrote for Marissa," the queen observed.

"Talk about a sure-fire hit," the matador declared.

"As you know, he'll be recording it and the other songs he wrote while he was away," Sterling said. "It was a very painful year for him, but he used it well."

"As did you," the shepherd said quietly.

"Yes indeed. Absolutely," they all murmured, nodding.

"You not only found someone to help and used your head to work out a solution to her problem, but you also used your heart," the Native American saint said, clearly proud of Sterling.

"And you saved Charlie Santoli from the destructive life he was leading," the nun added.

There was a pause.

Then the monk stood up. "Sterling, the celebration of the birth of our Savior is about to begin. It is the judgment of the council that you have earned not only a visit to heaven, but your permanent place there. It is time for us to lead you through the gates." He turned toward the door.

"Wait a minute," Sterling said. "I have something to ask you."

The monk stared at him. "What could you possibly have to ask at this moment?"

"I am so grateful to all of you. As you know, I long to be in heaven. But I so enjoyed this experience that, by your leave, I would like to return to earth every Christmas and find someone who needs help. I never knew how good it could feel to really make a difference in other people's lives."

"Making other people happy is one of the great joys of the human condition," the monk told him. "You have learned your lesson even better than we realized. And now, come along."

✳

As they approached, the heavenly gates opened wide before them, revealing a light brighter than a thousand suns, brighter than anything that Sterling had ever been able to imagine. A profound inner peace permeated his being. He was going toward the light; he was part of the light. The Heavenly Council stepped aside, and slowly and reverently he continued to walk forward. He was aware that there was one large group of people who were gathered together.

He felt a hand touch his. "Sterling, let me walk with you."

It was Annie.

"The other newcomers are just ahead of you," she whispered. "They all came together. Their lives ended tragically, and although they themselves have found eternal joy, they are deeply concerned for the loved ones they left behind. But they will find their own ways to send help and comfort to them."

Annie paused. "Oh listen, the celebration is beginning."

Music filled the air, rose toward a crescendo. With the angels and saints and all the other souls in heaven, Sterling lifted his voice in song as they continued walking toward the light.

"Glory to the newborn King . . . "

Deadline

Books by Fern Michaels:

Betrayal
Southern Comfort
To Taste the Wine
Sins of the Flesh
Sins of Omission
Return to Sender
Mr. and Miss Anonymous
Up Close and Personal
Fool Me Once
Picture Perfect
About Face
The Future Scrolls
Kentucky Sunrise
Kentucky Heat
Kentucky Rich
Plain Jane
Charming Lily
What You Wish For
The Guest List
Listen to Your Heart
Celebration
Yesterday
Finders Keepers
Annie's Rainbow
Sara's Song
Vegas Sunrise
Vegas Heat
Vegas Rich
Whitefire
Wish List
Dear Emily
Christmas at Timberwoods

The Godmothers Series:

Deadline
Late Edition
Exclusive
The Scoop

The Sisterhood Novels:

Home Free
Déjà Vu
Cross Roads
Game Over
Deadly Deals
Vanishing Act
Razor Sharp
Under the Radar
Final Justice
Collateral Damage
Fast Track
Hokus Pokus
Hide and Seek
Free Fall
Lethal Justice
Sweet Revenge
The Jury
Vendetta
Payback
Weekend Warriors

Anthologies:

Making Spirits Bright
Holiday Magic
Snow Angels
Silver Bells
Comfort and Joy
Sugar and Spice
Let it Snow
A Gift of Joy
Five Golden Rings
Deck the Halls
Jingle All the Way

FERN
MICHAELS

Deadline

KENSINGTON PUBLISHING CORP.
http://www.kensingtonbooks.com

KENSINGTON BOOKS are published by

Kensington Publishing Corp.
119 West 40th Street
New York, NY 10018

Copyright © 2012 by MRK Productions
Fern Michaels is a Registered Trademark of First Draft, Inc.

All rights reserved. No part of this book may be reproduced in any form or by any means without the prior written consent of the Publisher, excepting brief quotes used in reviews.

All Kensington titles, imprints and distributed lines are available at special quantity discounts for bulk purchases for sales promotion, premiums, fund-raising, educational or institutional use.

Special book excerpts or customized printings can also be created to fit specific needs. For details, write or phone the office of the Kensington Special Sales Manager: Kensington Publishing Corp., 119 West 40th Street, New York, NY, 10018. Attn. Special Sales Department. Phone: 1-800-221-2647.

Kensington and the K logo Reg. U.S. Pat. & TM Off.

Library of Congress Control Number: 2011937863

ISBN-13: 978-0-7582-6603-3
ISBN-10: 0-7582-6603-0

First Hardcover Printing: January 2012
10 9 8 7 6 5 4 3 2 1

Printed in the United States of America

Deadline

Prologue

"How can we go to the governor's mansion if it no longer exists?" Mavis asked Sophie, as the Citation X gently lifted off the runway at LAX. "I read about it on the Internet this morning, when I was checking my Web site." Mavis's line of funeral attire, Good Mourning, had blossomed almost overnight since its inception, but she continued to monitor her Web site for each individual order received. Now more than ever, she lived on the Internet.

Sophie rolled her chestnut eyes upward, showing only the milky-colored whites. "It still exists; just more of a tourist attraction these days. Ronald Reagan was the last governor who lived there. The *gov-er-na-tor* stays at the Sterling Hotel, which is where we will be staying for the next few days or however long it takes to assist the first lady of California with her nightmares." A slight smile lifting the edge of her full lips, Sophie mimicked the instantly recognizable accent for which the famous former actor turned governor was so well known.

"Stop being so damn dramatic. You may be a drama queen, but you're not an actress," Toots called out from the seat in front of Sophie and Mavis.

"I didn't say I was," Sophie tossed back.

"Stop!" Ida intervened. "I don't want to hear any smart comments today. I've about had it listening to the two of you squabble."

Laughter bubbled throughout the private jet.

When the four women had boarded the luxury jet, all of them agreed that California's governor flew in style. The cabin was decked out in creamy leather reclining seats, solid cherry cabinetry, and all the latest gadgets, including an Apple iPad2 equipped with high-speed Internet, and built-in telephones—just in case the governor had to make a call and was unable to move about the plane.

Theresa "Toots" Amelia Loudenberry, Sophie Manchester, Ida McGullicutty, and Mavis Hanover, the last three being Toots's daughter Abby's godmothers, were en route to Sacramento, the state capital. Sophie, in her newfound celebrity, was slated to perform her magic, said *magic* consisting of holding a séance for the Peabody- and Emmy-award-winning first lady. She had begun to be plagued with nightmares about her famous uncle, John F. Kennedy, the thirty-fifth president of the United States, who was assassinated when she was eight years old. When she'd heard of Sophie's success in abolishing ghosts and other *un*worldly beings, she'd personally called to ask for her assistance.

"Oh hush, Ida! If I wanted your opinion, I'd ask." Sophie smirked. "And I really, really do not."

There was a long-standing war of sorts between Sophie and Ida. Though neither would ever voluntarily admit it, if pressured, both would confess to loving the other. It was just that they didn't *like* each other.

"Now now, girls, let's not fuss. We've got a long flight ahead of us, and I, for one, want to relax before we're introduced to California's first couple. I don't want to appear haggard," Toots explained.

Mavis, the most upbeat and positive of the group, said

softly, "Oh, Toots dear, you could never look haggard! I believe you're the most gorgeous woman I know."

Toots smiled at Mavis. "You are too kind, but thank you anyway."

Ida muttered something decidedly unkind.

As usual, Sophie and Toots ignored her when she mouthed off.

"Hey, this flight might not be as long as you think. Listen to this." Sophie held up the brochure she had removed from her seat pocket. "The Citation X can fly through a half dozen time zones before refueling, and it has a Rolls-Royce engine. Whew! This is some aircraft."

Ida spoke up. "That *is* good news. The less time I'll have to listen to you three run your filthy mouths, the happier I'll be."

Sophie raised her hand above her head so Ida could see her middle finger standing proud and tall. "And it says the bathroom is marble."

Coco, Mavis's spoiled female Chihuahua, growled from her royal seat, aka Mavis's lap. "Ida, I believe you've upset Coco. She knows full well that I don't say nasty things the way the rest of you do." Mavis grinned, before adding, "Or at least not nearly as often."

It was hard to imagine the woman Mavis had been just two short years ago. A retired English teacher and widow for seventeen years, she'd lived in a little clapboard house near the ocean in Maine before Toots had e-mailed her and invited her to Charleston, South Carolina, Toots's hometown. She'd been a heart attack waiting to happen when Toots rescued her, and, yes, that was exactly what Toots had done, rescued her. If she hadn't, Mavis would probably be six feet under that very moment. Guided by Toots and a personal trainer, Mavis lost over one hundred pounds and exercised daily as though her life depended on it, which it likely did.

Ida, a native New Yorker and a high-society snob, had been a complete and total nutcase. Recently widowed when Toots invited her to come to Charleston, the elegant former photographer suffered with OCD, obsessive-compulsive disorder, and a debilitating fixation on germs. Thomas, her spouse of more than thirty years, was thought to have died from the bacterium E coli found in a tainted piece of meat Ida had purchased from her favorite butcher shop.

Circumstances being what they were, Ida's psychological disorder had caused her to become a total shut-in. Her world of Clorox and sanitizing had quickly ended when Toots sent her to a famous doctor in California who specialized in treating her disorder. Not only had she been cured of her compulsion in a matter of weeks, but she became romantically involved with her savior, who turned out to be no doctor at all but an imposter. He'd almost bilked Ida out of three million dollars to boot. To see her now, minus her cleaning kit, was a true miracle.

Sophie, also a native New Yorker, an RN and a former pediatric nurse, had been recently widowed as well. Walter, her abusive alcoholic husband, died from cirrhosis of the liver. No big surprise there. Planning ahead and looking forward to the day he died, Sophie had taken out a five-million-dollar life insurance policy on him before it was too late and was now quite comfortable.

Toots, an expert at planning funerals—or *events* as she liked to think of them—had a great deal of practice over the years, and helped Sophie arrange a quick *event* for Walter. Toots sang an off-key "*Ave Maria*," they said their Hail Marys, baked Walter's remains, then spent the rest of the day shopping before jetting back to Los Angeles, where Toots had fulfilled a secret lifelong dream when she purchased *The Informer*, a tabloid newspaper where her daughter, Abby, was working as a reporter.

Two years later Abby, now editor in chief of the tabloid, still had no clue her mother was the real power behind LAT Enterprise, the corporation that owned the paper. Abby seemed content to accept her new boss's preference for communication—e-mail and FedEx—so until Toots had a darn good reason, she had no intention of revealing her own involvement as the corporate owner of *The Informer* to Abby.

Knowing she'd have to stay in close contact with her daughter, Toots purchased a beautiful three-story hillside minimansion in Malibu. It had been inhabited by a former pop star, whose idea of decorating was hot pink and purple. One of the guest bathrooms actually had a mirror in the shape of a guitar, and blue rhinestones on the baseboards. Toots guessed it was a sad tribute to the King himself, dearly departed Elvis.

Prior to the pop star, the house had belonged to Desi Arnaz and Lucille Ball. Toots, along with her dear friends, had moved into the Malibu beach house while it was being remodeled. It was during the remodeling that she experienced a paranormal phenomenon in her own bedroom.

She remembered that night as being the most frightening of her life.

Awakened by a pounding heart and an eerie chill in the horrid purple bedroom she'd referred to as a hooker haven, and paralyzed by a fear unlike anything she'd ever experienced, Toots had been unable to move from her bed. Next—she still had difficulties believing this—what seemed to be four clouds, in an eerie, translucent shade of blue, clustered around her bed. Inside the cloudlike puffs were faces. Yes, she knew how insane it sounded, but she'd seen it with her own two eyes and it was what it was. Afterward, she remembered thinking she could've had hallucinations from a bad case of indigestion or, perish the thought, even a brain tumor. She had read somewhere about tumors on the brain causing pressure that gave rise to hallucinations. But it had been nothing like that at all.

Recalling the faces, she realized they were familiar to her, but in her traumatized state, she was unable to identify them. In a matter of seconds, the foglike clouds disappeared. Scared and shaken, she'd told Sophie what she'd experienced. Having had a lifelong interest in the paranormal, Sophie hadn't been shocked when Toots told her what had happened. Of course, now they knew the remodeling in the bedroom had stirred up the spirits of famous movie moguls Aaron Spelling and Bing Crosby, who in life had an ongoing feud over a piece of land. Sophie had suggested a séance. Successful in her attempts to contact and communicate with the dead, Sophie had become a celebrity in the world of paranormal events and ghosts. So there they were, flying in a private jet on their way to the governor's mansion to assist California's first lady with her recurring nightmares.

Toots reclined in the luxurious leather seat, content with her life and that of Abby's three godmothers. Since the girls had temporarily relocated to California and South Carolina—temporarily being two years—their lives as senior citizens had been one big roller-coaster ride. A few rough spots along the way, but thrilling nonetheless.

Toots glanced at each of her friends, who were really more like sisters. Abby's three godmothers were quiet, each lost in her own private world. They had been friends for more than fifty years. She treasured her friendship with each woman. Each was unique and individual in her own right. Toots could only hope they'd have another fifty years together.

The copilot's deep voice came over the intercom, announcing they were about to begin their descent into Sacramento International Airport. "Ladies, I'm going to have to ask you all to buckle up. The ceiling is down to two hundred feet with some fog and light rain. We'll be making an ILS approach, so it could get bumpy. Please secure any open containers and that little dog."

Ida, an uncomfortable flier on a good day, turned ten shades of white. "What does that mean? I knew I should've taken a commercial flight. I hate these small planes."

"Private jets have the same stupid-ass rules as the commercial airlines," Sophie said as she adjusted her seat belt.

Mavis put Coco in her carrier and placed it beneath the seat. The little pooch growled, then went into a series of earsplitting barks before settling down. "She just hates that crate, but we have to follow the rules. They're for our own protection." Mavis darted a glance at Sophie.

"Oh crap, Mavis, I know that. I just like to complain. At least we didn't have to go through security and get felt off. I bet Ida wouldn't mind going through security, would you?" Sophie said, trying to distract Ida.

When Ida didn't respond to her teasing, Sophie continued. "Ida, clear something up for me. Is it 'felt off' or 'felt up'? I've heard both, but I'm not sure which one to use."

Toots cackled, Mavis smiled, and Ida answered Sophie, her voice trembling with fear. "Either. Personally, I like to think of it as getting 'felt off.' I'm surprised at you, Sophie, with your infinite well of useless information, that you would even ask such a question." To her credit, Ida didn't react to Sophie's tormenting her as she would have a year ago. She was learning to be a true Southern smart-ass.

"It certainly has been in the news a lot lately, those perverts trying to cop a feel. People have no respect for one another anymore," Toots said disgustedly.

Suddenly, the plane lurched to the left.

Ida shrieked. "What's happening?"

Unlike a commercial jet, the private plane did not have a closed cockpit. Ida strained to see into the cockpit and gasped when she saw nothing but clouds rushing past the windscreen. "Oh my God, how are they going to land this plane? The windshield is covered with clouds! I should have stayed home." Ida bowed from the waist, closed her eyes, and held on tight.

Toots observed Ida, whose normally composed face was etched with fear, fingernails digging into the expensive leather armrest. Toots knew full well there was nothing to fear. One of her eight husbands, she couldn't remember exactly which one in the sequence, had been a pilot. To take Ida's mind off her fear, she said, "I remember doing this many times; it really isn't as dangerous as you think. See all those little gauges?" She pointed to the instrument panel, which was clearly visible from their seats. "One of those little round things has two needles on it. One goes up and down, and the other moves left and right. As the pilot approaches the airport, the needles will begin to intersect each other. Keeping them centered—it's somewhat similar to the crosshairs on the scope of a rifle—will align the plane directly on the center of the runway at exactly the right height and allow the pilot to make a normal landing even though he can't see."

Incredulous, Sophie asked, "How in the hell do you know that? Or is that something you're just making up so Ida won't be afraid?"

"Trust me, when you've been in a plane that's even smaller than this one, a four-seater, and you're in the co-pilot seat and cannot even see the wings of the plane, you remember stuff like that. Plus, I think it was Joe, number four or five, who was obsessed with flying and explained everything to me when we flew together. I listened, too, just in case he kicked the bucket. By then, I was already quite experienced in the widow department."

The turbulence ended as quickly as it had begun. Below was the view of a beautiful runway lit up like a festively decorated tree on Christmas morning. Seconds later, the wheels screeched, and they were safely on the ground.

The copilot announced their arrival, and within minutes the cabin door was opening and the automatic stairs descending for their immediate exit.

"This sure beats commercial flying. I always hate when the passengers jump up like pigs running to a feeding trough. Not to mention all the offending body odors you have to endure."

"You're disgusting, Sophie," Toots said.

Their arrival was met with all the pomp and circumstance afforded visiting dignitaries, complete with a meticulously placed red carpet leading to a sleek black limousine.

The chauffeur was retrieving their luggage from the baggage compartment when a well-dressed woman in her mid-thirties emerged from the limo. She greeted the quartet as they approached the vehicle. "I'm Cynthia Johnson, the first lady's personal assistant. How was your flight?"

Returning to her role of society snob, Ida was the first to speak. "It was perfect from takeoff to landing. It was so kind of the governor to send his jet for us."

Sophie looked at Toots and Mavis, rolling her eyes. "Is this the same woman who left fingernail marks on the armrest five minutes ago?"

Ida shot her a *shut-up-or-die* look.

"I'm not the biggest fan of flying myself," Cynthia said to Ida. "Sophia?"

"That would be me," Sophie said, shaking hands with the woman. "These are my friends, Toots, Ida, and Mavis."

"I'm glad you all could accompany Sophie. I'm sure you will enjoy the amenities at the Sterling Hotel. You have carte blanche, courtesy of the governor." Cynthia looked at her slim gold wristwatch. "We'd better get going."

Half an hour later, when they arrived at the hotel, they were greeted by the governor himself.

Chapter 1

After dinner with the first couple, Ida, Mavis, and Toots went to their rooms while Sophie met the first lady in her private suite. Slender, with a head of thick brown hair, and sparkling brown eyes, the former journalist was as bubbly in private as she was in public. Sophie liked her immediately.

"I'm not sure where to start. I've never done anything like this before. When I heard about your success, I knew it was something I had to try. The nightmares are so real, I must admit, I've been terribly ill at ease."

Sophie could feel the woman's uneasiness. "There are numerous ways to communicate with those who have passed. Why don't you tell me about your dreams first, then we can decide what is best for you."

"All right. I'm sure you know the story behind my uncle's assassination; the entire world still speculates on exactly what happened in Dallas that day. I was just a child, yet my memory of that day is very clear."

Sophie listened intently.

"I remember my mother had just returned from a trip, but I don't recall where she'd been. She was crying so hard; I'd never seen her cry before. She was always such a strong woman. It scared me to see her like that. The house was instantly occupied with Secret Service. We were told we couldn't do anything without one of them present." The first lady paused and removed a tissue from the box on the table to her side. "Of course, I was aware our family was in the public eye, but I wasn't used to having strangers swarming all over our home. But this doesn't matter. You didn't come here to listen to my childhood memories.

"The dreams, the nightmares started about a year ago. In my dream, I am walking in a tunnel, and there are hundreds of people around me, pushing and shoving one another in their attempt to get to the end of the tunnel. Two men seem to hover above the crowd. They have guns, and on their faces are horribly wicked smiles. Then there is a very loud noise, and in my dream I know it's a gunshot. I try to get away from all the people, but I'm frozen, my legs won't move. Those evil men above me have some sort of invisible hold on me. I struggle, and still can't move.

"Once again I hear the same loud noise, the one I know is a gun being fired. I have to get out of that tunnel because I know if I don't, someone will die. I continue to struggle, but I'm not going anywhere. Maniacal laughter is followed by a vision, or a flash—I'm not sure what it is—of my uncle's face. He is trying to tell me something of great importance. And then I wake up."

Understanding, Sophie nodded. "I'm not an expert at dream interpretations, but I've studied enough to have a basic knowledge of certain symbols and what they most commonly represent."

"I know this isn't a scientific method."

Reassured, Sophie continued. "Dreaming that you're running usually indicates an issue you're trying to avoid. Some experts"—Sophie made air quotes as she said it—"would say you are not taking responsibility for your actions. In your case, it seems you're trying to run from an attacker, or some type of impending danger. That usually means you have a fear that needs to be confronted.

"Another theory suggests that dreaming you're running and you can't make your feet move often signifies lack of self-esteem and confidence. I think we can agree you're a very accomplished woman, and this is probably not an issue for you.

"On the other hand, when you dream you're running alone, it sometimes refers to your determination and motivation in the pursuit of your goals. I could go on and on as there are varied interpretations. You say you are in a tunnel, and that often signifies determination." Sophie paused, unsure if she should say more.

"Please, go on."

She took a deep breath, ran a hand through her loose hair. *This might be touchy*, she thought, *but what the hell*. "It's possible your dreams and nightmares of the faces and gunshots are relevant to the assassination. Dreams of witnessing an assassination usually indicate you should be paying attention to some small detail."

The first lady brightened. "That's exactly what I feel sometimes. Maybe there is an important detail I'm subconsciously aware of?"

The last thing Sophie wanted to get involved with was another conspiracy theory concerning the former president's death. Way too heavy for her. "It's possible your nightmare is warning you not to overlook the seemingly insignificant things in your life." She didn't want to come off as a street corner fortune-teller, and knew her words were much too general. But Sophie wasn't stupid enough to think she could offer the first lady an instant cure-all solution to how and why those images plagued her dreams.

However, she'd been extremely successful contacting those who'd passed over to the other side, and *they* might offer an explanation.

"I suppose that could be true, but there are so many details in my daily life that are insignificant. How am I supposed to differentiate one from the other?"

"I don't have an answer for that. All I can do is help you open the door and see what happens," Sophie explained.

"Yes, of course. I don't mean to suggest anything more. It's just such a relief to have someone to discuss this with, someone who doesn't think I'm making more out of my nightmares than I should be."

Sophie reached across the small glass table that separated them. She took the anguished woman's hand in hers. "I'm honored you invited me. When would you like to hold the séance?" It was too late that night, plus Sophie was tired. She had learned that when she was tired, she wasn't nearly as successful at making contact, but if the first lady wanted to try, she would.

"Is there a particular time that's . . . better to make contact?"

Sophie smiled. "Not in my experience. If a spirit wants to make contact, it will no matter what time of the day or night. There are a few items I require, so I brought them with me. We will need a quiet room where we won't be disturbed."

"Yes, I thought so. If it's all right with you, I've made arrangements to use one of the rooms at the governor's mansion. It's undergoing renovations now, so it is closed to the public."

Sophie looked skeptical.

"We give tours. Though Ronald Reagan was the last governor to actually live there, it's quite the tourist attraction now."

Understanding, Sophie nodded. "You say there are renovations going on? This could be a good thing. Structural disturbances seem to appeal to the other side. How about tomorrow at noon?"

"I'll arrange for the limo to pick you up at ten o'clock." The first lady hesitated. "What about your friends?"

"They're part of the package."

"I see. They will be discreet?"

"I would trust them with my life," Sophie stated confidently.

The first lady stood, indicating their time together was over. "I can't thank you enough, Sophie. I hope you can help me."

"I will do my very best."

Sophie stepped into the hallway, where several members of the governor's staff waited. A tall man in his late thirties escorted her back to her room. On any other occasion, Sophie would have joked around, but this was neither the time nor the place. When he reached her room, he stepped aside while she unlocked the door.

"Good night, ma'am."

"Nighty, night," Sophie said quietly.

And what a night it had been. She couldn't wait until morning.

On their way to the old mansion, the first lady gave them a brief history of the thirty-room structure.

"A wealthy hardware merchant by the name of Albert Gallatin had the home built in 1877. It wasn't until 1903 that the state of California purchased the house to use as the official governor's mansion. It's quite charming. We still have many of the furnishings from some of the former governors." On the short commute, she filled them in on details that were irrelevant, but Sophie knew she was talking so much because she was nervous.

"I think it sounds like a wonderful home. Why doesn't the governor live here now?" Mavis asked, her cheerful voice a welcome respite.

"When Reagan left office, the state built a new residence in Carmichael—not far from Sacramento. When Governor Brown took office, he refused to live there, and the house was sold by the state in 1982. The mansion is now considered a United States Historic Site, and is listed on the U.S. National Register of Historic Places. We're content to commute."

"My home in South Carolina is on the National Register, too," Toots said. "I love old houses."

Sophie wanted to add that if it weren't for that old beachside dump in Malibu Toots had purchased, none of them would be riding in a limousine to a former mansion, but she refrained.

Without too much fanfare, they made their way inside the musty old mansion, where they were led to a small room on the third floor. The drapes were drawn, and, as Sophie had requested, a round wooden table with five chairs sat in the center of the room.

"It will take me a few minutes to arrange my things, so if you want to wait outside..." She hated telling this powerful woman to wait, but she didn't want her observing the setup ritual.

From her carry-on baggage, Sophie removed the old purple silk sheet that had been left at the beach house by the former pop star and seemed to be a symbol of good luck. Whatever it was, Sophie wasn't going to mess with it. She'd never covered a séance table with anything else and saw no reason to make any changes in her way of conducting a séance.

She removed seven candles from a box. She knew the first lady would ask her why seven candles. There was no particular reason other than seven had always been Sophie's lucky number. She placed six candles around the room and one on the table in front of the chair from which she would lead the séance. She also had a supply of rocks glasses that she felt were good-luck items and centered one in the middle of the table, where everyone could reach it easily.

She placed a legal pad and several pencils to her right, close to where the first lady would be seated. Sophie did not want changes in anything. It would scare the ghosts away, or so she feared.

Toots, Ida, and Mavis positioned their chairs in their usual order. Toots sat directly to Sophie's left, then Ida and Mavis, who would be seated on the other side of the first lady. *This works out perfectly,* Sophie thought, *because I don't want Ida seated next to me.* God forbid Ida put on some phony act just to focus attention on herself.

With the scene set Sophie stepped out of the room and told the first lady they were ready.

"You may sit here," Sophie said, pointing to the chair to her right, "and we will begin."

When everyone was seated, Sophie took her seat center stage, or rather center table. "I always like to explain what a séance is to those who have never attended one. I think the spirits like the formality of the introduction," Sophie joked. She cleared her throat.

"The séance is the coming together of a number of people for the purpose of seeking communication with those who are no longer of this world. Temperaments of those attending séances should be varied as much as humanly possible. While we may share common interests, we must all have open minds in order for any supernormal phenomena to occur." Sophie focused her attention on the first lady. She didn't want to totally freak her out.

"Is everyone ready?" Sophie asked.

All of the women indicated they were.

"I usually open a séance with a prayer of sorts, then I ask if there is anyone who would like to make contact with our guest." She looked at the four women, then took the first lady's hand in her right hand and Toots's hand in her left. Sophie bowed her head in prayer, asking that the room be blessed and that no evil enter their sacred space.

"Let us all take a deep breath, relax and open our minds and hearts to the possibility of another dimension, a place where lost souls are trapped. Now let's place the tips of our fingers against the glass in the center of the table. This is how we communicate with the spirits."

Each woman touched the glass with her fingertips. Sophie closed her eyes and began to speak in a soft, almost seductive tone. "We are here to contact a family member of . . ." Sophie whispered the first lady's full name. She waited several minutes, hoping the silence and the dim lighting would tempt the spirits to reach out and make contact with her.

"If there is a spirit here in this room, move the glass in the center of the table to my right, toward the first lady of California."

All eyes were focused on the glass. When nothing happened, Sophie spoke again. "Our guest is plagued with nightmares, and she needs help to understand their meaning. Again, if there is a presence in this room, move the glass in the center of the table to the right." Again, the women focused on the glass.

A sharp intake of breath came from the first lady when she saw the glass move ever so slightly to the right. Sophie gave her hand a reassuring squeeze. "We've made contact."

"If you are here on behalf of our guest, move the glass to the left."

Suddenly, the glass lurched to the left.

The temperature in the small room became icy, and the candles flickered as though a gust of air had passed over them.

"Thank you." Sophie figured it never hurt to let the spirit know its presence was appreciated and welcomed.

"In her dreams, she is in a tunnel filled with people. She tries to run, yet she is unable. There are gunshots. There are faces of two men in her dreams. Are the events that led to your death related to her dreams? If the answer is yes, move the glass to the right. If the answer is no, move the glass to the left."

All eyes were focused on the glass.

As if an invisible hand swooped down and took the glass, it flew across the room, shattering against the ancient plaster walls.

"Oh my God!" the first lady cried.

Toots, Ida, and Mavis didn't move. They'd come a long way since their first séance.

"This is no cause for alarm. I think the spirit is trying to tell us he is angry. Mavis, there is another glass in the box on the floor behind you. Would you please get it and place it in the center of the table?" Sophie asked.

Mavis slipped out of her chair quietly, located the box, took out the glass, and centered it on the table. As soon as she was seated, Sophie continued, "Let's put our fingers on the glass."

They did as instructed.

"If you're angry, move the glass to the right."

Within seconds, the glass moved to the right, stopped, then moved to the right again.

The chilled room was deathly silent.

"I think it's time for us to try another method. I think I only have a few extra glasses," Sophie said, trying to lighten the atmosphere.

"I don't understand," the first lady stated.

Sophie pointed to the legal pad and the stack of pencils on the table. "There is something called automatic writing. This allows the spirit to communicate through the medium. This technique has been very successful in the past."

Sophie neglected to say that she'd solved a murder using automatic writing. Ida's deceased husband was thought to have died from E-coli from eating a piece of tainted meat. During a séance, his spirit had provided them with enough information to give to law enforcement to prove his death was not an accident.

"All right. Just tell me what to do," the first lady whispered, her fear evident.

"You don't have to do anything except concentrate and allow the spirit to work through me. Automatic writing is essentially writing that's done in an altered state of consciousness, and directed by the spirits of the dead. The spirit will literally manipulate the pencil in my hand. I will be unaware of what is being written and will ask that you not look at the paper until we're finished."

"Exactly how does one put oneself into a trance?"

Sophie had never had her methods questioned so thoroughly, but understood the first lady's skepticism and did not resent it at all.

"I'm going to take several deep breaths, then close my eyes. It's like self-hypnosis. Now, you will all join hands, clear your minds, and relax."

Sophie dropped her head to her chest and began to inhale and exhale. She allowed herself several minutes to reach her self-imposed hypnotic state.

Suddenly, she grabbed the pencil in her left hand. She began to move it across the top of the legal pad. She drew four small squares, two on the top and two below. They were precise, perfectly aligned. Then she drew a large square around the four squares. Her hand whipped across the page, where she proceeded to sketch what appeared to be a small hill. At the bottom of the page, in a childlike scrawl, she wrote in block letters:

O. L. H.
H. O. L.
L. H. O.

She dropped the pencil, only to pick it back up with her right hand. Sophie was right-handed. Skipping all over the page, she made dozens of question marks.

She ripped a page from the tablet, and using her left hand again, drew four small squares, two on the top and two below as she had done only minutes before. On the bottom right of the page, she began to sketch slowly, then quickly, as though she was running out of time. Her head lolled to the side, she dropped the pencil, and her body collapsed in the chair.

The temperature of the room returned to normal, and the flames on the candles stopped flickering.

Toots got up and opened the drapes, while Mavis blew out the candles. Ida remained seated. The first lady looked to be in a state of semishock. Sophie stretched her arms out in front of her, then picked up the tablet.

She studied the writing on the second page. "Where is the first page?" she asked.

"Here, you tore it out." Toots gave her the paper.

Sophie spent a few extra minutes mulling over the papers. "I'm not one hundred percent sure what this means; I don't know how it's connected to your dreams. Maybe you can see something I'm not."

Handing the papers to the first lady, Sophie watched as the governor's wife reviewed the content. When she spied the miniature drawing of the face on the bottom right corner, she gasped.

"I can't believe it! It's the same face from my dreams! And this, look." She tapped her finger against the paper. "Do you have any idea what this is? I'm sure this has something to do with my uncle's assassination. Maybe he's been trying to tell me something in my dreams."

Sophie nodded. Toots, Ida, and Mavis listened intently.

"I wasn't there when it happened, but I've seen hundreds and hundreds of pictures and newsreels from that day. This is the grassy knoll on the hill in Dallas. And this"—she again tapped the paper with her fingertip—"is the window from the depository." She turned the paper around in order for Sophie to see it. "What do you think?"

The three other women stood behind Sophie while she viewed her cryptic writings.

"I'll be right back," the first lady stated as she hurried out of the room. In less than a minute, she was back in the room with a large book in her hand. Quickly flipping through the pages, she stopped when she found what she was looking for.

She laid the book on the table next to the paper that displayed Sophie's handiwork. "This can't leave this room, ever. Look, you know who this man is?"

No one said a word. The significance hit the wall like a ton of bricks.

The sketch of the face at the bottom of the paper was a replica of Lee Harvey Oswald.

Chapter 2

The next morning, the first lady accompanied them on the ride to the airport, where they would board her husband's personal jet for the return flight to Los Angeles. "I haven't slept as well as I did last night in such a long time, and I have you to thank," she said to Sophie, who was feeling quite proud of herself.

When the séance had ended the night before, Sophie concluded that the former president was trying to tell his niece there were no complex conspiracies, that the conspiracy theories about his death were just that and nothing more. The face from her dreams, the same face that Sophie had sketched, was that of the man responsible for his assassination.

"I was glad to help," Sophie said.

If her findings were accurate, she would forever hold a place in history. However, the information would never be made public. Sophie was content with the results even though they had not been quite as detailed as those of some séances she had performed in the past. Maybe those seemingly insignificant things in the first lady's life were just that. Insignificant. Personally, Sophie thought the poor woman's life was filled with too many complex details, which led her to deny the simple truth concerning her uncle's death. Someone was trying to tell her that, hence the nightmares.

Their return to the airport wasn't accompanied by quite the pomp and circumstance of their arrival. The same luxury jet awaited them, and the pilots greeted them as though they were old friends.

From inside her carrier, Coco growled at the two men, then stuck her tiny tongue out as though she were a naughty child. Everyone laughed. The chauffeur assisted the copilot in storing their luggage in the cargo hold of the small jet. Sophie and the first lady said their good-byes, and Sophie shook hands with Toots, Ida, and Mavis, thanking them for their discretion. In a matter of minutes, the four friends were back inside the aircraft and strapped in for the flight to LA.

Arriving back at Malibu, courtesy of yet another limousine, they piled out of the vehicle, glad to return to the beach house. For the past forty-eight hours, Sophie and Toots had refrained from their usual chain-smoking, settling instead for the nicotine gum Mavis was always pushing. It'd been Sophie's idea, telling Toots it probably wasn't politically correct to chain-smoke in the presence of the first lady, knowing she and her husband were health nuts.

"I don't know about you, but if I don't have a cigarette soon, I'm going to croak," Sophie said as she hustled toward the beach house.

"Oh dear, and here I thought you both were happy chewing your nicotine gum. Why don't you try that for a while? It can't be as bad for your lungs as those nasty old cigarettes you smoke," Mavis said sweetly.

Toots placed an arm around Mavis's shoulder as the two of them walked up the steps to the beach house. "Our cigarette habit is as bad as your junk-food habit was. I know it isn't healthy, and so does Sophie. At this point in my life, I don't feel like I'm quite ready to give up the habit, but I promise I will continue to chew that nasty rubbery nicotine gum just for you, Mavis. How's that?"

"I suppose it will have to do," Mavis said. "I do wish you two would stop."

Ida, who lagged behind, spoke up. "Sophie and Toots don't have the power to overcome their addiction."

Toots turned around and looked at Ida. "I don't want to overcome any of my addictions, Ida. I like sugar, I like cigarettes, and I like an occasional drink. So there. Why don't you consider giving up men?"

"You can be such an ass." Ida's words weren't said maliciously, as it was just the type of relationship they shared. Two old women bitching at each other for anything and everything. Toots was quite fond of Ida and vice versa.

Toots flipped her the single-digit salute.

Once everyone was back inside the beach house, they went to their respective rooms. They had established a routine since their temporary relocation to Los Angeles. Mavis was the official chef since she'd lost all that weight, and had become very adept at serving them healthful and delicious meals. Toots, of course, had to have her sugar-laced bowl of Froot Loops at least once a week, but she managed to do so without letting Mavis know about it. Ida, no longer obsessed with germs, had focused her energy on her old passion, photography. Toots admitted that Ida was quite good at it and encouraged her to pursue her interest. Beyond that, Mavis and Ida had become quite successful with funeral parlors throughout the country.

Mavis had designed a line of clothing called Good Mourning. They were clothes mourners could wear not only during the rituals intended to ease the journey of the dearly departed into the netherworld, a world in which Sophie seemed so comfortable, but even after the mourners' loved ones had crossed over.

Ida, a stunning woman extremely skilled at applying makeup, took an interest in Mavis's project when Mavis went to a conference in San Francisco, where she learned how to lay out the dead. In the course of their activities, Ida developed her own line of cosmetics, Drop-Dead Gorgeous.

Mavis, in her desire to help the dearly departed look their best, had also designed a line of clothing for the dead. Her success was so great, she had had to hire a team of seamstresses, then rent a warehouse from which to operate the company. While most of her orders came from the Internet, she had become quite well-known among morticians and funeral directors.

They had all come quite a long way since Toots had sent them that e-mail two years ago inviting them to Charleston right after her eighth husband, Leland, a wealthy cheapskate, had kicked the bucket. She'd felt herself at loose ends, something in her wanting to make a dramatic change in her life. Abby's phone call telling her that *The Informer* was going up for sale had catapulted her into the life she now shared with her three childhood friends. She was truly a happy camper.

While she and the girls were in California, Bernice, her dear friend and housekeeper for more years than she cared to remember, remained in Charleston. During a visit home, to Charleston, Toots had learned of a bakery that made the most perfect pralines. Bernice, the Queen of Superstition, told her that at the grand opening of the bakery, The Sweetest Things, a man had died of a heart attack while waiting in line. Bernice was sure that anyone who came in contact with the bakery or the young girl who owned it would suffer a tragedy of their own if they purchased any baked goods.

It was all the encouragement Toots needed to go check out the bakery for herself. She, along with Mavis, Sophie, and Ida, met the owner, whose name was Jamie. Toots had taken one bite of her pralines and knew instantly that the young woman had a talent. After she had learned that Jamie was about one week from closing down, thanks to the bad publicity over the man who died while waiting in line, Toots suggested she and Jamie go into partnership together. The venture was now extremely successful. Tourists and locals waited in line for hours to purchase her pralines, which were famous statewide.

And Jamie had been living in Toots's guesthouse ever since. She had offered to move now that she was financially stable, but Bernice had become quite attached to the young girl and insisted she stay. Toots agreed. Jamie was like a second daughter. But she was the daughter Bernice had never had. Having a grown son who spent most of his adult life traveling the world searching for who knew what, Bernice was beyond heartbroken by her son's neglect. Toots suspected there was more to the story but didn't voice her thoughts to Bernice. For now, she was happy and content to help Jamie with the bakery. She knew enough not to mess with a good thing.

Toots unpacked and took a quick shower. She slipped into a pair of old jeans she'd had for longer than she cared to remember, topped with a gauzy pale peach blouse. She twisted her heavy auburn hair into a topknot. Sucking in her cheeks, she filled hollows with a matte bronzer a shade deeper than her skin, accentuating her high cheekbones. A touch of mascara, and her favorite coral-colored lipstick, and she was good to go. Since starting her bicoastal lifestyle, as she liked to think of it, she'd been a wee bit more conscientious about her appearance. She slipped her feet into a pair of Kelsi Dagger embellished leather flats, grabbed her package of Marlboros, and headed out to the deck, where the four friends had agreed to meet.

Sophie had arranged the blue-and-white-covered deck

chairs in their favorite positions, side by side, with the giant seashell ashtray on the table between them. Toots reclined next to Sophie, lit a cigarette, and took a deep, satisfying puff.

"I don't see how we managed to do without these damned cigarettes for forty-eight hours."

"Yeah, well, I can't either, but I thought it proper given the circumstances. Plus, it seemed to make Mavis happy," Sophie said.

Toots blew out a large stream of light gray smoke, her throaty laughter deep and rich. "You know, we have cut down quite a bit."

"I know. But you know as well as I do that cutting down isn't the same thing as quitting. I'm thinking about it, really." Sophie had a smile on her face.

"I suppose if you do, I'll have to give it a more concerted effort."

At that moment, Mavis stepped out on the deck, carrying a tray full of tropical delights. "I thought you girls might want a snack."

She placed the platter on the large patio table. Bowls of fresh pineapple, kiwi, and strawberries, were topped with slices of grapefruit—the day's snacks. Mavis had arranged the fruit so perfectly, it would've looked at home on the cover of *Bon Appétit.*

Ida, the queen of sophisticated fashion, chose that moment to grace them with her presence. She was wearing a feminine, billowy yellow skirt with a matching blouse and gold kitten-heeled sandals. As always, her blond hair was coiffed in a perfect pageboy.

"I just checked my e-mail, and I have fourteen requests from funeral parlors wanting to carry my line of Drop-Dead Gorgeous cosmetics," Ida informed them as she helped herself to a bowl of fruit.

"That's fantastic," Mavis said. "I must admit, I looked at my e-mail, too. There were more than a hundred orders. I still can't believe my new career. While it's sad, I feel good about sending people's loved ones off in style. I always thought it was such a morbid thing to have to pick out an outfit in which to bury a family member. Now, funeral parlors can offer my services, saving the family the pain of searching for that final dress or suit. When Herbert died, he only had one suit, so there wasn't really any choice to make."

"Can we talk about something else besides dead people?" Toots asked.

Everyone laughed.

"Has anyone spoken to Abby?" Mavis asked.

Now that she was editor in chief at *The Informer,* Abby spent most of her time behind a desk. However, when the opportunity arose and she was needed, she pounded the pavement just like the reporters, in search of the next big story.

"I tried to call her right before I got in the shower. All I got was her voice mail. I left a message to tell her we were back at the beach house and would be home all evening if she wanted to bring Chester by to visit with Coco." Chester was Abby's German shepherd, who just happened to be madly in love with Coco.

On hearing her name, Coco popped out through her newly installed doggie door onto the deck. She growled, then barked. They all knew she had recognized Chester's name.

Mavis picked up the little dog and placed her in her lap. "Coco would love to see her sweetie, wouldn't she?"

Alert, her ears perking up, Coco stared at the door, most likely searching for Chester.

They spent the next half hour discussing dogs, cats, and

food. Toots and Sophie smoked three cigarettes each and Mavis went back to the kitchen, where she made a pot of coffee and brought it back out to the deck.

The sun was low on the horizon, a brilliant red and yellow ball sinking into the waters of the Pacific Ocean. Foamy white waves curled onto the bisque-colored sand. The early-evening air was warm, yet the breeze off the ocean provided just the right amount of motion to make everyone comfortable. The four women continued to relax on the deck and enjoy their coffees and light conversation.

As they were about to get into a lengthy discussion on the merits and demerits of plastic surgery, the telephone rang. Expecting Abby's call, Toots had brought it outside with her. She looked at the caller ID and picked up on the second ring. "Abby, you got my message. How are you?"

"I'm great. How are the three Gs?" Abby asked, affectionately referring to her three godmothers.

"Ornery as ever. You should know that," Toots teased.

"How was Sacramento?"

Abby knew they'd gone to Sacramento, but had no clue why. Toots hated being dishonest or evasive, especially to her daughter. But being a newspaper editor, Abby would know how important protecting one's sources was. What they'd just done required absolute silence.

"It was a quick trip, nothing exciting. We all had a little bit of business to attend to," Toots explained to her daughter. "Is there any juicy Hollywood gossip these days?"

"Actually there may be. I don't know if you'd call it juicy gossip, but, apparently, Laura Leigh is missing."

Laura Leigh was a midlist actress in her early twenties who often guest starred on some of the more popular sitcoms. She'd had a starring role in a B-grade horror flick a few months earlier and had appeared on all the late-night talk shows. While the movie wasn't a blockbuster by any means, she'd gained quite a following among teenagers. It was said there would be a part two, and possibly a part three, to follow. Shades of *Halloween*.

"Oh my God! Exactly what do you mean by *missing*?" Toots placed her hand over the receiver and told the other three what Abby just told her.

"Missing, as in she hasn't been seen for three days," Abby said. "She was supposed to meet with her agent, and apparently the meeting was crucial to her career. She never showed, and now this."

"It's probably some publicity stunt. Are the police involved?"

"I'm sure they are. Her family just landed at LAX about two hours ago. I had one of the reporters waiting there, hoping to get something for the paper, but her parents and younger sister wouldn't talk. I hate to think Laura would pull such a stunt, upsetting her family like this. They all looked incredibly worried. I've got a reporter waiting at her house in case she shows up. It would be great for *The Informer* if we could get a scoop about her return. It seems that she frequents a couple popular bars in downtown Los Angeles. I've got two reporters staking out those places now. This could be really big news, especially if it's a stunt, which it probably is. I think she liked all that publicity she received a few months ago, and now that it's died down, maybe she's looking to add a little more excitement to her life."

"What a terrible thing to do, especially to her family. If she wants publicity, she should make better movies, something with a real plot and story line. Not those horror vampire slasher movies. Though I know they're quite popular with the younger set."

"Mom, can you hang on for a minute? I think I have another phone call coming in."

"Sure."

"Abby's got reporters staked out at all the hot spots that Laura Leigh frequents. It seems no one has been able to locate her for the past three days," Toots explained to Sophie, Ida, and Mavis, who were engrossed in anything their goddaughter had to say. Toots heard the click and held up a finger indicating Abby was back on the phone.

She was met with silence. "Abby, are you there?"

"Yeah, uh . . . I'm here."

"What's wrong?" Toots asked anxiously. "I can hear it in your voice." She knew her daughter better than anyone in the world and recognized when Abby was worried.

"I'm not sure if anything is wrong. It was just a call from one of my sources at the Los Angeles Police Department. Apparently, Laura Leigh's family is there giving statements." Abby paused, then went on. "I'm not sure if I believe what I just heard or not."

"I am your mother. Do not do this to me. If there is some super-duper juicy gossip, especially something that you're going to report in *The Informer,* I want to know before it's in print."

"Mom, you know I don't like to reveal what my sources tell me until I've confirmed it, but I'm going to make an exception to the rule this time. Promise me you will not reveal one word of this to anyone."

"Not even your godmothers, Abby?" Toots asked.

She heard her daughter's intake of breath.

"I suppose you can tell them, but please explain to them how important it is to keep this to yourselves until I have confirmed it."

"That's a given, Abby, you should know that by now. I'm surprised you would even say such a thing," Toots chastised her daughter.

Sophie, Mavis, and Ida stared at Toots, even more intrigued now that they had heard her end of the conversation.

"According to my source, and at this point I have no reason to doubt the person since the person is the one who read the missing persons report on Laura Leigh, it seems that Chris Clay was the last one to see her alive."

Chapter 3

Toots felt like she'd been sucker punched. "There has to be a mistake. And why would you say *alive?* she asked Abby. "Do they believe she's dead?"

Chris Clay was Toots's stepson, an entertainment attorney who practiced in Los Angeles. She had high hopes that someday he and Abby would stop denying what they felt for one another and become a couple. Chris was the most upstanding guy in the world, just like his father, Garland Clay, had been. Toots couldn't recall his number in her lengthy list of marriages, but next to John Simpson, Abby's father, he was the second love of her life.

"I'm just reading what the report said, Mom. It's cop talk."

"Have you spoken to Chris?" Toots asked, as she moved from the deck into the kitchen, with Abby's godmothers trailing behind her.

"No. But I'm going to hang up and call him right now. Give me half an hour, and I will call you back." Abby clicked off.

Toots nodded, then placed the phone back in its stand on the countertop.

"Toots, what is it? You look like you've seen a ghost.

No, scratch that; been there, done that. You look like shit," Sophie said with her usual tactlessness.

"Abby says her source at the police department called and gave her a tip. It seems that Laura Leigh's family was brought in for questioning. I don't know if this is true or not. I'm only repeating what was told to Abby. Apparently, Chris was the last person seen with Laura."

A hush fell over the homey blue-and-white kitchen, where Mavis was busy pouring everyone another cup of coffee. "I don't understand," she said. "Why would they think he had something to do with her disappearance?"

Toots's hands shook. "That's what Abby is trying to find out. She's going to call back in half an hour." Toots got up from the table and walked over to the cabinet where they stored the liquor. She reached for a bottle of whiskey and brought it back to the table. After she finished the last of her coffee, she poured a liberal amount of the liquor into her coffee cup. Sophie, Mavis, and Ida followed suit.

Ten minutes later, the telephone rang again. Toots looked at the caller ID before picking up. "What did you find out?" she asked Abby, without bothering to say hello.

"I called Chris's house and his cell phone. I even sent him an e-mail. I haven't heard anything yet, but it's just been a few minutes. If I don't hear from him soon, I'm going to go look for him myself."

"You're not going alone. Name a place and we'll meet you there. This is family, not some silly movie star," Toots said.

"Mom, stop. I'm sure we're all overreacting. You know and I know that Chris would never get involved with anything even remotely shady. He's probably just with a client and can't be interrupted. I'm sure he knows what's going on. He is an attorney, you know? He has his share of sources just as I do. It's probably nothing, but when I got the phone call, it just alarmed me. I shouldn't have said anything until I knew something for sure."

"You did exactly what your gut instinct told you to do. You're that much like me. I hate to ask, but was this Laura Leigh more than just a friend? I certainly hope not."

She heard her daughter's deep sigh.

"I wouldn't know."

Toots was sure Abby was holding out on her. She didn't blame her. Abby's relationship, or her lack of one, with Chris was none of Toots's business. She just didn't want Abby to get hurt. She certainly didn't want Chris to get caught up in some Hollywood scandal, something that had the potential to ruin his career. She would not sit by and do nothing. If, God forbid, Chris was in any kind of trouble, something she really doubted, she would spend every dime she had in his defense. After all, he was her son.

"There must be something we can do. I hate sitting here waiting, not knowing," Toots said.

"Good thing you don't work at the paper, Mom. Sitting and waiting is ninety-five percent of our job."

Toots about fell off her chair. Poor Abby. If she only knew. "Of course, I understand that. This is different. This is family."

"Sorry, Mom. I know you mean well. But I really think I've overreacted. Let's just wait until I hear from Chris himself. If he thought either of us was poking around in his affairs, he would have a shit fit. As soon as I hear something I'll call you back, I promise," Abby said.

"Please do, I'm very concerned."

"Okay. I will talk to you later," Abby replied, before disconnecting.

For the second time that evening, Toots placed the

phone back in its stand. Worried, feeling as though she should be doing something, anything, she began to pace the length of the kitchen. Spying her pack of cigarettes lying on the kitchen table, she grabbed it and went outside to the deck. Sophie, Mavis, and Ida trailed behind like little ducklings following the mama duck.

"What's going on, Toots? Is Chris in some kind of trouble?" Sophie lit a cigarette and blew a thick cloud of smoke over her shoulder.

They took their usual places while Toots filled them in on what Abby had learned.

"I saw something about that girl on the Internet, but I'm ashamed to say, I deleted it, thinking it was another one of those e-mail hoax things that does nothing more than spread viruses," Mavis said, her words regretful.

Toots nodded. "I understand. I wouldn't have paid one bit of attention to it, either. But it is what it is, and we will have to deal with it, one way or another.

"Sophie," Toots said, releasing a wide ring of white smoke, "have you talked to Goebel lately?"

Goebel Blevins, a former New York City detective for over thirty years, now turned private eye, had been instrumental in locating the murderer of Thomas, Ida's dead husband. Chris had recommended him as he'd used him on more than one occasion. He was damn good at what he did.

"Not that it's any of your business, but yes, I've spoken with Goebel. He e-mails me daily. I've even read for him a few times. He's got good karma." Not only did she perform séances, Sophie was quite the psychic, and her ability with tarot cards was uncanny. She had accompanied Goebel in a sting operation of sorts, and they'd hit it off.

"I like that man," Ida said out of the blue. "He's shaped up quite nicely since Mavis suggested her diet."

Sophie whirled around, almost knocking the giant seashell ashtray over. "Listen you . . . you fornicatress, you, he's not up for sale. You got that?"

Indignant, Ida lashed back. " 'Fornicatress'? Why, I should smack that filthy cigarette from your dirty mouth. How dare you call me such a name!"

Toots tried to hide her smile but couldn't. "Now is not the time, children. Ida, for the record, I do believe Sophie and Goebel are quite fond of one another. Let's not start a war. We have to help Chris."

Toots looked at the three women gathered on the deck and fixed her gaze on Sophie, who was still fuming. "Why don't you call Goebel, see if he's up for a trip out West? I would like to have him close by just in case. Tell him I'll foot the bill, first-class all the way."

"I can do that. As a matter of fact, I'll do it right now." And without further ado, Sophie hopped off the deck chair, marched through the open sliding glass doors, and headed upstairs to her room.

Toots, Mavis, and Ida were so quiet you could hear a pin drop. Ida's prim voice broke the silence. "A woman has a right to comment on a man's looks. It doesn't matter if he's spoken for or not. The man has done a complete 360. I was simply paying him a compliment."

"Yeah, just don't do it in front of Sophie. She's a bit sensitive where he's concerned. Remember, Walter, the old bastard, was the only man in Sophie's life. If she gets a second chance at her age, I say more power to her. So leave it alone, Ida. Don't antagonize her, and I'll make sure she doesn't do the same to you. Sometimes, you both act like little children." Toots huffed.

"Yes, we certainly shouldn't be arguing at a time like this. Poor Chris. I hope nothing has happened to him," Mavis commented.

Toots leaned forward, scooting to the end of the deck

chair. "Let's not think that way. I'm sure it's just as Abby said. His name was mentioned on the police report, and maybe he was the last person to be seen with Laura Leigh publicly. We don't know that anything has happened to her, much less to Chris. I'm sure this means absolutely nothing. Starlets like publicity. Some will go to great lengths to be mentioned in Jay Leno's monologue. Let's just hope this young woman is found unharmed. Let her agent deal with her."

Sophie padded back out to the deck, her cell phone stuck to her ear. "Here, I'll let Toots tell you. She spoke to Abby."

Sophie handed Toots her cell phone. "Hello, Goebel. It's great to hear you, too. Yes. Of course. Anywhere you like, just name it." Toots's auburn topknot bobbed up and down as she spoke. "I'll take care of the arrangements right away." She handed the cell phone back to Sophie, then went inside.

Picking up the phone, she placed a call to her travel agent, explaining the travel requirements for Goebel. Ida and Mavis followed her, and as was becoming normal, they all gathered around the kitchen table.

"I'll make another pot of coffee," Mavis said.

Toots clicked off the phone and sat back down at the table. "Goebel will be here tomorrow afternoon. I've booked him a suite at the Beverly Hills Hotel. Ida, I want you to be on your best behavior. We need to focus on helping Chris." She allowed Mavis to pour her a cup of coffee. "That is if Abby calls."

Taking a sip of the hot brew, Toots winced and reached for the sugar bowl and creamer. She generously filled her cup with half-and-half, then added three large tablespoons of sugar. She desperately needed a sugar fix.

"Good thing you're not a diabetic," Ida said sarcastically.

"Kiss my ass," Toots offered with a grin.

"You keep asking me to kiss your old ass, and by now I would think you would know better. I am not that kind of woman," Ida singsonged.

"You're not now. However, that's apt to change after spending several years in California. Who knows which way you'll go," Toots teased poor Ida. "We do see a lot of same-sex couples out here, much more so than we would in Charleston. But that's the South for you; they are a bit behind the times. Not that it's my cup of tea, but I say, whatever floats your boat."

"Why are we talking about sex again?" Mavis asked timidly.

Loving to see the shocked look on poor Mavis's naive face, Toots said, "I'll give you my usual stock answer. None of us is getting laid."

"You will never find a sophisticated man with that gutter mouth of yours," Ida added smartly.

Toots was in the middle of swallowing and almost choked at Ida's words. Mavis ran around the table and smacked her on the back. Toots took several deep breaths before speaking again. "First of all, let's get one thing straight; I am not looking for a man. Remember, I've had eight husbands, all of whom, I might add, were almost as sophisticated as they were wealthy. Might I also add, dear Ida, you will never find a man to stick around if you continue to hop in and out of bed with them. You know that old saying, about milking the cow, why bring it home?"

"Girls, girls! Now is not the time. You both still act like you're in eighth grade. I wish you would learn to get along better. I so hate when the two of you fuss. For one thing, Coco gets upset when she hears loud noises."

At the mention of her name, Coco jumped up on her hind legs and wrapped her two front paws around her mistress's leg.

"See?" Mavis said. "Even she's asking you to stop."

At that moment, Sophie came back inside with a smile as big as the moon on her face. "Goebel says he'll be here tomorrow; he just received the e-mail from your travel agent, Toots. I do love the instantaneous e-mail stuff. He'd heard about the missing girl but almost croaked when I told him Chris might be the last one to have seen her. If something bad has happened, Goebel will be the one to find it out. The man is sneaky and sly. Just my kind of guy."

Toots hadn't seen Sophie's eyes sparkle as they were now since high school, long before she had met that old bastard Walter. It was high time she had a man who would treat her respectfully. She'd spent the better half of her marriage being Walter's punching bag.

Though Toots disliked anyone speaking ill of the dead, when it came to Walter, she made an exception. He had been a worthless alcoholic who'd spent his entire life making her very best friend miserable. If Sophie and Goebel became an item, Toots would cheer them on. Ida was absolutely right. Eighty-five pounds lighter than when they first met him, Goebel was quite the hunk.

Toots looked at the clock. It had been almost an hour since she'd heard from Abby, and she was starting to get worried. She'd no sooner had that thought when the telephone rang. She looked at the caller ID.

Abby.

Again not bothering to say hello, Toots begged, "Please tell me he's all right."

"I wish I had something to tell. I've called his house, his cell, everything. He hasn't read the e-mail I sent either. I checked. I wish the shit would return my calls." Abby sounded as worried as Toots.

"No news is good news they say. Have you spoken to your source at the police department? Maybe they've

taken Chris in for questioning. I see them do that on television all the time. Maybe they've got him hidden away in
one of those interrogation rooms just waiting for him to
crack."

Abby laughed. "Mom, this isn't *Murder, She Wrote.* If
Chris were being questioned, I would know."

"How?"

"Remember, I have that source? If Chris had been
brought in, my source would have told me. If anything
happens at the police station, my source promised to let
me know as soon as possible."

Toots took a swig of her cold coffee. "I feel so bad for
that poor girl's family. If this is a stunt, she ought to be
kicked out of the Screen Actors' Guild, or whatever the
Hollywood union thing is."

"We'll have to wait until we hear from either Chris or
Laura. I did have my source e-mail a copy of the missing
persons report. I looked it over, and it's just what one
would expect. Name, address, date of birth, date she went
missing, age, location of the person she was last seen with,
which said Chris Clay. Said they were both at the Hot
Wired Lounge. I'm sitting in the parking lot right now."

"Abby, you should let one of those cub reporters stake
that place out. If a young girl did go missing from Hot
Wired, I don't think it's a good idea for you to be there
alone," Toots said.

"Chester is with me. You know how protective he is.
I'm fine," Abby said reassuringly.

"I want you to stay on the phone with me until you
leave. If you believe anything untoward is about to take
place, I want you to stomp on it and get the hell out of
there. I don't have a good feeling about this, Abby."

"Mom, I could be here for hours. My cell phone battery
won't last that long."

"Abby Simpson, I cannot believe you of all people

would not have either a charger in your little MINI Cooper, or a backup battery. I don't like this Abby, not even a little bit. The news is full of women who've disappeared. If something did happen to Laura Leigh, and she was last seen at Hot Wired, it's not your job to investigate. Leave that to the authorities."

Toots paused, remembering she'd sent for Goebel Blevins, just in case. She hoped like hell she wouldn't need his services, but having him in the same city would be reassuring.

"Mom, I'm going to pretend I didn't hear what you said. I am almost thirty years old, for Pete's sake! I know how to take care of myself, trust me. Remember, I've lived in LA on my own for quite a few years. As I said before, this is probably some stupid Hollywood stunt. I did hear through the grapevine that Laura Leigh might not get the lead in part two of her vampire flick."

"You're not just saying this to make me feel better, are you?"

"Mom! Stop it already! I am fine. Okay? I am here searching for Chris, not Laura Leigh. I am going to hang up. If I have any new information, I promise you will be the first—well actually you'll be the second—person to know. Okay. I am hanging up now, Mother. Good-bye."

Stunned, Toots hit the END button on the telephone. Sophie, Mavis, and Ida all stared at her as if her hair had just turned fifty different shades of green and she had sprouted horns.

"What?" Sophie asked.

"I believe my daughter just hung up on me for the first time," Toots said, her voice betraying her surprise.

Chapter 4

Abby and Chester remained at their post in front of the
swanky nightclub. As the minutes passed, she became
more worried than she'd let on to her mother. She knew
Toots meant well handing out advice, but Abby was an
adult and knew how to handle herself. She'd call her and
apologize. She dialed the number to her mother's beach
house. It wouldn't matter how late because Abby knew
her mother wouldn't go to bed until she'd heard from her.
Abby had to admit it was nice having her and her godmothers close by. She wasn't sure how long they would
stay in Los Angeles this time, but under the circumstances,
knowing they had her back was comforting.

Her mother answered on the second ring.

"Mom, it's me again. I'm still parked at Hot Wired, and
I haven't seen Chris or Laura. I sent a couple of e-mails,
tons of text messages, and I've called his house so many
times I've overloaded his answering machine to the max. I
just wanted to tell you how much I love you. I'm sorry I
hung up on you earlier. I feel like . . ." She wanted to say
she felt like her world was slowly falling apart, but refrained. She didn't want to worry her mother or godmothers
any more than she already had. Abby was certain they

were more than concerned about the situation with Chris and the missing actress.

"Apology accepted. Now, it's after one in the morning, Abby. Why don't you call it a night? I hate the thought of you being out there all alone, with all this uncertainty."

"I'm fine, I promise. But I am getting concerned about Chris. It's not like him not to respond to text messages. I've sent so many of them, he'll probably think I've gone stark-raving mad, like a stalker or something. He still hasn't checked his e-mail, either, and that is really odd."

"Do you want me to come to Brentwood?" Toots asked.

Abby had purchased a nice little ranch house in Brentwood. Before she'd been appointed editor in chief at *The Informer*, she had spent most of her free time remodeling her house. It had turned out quite nicely.

"No, it's too far for you to drive. It's late. I'm going home, Chester hasn't had his dinner yet. I will be fine. I just wanted to check in and tell you I was sorry."

"Promise to call me when you get home? I need to know you're safe before I can even think about going to bed. Your godmothers are still awake, too."

"Of course I will," Abby said, then clicked off.

Her mother was just as concerned about Chris as she was though their lines of thinking weren't the same. Abby was wondering about the possibility that Chris and Laura had taken off for a romantic holiday. As an entertainment attorney, Chris found himself escorting some of Hollywood's most sought after actresses to all sorts of events. He'd told her more than once it was a job requirement that he wasn't very fond of, but Abby wasn't sure if she believed him or not. What guy in his right mind wouldn't want a sexy starlet hanging on his arm? Chris denied any attraction to the women he escorted, telling her it was only work to him and that there were lots of other things he would rather do with his evenings, but Abby still wasn't one hundred percent convinced. Yes, she and Chris had gone out on more than one occasion. Yes, she was very attracted to him. And she thought he was attracted to her, too. While neither claimed exclusive rights to the other, Abby was pretty sure Chris felt the same way she did. Abby sometimes felt like they were playing a game. *You show me your feelings, and I'll show you mine,* yet both remained poker-faced, waiting for the other to make the first move.

As she pulled out of her parking place across from Hot Wired, she told herself that if she found Chris, she would tell him how she felt. Well, only if he wasn't involved with the missing actress. If he was, she would continue in her role as nagging younger stepsister even though she'd never really had a sibling-like relationship with him. He'd gone away to college before Abby was old enough to get to know him. By the time he graduated from college, she was in college herself, studying for a career in journalism.

And now she was out searching for him like some lovesick teenager. The streets of Los Angeles had settled down for a few hours as the has-beens, wannabes, and were-nots partied in the dozens of clubs LA offered. The club-hopping traffic would only last for an hour or so more. Come sunrise, all the main highways would have bumper-to-bumper traffic and the infamous LA freeways would become elongated parking lots if a single car were to overheat, stall, or become involved in an accident. It was the perfect time for her to call it a night.

She wound her way through the back streets, heading toward the main highway to Brentwood. Chester, head on his giant paws, yawned. "When we get home, I'm making you bacon and eggs, Buddy."

Poor Chester, Abby thought. He was the best friend a girl could ask for. Didn't matter that he was a German shepherd, he was her family. He hadn't made a sound all night, except for the one time she let him out to take care of business. He recognized the word *home*. Rising in the seat, he peered out the open window, searching for the house. When Abby pulled her bright yellow MINI Cooper into the driveway, Chester growled.

She unlocked the dog's seat belt, and he bounced out of the car, running to the backyard. She waited at the gate while he did his thing. If it were daylight, Chester would be searching for squirrels, but for some reason, at night the desire to chase the bushy-tailed rodents completely disappeared.

Inside, with the doors safely locked and Chester at her heels, Abby flipped on several lights as she walked to the kitchen. The solid cherry floors she'd sanded herself glistened in the light, warm and comforting. She pulled down the shades on the French doors that led outside to an enclosed courtyard. She wasn't going to give a Peeping Tom an opportunity, not that she ever had that particular problem, but with everything that was happening, she was on edge.

Her mother's warning was ringing in her ears, and she had to admit it was possible there was someone out there abducting young women. That led to the thought that if there was, maybe he or she only went after Hollywood starlets. If so, she was perfectly safe and could relax again. Mentally kicking her butt for such a terrible thought, she tossed her purse and Chester's leash on the small kitchen table.

"I promised you bacon and eggs, and I'm going to join you." Realizing she hadn't had a bite to eat since lunch, Abby removed a bright yellow bowl from the cupboard, along with eggs, bacon, and milk from the refrigerator. Using a cast-iron skillet that had a permanent place on the top of her stove, she sprayed the skillet liberally with cooking spray and turned the heat on under it, cracked five eggs into the yellow bowl and added a dash of milk. She whipped the mixture into a frothy pale yellow foam, carefully placed four slices of bacon on a paper towel, tossed it in the microwave, then poured the eggs into the sizzling skillet.

Chester stood beside her, his black nose twitching.

"Smells good, huh?" Abby said as she removed the bacon from the microwave. She stirred the eggs until they were plump and fluffy. "This has to cool, Bud; I like it hot, but I'm afraid you're gonna have to wait a few more minutes." She scooped a large portion of scrambled eggs onto a paper plate, along with three slices of bacon, and placed it inside the freezer.

She took her plate to the table, Chester still at her heels. While she waited for Chester's dinner to cool in the freezer, she booted up her laptop, hoping against hope to find a reply from Chris. Her cell phone had died as soon as she'd hung up with her mother. Maybe Chris had tried to get in touch with her. She looked over her shoulder at the light on her answering machine, but the red light was as still as the night—not one single message. She wasn't sure if that was good or bad.

She removed Chester's meal from the freezer and transferred it from the paper plate to his doggy dish. Chester was very finicky and would only eat from his dish. He wolfed down the bacon and eggs in a matter of seconds, then took several loud slurps of water from his bowl.

"I like a man with table manners," Abby said to him. His noisy lapping always made her smile.

After she was finished eating, Abby checked her e-mail, still hoping for a response from Chris. She skimmed down the list. Nothing. Checking to see if he'd even read her e-mails, again she was disappointed when she saw the NOT READ icon on her screen.

"This is not good, Chester. It's been three days since Laura went missing. If Chris was last seen with her, has he also been missing for three days?" Abby often spoke to Chester as though he could understand her.

As he always did, he tilted his furry head to the side, his deep brown eyes locking with hers. "Woof!"

"Whatever that is in doggy-speak, I agree."

What Abby wished she knew was if Chris had been missing for three days, too. She hadn't spoken to him in a week, so she had no clue. He worked out of his condo and didn't have a secretary or an answering service he checked in with, so it was a distinct possibility that he was missing as well. Should she file a missing persons report? No, you had to be missing for twenty-four hours. For all she knew, Chris was kicked back on his patio watching the stars.

Maybe he'd removed himself from the world of instant connection for a few days. He and Abby had discussed that very thing at great length. While both admitted they did not know how they survived before the World Wide Web, both agreed it was sometimes too invasive. They'd talked about taking a break from the high-tech world, maybe going away for a few days without a cell phone or a laptop. But that was as far as they'd ever gotten, talking about it. Maybe Chris had taken the much-needed break. Maybe he was simply holed up in his condo with the telephone unplugged.

Deciding there was only one way to find out, she tossed her paper plate in the garbage can. "Chester, my friend, we are going to do a little wee-morning snooping." Picking up his leash from the table, along with her purse, Abby headed for the front door. Chester followed. "I'll pay you back big-time for this. When things calm down, we'll go visit Coco." At the mention of the little Chihuahua, Chester ran in circles, jumping up and down as though he were performing in a circus act.

"Soon, Buddy. Right now, I need your protection. Just in case." With that, she left, not bothering to turn off the lights. The hell with the electric bill. Her salary had doubled since she'd taken the position of editor in chief. She could afford to leave the lights on for a few hours without worrying about the meter going crazy.

Back inside her MINI Cooper, Abby fastened Chester's seat belt, then her own. She'd grabbed her cell phone charger on the way out and plugged it into the cigarette lighter. When she took her phone out of her purse and plugged it in, she saw the lightning bolt in the upper right-hand corner of the screen, indicating a positive charge.

Hoping she wasn't embarking on another wild-goose chase in the same twenty-four-hour period, Abby sped off into the night to search for the man who, even though he wasn't aware of it, held her heart in his hands. At least she didn't think he was aware of it. But that didn't matter. What did matter was that she find Chris. As the hours and minutes passed, she was becoming more creeped out than ever.

Chris's condo wasn't all that far from Brentwood. That time of night, or rather morning, it would only take twenty minutes to get there. Abby's schedule was so screwed up, she knew she'd never be able to work a normal nine-to-five job. Writing for the tabloid press required one to be ready in a moment's notice. Being in Hollywood meant most of the breaking news was late at night or in the wee hours of the morning.

Seventeen minutes after she left her house, she was pulling into the condo's guest parking. Hooking Chester's leash to his collar, she led him out of the car on the driver's side. One door slamming that time of morning was enough. Hopefully, Chris didn't have nosy neighbors.

Abby led Chester down the narrow sidewalk. Careful not to make any unnecessary noise, she practically tiptoed up the two flights of stairs. The sound of Chester's nails clicking on the cement was magnified in the still night air. When they reached Chris's condo, before knocking on the door, she peeked inside the small pane of glass at the top of the door.

She couldn't see much. There were no lights on, but she could tell by the moonlight filtering through that the sliding glass doors were open. Smiling and ready to kick his butt and take names later for causing her to worry, Abby gently knocked on the door so she wouldn't startle him. It was three in the morning, the witching hour, as Sophie referred to it, not the most appropriate time to pop in and say hello.

When there was no response to her light knocking, she knocked harder and was surprised when the door opened. "Chris?" She pushed the door to the side but remained outside. Seeing that she was right, and the sliders were open, Abby entered the condo. "Chris, are you here?" She waited for a minute, thinking he might be in the shower. When there was still no response, she pulled on Chester's leash. "Come on, boy," she whispered. "I don't feel good about this."

Carefully, she made her way through the living room without knocking anything over, though she had to admit Chris's furnishings were sparse; there wasn't much she could knock over except for a couple lamps. The moonlight illuminated the terrace. Two deck chairs cast dark shadows on the terrace. Abby dropped Chester's leash to the ground, gave a hand signal indicating he should stay, then stepped outside.

And nothing. Two chairs, a glass-topped table between them. "What the hell?" she whispered. Two half-empty wineglasses were situated on the table. She picked one up, brought it to her nose. Red wine of some kind. She strained to hear something, anything, that would give her some clue if Chris was inside his condo. If he was in bed with one of those starlets he claimed to dislike so much, she didn't want to be the one to catch him.

Heart pumping, Abby went back inside, down the hall, and peered inside the guest bathroom. She didn't want to turn on the lights yet, so she ran her hands along the inside of the shower door, checking to see if anyone had showered recently. Dry as a bone. She ran her hands along the vanity. What did she hope to find? A tube of lipstick? A hairbrush? A box of tampons? Anything to indicate Chris was inside with a lover?

Her search of the guest bath produced nothing. If she were brave enough to turn on the light—she wasn't—she would most likely find the same ugly beige guest towels, a soap dish that had three soaps in the shape of a seashell, and a box of Kleenex. She remembered this from the last time she was here; she recalled thinking he could use a decorator's services.

In the darkness, she couldn't see anything out of place, so she continued her search. She knew Chris used the second bedroom as an office. Cautiously, she turned the knob, pushing the door open, and was greeted by total darkness. No wandering fish on a screen saver, no nightlight, nothing, nada, zilch. Not even the moonlight filtered through the closed blinds. She stepped completely inside and walked over to his desk, which faced the wall opposite the window. His MacBook Pro and MacBook Air were on the desk. Abby knew Chris well enough to know that, as a rule, he didn't take off without one of his precious Mac notebooks.

Weird.

She left the office, careful to close the door behind her. Next on her list, the master bedroom. She heard Chester's collar rattling in the living room. *Damn!* She'd told him to sit, and Chester always followed her commands unless . . .

She hurried back to the living room to find Chester waiting by the front door. "You're kidding, right?" Chester never stood by any door unless he had to pee.

The German shepherd growled. "Okay. Just give me a minute. You stay," she said before racing back down the hall.

She was taking a big risk by sneaking into Chris's bedroom, but she'd worry about the consequences later. If she saw he was in bed alone, well, she might join him. Then kick his ass for causing her to worry. If he was in bed and had company, Abby knew her heart would shatter into a million little pieces.

She drew a deep breath once she was outside Chris's bedroom. Maybe she should knock first, just in case he wasn't alone. Maybe she should turn around and go home. Forget about Chris. Forget about Laura Leigh.

Abby's reporter's instincts were on high alert. She couldn't walk out of there without some kind of answer. So, before she had a chance to change her mind, she took the brass knob in her hand, and slowly began to turn it to the right.

Before she could turn the knob all the way and thrust the door aside with the expertise of a professional prowler, a buzzing in her hip pocket almost caused her to have a heart attack. Quickly she took her cell phone out of her pocket. It could be Chris. She looked at the caller ID.

Shit, shit, and double shit!

It was her mother. She had to answer.

Chapter 5

Abby punched the bright green TALK button on her cell phone. In a hushed whisper, she said, "Mom, I'll call you back." She hung up, then turned her phone off. For all she knew, Chris and some skanky chick were in the bedroom laughing at her at that very moment. She'd explain everything to her mother as soon as there was something to explain.

That was when she remembered she'd promised her mother she'd call as soon as she got home. *Poor Mom and the three Gs.* They were probably imagining all kinds of terrible things. At least her mom knew she was alive. Content with that for the moment, she reached for the doorknob and, without a moment's hesitation, turned it all the way. Pushing the door aside, Abby entered the room.

Bathed in silver moonlight, the master bedroom appeared empty. She walked over to the bed, saw it hadn't been slept in, and breathed a sigh of relief, then shuddered at her thoughts. Just because his bed was empty didn't mean anything other than he wasn't in it at present. She looked inside the master bath and discovered that it, too, was empty. She yanked the shower curtain aside, just in case. Anthony Perkins's role in Alfred Hitchcock's blockbuster 1960 movie *Psycho*, which she had seen a zillion times on late-night TV, had left its mark on her. She rarely looked at a shower curtain without imagining someone behind it. Childish, yes, but still frightening. There was, of course, nothing in Chris's shower except the usual array of items. Soap, shampoo, a razor, and a can of Edge shaving cream.

She spotted a night-light on the side of the vanity, and, without giving it another thought, flipped the switch. A warm, golden glow filled the bathroom. Abby looked around, searching for evidence of a female. She opened the medicine chest. A tube of Crest toothpaste, a blue-and-green-striped toothbrush, a bottle of Tylenol PM, and a small tube of Neosporin antibiotic ointment. *Nothing mysterious here,* she thought, closing the medicine cabinet and turning off the night-light. She glanced around the grayish black room. Chris was definitely not at home.

She hurried back to the entryway, where Chester was waiting patiently. She looked around one last time before slipping out the front door. Once she was downstairs, she released Chester. While she waited for the dog to investigate each and every shrub, her mind raced.

It was obvious Chris had been home at some point in the past few hours. Two half-empty glasses of wine proved that. His front door wasn't even locked. How could she explain that? Chris wasn't stupid. He would never leave his condo door unlocked.

Chester finished his business, then returned to Abby, waiting by the car. After she unlocked the door, and the big pooch hopped in, she leaned across the bucket seat and fastened his seat belt.

"Woof! Woof!" Suddenly Chester tried to break free from his belt.

"Hey, boy, what's up?" She scratched him between the ears, something that always calmed him. When he didn't settle down, Abby knew something wasn't right. Chester's

instinct was almost as honed as her own. She quickly un-
hooked the seat belt, then took the leash off and placed it
on the floorboard.

Stepping aside so the big dog could jump out of the car,
she followed him, running behind to keep up. Chester
raced toward the beach. As they came closer to the beach-
front, Chester stopped, ears perked up in attention. Abby
strained to hear what he was hearing, but couldn't. Her
hearing wasn't as fine-tuned as Chester's, but mere seconds passed before she heard what he'd been able to hear
from the beginning.

Laughter from the beach. Abby stopped, and grabbed
Chester's collar to restrain him. She was able to discern the
laughter as female, followed by a male voice. Why hadn't
she thought of this? How stupid could she be? This explained why Chris's front door was unlocked. Explained
the two half-empty glasses of wine on the terrace. Chris
and whoever he was with had been taking a moonlight
stroll on the beach. The dirty rotten shit! How dare he do
this to . . . Toots! Abby was worried sick about him, too.
She had spent her entire night searching for him, staking
out that stupid club, and she'd lost count of how many
e-mails and text messages she'd sent. Her first thought was
to get the hell out of there before he saw her.

Remembering what was on Laura Leigh's missing persons report, she changed her mind. If Chris knew anything
about it, he needed to come forward, tell his side of the
story, clear up the mystery that was going to generate big
headlines if Laura wasn't found soon. Or maybe he already knew that. Maybe it was part of his attorney-client
relationship. Chris was well-known, had been voted one
of Hollywood's most eligible bachelors. His name would
pack quite a punch on its own. Add a B-grade actress, and
the story would blossom into front-page news. Hell, it was

news already. Abby had sent her own team of reporters in search of a lead.

Two figures emerged from the beach. She waited in the parking lot, having decided to confront Chris and tell him his ass was about to be on fire, and she was the one who was going to light the match.

As she waited for him and his female "friend" to reach the stairway—the only way to enter the condo—she felt her heart crack, splitting in half. All those sweet words he'd said, all those damned fantasies she'd had were just that. Fantasies. Christopher Clay was not interested in her. Pure and simple.

She heard the couple giggling like teenagers as they came around the corner. Leaving Chester in the car, Abby hoofed it back to the stairs, and called out, "Chris, I need to talk to you now!" Shaking, she waited for him to yell at her, tell her to mind her own business, something, but all she heard was whispering, then someone cleared his throat.

"Look, I don't know who's out there, but this isn't Chris," replied a male voice that definitely didn't belong to Chris.

Abby stepped out of the dark shadows, walking toward the staircase. Going with the obvious, she demanded, "Who are you? And what are you doing here?"

"I believe I should ask you the same thing. Who are you and what are *you* doing here?" His voice was cold and hard.

Her heart raced unnaturally. For a second she thought it might explode. She knew how odd it appeared, her being at Chris's condo at three o'clock in the morning, but no more so than a strange man and woman giggling on the beach. "I'm Chris's stepsister." As if that gave her an official right to barge in anytime she felt like it.

Abby could feel the tension in the air disappear. The guy took a deep breath, released the young woman's hand he had been holding, and stepped forward with his hand held out to Abby. "I'm Steve, I went to school with Chris. He didn't tell me he was expecting you. Come on inside." Almost as if it were an afterthought, he said, "This is Renée, my fiancée."

Abby nodded at the young woman, started to follow the couple, then stopped. "Look, I can't go inside. My dog is in the car, and I have a phone call I have to make. If you can just explain why you're here, I'll leave." She wasn't sure if she should reveal the information about Chris's disappearance just in case this guy had something to do with it. Though she had to admit she'd heard Chris speak of him before, and was quite sure Steve was who he said he was. Still, she wasn't going to take that chance.

Steve turned around when he reached the top of the stairs. "If you must know, Chris loaned me his condo for the week. He said he had plans and wouldn't be here anyway."

Abby's mind raced. Plans? As in going-out-of-town plans? If so, he certainly hadn't told her or her mother. *Not that he had to, but it would have been nice, a common courtesy,* she thought. When Chris found out she'd been there at that ungodly hour, he would never let her live it down. Deciding to accept the explanation, she felt her face turn a deep shade of red at the thought of what she must look like. She was glad for the darkness. "Did he mention where he was going?"

"No, and I didn't ask," Steve said. "I gathered he didn't want anyone to know."

Abby wanted to ask how he "gathered" Chris didn't want anyone to know, but future humiliation prevented her from asking. She nodded. "Well, then, I have to go.

My dog is waiting. Could you do me a favor?" she asked timidly.

"I can try," he said.

"When Chris returns, don't mention this visit."

"Uh, sure, no problem."

Without another word, Abby headed for her car. Chester was waiting, his tongue hanging out the side of his mouth. His tail wagged so fast it created a breeze. She started the engine and shifted into reverse. She hit the accelerator so hard, her tires squealed.

Shit! Now she was sure someone would tell Chris about the bright yellow MINI Cooper peeling out of the parking lot. *Big mystery*, she thought, knowing Chris would recognize her car. Why hadn't she bought a silver Toyota like the rest of the world? At that point, it didn't really matter. She'd learned absolutely nothing.

Not true, Abby. She'd learned Chris was really out of town, but didn't know where or with whom. Remembering her promise to call her mother, she removed her cell phone from her pocket and hit the speed dial.

"Abby, I was just about to call the police! Where in the world are you?" her mother exclaimed, her voice laced with worry.

Did she really want to go into all the details right then? No, but knowing her mother could be relentless when she was upset, Abby decided there was no time like the present. "I went to Chris's condo, looking for him."

"Did you find him?" Toots asked.

Abby hit the SPEAKERPHONE icon. The clubs were closing, and traffic was heavier. Tired, and beyond worried, she needed to focus her attention on her driving.

"No, but get this. There's a guy named Steve staying at the condo. He brought his fiancée, a woman named Renée. Chris told him he would be gone for a week, but neglected to say where or with whom."

"That sounds just like something Chris would do. He's very private. His father was the same way. Never told his left hand what his right hand was doing," Toots said.

Incredulous, Abby asked, "You don't think this is suspicious? Chris is gone for a week, and Laura Leigh just happens to disappear?"

"No, not really. It is odd that Chris was reported as the last person she was seen with. Maybe they were at the same nightclub, and he walked her to her car. He is a gentleman. Chris would do that," Toots explained, though Abby wasn't buying it, not one little bit. There was something going on with him, and she planned to find out exactly what.

"This has nothing to do with Chris being a gentleman, Mom. No one seems to know where he is. An actress is missing and Chris's name is mentioned in the report." Abby swerved to avoid a bag of garbage in the middle of the road. "I'm almost home. Can I call you tomorrow? I need to get a few hours' sleep. I can't let my employers find me asleep at my desk or at home when I should be editor in chiefing at the office. I promise if I hear any news, I'll call you."

"All right," said her forgiving employer, who had to resist the urge to tell her daughter to take the day off, "but promise you won't forget to call. We were so worried, Abby."

She heard the concern in her mother's voice and felt a pang of guilt for not calling when she said she would. "I promise," Abby said, before ending the call.

She pulled into her driveway, suddenly exhausted. She removed Chester's belts and buckles and for the second time in three hours, let him leap across the seat and visit the backyard. Abby looked at her watch. Almost 4:00 AM Definitely time to hit the sack.

Chapter 6

Toots spent the next three-plus hours tossing and turning. She glanced at the digital clock next to her bed—7:30. Knowing there was no way she would go back to sleep, she decided to get up and start the day. She took a quick shower, and dressed in a pair of black slacks with a gray blouse. She twisted her hair in its usual topknot, added a smear of blush to her cheeks and mascara to her eyelashes, and went downstairs to start the coffee.

She had high hopes Sophie, Mavis, and Ida would sleep in after staying up so late waiting to hear from Abby, but tossed them right down the drain as soon as she heard the familiar creak on the staircase. Expecting it to be Sophie, Toots was surprised when she saw Ida, dressed to the nines in one of Mavis's remakes of a sixties-style Coco Chanel shift dress Ida had worn in her younger days. It was black with white trim, sleeveless with an empire waist, and she was the only sixty-six-year-old woman Toots knew who could pull it off without looking like she was trying to act twenty years younger.

"I smell coffee," Ida said as she sashayed over to the counter next to Toots.

"Help yourself," Toots replied as she filled her cup with half and half, along with her usual three giant spoonfuls of sugar. She watched as her friend poured coffee into a cup, adding about two grains of sugar. Rolling her eyes, Toots walked over to the table. Seated in her regular chair at the head of the table, she continued to watch Ida. "Did you ever think of becoming an actress?"

Ida brought her cup to the table. "Why do you ask?"

"Well, you're up at seven-thirty in the morning, fully dressed, and you have makeup on. That's how actresses always look on television. Just a thought I had, nothing important."

"Is this your way of asking me why I'm dressed so early?"

Toots rolled her eyes again. "Actually, it isn't." Under no circumstances would she give Ida the satisfaction of asking why she was dressed like she had stepped right out of the star's dressing room, no matter how curious she was. Instead, she took a sip of her coffee and cringed at the bitter taste despite its being laced to overflowing with cream and sugar. She really didn't like the imported coffee beans Mavis had switched to. Give her good old Maxwell House any day of the week. This crap was certainly not good to the last drop.

Ida took several sips of her coffee before speaking. "I have a nine o'clock hair appointment at Neil George Salon. They're the most posh salon in Beverly Hills. At least for the moment."

Toots's instinctual alarm went off. She knew what Ida was up to. It didn't take Albert Einstein, or even a plain old rocket scientist, to figure it out. Ida wanted to make damn sure she'd look her best before Goebel arrived in the afternoon. Formulating a plan, Toots's thoughts brought forth an evil grin. "You know, I have been looking for a new salon. I need my ends trimmed and a bit of a color touch-up. Would you mind giving me their number so I can schedule an appointment? I would appreciate it."

Toots's eyes danced with delightful mischief. She was not going to let Ida get one up on Sophie.

"I thought you always colored your own hair," Ida said, "but of course I'll be happy to give you their number. You might want to consider adding some highlights to your hair. It's become quite dull."

Toots wanted to bitch slap Ida but managed to refrain. She'd let Sophie have that pleasure. Ida obviously thought she was Mrs. Senior America—if there was such a thing. Ida was indeed beautiful, and she certainly knew it, but Toots thought her vanity had an ugly quality to it that detracted from her beauty. She laughed out loud.

"I'm glad you think it's funny. Remember, we are in Hollywood, and looks matter. I, for one, am not dead yet. As a professional makeup artist, I do have a certain image to uphold."

"For all of those dead people you glam up? I'm sure they appreciate looking their best before they get baked," Toots joked. Actually she was quite proud of Ida, who had come a long way in the past two years. Her Drop-Dead Gorgeous line of cosmetics was quite successful. Toots also wanted to add that her clients probably didn't care about Ida's looks, but bit her lip. She'd gone far enough that morning.

"Don't let Mavis hear you talk this way. You will hurt her feelings," Ida informed her.

"I wouldn't even think of it," Toots said.

"Think of what?" Sophie said as she padded into the kitchen. She helped herself to a cup of coffee before settling down at the table.

"Hurting Mavis's feelings," Ida offered up.

"Why would Toots want to hurt Mavis's feelings? Why would anyone want to hurt her feelings? She's the most honest, kind, and loving woman I know." Sophie shot Ida a dirty look.

"I simply commented on Ida's dress. She looks like a movie star ready to make her first appearance of the day before a camera," Toots explained to Sophie.

Sophie looked at Ida and rolled her dark brown eyes up at the ceiling. "Maybe from a silent movie."

Toots couldn't help herself, she burst out laughing. Sophie joined her. Ida stuck her nose up in the air.

"You have no class, Sophie Manchester," Ida stated in a matter-of-fact voice.

"I know. I gave it all to you, which is why you have so much," Sophie teased. "Speaking of class, who's going with me to pick up Goebel?"

"I suppose I could accompany you," Ida said. "I should be finished with my hair appointment. He arrives around one o'clock this afternoon?"

Toots saw the look on Sophie's face. Rather than giving Sophie a chance to go ballistic at Ida's "generous offer," Toots kicked Sophie under the table just in time to prevent her from doing just that. Sophie caught her eye, whereupon Toots winked and gave a slight nod.

"I think that's very generous of Ida, Sophie. As a matter of fact, I think we should all go with you to the airport. You might get lost."

Mavis and Coco chose that precise moment to enter the kitchen. The little Chihuahua danced from one foot to the other, then raced through the doggie door and was back within a matter of minutes. "She's such a good girl," Mavis said, reaching down to stroke the little brown ball of fur. She filled Coco's dog bowl with sliced turkey breast and her water bowl with natural spring water. Since Mavis had gone on a health kick, she'd insisted that Coco follow suit. The dog certainly didn't seem to have any problems with her new diet.

Mavis poured herself a cup of coffee, then started a second pot. It was a house rule that whoever drank the last cup had to start a new pot. Among the four of them, they often went through five or six pots a day.

As soon as Mavis sat down, Coco jumped onto her lap and peered over the table, her miniature head tilted up as though she were snubbing them. Toots was convinced the dog had been royalty in another life.

"Sophie, you need to read for Coco," Toots said.

They all laughed.

"I've never tried to contact an animal." Sophie took a slurp of her coffee. "Do you realize how insane that sounds? If anyone were to hear our conversations, we would all be committed."

When the second pot of coffee was ready, Toots refilled their cups, then sat back down, her look and tone serious. "I've been trying to put this off, but I'm afraid I can't any longer." Grabbing the remote control in the center of the table, she aimed it at the small television set on the counter-top across from them. "I want to see if there's any more news on that missing girl." She didn't add, *and anything about Chris.* She hadn't heard from Abby yet that morning, not that she expected to less than four hours since she last spoke to her daughter, so she was going to go with the "no news is good news" attitude until she heard otherwise.

She flipped to a local station. They all focused their attention on the female newscaster.

"*It has been four days since Laura Leigh was reported missing by her agent, Leo Goldenberg. The actress was featured in the teen hit* Bloody Hollow. *Sources say she is being considered for the leading role in part two, as of yet unnamed. She was last seen leaving Hot Wired, a local nightclub frequented by Hollywood's hottest stars, with Christopher Clay, a popular Los Angeles entertainment attorney. Laura Leigh is five-three, 115 pounds. The much-adored starlet has blue eyes and blond hair.*"

A picture of Laura Leigh filled the screen—a still shot from *Bloody Hollow*. Her face was powder white, her eyes gold, and her hair a deep shade of burgundy. Another image filled the screen, this one a more accurate portrayal of what the actress looked like out of makeup. Her long blond hair was styled in loose curls. She was smiling at the camera, her bright blue eyes shiny and clear.

"Miss Leigh's vehicle, a 2011 Barcelona Red Metallic Toyota Prius, license plate IMASTAR, *has not been located. A spokesperson for the Los Angeles County Police Department said a search warrant for the vehicle was issued yesterday. Her apartment in Los Angeles was searched. The spokesperson reported there were no signs of a struggle, and it did not appear as if Miss Leigh had taken any belongings from her apartment. Police are searching for Christopher Clay, who was the last person seen with Miss Leigh. Mr. Clay is wanted for questioning. He is not considered a person of interest at this time."*

A photo of Chris, the same one used when he was voted one of LA's top ten bachelors, filled the screen. He was smiling, his sandy hair windblown and his eyes sparkling.

"A one-hundred-thousand-dollar reward is being offered for information leading to the actress's safe return."

Toots turned the television off. No one said a word. Grabbing her cigarettes, she went outside to the deck. Sophie followed her. Each sat in her own deck chair and lit up.

The breeze from the ocean was still cool, the air quiet and gentle. Hues of violet, pale pink, and burnt orange rose from the aquamarine water. Seagulls cawed in the early-morning air. Lights from a variety of water vessels flashed in the distance. Waves crashed on the oyster-colored sand, white and frothy like a French latte.

Toots gazed out at the beach, her thoughts reflecting the fright she felt.

"You know Chris had nothing to do with that girl's disappearance," Sophie said gently.

Toots nodded and couldn't help it when a single tear rolled down her cheek. "I know, but I'm afraid, Soph. What if something terrible really has happened to that poor girl? What if Chris is accused of . . . of harming her? I've dealt with a lot of problems in my life, but nothing like this. Don't tell anyone, but I've tried his cell phone, his house, and, like Abby, I've sent a dozen e-mails. Chris always answers me, almost instantly. You know that."

Sophie placed her hand on Toots's. "There is a perfectly logical explanation for this; I can feel it in my gut. That probably doesn't help now, but you know I'm rarely wrong, or at least my gut isn't."

Toots felt a bit encouraged. Sophie was right. Her gut was almost one hundred percent accurate. Toots had witnessed it many times. "Do you think there is anything you can do, you know, spirit-wise, to help locate this Laura Leigh?"

"I can certainly try."

"Then let's do it, right now." Toots jumped off the deck chair. "Before Ida has to leave. She's going to get her hair done at some high-class hair salon in Beverly Hills. She has to be there at nine o'clock."

"I wondered why she was all gussied up so early. I thought maybe the FedEx guy was making an early delivery. Ida's such a slut." Sophie crushed her cigarette out in the seashell ashtray.

"Not that I'm aware of, but don't say I didn't warn you; I think Ida's set her eyes on Goebel. Now that he's lost all that weight, he's a good-looking man. Not that he wasn't handsome before. She hasn't been with a man since Patel, at least not that I'm aware of."

Sophie lit another cigarette and passed it to Toots, then lit one for herself. "Goebel isn't interested in her, trust me.

She's too prissy for him. I'm not worried, okay?" She blew smoke out in one big puff.

"Remember, Ida likes a challenge. She is beautiful"— Toots turned to her friend—"but not nearly as beautiful as you."

"Oh, stop with the sappy shit. I know Ida's easy on the eyes. I'm fine with that. Hell, we're all easy on the eyes, especially for seniors."

They laughed at Sophie's conceit.

"Now, before we go back inside, I have something to tell you." Toots whispered just in case. "I am going to get even with Ida. I have her new hairdresser's phone number."

When Toots told Sophie of her plan they giggled just like they had in high school. As soon as they thought their laughter was under control, they would look at one another and start all over again.

Poor Ida, Toots thought. *She is in deep shit.*

Chapter 7

Abby jerked upright, momentarily disoriented. Seeing that she was at home in her living room, safe and sound, she leaned back, remembering the events from last night. When she had returned from Chris's, she'd been too tired to bother changing into her pajamas and crawling beneath the sheets. She'd lain down on the sofa, with Chester at her feet, and fell asleep as soon as her head hit the cushion.

Forcing herself into a sitting position, she cringed at the way she felt. Her neck was stiff, and her mouth was as dry as the Sahara during a drought. Chester, who had been disturbed by her movement, slowly hopped off the couch and headed for the back door. She unlocked the door and waited while Chester watered the lawn. When he finished, she whistled, and, now fully awake, he came running. "No squirrel watching today, Bud. We've got work to do."

In the kitchen, Abby prepared her morning pot of coffee, then filled Chester's dish with kibble. She rinsed his water dish, refilled it with tap water, and said, "I'll be right back." Then she grabbed her cell phone from the coffee table and punched in Chris's cell number. When it went straight to voice mail, she clicked off, as there was no point in leaving yet another message. There was no point in calling his house, either. She booted up her laptop, hoping against hope that he had sent her an e-mail. She scanned through the long list of e-mails, searching for his name, and again found nothing.

Knowing there wasn't anything she could do just then, Abby placed a quick call to *The Informer* to tell Josh she would be there later in the morning. She went back into the kitchen, poured herself a cup of coffee, then headed for the blessed relief of a shower.

Stripping off her grimy clothes, she turned the water on and pulled the knob up for the shower. It took a couple minutes for the water to get hot enough, something she kept promising herself she was going to remedy later, but for now it was the least of her worries. Squirting grapefruit-scented body wash onto a mesh sponge, she quickly scrubbed, gave her hair a ten-second wash and rinse, then stepped onto the bath mat.

Wrapping a huge bath sheet around her and a towel around her head, she wiped steam from the mirror with her hand. She brushed her teeth, savoring the fresh feeling. After smearing a light moisturizer on her face, she attacked her tangled hair.

In her bedroom, she grabbed a pair of Levi's and a black turtleneck T-shirt. She dressed quickly, then returned to the kitchen. Looking at her answering machine, she saw the red light flashing. Crossing her fingers and hoping for the best, she hit the PLAY button. Two calls from her mother. *Poor Mom,* Abby thought as she fast-forwarded through her messages. A call from Angelina, wanting to know next week's assignment. She flashed through that, too. The last message was from a solicitor trying to sell her an ownership of a time-share unit in Florida. Still nothing from Chris.

Damn. She was getting more worried by the hour. It was way out of character for him. She looked at the clock and quickly punched in her mother's cell number.

When there was no answer, she tried calling the beach house. When she still didn't get an answer, she tried Sophie's cell phone. No answer. She tried Ida's and Mavis's numbers, and they didn't answer either. Something was going on, big-time.

"Chester," Abby called. "Let's go." She yanked her purse off the coffee table, then went back into the kitchen to turn off the coffeemaker and lock the back door. Grabbing her laptop, she didn't bother putting it inside the case. In less than a minute, she was squealing out of her driveway. Early morning and neighbors be damned.

The morning traffic in Los Angeles was horrific, more so than normal. Waiting for traffic to move, she searched for a radio station that offered news. When she located KABC, the sister station of her favorite local television station, she cranked up the volume.

"*Miss Leigh's vehicle, a 2011 Barcelona Red Metallic Toyota Prius, license plate IMASTAR, has not been located. A spokesperson for the Los Angeles County Police Department said a search warrant for the vehicle was issued yesterday. Her apartment in Los Angeles was searched. The spokesperson reported there were no signs of a struggle, and it did not appear as if Miss Leigh had taken any belongings from her apartment. Police are searching for Christopher Clay, who was last seen with Miss Leigh. Mr. Clay is wanted for questioning. He is not considered a person of interest at this time.*"

Abby almost lost control of the car. A person of interest? She hated that terminology because she knew in the public's mind that meant "suspect." Knowing there was nothing she could do except focus her attention on the road, she flipped to another radio station, one that played classical music. She turned up the volume, then rolled down the driver's side and passenger windows. Chester stuck his head out the window, his nose twitching in delight.

Fearing something horrible had happened to her mother and godmothers, Abby drove eight miles over the speed limit, crossing her fingers that the California Highway Patrol wasn't shooting their radar gun along that particular strip of the Pacific Coast Highway. Abby paid no attention to the scenic drive. When she had first moved to Los Angeles, she couldn't get enough of the beach, but the novelty had quickly worn off. She was lucky if she made it to her mother's beach house once a week.

Her heart slowed a bit when she reached the turnoff to Malibu. It was so unlike her mother and the three Gs not to answer their phones. Abby was always in contact with them and knew for a fact they never went anywhere without their cell phones, especially her mother. So why weren't they answering? She swerved to the right, making the final turn. In three minutes flat, she pulled into Toots's driveway and flew out of the MINI Cooper, with Chester racing ahead of her. Knowing that Coco was on the other side of the door, Chester jumped on his back legs, his paws scratching at the door. "Down boy," Abby whispered. She wasn't sure what was going on behind the door, but knew enough to know she didn't want to warn anyone of her presence. She fumbled with her key ring searching for the house key, and when she finally located it, she quietly inserted the key into the lock. Turning the knob, she slowly pushed the large door inward, preparing herself for what, she didn't know, but her senses were on high alert.

Knowing how all four women always gathered around the kitchen table, she went there first. Seeing four cups, napkins, and the sugar bowl and creamer, Abby knew they couldn't be far away. She peered out to the deck, but there was no sign of them there. It was still early, just after eight o'clock, too early for the four of them to be out and about.

Chester's nails clicked on the hardwood floor, so if anyone was in the house and heard the sounds, Abby figured they would've made their presence known already. From her vantage point in the kitchen, she was able to see that the door to the dining room, the room reserved for Sophie's séances, was closed. She headed over to the door and placed her ear against the wood. She heard Sophie asking the spirit world to guide her. Abby smiled, relieved and thinking she should have known. Where else would they be at this time of morning without their cell phones?

Having solved that mystery, she went back to the kitchen and made a fresh pot of coffee. She knew their habits, and hadn't had nearly enough caffeine herself. Chester continued to hang out by the door, knowing Coco was inside, most likely sitting on Mavis's lap.

Abby removed the cups from the table and replaced them with clean ones. She refilled the creamer and the sugar bowl. Her stomach growled even though she'd had bacon and eggs late last night. In the fridge, she saw the usual platter of Mavis's fresh fruit and helped herself. When the coffee finished perking, she poured herself a cup and sat down at the table to drink it in peace. Since she knew better than to interrupt the séance, she made herself comfortable and waited. In the meantime, she used her mother's house phone and tried to call Chris again. Still no answer. Abby was beginning to think he was spending the week with some unknown female. If he was, she was never going to speak to him again. And if he wasn't? That simply didn't bear thinking about.

In the dining room, Sophie tried every trick she knew and was unable to make contact with any spirit, good or bad. She even tried her self-induced trance, and still nothing worked.

"I give up," she finally said. "Apparently my stars aren't

properly aligned, or the moon isn't in the seventh house. We can try later; maybe Goebel will join us."

Mavis stood up, one arm clutching Coco, and walked around the room, blowing out the candles. Toots put the rocks glass in the box on the floor. Ida watched.

At that moment, Coco started squirming, trying to jump out of Mavis's arms. "Coco, settle down," Mavis soothed. "I don't know what is wrong with her."

"Listen," Toots said, leaning against the heavy door.

They gathered at the door, and the little Chihuahua went crazy.

Toots opened the door. Chester stood there in all his glory, his bushy tail wagging ninety miles a minute. Coco practically sprang out of Mavis's arms. Stepping out of the room, Toots bypassed the two lovebirds.

"Abby Simpson, why didn't you tell me you were coming?"

"Trust me, I tried. I called the house and all of your cell phones. I was afraid something had happened. Isn't it a bit early for a séance? I thought you reserved those for evenings only."

Sophie came over to the table and kissed Abby's cheek. "*I* can do this anytime. It's the *spirits* that seem to be so damned finicky today."

Abby took a bite out of a strawberry. "Does this early-morning session have anything to do with Chris?"

Toots poured a fresh cup of coffee for herself, and sat next to Abby. "I take it you haven't heard from him either. I've tried his cell number and sent dozens of e-mails. I'm really starting to get worried."

"I know. I haven't heard a single word. It's just not like Chris to do this. Loans out his condo for a week, doesn't mention a thing, then boom, he's missing, along with one of his clients. I've got a reporter staking out Laura's apartment, and tonight I'll go back to Hot Wired and The Buzz, see what I can learn."

"Should we file a missing persons report?" Mavis asked. "I would hate to think we're not doing everything we can to locate Chris."

Abby shook her head. "He's not officially missing, or that's what the police would tell us if we tried to file a report. He loaned his condo to a friend, said he had plans. The cops won't waste their manpower, trust me."

"It doesn't matter," Sophie said. "Your mother has called Goebel. He's arriving this afternoon." Sophie looked at Toots. "Oops. I hope it was okay to mention this?"

"Yes, of course it is," Toots answered. "Abby, I called Goebel last night. He'll be here this afternoon. He can poke around, see if there is any connection between Chris and Laura Leigh. You know he was a detective for the New York City Police Department for over thirty years."

"Isn't he the guy that solved Thomas's murder?" Abby asked even though she knew full well that he was.

"The one and only," Ida said, joining in on the conversation. "I hate to be a party pooper, but I have a limo coming to take me to the salon, and it should be here any minute. Abby, you'll call me the minute you hear any news?"

"If you don't hear it from me directly, then I'll call Mom."

Ida sashayed to where Abby sat. She gave her goddaughter an air kiss, then grabbed her purse and left.

"That's the strangest woman," Sophie said. "I'm going to smoke, Toots. You wanna join me?"

"Yes, but I have a phone call to make first." She winked at Sophie, then went upstairs to make her call in private.

Mavis and Abby followed Sophie outside, where she lit up one of her Marlboro Lights.

"I wish you and Mom would give up that nasty habit," Abby said. "It's almost a crime to smoke nowadays. Did you know that in New York City, they are talking about banning smoking outdoors in parks, on beaches, and in other outdoor areas? "

"I know, kiddo, but we've cut down, haven't we Mavis?"

Mavis nodded. "They certainly haven't been smoking as soon as they wake up. I'm going to continue to nag them until they give up their nasty habit and overcome their addiction. If I can give up all those potato chips and ice cream, I know they can do this if they set their minds to it."

"Set their minds to what?" Toots asked, stepping outside.

"Abby wants us to stop smoking," Sophie said, crushing her cigarette out.

"I know, and I am going to give it serious thought. We aren't smoking quite as much as we used to." Toots conscientiously refrained from lighting up. If it bothered Abby that much, she wouldn't smoke in front of her.

"I'm glad," Abby said.

"Did you see the news?" Toots asked Abby. "If Chris is out there somewhere, I wish he would call one of us and at least let someone know he's alive and not with that barely out of her teens starlet. Of course, I hope she isn't in danger, either. This is just not right!"

"I heard a report on the drive over. If he doesn't show up soon, or call someone, and if Laura Leigh isn't located, theories about Chris's involvement are just going to garner more and more attention. And that is not something someone in Chris's position needs."

Toots teared up again. "If he's able to, Abby. For all we know, he could have been in a car accident. He could be lying unconscious somewhere, or, God forbid . . . I won't even say the words out loud. Are they looking for his vehicle, too?"

"I don't know, but I'm certainly going to find out. Or at least give it my best shot. My source at the police station should be on duty now. Give me a minute."

Abby reached for her cell phone. She punched in the number and walked to the edge of the deck, out of hearing distance. Protecting her source.

The tension was as thick as the puffy clouds burgeoning above the ocean as they waited to hear any news. No one said a word while Abby was on the phone.

As soon as she finished speaking, Abby rejoined them. "Officially, they're not searching for Chris's car, but my source says not to rule out a BOLO—be on the lookout— for his car if he doesn't show up soon."

Crestfallen, her pretty face distorted with worry, Mavis asked, "What does that mean?"

Leaning on the railing, Abby sighed and shook her head. "I don't know. It could be they're simply looking for him as a witness, or they have something more than they're reporting, keeping it under their belts. I don't know. It just pisses me off! I've said it a hundred times, and I'll keep saying it; this is not like Chris. He can be an ass, but he wouldn't deliberately cause any one of us to worry unnecessarily."

Toots placed her arms around her daughter. "I know he wouldn't, but we have to hope for the best. Sophie said her gut wasn't giving off any bad vibes. And you know how reliable her instincts are. She's always on the money."

Abby smiled, but the emotion didn't reach her eyes. "That's encouraging."

Sophie spoke up. "Goebel kicks ass and takes names later, Ab. He cuts through the flesh and goes right for the bone. He's got a lot of contacts all over the country. We just have to be patient and not think the worst. Okay? And I told you, I really don't have a bad feeling about Chris, or the girl, for that matter. If I thought the police would listen to me, I'd tell them so myself."

Abby nodded. "I suppose you're right. I'm going to the office; I've still got a paper to run. Mavis, do you mind if I leave Chester for the day? He's been cooped up in the car too much."

"I would love to have Chester stay. I'll take him for a walk on the beach."

Abby blew her godmother a kiss. "Thanks. Mom, if you're going to hide in the séance room, let me know in advance, okay? I've got enough to worry about just now."

"You're becoming me, dear. Yes, I'll make sure to call. You be careful, Abby. If you're going to stake those clubs out tonight, let me know."

"I will, I promise. Tell Goebel I'm looking forward to meeting him."

Abby said good-bye, gave Chester a rub between the ears, which, with Coco curled against him, he totally ignored. "Okay, Bud, you be good."

She knew Chester was in good hands. Her mother and the three Gs were safe. Now, if she could only locate Chris, her life would be close to perfect.

Chapter 8

Toots, Sophie, and Mavis had just finished a light breakfast when they heard a car door slam. "The queen of cosmetics has returned," Sophie said.

Coming to Ida's defense, Mavis piped up, "Stop it, Sophie. She's doing a wonderful job. The customers love her."

"They're dead, Mavis. Of course they love her," Sophie teased.

"The morticians," Mavis explained. "She has a way with them."

"Both of you stop," Toots interjected.

No one uttered a single word when Ida entered the kitchen. All three women stared at their friend, looked at each other, then doubled over with laughter. Ida glared at them, her eyes practically bulging out of her head, her breathing as rapid as if she were hyperventilating.

"You!" she accused, pointing at Sophie. "I know you had something to do with this! Look at me, I am ruined! It will be weeks before I'm able to show my face in public! How could you?"

The three women looked at Ida, their mouths hanging open like three treasure chests. Her normally perfectly coiffed pageboy had been replaced by a pixie cut, and her formerly platinum-dyed hair was bright pink.

They giggled, pointing at her magenta-colored hair.

Between their wild hooting and laughter, Toots managed to say, "It wasn't Sophie."

The old cliché about a picture being worth a thousand words didn't begin to do justice to the expression that came across Ida's face.

Ida's complexion went from white to an ashen gray. *Not a good match for her new hair color*, Toots thought, as she struggled mightily to keep a straight face. "I did it, Ida. It was me. Sophie had absolutely nothing to do with it." Toots risked a glance at Sophie, whose ear-to-ear grin displayed her glee at Ida's plight.

Truly at a loss for words, Ida stood gaping at them, her mouth an angry red slash. "Exactly what is that supposed to mean?"

"Just what I said. I called Neil George Salon and told them to give you the latest Hollywood hairstyle, my treat. How could I know they were going to turn you into one of those little pink baby chicks we used to get at the carnival?" Toots looked again at Sophie and Mavis and tried to get her bearings so she wouldn't burst out laughing again. "No, I did not. How could I?"

Ida threw her hands up in the air. "I don't believe you. I know you too well."

Toots aimed her index finger at Ida. "That's your choice. I simply asked they give you the latest, most popular hairstyle. I didn't specify your age, which I suppose I should have, given the circumstances. I will call the salon and tell them they've made an awful mistake. As a matter of fact, if they can, I'll see if we can drop you off when we leave for the airport."

"And miss Goebel's arrival? I don't think so," Ida said, before stomping upstairs. "And don't talk about me behind my back. My hearing is quite good," she tossed over her shoulder.

Toots turned to the others, whispering. "She's up to something. And it isn't good."

"If she thinks she's got a chance with Goebel, she'd better think again. He is not impressed with her kind. Told me so himself. He'd rather date . . . *Bernice* than Ida," Sophie said forcefully. "I don't understand where she thinks she can just move in on someone's territory! She's a true slut."

"Bernice wouldn't give Goebel a second look, just so you know. She's had the hots for Malcolm Moretti for over twenty years. He owns the butcher shop she frequents. Says he gives her his best cuts of meat," Toots said, wiggling her eyebrows Groucho Marx style. "Actually, she's been seeing him on the sly and doesn't know that I know, so when we're in Charleston, keep this between us."

"So does this mean you're planning a trip south?" Mavis asked. "Hello."

"Absolutely not. Until I know what's happened to Chris, I'm staying right here," Toots assured them.

"There is a simple explanation. I just know it." Sophie grabbed her pack of cigarettes from the kitchen table and went to the sliding glass doors. With one foot inside and the other on the deck, Sophie lit up, blowing the smoke outside.

"I hope there is. If he's off with some bimbo, he is really going to be in a heap of shit with Abby. She's crazy about him, and I could see the worry etched in her face. Those two have something going on, big-time. If they'd only acknowledge it and make me a grandmother, I would be the happiest woman alive." Toots brushed past Sophie and stepped outside, whereupon Sophie stepped fully onto the deck.

"I think they're cute together, but don't tell Abby I said that," Sophie said.

"She's too independent for her own good," Toots observed. "At this rate, I'll be six feet under before she decides to settle down, let alone get married and have children. Of course, I want her to do the marriage thing once. Not eight times. Why do you suppose I felt the need to marry so many times?"

Sophie took a deep draw on her cigarette and blew the smoke out through her nose. "I think you're the nurturing kind. You attract men you can take care of. Or at least that's my take on it."

Toots appeared to be in deep thought. "Who knows? I do know that I won't be adding a number nine. I don't have time for a relationship anyway. Speaking of relationships, just how close are you and Goebel?"

"I haven't slept with him if that's what you're asking. I'm sixty-six years old, Toots, I'm not sure I could ever again have an intimate relationship with a man. It's been my experience when you give that part of yourself, he thinks he owns you. I wasted too many years of my life on Walter. I enjoy Goebel's company, he's a great friend, and for now I'm not looking for anything else. Does that answer your question?"

Toots crushed her cigarette out in the seashell ashtray. "Yes. Now, if we don't get our asses in gear, Goebel will have to take a taxi. Do you want to invite Ida along for the ride?"

"Sure, why not? I thought she was going anyway. Just because her hair is hot pink, why should that matter?" Sophie teased.

Toots stood brushing the ashes from her slacks. "It shouldn't, but maybe you don't want to be seen in public with her."

"I don't care, but I have to ask, did you really tell her

hairdresser to give her the latest style, or did you give them specifics?"

"Let's just say I gave them the idea and leave it at that."

The two women looked at one another before both hooted with laughter.

After sending her two ace reporters Brandy Collins and Chuck Pierce to stake out Hot Wired and The Buzz, Abby called May Marchand, who'd spent the night staking out Laura Leigh's apartment.

"Anything to report?" Abby asked, concise and to the point.

"Absolutely nothing. Not even a newspaper delivery. The media is all over the place, though. *Entertainment Tonight, E!,* and *Inside Edition* all have their big guns out. Sure looks like this is turning into a major media event," May said.

Abby took a deep breath. *Damn.* She knew this was going to happen. If the major networks were parked and waiting, then the story was going international. They didn't send the big guns out for petty news. Against her better judgment, she decided she had to cover the story herself. Rules be damned. "Stay there until I arrive, then you can call it a day."

Before she had a change of heart, Abby sent LAT Enterprise an e-mail.

TO: LATEnterprise@yahoo.com
FROM: ASIMPSON@THE INFORMER.com

The Informer is covering the disappearance of Laura Leigh. It has been brought to my attention that this same story is being covered by *Entertainment Tonight, E!* and Inside Edition. Sadly, as I'm sure this has been or will be reported, I have a personal relationship with a party who is being named a person of interest in Miss Leigh's disappearance. Therefore, I will be covering this story myself. Joshua Walden will be acting editor in chief should this story require my daily absence from the paper.

Respectfully,
Abby Simpson
Editor in Chief

Before she had a chance to change her mind, something she seemed to be doing quite a bit lately, Abby clicked the SEND button. Now, all she had to do was tell Josh, her resident computer guru, that he might have to act as temporary editor in chief. He was going to love that.

She called his office. "Yep? Whacha need?" Josh asked.

Abby suddenly wondered if she'd made a mistake, but it was already too late. She'd give Josh a quick course in telephone etiquette and the duties of the editor in chief. "Hey, Josh, can you come down to my office ASAP? I need your help." Abby placed the phone down before he had a chance to respond. *He really doesn't have a choice,* she thought as she cleared the clutter from her desk.

Minutes later, Josh knocked on her door. "What's so important?"

"Josh, tell me your level of education."

"I have a master's degree in computer science. I thought you knew that."

She did.

"I don't know if you've been hiding in the Batcave the last few days or watched the news or if you've read *The Informer*. That actress, the one in that silly vampire flick, Laura Leigh, is missing. I'm not going to go into any detail, but this is a story I have to cover myself. I need you to act as editor in chief in my absence."

Josh, tall and lanky, with dark brown hair to his waist and a pierced tongue, did not begin to fit Abby's idea of what an editor in chief should look like, but right now he was all she had. He knew the inner workings at the paper as well as she did.

"Are you serious?" he asked, taking a seat in Chester's Barcalounger.

"As a heart attack. You won't have to deal with the public; I just need someone here to oversee the assignments for the junior reporters. You can tweet me with any questions you have."

Josh smiled. "I didn't know you were tweeting. You're really stepping into the twenty-first century, Abs."

She hated it when he called her Abs.

"I'm glad you approve. Now this is my plan."

Abby spent the next hour going over future assignments for *The Informer,* instructed him that all e-mails from LAT Enterprise should be forwarded to her immediately, no matter how trivial they might seem to be. He was to answer the phone properly.

She explained that he would be acting editor in chief until further notice. With the new responsibilities, Josh's slang cleared instantly. *There is hope after all,* Abby thought as she went down a detailed list of upcoming events for Hollywood's finest.

"If you need me, don't hesitate to call my cell," Abby admonished as she stood and headed for the door.

"Okay." Josh plopped down on her just-vacated chair.

Abby smiled. "Don't get used to that chair, okay?"

Josh laughed. "It's too small, Abs. I won't."

Abby shook her head and wiggled bye with her index finger. She trusted Josh. Yes, he was a bit rough on the exterior, but he had the IQ of a genius. He just needed to work on his people skills. Hopefully, she would find Chris soon, and the mystery surrounding Laura Leigh's disappearance would be solved. She crossed her fingers.

Back inside her MINI Cooper, Abby ran down her mental to-do list. First, she needed to go to the police station. Depending on what she found out from her source, she would decide her next move. She wanted to go back to Chris's condo to question his friend, certain he had seen the news by now. If he knew where Chris was hiding, she would get it out of him or die trying.

Winding through the noontime traffic, Abby arrived at the Los Angeles Police Department main headquarters in record time. She checked her cell phone for any text messages, tweets, or e-mail before entering, knowing that her cell phone would be scanned and probably scrutinized by the police officer who manned security. They were noted for being nosy.

Inside police headquarters, the unforgettable odor of burnt coffee tinged the stagnant air. A sense of hopelessness clung to the ash gray walls. Fluorescent lighting cast a pallor on the aging officer who oversaw the scanning machine. He tossed a round plastic tray toward Abby as she stood in line behind a deputy district attorney who was known as a female ballbuster. Abby liked her.

Without being told, Abby placed her cell phone, car keys, and watch in the circular tray. She placed her treasured briefcase on the conveyor belt and watched the cop use chopsticks to poke and paw through its contents before placing it back on the belt to make its way through the scanner. She really thought that was unnecessary, but she knew most of the officers at that particular post were downright nosy. Briefly, she thought they'd make ace reporters, then decided not. What they were was hateful.

"Looking for a locked-up star are we?" the cop asked while she put her watch back on.

"No, I was hoping to visit that crooked cop they arrested last week. You remember, the one who pulled women over for speeding, then raped them?" Abby saw the cop's face redden. "A friend of yours?" she couldn't help adding.

He pushed her briefcase to the end of the belt, ignoring her last remark. *Serves him right,* she thought as she gathered the rest of her things. She traveled down several long hallways before locating her source's office.

When her source spied her lingering in the doorway, Abby was motioned to follow. Down another long hallway they went until they stopped in front of the supply closet. Abby grinned. If circumstances were different, she might've made a joke about such a clandestine meeting place, but they weren't, and she didn't.

She entered the dimly lit closet, closing the door behind her. "You have something new?"

"Yes, they've just issued a BOLO for Mr. Clay's Toyota Camry. It went out about an hour ago."

Damn. Abby knew that was coming. "Thanks. I'll return the favor." Her source took payment in advance copies of *The Informer.*

If only the powers that be accepted that kind of payment. With luck, she would find Chris before the police did. And when she did, he was going to have hell to pay.

And then some.

Chapter 9

Toots studied her surroundings as she waited with her friends to be seated on the patio at the Polo Lounge. Giant urns with bright pink azaleas, white wrought-iron tables decorated with forest green cushions and color-coordinated tablecloths were scattered all across the brick-work. A giant old Brazilian pepper tree grew in the center of the patio. Not much had changed since her last visit.

Miguel, their favorite waiter, spied them waiting and insisted they follow him. Their "special" table was empty. In a thick Spanish accent, he said, "Before that pissy hostess seats someone else, you come with me."

The hostess, a petite girl barely five feet tall with long red hair, rolled her eyes at Miguel, and muttered, "He thinks he owns the place."

Miguel raised his fist high in the air as soon as the hostess looked away. They all laughed.

Once they were seated, Sophie flushed with excitement, her eyes sparkling like brilliant diamonds whenever she looked at Goebel. Toots was sure it was a love match in the making even though Sophie wouldn't admit to it.

"So this is the famous Polo Lounge. I've been to LA many times, but I've never made it here. How's the food?

Not that I'm going to be ordering anything fattening,"
Goebel assured everyone as he smacked his now-flat stomach. "That diet Mavis put me on was the best thing that
ever happened to me. Well, except for"—he winked at Sophie—"this brunette bombshell."

Ida looked really pissed off. She was used to being the
center of attention, especially where a man was concerned.
With her new "do," Ida had received quite a bit of attention as they walked to their table. It just wasn't the type of
attention she was used to. Toots had offered to take her
back to the salon first thing in the morning and insist they
give her something more age appropriate, but Ida had de-
clined. Personally, Toots thought Ida kind of liked looking
different, liked the attention she received. Her hair color
matched that of the azaleas in the giant urns.

"I've never thought of Sophie as a bombshell," Ida said
smartly. Since picking up Goebel from the airport, she
hadn't muttered more than a dozen words.

"Thank God," Sophie said. "I would hate to think I'd
played a role in any of your fantasies."

Goebel chuckled. "I don't think Ida's that kind of girl,"
he said in her defense.

"Well, you don't know her like I do, now, do you?" Sophie retorted playfully.

"Please, let's not fuss in front of Goebel," Mavis
begged. "He isn't here to listen to us squabble about one
another."

"She's right," Toots said. "We need to find Chris. That's
why Goebel's here."

After they placed their orders, Goebel took out a small
black notepad and pen, preparing to take notes. "Why
don't we start with what we know."

Toots shook her head. "Unfortunately, there isn't much
to tell you. As you already know, Chris is an entertainment

attorney here in LA, has been for a number of years. He's very casual about his practice. He doesn't even have an office. He works out of his condo."

"Okay, stop there. Are you telling me Chris no longer has an office in that building over on Whitley, just off Franklin? When did he move out of there? And why? Seems odd for an entertainment lawyer in LA, the capital of appearances that are not only everything but the only thing, to work out of his condo." Goebel looked to Toots for an answer.

In the two years since she had come to LA, she hadn't really given Chris's lack of a downtown office any serious thought. It certainly wasn't for any financial reason. He had a very successful practice that earned him a nice piece of change, but compared to the sizable fortune his father had left him, what he earned really was just that, a piece of change.

"I'm clueless. Now that I think of it, I remember he did have that office you spoke of. Maybe he decided it's just more convenient to work out of his place. Most of his clients are Hollywood's up and coming. He takes them out to the popular nightspots. Most of his clients know about the situation going in and seem to be happy with the arrangement. Of course, I'm really guessing, which is to say I do not actually know the answer. It's certainly not because he can't afford the usual trappings of a successful law practice. Not only does he have a substantial income, but is quite well-off apart from that. For all I know, he may have a completely different answer. I've never had a reason to give it much thought."

Miguel appeared with their entrees, stopping further discussion. For the next few minutes all that could be heard was the clink of silverware clattering against their dishes. When they'd finished, Miguel appeared with a pot of coffee, the sugar bowl, and lots of half-and-half.

"Thank you," Toots said, as he filled their cups.

When they were alone again, Goebel resumed his questioning. "Does he make it a habit of getting involved with his clients? Romantically?"

Sophie, Ida, and Mavis eyed Toots like she had a horn growing out of her head. "Don't look at me that way! Goebel, I can't be one hundred percent sure about Chris's involvement with past or present clients. What I can tell you is he's a man of integrity. He's not what Hollywood would call a . . . man whore." Toots paused, turning to Ida. "Is that what they call them?"

Ida shot daggers at Toots. "I wouldn't know. Ask Sophie."

Without making a big production of it, Sophie wiggled her middle finger at Ida.

Ida smirked before taking a sip of her coffee. "Someday that finger is going to fall off. And then you'll wish you hadn't used it so much."

They all laughed. Even Ida. Things were looking up in that department.

"I think the word is *gigolo*, ladies. But anyway, what you're saying is that you don't think Chris makes a habit of getting involved with his clients."

"I don't know. That's what you're here to find out," Toots said.

Miguel brought their tab to the table, Goebel reached for it, and Toots let him. It'd been a long time since a man had picked up her tab.

"Thanks," she said after the waiter left. "Once you're checked into your room, do you want to come to the beach house?" They hadn't made any plans other than a late lunch at the Polo Lounge.

"If you ladies wouldn't mind, I would like to take a quick shower first. That east-to-west flight is quite long." Goebel stood and they all headed toward the exit.

Sophie piped up, "We'll go smoke while you're doing your thing, then we can head for the beach house. Is that okay with the rest of you?"

"Since when did you start to care?" Ida asked.

"Oh for crying out loud, get off your pity-party trip. We're going to smoke. If there's something else you'd rather do while we're waiting, please, don't let me stop you," Sophie said.

Ida seemed to instantly perk up. "Well now that you mention it, there is something I would like to do."

Toots reached for Ida's arm, then pulled her close, and whispered in her ear. "Don't you dare follow Goebel to his room."

Ida turned as pale as a ghost. "Why . . . I can't believe you would even say such a thing!"

"Girls, please," Mavis interjected.

"I know that's what you're thinking. He's off-limits, Ida," Toots said, all traces of her earlier humor gone.

They waited for Miguel to return Goebel's AmEx gold card.

"Like Jerry was off-limits?" Ida shot back.

"I can't believe you have the nerve to bring him up. It's been more years than I care to remember. If memory serves me correctly, he came after me, not the other way around. And you'd already moved on to someone else. I can't recall his name." Toots huffed.

During their exchange, Sophie hadn't uttered a word, until she said, "I'm going to pretend I didn't hear that. Now here comes Goebel. Ida, keep your frigging hands off, okay? I promise that's the only time I'm going to say this. Do you understand?"

"I can't believe you think I would stoop so low," Ida said. "It's not like I have a hard time attracting men."

Sophie smacked her forehead. "How could I forget? Once a slut, always a slut."

Goebel joined them. "Are you sure you gals don't want to come to my room? It'll only take me a few minutes to clean up."

Toots spoke up before anyone else had a chance. "We'll wait out front. Just meet us there whenever you're ready. Sometimes we chain-smoke."

He nodded, then grabbed Sophie and gave her a quick hug. "Don't be giving the eagle eye to any of those hot young studs I saw working the valet parking, okay?"

Sophie grinned. "Never."

Goebel scurried off to his room.

Outside in the hotel garden was an area with four benches and three giant ashtrays reserved for smokers. "I miss this place," Mavis said, taking a seat on the bench opposite Sophie and Toots. Ida remained standing.

"Yeah, me too. Maybe we can have another spa day sometime in the near future. I might consider getting a bikini wax," Sophie said between puffs of smoke.

They all laughed, except for Ida.

Toots smoked, preferring to remain quiet. The chatter was getting to be too much for her. Even she had her limits as far as keeping her worries undercover. She was beyond being concerned about Chris, having reached the stage of downright panic on the way to the screaming meemies. Crossing her fingers that Goebel could find him before he became even more involved, Toots couldn't wait for Goebel to get started.

Fifteen minutes later, a freshly showered Goebel met them in front of the hotel. Sophie's eyes lit up like a vault of jewels. "I was getting ready to come looking for you."

He looked at his watch. "Twelve minutes, Sophie. That tickles me if you want to know the truth."

"Why does that tickle you?" she asked.

Goebel placed his hand on her lower back, guiding her

toward the exit. "Look, sweetheart, twelve minutes isn't a long time to get all snazzed up. At least I don't think it is."

"It isn't. Leland used to take at least an hour just to shower," Toots said. "I often wondered what took him so long."

While they waited for a young man from valet parking to bring Toots's car to the covered portico, Sophie commented, "Surely, after eight husbands, you're not that stupid."

"What's that supposed to mean?" Toots questioned.

Mavis giggled, and Ida actually laughed.

Sophie being Sophie said, "Do you really want me to tell you?" She looked at Goebel, who was wearing a smile the size of the moon. "In front of Goebel?" she added, a wicked grin on her face.

Stains of scarlet dotted Toots's cheeks. "I can see where you're headed. Right to the gutter. Why am I not surprised?" She shook her head. When she saw her newly purchased black Cadillac Escalade, she breathed a sigh of relief. No one but Sophie would think of such a thing at such an inopportune time.

The valet attendant hopped out of the SUV and opened the rear passenger doors for Toots, Mavis, and Ida. Sophie drove, and Goebel rode shotgun. Toots was glad she'd purchased the oversized vehicle. They needed the extra seating. Goebel took a handful of cash from his pocket and handed it to the attendant. Toots saw this and liked him even more. He wasn't cheap. Sophie had scored bigtime. Toots was happy for her even though there was no way in hell Sophie would admit to anything more than friendship. *Give her time,* Toots thought. *Give her time.*

Once they exited the Beverly Hills Hotel, Sophie pointed the Escalade northwest, then made a left onto Santa Monica Boulevard. A few turns later, they were on the Pacific Coast Highway, headed for Malibu. With rolling hills on one side and miles of beach on the other, the scenic drive still had the power to evoke jaw-dropping stares.

"This sure as hell ain't New York," Goebel commented. "If I lived here, you'd have to drag me away from the beach. Hell, I might have to think about gettin' a place of my own."

Sophie took her eyes off the road for a second to stare at him. He winked at her. "Besides, I'm getting too old for those harsh New York winters," he added.

Mavis piped up, "I don't miss Maine's cold weather either."

Sophie was silent, content to drive. For the next half hour, they chatted about the pros and cons of West Coast versus East Coast living until Sophie made the turn that led to the beach house.

Goebel whistled. "Nice digs, Toots."

"You wouldn't have thought so if you'd seen the place before we remodeled. I think we've referred to it as 'hooker haven.' "

"Ida's bathroom looked like a reject from Graceland," Sophie said as she parked in front of the beach house. "The pop star who'd lived here apparently had a thing for Elvis Presley."

Goebel hooted, then jumped out and hastened to open the two passenger doors, then the driver's door for Sophie. *Chalk up another point in his favor,* Toots thought. If he could just locate Chris before the situation got even more out of hand, Toots would add another point to his growing list of positive attributes.

Loud barking sent Mavis rushing to the front door. She fiddled with her key ring—Toots had had keys made for all of them—jostled the knob, then pushed the door open. "Oh my sweet little girl and godson, you couldn't wait to see me now, could you?"

Chester and Coco had spent the afternoon by themselves at the beach house, but neither appeared as though they cared. Once they sniffed Mavis's hand, they took off, stopping only when they reached their favorite corner of the kitchen.

Goebel, Sophie, Toots, and Ida followed the canines to the kitchen. Mavis began to prepare a pot of coffee.

"Okay, let's see what we have here," Goebel said as he removed his little black notepad from his shirt pocket. He flipped through the pages and took his pen out of his pocket before sitting at the kitchen table. "This okay?" he asked, nodding at the table.

"It's command central." Toots sat in her usual place at the head of the table. "We seem to wind up here or on the deck." She pointed to the wall of sliding glass doors that faced the beach.

Goebel eyed the view. "I'll check that out later. While it's still fresh, I need you to tell me every single thing you know about Chris's disappearance—again. Sorry."

Toots repeated what little she knew. Something told her it was going to be a very, very long night.

Chapter 10

Abby's intent was to go back to Chris's condo and question Steve and his fiancée, Renée, one more time, but she changed her mind when she received a call from the source she'd just left behind.

"Apparently, the suspect had his vehicle towed. It was parked on the side of Sunset Boulevard. His mechanic called the station not long after you left, and explained that he listens to a police scanner."

Suspect!

She used her shoulder to hold her cell phone against her ear, and scanned her rearview mirror. *Shit! This isn't good.* Making an illegal U-turn, she headed in the opposite direction. "Can I see his car?" She knew it was stupid to ask, but she had to, just in case.

"You know I can't allow that, Abby. I'm already pushing the line as it is. The mechanic did say the car had a terrible oil leak, said it was completely out of oil."

Now that sounded like Chris. He was not into vehicle maintenance at all. "And that's it? Was there anything"— she hated to even think the word, let alone say it out loud, but she really didn't have a choice—"incriminating?"

"If you mean trace evidence, hairs, fibers, body fluids, no. They haven't had the vehicle long enough to fully process it yet," her source explained. Though Abby knew all about the basic procedures, she didn't like to think of them in the same context with Chris.

"You'll call me as soon as you know something . . . solid?"

"I will."

Abby hit the END button and tossed her cell phone onto Chester's empty seat. There would be no point in returning to the police station, so she headed to the beach. Josh was in charge for a while. It would do him good to use his human skills. He spent way too much time in cyberspace. Maybe between her and Goebel, they could put their heads and skills together and come up with a clue before it was too late.

They'd just sat down for their first cup of coffee to discuss Chris when Sophie's cell phone rang. She didn't answer, and it rang again. "Answer it, Soph. It might be Abby."

Sophie answered the phone. "Yes, this is Sophie Manchester. Yes. Yes. I am." Sophie's brown eyes doubled in size. "Now? Well, I suppose I could. Can you hold on for one minute?"

They stared at Sophie. She placed her hand over the minispeaker on her cell phone. In a loud whisper, she said, "You are not going to believe who this is."

"Chris?" Toots exclaimed.

Sophie shook her head. *Sorry,* she mouthed to Toots, and the others, who watched her like a hawk.

"Yes, of course. I can be there in an hour." Sophie clicked the END button on her phone, placing it on the table.

All directed their gazes toward Sophie.

Amazed, Sophie turned to the group clustered around the table. "You won't believe who just called. I don't believe who just called."

"Don't keep us in suspense," Ida said, her hot pink head raised a notch above normal.

As though she were in a stupor, Sophie stated, "That was Laura Leigh's mother."

Except for Chester's panting, the kitchen was completely silent. Four pairs of eyes stared at Sophie.

Toots was the first to speak. "What did she want? Surely she doesn't suspect Chris of anything? How did she make the connection?"

"It seems she's heard about me through the Hollywood psychic line. She wants me to do a tarot reading for her. She doesn't have a clue that I have a connection to her daughter's disappearance. Not that I have a connection, but you get the picture."

"You're going to do this?" Toots asked.

"Of course I'm going to do it. She wants me to meet her at the Huntley Hotel in Santa Monica in an hour. I take it you don't think this is a good idea?"

Toots shook her head. "No . . . I mean yes, I think it's okay. It might even help us to find Chris. What do you think about it, Goebel?"

"I think she should get her ass out of here."

Sophie nodded. "Yes, I'm going. I'll need to gather my things. I normally go to a reading with a bit more notice. Give me ten minutes, and I'll be ready to go." Sophie whirled out of the kitchen like a spring storm.

Five minutes later, she returned, wearing a pair of black trouser pants with a pearl-colored silk blouse. She left her dark hair loose. With her olive complexion, prominent cheekbones, and full lips, Sophie looked like a woman ten years younger. A smudge of cranberry lipstick and mascara was all the makeup she needed to take off another five years.

"Who wants to come with me?" she asked.

"As much as I hate to say this, I think you need to go

alone. This missing girl Laura is in the public eye, which means that as soon as the media gets wind of what the family has asked of you, they're going to scrutinize you and whoever you're with." Goebel held his hand out in front of him. "I realize you're already in the public eye. I think the longer we can keep the connection between you and Chris out of the media, the better off we'll all be. What say you, Toots? Ida? Mavis?"

"It's just as well. Mavis and I have a client to dress this evening," Ida said.

Perplexed, Mavis looked at her. "We do?"

Ida's expression revealed the confusion she felt. "I forwarded the e-mail to you two days ago, remember? It's that crazy star who hanged himself! I can't believe you've forgotten! We have to be there by eight o'clock. We'll need at least three hours."

Mavis looked as confused as Ida. "I'm ashamed of myself. The only e-mails I've really digested lately are orders coming in for the Good Mourning line. I suppose I might have deleted it, Ida." Mavis watched the group at the table. No one seemed upset except Ida.

"You have to take this seriously, Mavis. If we're to work as freelance funeral dressers, we have to be able to communicate," Ida admonished.

"I'll get ready." Mavis called for the two dogs. They followed her upstairs.

Out of earshot, Toots said, "You need to be gentle with Mavis. She isn't an old hard-ass like the rest of us."

"If she wants to run a successful . . . whatever it is we do, then she must pay close attention to every detail. It's the same as you communicating with *The Informer.* Everyone who is anyone either communicates by e-mail or text messages. I'm just playing the game, Toots," Ida said in her queenlike manner.

Toots wanted to bow, but successfully resisted the urge.

"I understand, but cut Mavis some slack. She lives under the same roof as you do. It wouldn't have hurt to actually tell her." Toots was all for electronic communication, but Ida took it a step too far, as she did most things.

"Ladies, I hate to be a party pooper, but Sophie needs to go. Ida, can Sophie drop you two off on her way?" Goebel asked.

Ida gave an impatient shrug. "I suppose she could. It's at Evergreen Funeral Parlor in Santa Monica. They're not far from the Huntley Hotel."

"I'm gonna need a vehicle myself," Goebel said as though he'd just realized it.

"I still have the Thunderbird. It's in the garage, and you can use it. Where will you go?" Toots questioned.

"I made a few phone calls before I left. There isn't a lot to work with yet. I can poke around in a few places, see what I can find."

As though she were suddenly struck by lightning, Toots jumped up from the table and grabbed the remote. She turned the TV on and found the local news station she'd watched earlier. "There should be an update soon. It's after six o'clock." She raised the volume. The glossy-lipped reporter she hated filled the screen.

"*Police have located and impounded Chris Clay's Toyota Camry. When asked if there was any evidence indicating a crime had been committed, Chief Roberts said the vehicle was currently being combed for possible trace evidence.*"

She turned the TV off. "Why doesn't Abby know this? She's a reporter!" Toots's hands shook as she reached for her cell phone. She dialed Abby's number. Abby picked up on the first ring.

Toots didn't bother with hello. "Abby, they've impounded Chris's car."

"I'm in your driveway," Abby said.

Seconds later, she bounded through the front door and entered the kitchen.

Goebel spoke up. "You must be Abby. I'm Goebel." He held his hand out to her.

"I've heard a lot about you; it's good to finally meet you. I take it you know all about Chris and the media's trying to connect him to Laura Leigh's disappearance?"

"I know what your mother told me, and what the news is reporting." He looked at the small television set on the countertop.

"They're searching Chris's car for trace evidence. His mechanic called in when he heard the BOLO on the police scanner. He said the car was totally out of oil. It was on the side of Sunset Boulevard, and Chris had it towed, according to the mechanic."

"I don't understand. Why . . . what?" Toots asked.

"That's what I intend to find out. Goebel, do you have a contact at the police department? I have a source, but my source has the same information the media has, at least I think so. Damn Chris, if he would only answer his phone! I've called, texted, e-mailed, and nothing. I hope to hell wherever he is, he's having one good time. When I get my hands on him, I personally plan to kick his ass all the way to hell and back." Abby was shaking with anger, yet tears pooled in her bright blue eyes.

Toots embraced her. "We have to keep good thoughts, Abby. Chris would never intentionally cause either of us to worry. Unless something has happened to him, I'm sure there's a reasonable explanation for this."

"Right, Mom! And Laura Leigh? How do you explain that? Chris was the last person she was seen with. I don't know about you, but from my standpoint, it doesn't look so good." The tears began to fall from Abby's eyes, leaving damp circles on her black turtleneck.

Toots cleared her throat. It wasn't the time for her to

fall apart. She had to be strong for her daughter. Later, when she was in the privacy of her own room, she could fall apart all she wanted, but not now. Abby needed her.

"Listen to me, Abby, Goebel will find out where he is, trust me. If he can take"—she searched for the right word—"instructions from a damned spirit and solve a murder, finding Chris will be a breeze. Right, Goeb?" Toots said, shortening his name.

"A piece of cake," he replied.

Abby grabbed a paper napkin from the table and blew her nose. "Then let's stop talking about it and do something!"

Goebel appeared uncomfortable. Toots, ever the caregiver, hated it, but it was what it was. "Abby's right. We've talked this to death. Maybe Sophie can learn something from Laura's mother when she reads for her."

Sophie, who'd been silent during the exchange, spoke up. "I have to go now or I'm going to be late. Ida, can you go tell Mavis to speed it up?"

Ida nodded and went upstairs, returning a minute later with a well-dressed Mavis, the two dogs trailing behind her.

"Okay. As soon I learn something, I'll call. Everyone keep your cell phones on." Sophie tucked her tarot cards inside her tote bag.

"We can't possibly take phone calls when we're at the funeral home. They're having a viewing tonight," Ida said, without much feeling for what they were going through.

"Vibrate, Ida, put your frigging phone on VIBRATE. I'm sure whoever you're decking out won't mind. Now let's go before I miss this opportunity and your stiff gets even stiffer." Sophie hugged Abby, gave Toots their special look, and winked at Goebel.

When they left, Coco and Chester ran back to their favorite corner of the kitchen. Chester stretched out on his side, and Coco tucked herself in the space between his front and hind paws. They appeared to be spooning.

"Woof! Woof!" Chester saw Abby. She stooped down to receive his doggie kiss. He licked her face, where traces of her tears still shimmered.

Coco growled. Chester belonged to her right now, and she was letting them know it. Abby fluffed her between the ears. "You be a good girl, okay?" Coco barked, then turned away from Abby and back to her hero, Chester.

Toots led Goebel to the garage, where the Thunderbird was parked. "It's full of gas; keep it as long as you need it. Of course, if you have any news, call me." She handed him her cell phone number and house number on a scrap of paper. "You need anything, please let me know, Goebel. Chris is my son."

Without another word between them, Toots went back inside where Abby was sitting on the floor with Coco and Chester.

Putting on a cheerful front for her daughter, Toots took a deep breath before speaking. "Let's keep our fingers crossed, Abby. And anything else we can cross."

She had lost eight husbands. She did not want to experience the loss of a child. It would be devastating, worse than any kind of grief in the world.

Toots could not go there.

Chapter 11

Sophie arrived at the Huntley Hotel with two minutes to spare. She'd dropped Ida and Mavis off at Evergreen's, which was on the way, but still didn't have much time to prepare for her new client, Angela Leigh, mother of missing actress Laura Leigh.

Inside the hotel, the lobby was modern—lots of white walls and aquariums filled with odd-looking white fish, swimming as though they were in their natural habitat. Ultramodern furniture in earth tones, and sea-colored sofas lined the wall opposite the aquariums. Briefly, she wondered how much a room like that would set her back, then gave a shrug. Who cared? She wasn't staying there, and if she wanted to, she could sure as hell afford it.

She'd been instructed to see the hotel concierge upon arriving, so spying the desk, she hurried to ask where she was to meet her client. She knew the meeting was on the QT, big-time.

Sophie spotted the alcove leading to the birdcage elevator, which she had been instructed to take to the fifth floor. The enclosed glass elevator on the outside of the hotel offered a spectacular view of Santa Monica Beach. A smattering of lights touched the horizon, and tips of white sails bobbed in the glow of the red-orange setting sun. Something told her Goebel would admire the view as much as she did.

When she reached the fifth floor, the elevator doors swished open. Plush white chairs faced one another, teak side tables topped with sculptures of sea life formed a sort of urban-chic lounge. Floor-to-ceiling windows faced the ocean and the sunset's golden glow brought added warmth to the space.

A woman in her late forties, with short blond hair, a fake tan, and silver earrings the size of a bracelet was waiting for her in the lounge. She wore a short black sundress and shiny red heels at least four inches high. *Cheap* came to mind as Sophie followed her. Their shoes made soft mushy sounds in the grasslike carpet. When they arrived at the room, Angela Leigh used a keycard to open the door. She stepped inside, not bothering to speak, offering nothing in the way of an invitation or a greeting. Sophie disliked the woman already.

"You can sit there," the woman instructed brusquely, speaking to Sophie as she might to a beggar from the streets asking for a handout. She pointed to a chair that matched those in the lounge area.

"I'll need a table," Sophie said. When the woman looked at her like she'd lost her mind, Sophie wanted to bitch slap her, but refrained. "You want me to read for you, I'll need a table on which to place the cards," she explained as she remained standing behind the large white chair.

"Here. Use this." The rude woman slid a cloth-covered ottoman between them.

Sophie removed her tarot cards from her tote bag but didn't bother spreading them out on the ottoman. Suddenly, she felt dizzy, the room becoming a blur of white. Reaching for the back of the chair to steady herself, she closed her eyes, hoping the waves of light-headedness would pass.

"Are you all right?" Angela Leigh asked her.

Sophie heard her, but felt like the voice was coming through a tunnel. She nodded that she was okay, but she wasn't. Carefully, she made her way to the front of the chair and sat down. Opening her eyes, she saw that the room was no longer spinning. Taking a deep, unsteady breath, she tried to clear her head. She'd never experienced anything like that before. Never. And it frightened her.

"I can't do this now. I'm sorry," Sophie said in a voice she hardly recognized.

"You want a glass of water or something?"

"No. I just need to sit here for a minute. I'll be fine." Sophie was unsure of anything at the moment.

"Does this have anything to do with my daughter's disappearance? Your behavior?"

Sophie felt like she'd been knocked in the head. She wasn't sure what to say because she didn't know. In her sixty-six years, she'd never experienced this . . . spaced-out feeling. The image she'd seen was as clear as the room she was in. But it was not this room. No, it was a scene she'd never witnessed in her life—unless it was in some past life.

As though she was viewing a movie, an image of a snow-covered mountain filled her vision. And something red and so bright it hurt her eyes.

Sophie was one hundred percent sure she'd just experienced her first true clairvoyant vision.

Trying to act like nothing had happened wasn't going to work. "Uh, no, I'm just a little dizzy. Look, I know you wanted me to read for you, but I can't. Not now. I'm sorry."

Angela Leigh sat in the chair across from Sophie. "I know I'm not the friendliest person in the world right now." She blotted her eyes with a tissue. "Laura always calls me; she would never just take off and not let me know where she was going. I'm afraid something terrible has happened to her."

Sophie felt bad for her earlier thoughts. Of course, the woman was suffering. Her child was missing. Forget the fact the daughter was a B-grade actress, and the mother dressed like a social-climbing high-school student. This was serious.

"I don't know if this will help you, but when I heard about your daughter's disappearance, I didn't get a bad feeling. I'm rarely wrong." Sophie knew it wasn't much, but at that moment it was all she could offer. She felt weak, as though she needed to lie down.

"No, it doesn't help. I was told you read tarot and held an occasional séance. I was expecting something that would help me locate my daughter."

Sophie just wanted to leave, get the hell out of there. She needed to think, needed to try to decipher the image she'd seen. "Again, I apologize. I'm not feeling well. It must be the fish I ate earlier. I can call you, reschedule this when I'm feeling better."

"I don't think there's time for that," Angela said. "Do you want me to call downstairs for someone to assist you?"

"No, I will be fine." Slowly, Sophie stood up. Other than being a little shaky, she was sure the worst of the dizziness had passed.

"Of course. I'll get the door."

"Thank you," Sophie said briskly. She hoofed it to the door as fast as possible. She needed to get the hell out of there and quickly.

Inside the elevator, she punched the button for the lobby. The second the doors swooshed open, she headed for the exit, and the car. Inside the Escalade, she tossed her tote bag in the passenger seat, but didn't insert the key in the ignition. She wasn't in any hurry to start driving. Mavis and Ida would be with their stiff for at least two more hours. That should give her enough time to recover from her . . . vision.

Suddenly, Sophie wished her old friend Madam Butterfly was still alive. Living in New York City, Madam Butterfly had been a mentor of sorts. Sophie had gone to her for readings off and on for years, and it was she who'd discovered Sophie's psychic abilities. At the time, Sophie had laughed at her, but as the years passed, Sophie knew that the "feelings" she had were more than normal intuition. It had frightened her, but she'd always remained interested in the world beyond, an after place. When the spirits decided to pay Toots a visit, Sophie's abilities had been reawakened. Calling those from beyond was as normal to her now as picking up the phone. Almost. But she didn't recall ever having such a clear and vivid vision. If she could figure out what it meant, it would be worth the physical agony she'd gone through.

She closed her eyes, trying to call up the vision. Snow, fresh and powdery—she could almost feel its iciness. Concentrating, she focused on the blinding white. It was endless. As she focused on the image, the flash of bright red appeared. It was slick and flat. The object was surrounded by snow. Her expression froze when it hit her.

Suddenly, Sophie's vision became quite clear to her. What she had seen was a vehicle, a bright red vehicle covered in snow.

The heady scent of roses and carnations filled the small viewing area at the Evergreen Funeral Home. Four rooms were used for viewing dearly departed loved ones. One room held seating for only twenty-four. Half of the seats were empty.

Mavis and Ida arrived just as the deceased's ceremony began. Out of respect, they joined the ten mourners as Lula Mae Travis made her last earthly appearance.

Friends and relatives each took a turn at the lectern, remembering Lula Mae. Each eulogized her at great length.

Ida looked at her watch, then leaned over to whisper to Mavis. "The woman was ninety-seven years old. Do you imagine they're going to rehash her entire life?"

"Shhh," Mavis said. "Give them a couple minutes."

Ida rolled her eyes, but kept silent. If they didn't get started on their client soon, they'd be there all night.

Tapping her high-heel-clad foot against the chair in front of her, Ida had a flash of the mourners mourning themselves. She spoke up, though this time she didn't bother lowering her voice as she doubted half the mourners could hear her anyway. "Let's just leave. We'll be here all night."

Mavis took her bag from the floor and quietly escaped through the dark green drapes that separated the viewing rooms. Once they were out of earshot Ida swore. "Damn, Mavis, we can't let ourselves get involved this way again. Remember, we're professionals."

"Yes, but we must always show compassion," Mavis said sweetly. "Remember Pearl."

Pearl May Atkins was the reason they were there in the first place. Mavis had attended the poor woman's funeral. When she saw there was no one to give Pearl a proper send-off, Mavis made it her mission to see to it that no one went to the hereafter without a decent farewell.

Mavis and Ida had trained in San Francisco, and now both were in demand. Mavis, for her unique clothes designed for easy dressing of the dead, and Ida, for her skill with makeup. Many had commented on her work, saying the deceased looked much better dead than they had alive. Ida was quite proud of her accomplishments.

The e-mail she had received from the owner of the funeral parlor said he was vacationing in Europe. Their services had come highly recommended. from morticians across the country who were raving over her cosmetics. He promised to refer them to other funeral parlors throughout the state.

They traveled down a long, dark hallway, where a sign pointed to the administrator's office. "Here," Ida said, stepping inside the office that consisted of a small dark green love seat with two matching wing chairs and a round coffee table in the center. Matching tables on either side of the love seat held imitation Tiffany lamps. Behind the love seat, a set of floor-to-ceiling shelves lined the wall. Each shelf held an urn, several small floral arrangements, and what appeared to be samples of materials for the inside and outside of the many choices of caskets Evergreen offered. Ida thought the entire setup exceedingly tacky.

"Who is our contact, and why isn't he here?" Mavis asked as she looked around the empty office.

Ida removed her BlackBerry from her purse and scrolled through her e-mail. When she found the original e-mail, she clicked on it. "His name is Barry Higginbotham. He's filling in for Mr. Greenfield, the owner, who's in Europe."

They each sat in one of the wing chairs. Ida looked at her watch. "He probably thinks we weren't coming since we spent so much time attending that service." Ida stood up and went to the door, where she peered out into the hallway.

A short man with a terrible toupee raced down the hall toward the office. He stopped and openly stared at Ida's bright pink hair. Stuttering, he said, "I'm s-s-sorry if I kept you w-w-waiting. The Travis family n-n-needed my attention. I'm Mr. Higginbotham. You must be Ms. M-M-McGullicutty." He held out a plump hand.

Ida instantly thought of germs. She did not want to

touch the little man's hands. They looked greasy, like he'd raked them through his oily black toupee. She forced herself to touch the top of his hand with hers, then inched away from him.

"Now about M-M-Mr. Frank." Mr. Higginbotham scooted behind the desk. He slid to the edge of the chair and placed both elbows on the desk. "It's a very s-s-sad case. As you know, the m-m-man took his own life. The family did not g-g-give me all the details, nonetheless there are some . . . uh, p-p-problems."

Mavis, who had remained silent, spoke up. "We are quite used to dealing with problem cases. As a matter of fact, we sort of specialize in difficult dressings."

Ida knew she was referring to Martha Wilkinson, their first client. The poor old woman's last request was to make sure she was buried with dentures in place, and she had been, just not the ones that belonged to her. The husband, in his late nineties, had mistakenly given the funeral director his teeth instead of his wife's. They'd almost had to break the poor woman's jaw to insert the extra-large dentures, but she had gone to the other side with a complete set of false teeth.

"T-T-That's encouraging, b-b-because . . . well, j-j-just follow m-m-me to the emb-b-balming room, and you can s-s-see for yourself."

Mr. Higginbotham scurried out of the office like a roach caught in the light. Ida and Mavis practically had to run to keep up with him. As they raced behind the little man to the embalming room, Ida suddenly had a feeling she'd made a serious error in accepting the assignment. She was beginning to think like Sophie.

At the end of the dark hallway was a door leading downstairs to the area where embalming and dressing took place. Ida grimaced at the iron odor that assaulted her. The room was like a crypt. Cold and lifeless. When

she was working, she tended to forget about the total mor-
bidness of her surroundings. She did her best to make the
deceased as presentable to the public as one could, under
the circumstances.

Two marble tables, stark and barren, stood in the center
of the white-tiled room. A single showerhead, used to
clean the occasional toxic mess, hung from the ceiling.
One of the tables held a body, with a white sheet draped
over the deceased. The sheet appeared to have something
beneath it, causing the center to rise slightly above the rest
of the body.

"This is M-M-Mr. Frank. His viewing is s-s-scheduled
for tomorrow a-a-afternoon."

Ida placed her case of cosmetics on the floor next to the
drain where body fluids were disposed of. Two years ago,
she would've been on the table herself, her fear of germs
killing her. Mavis hung the charcoal gray suit on a hook
on the back of the door, where a white jacket hung life-
lessly, like the body on the marble slab.

"I'll j-j-just leave you to take c-c-care of M-m-mr.
Frank," Mr. Higginbotham said. "I'll be upstairs if you
need me." Without giving either a chance to respond, he
hurried up the stairs.

Mr. Frank's body had been prepared at the hospital
morgue. His skin had been scrubbed clean, his hair sham-
pooed and conditioned. All the bodily fluids had been
flushed away into some secret foul place that existed in the
bowels of the hospital.

Mavis watched as Ida prepared her table, using a rolling
metal tray like those used in the hospital. Mavis would assist her, then together they would arrange the specially designed suit. "I don't have a photograph, so I'm hoping this
man doesn't need any stuffing," Ida said. They wouldn't
remove the white sheet until she had all of her cosmetics,
sponges, and brushes readied.

"That's so crude, Ida. He must've been a sad soul to do this to himself." Mavis's eyes filled with tears, something she did every time they had a laying-out to perform. She was softhearted, truly grieving for those who had passed.

"I don't mean to be crude, I just don't like it when I have to . . . patch them up," Ida said as she straightened her set of brushes.

"I'm sure we can cover his . . . wounds with the shirt's collar. I might have to make a few adjustments. So"—Mavis took a deep breath—"are we ready?"

Ida scanned her tray. All of her tools were where they needed to be. She had several shades of face makeup and powders lined neatly in a row. "Yes, I'm ready. Time to work our magic."

Mavis stood at the end of the marble table. Ida was on the right side, positioned in the middle near the corpse's stomach. She reached up and carefully pulled the white sheet off the lifeless figure. Dropping the sheet on the floor, Ida looked at the man, and screamed, "He's alive!"

Chapter 12

At loose ends while they waited for news of Chris, Toots and Abby took the dogs for an evening stroll on the beach.

Foaming waves rolled against the shoreline. Coco and Chester were in doggie heaven, each taking turns running to the edge of the water, sniffing around, then returning to walk alongside their human escorts. Both women were quiet, allowing the gentle, rolling sound of the ocean waves to soothe their frayed nerves. Lights from the assorted houses dotted the beachside. An occasional burst of laughter, mingled with varied accents, could be heard off in the distance.

Toots discovered they'd wandered farther down the beach than she had thought. "Let's head back now. Everyone should be returning soon. I hope Goebel or Sophie have some good news. I could certainly use some."

Abby called for Chester and Coco, who were frolicking in the sand about ten yards farther down the beach, but didn't bother putting their leashes back on. They knew the routine.

"Me too. I'm still at a complete loss. Chris just doesn't seem like the kind of guy who would take off without telling anyone. I know he likes his privacy, but this isn't normal. Tell me this, Mom, and don't sugarcoat it for my sake. Do you believe Chris could be involved in Laura Leigh's disappearance?"

Toots walked beside Abby, taking a minute to consider her question. She'd raised Chris since he was in his early teens. She'd been more than a bit surprised when he'd welcomed her with open arms as his stepmother. He'd lost his mother, and was thrilled when she and Garland married. He had never exhibited any disturbing behavior as a young boy. He made fantastic grades in school, never took up with a bad crowd, his friends were all decent, all with goals and ambitions and parents who cared. She and Garland had been very involved in their children's lives. Surely, if Chris had suffered from some mental disorder, something that could explain his possible involvement in the young woman's disappearance, she would've spotted it. She'd been around the block a time or two, knew what was normal behavior and what wasn't. Toots was positive Chris had not gone off the deep end. There had to be a plausible explanation for his apparent disappearance. Probably not a simple one, but plausible. They would have to be patient and wait. If Chris thought she and Abby were having this kind of discussion, he would be terribly hurt. No, Toots did not believe for even a second that Chris was in any way involved in Laura Leigh's disappearance.

"I just don't see him wrapped up in something so . . . torrid. To answer your question, I am one hundred percent sure Chris has nothing to do with Laura and the fact that she's missing."

Abby shook her head. "I wish I felt that way, too, but I don't. That's not to say I think he's . . . *harmed* Laura, but it's just too much of a coincidence for me to believe he isn't with her. They could be shacked up somewhere, who knows? Maybe they went to Vegas and got married. There are so many possibilities, they're endless." She said the last words quickly, her heart squeezing with each word.

Toots reached for Abby's hand. "I hope you're wrong." She paused. "Look, Abby, I know your feelings for Chris are more than friendly."

"Mom, let's not go there," Abby said, though she couldn't deny her feelings.

"Why not? I love you and Chris. You have my seal of approval. You didn't grow up together. You barely knew each other. Besides, I can see the way you two are when you're together. It's obvious you're both head over heels in love, so why not acknowledge it and accept it for what it is?"

"If it were that simple, trust me, I would. But it's not. Chris hasn't . . . I haven't . . . neither of us has admitted what we feel. I'm not sure I could at this point."

They continued to walk, their pace unhurried. Toots wanted Abby to experience the kind of love Toots had felt for Abby's father. If Abby wasn't convinced Chris was the love of her life, then so be it. After eight marriages, Toots felt she was in the position to offer her daughter sound advice. "You will know if he's the right one. It's simple advice, but it is what it is. When I met your father, I fell in love on our second date." Toots smiled at the memory. She and John had met on a blind date, hitting it off immediately. On their second, she knew he was going to play a very important role in her life. And he had. She'd had a perfect marriage, it just hadn't lasted long enough. *Only the good die young*, she thought, as she reminisced about Abby's father.

"Let's get through this first. If Chris is the man I think he is, he'll have a perfectly sensible explanation."

"At this point, I don't think any explanation will be 'perfectly sensible.' It's been too long. If he knows what's happening, he should've called. If he hasn't, I'm thinking he . . ." Abby paused. She didn't know what she was thinking. "I know something is wrong, Mom. I just know it. I can feel it in my gut."

"Of course. That's obvious. This isn't like the Chris we all know and love," Toots said.

"Maybe we don't know him as well as we thought. He's been in LA for a long time. People change. This is a totally different place from Charleston. Maybe Chris is being the person he thinks the world expects him to be," Abby suggested.

Toots considered her daughter's words. As much as she hated to disagree with Abby, she felt Chris was exactly the man he appeared to be. Just like his father. "I think you're wrong, Abby, but time will tell."

Lights from the deck shone in the distance, indicating the beach house wasn't far away. "I hope so," was all Abby could say.

Coco and Chester smelled home, and took off running, Chester stopping twice just to make sure Coco kept up with him. The two animals were madly in love. Abby could not help but smile. If only life were as simple for humans as it was for dogs.

"I'm sure Goebel will come up with something. He's the best, according to Chris. He knows Chris; maybe he has something up his sleeve." They walked up the steps leading to the deck where Coco and Chester sat panting. "I need to enlarge the doggie door for Chester," Toots announced as an afterthought. They'd had a small one installed for Queen Coco, but Toots hadn't so much as considered Chester when she'd chosen the dimensions.

"He's fine, Mom," Abby said. "I'll get them some fresh water. I know you want to smoke one of those icky cigarettes."

Toots smiled. Her Marlboros and lighter lay on the

table next to the seashell ashtray. "I just need a puff or two. Why don't you start a pot of coffee? I'm sure Goebel and the girls will want some when they return."

Toots looked at her watch. The others had been gone almost two hours already. She knew it would take Ida and Mavis at least three hours to prepare the body, and who knew how long it would take Sophie to make contact with the netherworld?

Sitting in her favorite deck chair, Toots lit up, and sucked the smoke into her lungs as if it were oxygen and she had just spent a minute underwater. She really wanted to quit, and someday she would. But it was not going to be that day. Or the next. When they located Chris and the missing girl, well then she might consider it. Maybe she would invest in one of those newfangled electronic cigarettes. They were all the rage—even though they seemed to carry some health risks, too.

Crushing her smoke out, she entered through the sliding glass door. Abby had busied herself making coffee, while Chester and Coco were curled up, side by side, in their favorite corner. Toots grabbed the remote and clicked on the television to the local news station that had been reporting on Laura Leigh's disappearance. The slick-lipped reporter she disliked filled the small screen.

Abby looked over her shoulder. "Mom, let's not listen to that crap she reports. We're lucky if one-tenth of what she reports is true."

"So far she's been on the money, Abs."

"Then it's the first time. She sends the reporters out and doesn't check their accuracy half the time. I can't believe the station allows her to report a quarter of the stuff she reads from the teleprompter. She doesn't even write her own copy most of the time."

Toots ignored her daughter. As she heard the reporter's words, she raised the volume.

"*Los Angeles police are currently searching the Toyota Camry owned by Los Angeles entertainment attorney Christopher Clay. Our sources tell us the vehicle is being thoroughly checked for trace evidence such as hairs, fibers, and possibly blood. If any blood evidence is found, it is highly possible Miss Laura Leigh is the victim of foul play. While Mr. Clay has not been named a suspect, one would assume, if evidence is found in his vehicle, he will be upgraded from a person of interest. Mr. Clay's mechanic called the Los Angeles Police Department after a BOLO—be on the lookout—for his vehicle was issued. The auto repair shop owner, David Williams of Poor Man's, said Mr. Clay's vehicle had been towed into the shop the same day Miss Leigh was reported missing.*"

Toots clicked the television off. "That bitch! She's ruining Chris's name before he's had a chance to defend himself. I think I will call the station and raise hell."

Abby brought two cups of coffee to the table, then removed the half-and-half from the fridge. "Don't waste your time, Mom. It won't do the slightest bit of good. People report her all the time. I'm sure she's sleeping with the owner of the station, so until that goes sour, it's useless."

"Then I'll file a slander suit against the station. I bet the owner won't hesitate to toss her out on her lipsticked ass then," Toots said indignantly.

"He's like Rag. When he feels things are beginning to heat up, and he displayed in a negative light, he'll toss Miss Chloe Brown out on her ass and hire another siliconed sweetheart to take her place."

Toots had a flash of buying the station. She'd hire her own team of news anchors, and they wouldn't be twenty-something bimbos. Something to think about later. She already had her hands full with *The Informer* and The Sweetest Thing, the bakery in Charleston she was half owner of. Not to mention running two households, and participating in Sophie's séances when the need arose. And her charities.

She had neglected participating in events the past couple years, but she continued to donate hefty sums of money to all. No, buying a television station wasn't a good move. At least not now, though she would give serious thought to it in the future. Something for Abby's future. Who knew, *The Informer* could go global, be the next *Entertainment Tonight*. Becoming a female version of Ted Turner would be quite a coup.

"And we thought KABC was the cream of the local crop," Toots added.

"It's okay, I watch it, too; I just know which reporter to listen to. Miss Chloe Brown gets all the hot stories because she's screwing the boss. Helen Woods is on the money. She does the eleven o'clock news."

"I'll keep that in mind." Toots sat at the table thinking a million different thoughts, none of them good.

Coco and Chester growled, their ears at attention. Both canines ran to the front door.

"That must be Goebel. It's still too early for the girls to return." Abby crossed her fingers, hoping he had something positive to report. A loud knock sounded on the front door, and the dogs went wild.

"Hey, you two, calm down," Abby warned. "I'll get it, Mom." She hurried to the front door.

It was indeed Goebel. Inside, he leaned over to scratch both dogs between the ears, and they followed him to the kitchen.

Her mind a zillion miles away, Toots practically jumped out of her chair when he entered the kitchen. She placed a hand over her thumping heart. "Did you find anything?"

Goebel pulled out a chair. Abby poured him a cup of

coffee, refilled her own cup, then sat down, waiting, hoping he'd found something, *anything* that would explain the insane nightmare.

He took a sip of coffee before answering. "No, and that's what's bothering me. I have a pal down at the police station, who owed me a favor from way back when. I called him as soon as I knew I was headed out West. According to what he said, they've gone over Chris's car with a fine-toothed comb, said it was a priority. And to quote him, 'They don't have jack shit,' " Goebel said with a gleam in his eyes.

"The news is reporting just the opposite." Toots repeated what the bimbo news anchor had reported.

"I don't think so. They've got every forensic specialist available examining that car. They haven't found anything suspicious, unless you call several wrappers from Pink's Hot Dogs evidence."

Abby's heart flip-flopped. *So Chris was hanging out at Pink's now?*

Stunned, Toots remarked, "That's it?"

"So far," Goebel said. "If you want my opinion, I think Chris and this little starlet are hiding away somewhere and don't want to be disturbed. From what I understand, Miss Leigh is very easy on the eyes."

Abby's heart flip-flopped again, then plummeted to her feet and back up. She was sure she felt an actual pain in her chest. Fearing Goebel was probably right, she gave up hope that anything would ever happen between her and Chris. When this was over, she would give serious thought to relocating. Suddenly, Charleston didn't seem all that bad.

A cell phone ring tone that Abby did not recognize sent her mother scurrying up the stairs. Toots called, "I'll be right back," as she raced up the staircase.

Abby raised her shoulders as if saying she hadn't a clue. Goebel nodded and sipped his coffee.

Upstairs, Toots searched for what she thought of as her "secure line"—a cell phone she'd purchased when she bought *The Informer*. For use only in the case of an emergency, she'd written in one of her LAT Enterprise e-mails. Abby and Chris were the only two humans on the planet who had the number, and one of them was sitting at her kitchen table, so that left Chris. The phone rang several times before she located it in her nightstand. She clicked the TALK button. "Hello? Chris? Is that you? Where are you?" She pulled the phone away from her ear, making sure there was still a connection. When she saw that the phone was dead, she gave herself a mental kick in the ass. The damned phone wasn't charged! *How could I be so stupid? A phone for emergencies that isn't even usable.*

Picking up the house phone, she quickly punched in Chris's cell-phone number. She was sure this was a good sign. The phone rang once, twice, and a third time. Toots always allowed the phone to go to voice mail, just in case. She let the phone ring for another thirty seconds. When she didn't get his voice mail, she was sure there were so many messages the phone could no longer handle any new ones. She tossed the phone on the bed and plugged her "emergency" cell phone into its charger. She hoped Abby didn't ask questions. Because if she did, Toots would have to tell her daughter another lie.

Chapter 13

Chris walked another thirty feet away from the cabin. He held his cell phone high above his head, hoping to catch a signal. The cell-phone service provider supposedly had the best coverage in the country. *Bullshit,* he thought as he continued to act like a satellite spinning around in the midst of a snowstorm. When he looked at the cell phone again, he saw he had one bar of power. Damn, he'd lucked out! Before he lost the precious signal, he called the one person he knew he could count on no matter what.

Toots. His stepmother.

He dialed her private cell number, knowing she would answer no matter what time of day or night it was. Since she'd taken over *The Informer,* Toots said she had to be available at all times even though Abby didn't have a clue her mother was the woman behind the mask. It would serve as *The Informer'*s emergency line of communication if the need to call and get an immediate response ever arose. As far as Chris knew, only he and Abby knew the private number. He shoved the phone closer to his ear to drown out the sound of the wind and listened, counting the rings. On the fifth ring, he let out a sigh of relief when he heard Toots's familiar "Hello."

"Thank God," he said. A static, crackling-like noise

sent his heart racing. "Toots, are you there?" He waited a couple seconds, giving her a moment to reply. When he didn't get a response, he looked at the screen on his cell phone. All he saw were the words NO SERVICE. He'd been shunted off to her voice mail.

Son of a bitch!

Furious beyond belief, Chris tossed the absolutely useless piece of plastic into a pile of snow. *What the hell am I supposed to do now? Wait until the spring thaw?* He should have his head examined for deciding to follow Laura Leigh. The spoiled-rotten brat was the client from hell. He should've paid attention to the rumors he'd heard, should have listened when his gut instinct told him to back off, stay away from the girl. But, she was an up-and-coming actress, and it was his job to represent Hollywood's best. Though he had to admit, if he were honest with himself, and he was on most occasions, she was really nothing more than a B-grade actress whom he'd used to make Abby jealous. He'd helped her get her first major role, and that should have been the end of it. Instead, he'd let Abby's lack of attention force him to use Laura in a way she truly didn't deserve. Sheer male stupidity.

Three times Abby had turned down his dinner invitation. Told him she had to work—each and every time he'd asked. He called her cell phone, called her office, her house, and nothing. Granted, he hadn't bothered to leave a message, but still, Abby had caller ID, and she was not stupid. After declining his dinner invitations, he'd thought of that night they'd shared at Pink's. He wanted to take her back to Pink's, sure that she would get the same feelings they'd had that night almost two years before. A night he had never forgotten, a night he often dreamed about, a night that caused him to wake up drenched in sweat at the memory of her touch. He knew she checked her caller ID, had seen her do it more than once. Chris knew she was totally dedicated to her work, but he also knew she had to eat sometime.

And now he was stranded on top of a mountain somewhere in the wilds of the Sierra Nevada range in the midst of a blizzard with a nutcase actress he didn't even like. No, check that. An actress he couldn't even stand. And the odds were looking better by the day that he would never get the chance to tell Abby how he felt about her.

All because he wanted to get Abby's attention, make her jealous!

Though it was useless to him now, Chris picked up the phone he'd tossed into the pile of snow and crammed it in his pocket. When he'd last listened to the weather report, he hadn't planned on being in the mountains, hadn't given any thought to the expected storm the forecasters were calling the *storm of the century!* How many of those had the forecasters predicted in the first ten years of the twenty-first century? Why did they have to be right this once? He sure as hell hadn't planned on being stranded in the middle of nowhere with a woman he could not tolerate!

The wind continued to howl, blowing icy bits of snow in his face. It felt as though he were being stung by a million angry bees. Heading back to the cabin, he lowered his head against the wind and pulled the collar of the jacket he'd been lucky to find at Johnathan's cabin high around the sides of his face. If he stayed outside any longer, he'd risk hypothermia. Counting the windchill factor, Chris guessed it had to be at least thirty below. Each time he'd ventured out into the bone-chilling cold in hopes of catching a signal on his cell, he'd allowed himself five minutes. Anything more was too big a risk. Hopefully, Toots would connect the dots when she saw his cell number on her private phone.

Disheartened, Chris had no other choice: go back inside

the cabin and spend the rest of the night listening to Laura Leigh expound on all she would do once they were rescued. He slowed his pace when he thought of the long night ahead. He couldn't believe he was in the position to be rescued. *How in the hell has it come to this?* What should have been a simple gesture had turned into a nightmare of mammoth proportions.

He'd been at Hot Wired waiting to meet a new client when he'd spied Laura Leigh sitting alone at a nearby table. Knowing it would be totally rude not to acknowledge her since she was, whether he liked it or not, a client, he'd picked up his glass of ginger ale—always with a twist of lime—and walked over to her table.

"Mind if I join you?" he'd asked.

Laura had seemed surprised to see him. "Sure. Why not?" She'd responded with about as much enthusiasm as a bank teller who had just been handed $10,000 in one-dollar bills.

Chris was sure she'd had more than her share to drink, but didn't want to ask her exactly how much for fear she'd think of him in a different light. Not the hip dude she assumed him to be. They'd been out in public together, and each time he'd had to force himself to act like he was having the time of his life, when, in reality, all he'd wanted to do was go home and call Abby.

A couple times he'd seen Abby while he was with Laura. He cringed when he remembered how he'd leaned close to her so it would appear as if he were kissing her neck. The cloyingly sweet scent of her perfume almost made him sick, but when he'd seen Abby storm out of the club, he'd been glad he'd made the move. Shown dear little Abby what she'd been missing.

Now it seemed that his childishness had come back to smack him squarely in the face. Trudging through knee-deep snowdrifts, Chris figured it served him right. Instead of playing stupid cat-and-mouse games with his feelings, and Abby's, too, he should've acted like the man his father and Toots had raised him to be. He should have stepped up to the plate a long, *long* time ago and told Abby how he really felt.

As he stomped his feet on the steps to get rid of the snow on his shoes, he wondered if he'd ever get the opportunity to tell her. Laura yanked the door open, preventing him from thinking about Abby and his lack of a relationship with her. His main focus returned—to get the hell off the mountain.

Alive.

"Where in the hell have you been? I am freezing to death! Did you find a way out of here? I hope you did because I can't stay in this shit hole another night! Look at me!" Laura shouted hysterically, as Chris shoved the large wooden door aside.

She followed him across the room to the fireplace. Warming his hands in front of the modest fire, he caught a quick glance at the wood supply. They had enough for another day, day and a half at best. Reasoning that Johnathan could afford new furniture, Chris eyed the solid oak table and chairs in the dining room. If push came to shove, he'd simply use the furniture for firewood and pay for the replacements himself. He'd worry about the fallout later.

The last person on earth Chris wanted to look at was Laura Leigh. Without her makeup, she looked like a twelve-year-old who could use a prescription for Accutane. Her actions were more like those of a toddler whose main pleasure was teasing her dog. Tossing his damp jacket across the back of a lounge chair, he took a deep breath. It was going to be another long, miserable night.

"I'm looking, Laura," he said out of sheer exasperation.

"And? I suppose you weren't able to get a connection?"

Chris made a silent promise to himself—he would never, never, ever represent Laura or anyone her age again. He'd retire first. Farming, coal mining, or even trash hauling suddenly held enormous appeal.

Wearing one of Johnathan's red plaid flannel shirts and a pair of gray woolen socks pulled up over her knees, her long blond hair pulled up high in a ponytail, she looked more like a two-year-old as she stomped her feet. "I asked you a question, dammit!"

Chris actually felt his jaw drop. He'd heard the expression "my jaw dropped" for years, but had never really given it much credence.

Until that moment. Until Laura Leigh actually stomped her foot and said what she said.

Shaking his head from left to right, he took a couple seconds to collect his thoughts. They were in this cabin because of her! He just needed to talk to her in a way that wouldn't cause another outburst. His patience almost gone, he said, "It's against the law to drive drunk, Laura. I'm sure that somewhere during your fun-filled, exciting life, someone or other told you that. And we're here because you threatened to blow up the studio, remember?"

Needless to say, Chris did not mention he'd lost a new client when he'd chased after Laura, trying to protect her from herself. Even if he said it, he doubted she would have paid the slightest bit of attention to anything other than her own misery.

Kicking at the dwindling pile of logs with her stockinged foot, Laura said, "Yeah and I didn't get the part in *Bloody Hollow, Two* because of you! Remember *that?*"

Obviously, we have remembered two different sets of events concerning the casting of Bloody Hollow, Two, he thought. It was his distinct recollection that the director, the producer, and everyone else right down to the catering staff, if you really wanted the truth, all claimed Laura Leigh was a nightmare to work with. She threw wild tantrums on the set, threatened to kill whomever her anger was directed at, and demanded hourly that her contract be changed. Yes, he knew exactly why she didn't get the second part. The big mystery was: Did she know?

"Spoiled brat" was too kind a way to describe her. Taking another deep breath to prevent himself from saying what he really wanted to say, Chris plopped down on the chair closest to the fireplace. "Laura, in spite of the delusions you have about show business, professionalism is required and respected, no matter who you think you are."

He grinned to himself, knowing that was sure to tick the girl off even more than she was already, but he didn't care. He was thoroughly tired of listening to her complaints. She was lucky he'd had the foresight to follow her when she'd left Hot Wired in a drunken rage. Even luckier that he'd convinced her to pull over and let him drive her home. But after ten minutes, Chris had known he couldn't take Laura to her house or his. He needed to get her away, someplace where no one would find her.

That was when he'd remembered he had the keys to Johnathan Kline's cabin near Mammoth Mountain. Forget that it was more than five hours away from Los Angeles. None of that had mattered. His main concern was getting her off the road and away from the publicity that was sure to follow if she'd acted on her threats. Lucky for him, he'd planned to attend a conference in San Francisco, so no one would be concerned about his whereabouts. His intentions were to leave Laura alone for a few days while he attended the conference. Then, when she'd had time to think about things, his plan was to take her home and let her face the music, minus him as her attorney. However, the umpteenth storm of the century had other plans for them.

Seething with uncontrollable rage, Laura picked up one of the logs from the box next to the fireplace. Hefting it over her shoulder, she prepared to swing it forward when Chris caught the end of the log in his hand. "Enough, Laura, dammit! Start acting like an adult." Easily taking the log from her hands, he tossed it into the fire, sending sparks flying up through the flue.

"Are you out of your mind?" she screamed.

"I could ask you the same thing." Chris stood up, looked around the room, threw his hands up in the air, then dropped them back to his sides. Frustration didn't begin to describe what he was feeling.

"Actually, I think we're damn lucky. We could be trapped in your car on the side of the road somewhere freezing to death. Instead, here we are in a luxurious cabin, with all the amenities. And you're complaining."

Chris turned his back on her and walked into the kitchen. He knew anything he said would not make a difference. Laura was an immature, self-serving, spoiled Hollywood brat. Knowing it gave her satisfaction to argue with him, he decided he would keep his mouth shut until they were able to drive away on their own or he was able to make a call using his cell phone. With that thought in mind, he opened the cupboard and removed two cans of tomato soup, thankful Johnathan kept the cabin supplied with plenty of staples.

He opened the soup with the electric can opener, again thankful for Johnathan's careful planning. The generator would keep the power on as long as their gas supply lasted. Chris guessed there was enough to last for another week if they were frugal. He scooped the thick glob of condensed soup in the saucepan, added water, then turned the burner on high.

Laura chose that moment to saunter into the kitchen,

stopping when she saw what he was doing. "Soup *again?* At this rate, I'll starve to death."

Chris smiled. The one positive attribute Laura had was her ability to chow down with the big boys. Although petite, she could consume as much food as someone twice her size. She was not one of those stars who ate like a rabbit.

"You're not going to starve." When the soup came to a boil, he turned the burner off and poured the bubbly red-orange liquid into two soup bowls. He grabbed a sleeve of saltine crackers and a jar of peanut butter from the pantry. He didn't cook this much when he was at home. He gathered the food up, placed it on a wooden tray, and carried it to the dining room table—the one he might have to use for firewood if their situation didn't change soon.

Rolling his eyes, he looked at the young girl. "Come on. You have to eat." He felt like he was babysitting!

Reluctantly, she slid into the chair across from him. "Whatever. Let's just call a truce, okay? I don't want to hear your mouth anymore."

Chris had never condoned physical violence of any kind, no matter what the circumstances. However, those past four days with Laura had given him a change of heart. Taking another deep, cleansing breath, he began to eat the soup. If he didn't do something soon, he thought he just might be tempted to give Miss Laura Leigh a good smack. More than a bit surprised at the direction his thoughts were taking him, he suddenly equated being stranded with her with being in a torture chamber.

"A truce, huh?" Chris repeated her words.

"Yeah, something wrong with that?" she asked hatefully, her eyes spewing sparks.

Another long, *long* night ahead, Chris swallowed the words he was about to say. Then and there, he decided, no matter what the weather, he was going to find a way off that mountain, come hell or high water. Sooner rather than later.

"Nope, Laura, not a single thing," Chris responded as he continued to eat his soup.

Tomorrow couldn't come soon enough.

Chapter 14

Mavis swallowed several times, her mouth suddenly dry as a bone. *Lord,* she thought, *that is not a word I should be thinking of right now.* Ida's face turned ten shades of white, her hands trembled like leaves in a windstorm, and she appeared utterly confused. Mavis cleared her dry throat, trying to sum up the situation.

"He's dead, Ida. All you have to do is touch him. See?" Hesitantly, Mavis touched Mr. Frank's foot. "He's as cold as an ice cube."

Ida looked at Mavis, then at Mr. Frank's private part, which stood at rigid attention. At a loss for words, she pointed to his . . . *problem.* Finding her voice, Ida whispered, "Then how, what is . . . *that?*"

In her studies, Mavis had heard of the *condition* but never expected to encounter such a problem. She spoke again, but with more authority. They were professionals, just as Ida had reminded her. "Though unusual, it's not unheard of." Mavis tried to recall verbatim the words she'd read. "It's called a terminal erection, or *priapism.* I remember reading this because . . . well, I have to admit I thought of you when I read about it." She paused, waiting for Ida to let loose on her. When nothing happened, she continued. "It's seen in corpses who've been executed, particularly those who died by hanging. I won't go into the technicalities of it, but I do remember reading about this condition when we were studying in San Francisco."

Ida stepped away from the marble table. Fearful she was about to faint or something, Mavis hurried to her side and placed a hand on her shoulder. "I can do this myself, Ida. Why don't you call Sophie, tell her to take you back to the beach house. I'll take care of this poor man." Knowing her skills with death makeup weren't quite as well developed as Ida's, Mavis would still do anything to spare her friend from regressing back to the fearful woman she used to be.

Ida shook her head, her hot pink hair the only bit of color in the sterile room. "Just give me a few minutes. I'm fine. Just a bit . . . stunned."

Quite shocked herself, Mavis knew it wasn't the time to show her feelings. The poor man had taken his own life. It was such a shame to have one's last viewing be one of utter humiliation. Though she'd read about the causes of this terrible . . . affliction, for the life of her she couldn't recall the cure. Several horrid images came to mind, and she quickly brushed them aside.

It suddenly occurred to her that Sophie was a registered nurse, so she would know what to do. Without another word to Ida, Mavis stepped away, allowing her friend a few minutes of privacy to collect herself. She dialed Sophie's cell-phone number, hoping she was finished with her tarot reading.

Sophie answered on the first ring. "Yes?"

Immediately, Mavis picked up on Sophie's mood. "Has something happened? You don't sound like yourself."

"I'm okay, just nothing I want to talk about right now. Are you finished with your stiff?"

Oh dear, Mavis thought, *if she only knew, she would not use that word.* She couldn't help but smile, then chastised herself for making fun of the dead. She was sure she would be punished for her wicked thoughts.

"Actually, we haven't even started. I think we might need your advice."

"I don't see how I can help, but go for it." Sophie sounded more like herself with each word.

Mavis tried to moisten her dry mouth but couldn't. She swallowed several times, knowing this was her body's way of telling her she was nervous. "I think you need to see our . . . problem. It's quite . . . a delicate one."

"I don't even want to know. Give me twenty minutes, and I'll be there. Make sure you're waiting outside for me. I don't want to go traipsing around a damned funeral parlor. Not now, especially after tonight's experience."

"Are you sure you're all right?" Mavis asked.

"I'll live."

"I'll be waiting for you out front in twenty minutes." Mavis hit the END button on her cell phone.

Ida remained in a state of semishock, still rooted to the floor. Mavis had to clear her throat rather loudly to get Ida's attention.

"Good grief! Is there something caught in your throat?" Ida asked, finally snapping out of her stupor.

"No, I just spoke with Sophie. I'll be right back," Mavis said quickly, then raced up the stairs, leaving Ida alone with the deceased and his problem. It probably wouldn't be a good idea to tell Ida what she had in mind.

Ever thankful for her smaller physique, Mavis hurried down the long hall, heading for the exit. Outside, the evening air was warm and a slight breeze lifted the ends of her hair away from her neck. She was very glad to have a few minutes away from the chilled room with the corpse and his terminal erection.

Minutes later, Sophie careened into the parking lot, making the tires squeal as she turned sharply into a parking spot. Mavis smiled. Only Sophie would make a grand entrance at a funeral parlor and live to tell about it.

Sophie jumped out of the Escalade. Pale and winded, she found Mavis at the entrance. Sophie placed a hand over her chest. "I need to ease off the cigarettes."

"You need to stop, yes," Mavis agreed, "but we'll discuss your nasty habit later. Right now we have a problem." She entered the funeral parlor, motioning for Sophie to follow her. "This is something you need to see," she added.

Sophie didn't utter a single word as she followed Mavis down the hallway. She was still trying to understand what her vision meant and how it pertained to Chris and the missing actress. When Mavis had called asking for her help, she'd been more than happy for the distraction. Still unnerved from her vision, she remained silent, deciding she would keep to herself what she had seen until she figured exactly what it meant.

They walked down a narrow staircase, stopping at the bottom of the stairs, where a large door stared back at them. Mavis pushed the door aside, allowing Sophie to enter in front of her.

The odors of sulfur and iron assaulted Sophie as she stepped fully into the chilled room. She gagged at the smell and was reminded of her earlier days, when she'd trained as a student nurse. A semester in the hospital's morgue assured her she would not be applying for a position at any of the local hospitals. She placed her hand over her mouth and nose. "This better be good," she said, turning to look back at Mavis.

In the center of the room lay a large marble table with a dead body on top. A bright white sheet covered the body, but Sophie noticed a rise in the center of the sheet. Almost like a tent, just smaller. "What do we have here?" she asked as she inched closer to the table.

Ida was sitting on top of several cardboard boxes in the corner of the room. Her expression was a million miles away. Sophie stepped away from the body, stopping to stand in front of Ida. She snapped her fingers in front of her eyes. "What is wrong, Ida? Are you going into germ mode again?"

Sophie snapped her fingers a second time. Ida jerked her head to attention, blinking rapidly as though she'd just come out of a trance.

Back in the moment, Ida spoke up, "What are you doing here?"

Sophie, relishing her role as a smart-ass, placed a hand on her hip, and pointed at the slab in the center of the room. "You tell me."

Mavis rushed to stand beside Ida. "I called her. She's a nurse, Ida, remember? She'll know what to do about Mr. Frank's . . . *issue*." Mavis said the last word in a whisper.

Bouncing up on her feet like an angry feline, Ida huffed. "I can't believe you brought her into this . . . mess. You know we'll never live this down!"

"Okay, now I'm really intrigued," Sophie said, suddenly thrilled for Mavis and Ida's dilemma as it took her away from her own.

"We might as well show her, Ida. We don't have that much time left. We said three hours, remember?"

Ida nodded and walked over to the marble table. Before anyone had a chance to comment, she whisked the sheet off the dead man as though it were a cape and she a matador facing an aroused bull.

Sophie edged over to stand next to Ida. Her eyes went straight to Mr. Frank's *problem*. Her mouth fell open, and she cracked a grin as wide as the table in front of her. "I've heard of this, but I've never seen it before." She gazed at the man's problem area, then turned to Ida. "I can't be-lieve you didn't take matters into your own hands, you know, take care of this?" She nodded at Mr. Frank. "I take it he tried to kill himself?"

"He did kill himself, Sophie," Ida said.

Shivering in the ice-cold room, Sophie nodded. "You know what I mean; I know he succeeded, that much is obvious. I just assumed . . . well never mind what I assumed. This postmortem condition isn't as uncommon as you think. I won't go into the medical details, but think of blood engorging in the lower extremities." Sophie watched Ida for a response, but it was actually Mavis who spoke up. Always kind and softhearted, she teared up.

"Oh that poor man! I imagine if he knew he would be . . . aroused by hanging himself, he might have chosen another way to end his life," Mavis said, her eyes full of unshed tears.

"I don't care what he was thinking. We need to fix this, and fast," Ida said, sounding more and more like her old self.

"Then you'd better glove up," Sophie stated in a matter-of-fact tone of voice, but her eyes sparkled, and she could not prevent a trace of a smile from lifting her full lips upward. "This is going to get messy."

Ida paused for a moment, then found a box of sterile gloves on the counter. She snapped them on and tossed a pair to Mavis.

"You want my help, pass a pair over here." Sophie wasn't one hundred percent sure what she could do, but she made the girls swear that whatever happened in that room would stay in the room. Kind of like what happens in Vegas, stays in Vegas.

To ensure their complete silence, Sophie asked them to gather around. "This warrants a secret handshake." She waited for Ida or Mavis to refuse. When they didn't, Sophie stepped back to the corner of the room, and stripped off her gloves. Ida and Mavis followed suit. Without another word, Sophie placed one of her hands out, then Ida and Mavis followed. When they had their hands piled on top of each other, they whispered loudly, "When you're good, you're good!"

They'd been doing the secret handshake for more than fifty years, and it still had the power to link them together, forever, all their secrets protected by the simple childish act they'd discovered as children.

The three women surrounded the marble table. Sophie stood at the center of the table, with Ida at the head and Mavis at the foot. Out of respect for his condition, Mavis had covered Mr. Frank's issue with the sheet before they'd stepped away to do their secret handshake.

Without another word, Sophie whisked the sheet off the body like it was a magic cape. Seeing the man's neck covered in eggplant purple, sea green, and the red marks where the rope had burned his neck, she placed the sheet on his upper torso, hiding the wounds. Taking her cue from Ida, who'd whisked a few tools off her makeup table, Sophie eyeballed the instruments. Seeing a small scalpel-like tool, she reached for it.

"This is going to be ugly, so I wouldn't look if you're the least bit squeamish," Sophie said.

"Considering what we do, I think we're both beyond squeamish right now, right, Mavis?" Ida asked.

"Of course," Mavis answered sweetly.

Sophie took a deep breath, closed her eyes, and intoned a quick prayer. *I can do this,* she thought. *I can't let the girls know the thought of slicing a man's dick off isn't as pleasing as I'd sometimes imagined it would be.* She told herself to pretend the man was Walter. To think of all those times he'd smacked her around, the time he'd broken her arm, and the hundreds of times his drunkenness had humiliated her.

Letting out the breath she'd been holding, she replaced

her gloves and secured the small steel scalpel in her right hand. With her left hand, she reached for the corpse's engorged body part, and, without further ado, made a small cut where no one would see. When nothing happened, Sophie looked to Ida.

"Can you finish him off?" she asked with a grin.

Ida's eyes doubled in size. "Why . . . how dare . . . you are a true bitch, Sophie Manchester."

Mavis watched the exchange between the two. "I'll do it if you'll tell me what I need to do."

Sophie and Ida looked at one another and burst out laughing. "Never mind," Sophie said. "I'll take care of this." She placed the scalpel back on the tray, grabbed the man's uncooperative part in her left hand, then squeezed.

Blood and urine and something else no one wanted to put a name to oozed out of the man's privates, which deflated like a balloon. Sophie reached for a handful of gauze, soaked up the fluids, then dropped the man's limp organ like a live grenade. She snapped off her gloves, tossed them in a bin behind her, then washed her hands at the small sink.

"Anything else, girls?" Sophie asked, as though it was something she did on a daily basis.

Mavis shook her head, and Ida rolled her eyes, saying, "I know I'll hear about this for the next fifty years."

"Only if you live long enough," Sophie added, smiling.

"That's it?" Mavis asked. "I thought there was more to the procedure."

"If there is, I'm not aware of it. And something tells me your stiff doesn't care whether there is or not, either," Sophie had to add.

"That's enough of your filth, Sophie. We have a job to do. You're welcome to stay and watch; otherwise, shut up and sit down," Ida said in an authoritative tone.

"This is your and Mavis's gig. I'll sit, thankyouverymuch." Sophie plopped herself down on the boxes in the corner while Mavis and Ida went to work.

Two hours later, the rope marks on Mr. Frank's neck were hidden and his *issue* was neatly tucked away in an adult diaper. He wore one of the suits from Mavis's Drop-Dead Gorgeous line of clothing. Ida's skill with makeup was undeniable, and the suit looked as though it had been custom-made for him.

No doubt about it, Mavis and Ida had found their niche.

Chapter 15

"Mom, you look like you've seen a ghost," Abby said. "Oops, forget I even said that; of course you have seen a ghost. More than once. You look terrible!"

Toots's mind was whirling with possibilities. She needed a minute to put them together. She pulled her chair out from beneath the kitchen table and sat down. "Abby, get me a glass of water, please."

Abby did as requested. "I heard a phone ringing, not your usual ring tone, Mom. What's going on?"

Toots didn't dare tell Abby about her private cell phone, fearing she'd give away her identity as owner of *The Informer*. So, not liking it, but knowing she had to keep the charade up a little while longer, she said, "I changed the ringer. I was sick of that old 'Take me out to the ball game' tune. I don't even like baseball. It made no sense to have that tune anyway—"

"Mom, you're blabbering. Stop, okay?" Abby placed a tall glass of ice water on the place mat in front of her mother.

Toots took a drink of water. "Yes, well mothers do that sometimes."

"Maybe other moms, but not you. Are you going to tell

me what's going on? Or do you want me to have Goebel resort to other means of torture?"

Goebel kept quiet for a few minutes, allowing them to talk without interrupting. He smiled at Abby when she mentioned his name. "Not something I would do," he chimed in.

"Please, I get enough verbal torture from Sophie," Toots informed them with a smile.

"She's got a mouth on her, that's for sure," Goebel said. "She's one heck of a gal, that Sophie."

Toots glanced at him. Yep, he was smitten. Big-time. *Good for them*, she thought. She just hoped Sophie was ready for a real man, one who'd treat her the way she deserved to be treated.

"Mom, are you okay?" Abby asked a second time.

Toots returned her focus to the here and now. "Yes, I'm just distracted, that's all."

"I can tell. So spit it out, Mom. Tell me what that phone call was all about. I know that's what has you in such a . . . *flutter*." Abby said the last word hesitantly.

Clearing her throat, then taking another sip of water, Toots knew she'd put off telling Abby and Goebel long enough. Why she felt the need to keep the call private, she didn't know, considering that half of LA was looking for Chris. She'd think of this as a good sign, the call coming to her. Meant Chris knew whom to call for help.

"I'm sure that was Chris calling." Toots looked at her daughter, whose eyes sparkled at the mention of his name.

Abby sat down in the chair across from her. Goebel leaned in closer.

"It was his cell number that showed up on the caller ID." Toots hated to tell Abby and Goebel about her phone's battery, but she had to. *It speaks volumes about my priorities,* she thought. "I haven't charged my phone for a few days, so the call was dropped." She waited for a reaction. When she didn't get one, she continued. "Chris's number came up, but there wasn't a message or anything." There, she'd said it, and now all they had to do was figure out where the phone call was placed from.

"You're sure it was Chris?" Abby asked in her reporter's voice.

"Unless someone else has his phone. It was his number."

"Let me see your phone," Abby said.

Just as Toots had expected, Abby wanted proof.

Toots hated to resort to such actions, but again, she reminded herself she didn't have much choice. "Do you think I don't recognize Chris's number? Good grief, Abby! I am not senile yet. I don't have to prove this. I can't believe you would even suggest such a thing." Toots was trying to appear indignant at her daughter's suggestion.

Abby rolled her eyes. "Of course you're not senile, Mom. I didn't mean to imply that you were. Go on, tell me what you were about to."

Toots took another drink of water. "That's it, Abby. There isn't anything else to tell. I heard the phone ringing, didn't get to it in time, and when I finally answered the phone, it went dead. End of story."

Goebel spoke up. "This is good. We can track down where the call was made through the pings in the towers and, hopefully, this will lead us to Chris. I have contacts, you know. Toots, let me have his number, and I'll get on it right away."

She recited Chris's number from memory. "Is that the same number you have?" Toots asked her daughter.

"Yes," Abby replied.

"Then let's allow Goebel to do his stuff, okay?"

Abby nodded. "Sure, Mom, but don't try to act like

you're telling me everything because I know you too well. I'll leave it alone for now, but later, you and I are going to have a talk, okay?" she admonished.

Toots wanted to spill the beans right there on the spot. She was not good at this . . . lying-to-her-daughter garbage. She could hide behind e-mails and FedEx letters until the cows came home, but lying face-to-face was a different matter entirely.

She would have to reveal that she was the face and fortune behind *The Informer,* eventually. Toots hoped when Abby knew the truth, enough time would have passed that her daughter would forgive her the lies she'd told. But that was for another time. She had to focus on doing whatever she could to help locate Chris before the press, especially one silicone-enhanced, lip-glossed Chloe Brown, destroyed him.

Wanting to say more but knowing it wasn't the time, Toots nodded in agreement. "When Chris is home safe and sound, we'll talk."

"You promise?" Abby asked, knowing Toots never broke a promise.

"I promise. Now let's focus on finding Chris. The sooner we locate him, the sooner we can have that talk." Again, Toots had the sudden urge to spill her guts right then and there, but didn't. *Soon,* she thought, *soon.* She'd been the puppeteer longer than she'd originally planned. It really was time to step out from behind the curtain.

While all this was going on, Goebel had been busy punching in info on his laptop and talking on his cell phone. He placed his hand over the speaker. "It won't take long to get the results. Told my buddy this was a life-or-death matter."

"Maybe you could come to work for me," Abby joked.

Goebel clicked off the phone and hit a few keys on his laptop before answering. "I'm too old to start a new career, but thanks. You ever need a background check or anything like that, you call me, okay?"

"Thanks, we have a guru at the paper who takes care of that type of thing, but if he's unable to make a connection in the future, I may take you up on that offer." Then, Abby reconsidered his offer. "Actually, there is something you could do for me, and I'll pay you for this myself. I've been secretly trying to find out who the mysterious name is behind *The Informer.* I've used every resource I have and I always come up empty. And I'd like to find that SOB who left me holding the bag, my former boss at the paper. Maybe after we locate Chris, you could help me locate the person who signs my paycheck."

Toots's heart rate shot up so fast, she thought she would faint. She grabbed the glass in front of her, drank the last of the water, then chomped on an ice cube. Her hands were shaking so badly, she put them under her legs so neither Abby nor Goebel would see them. She hoped Abby wouldn't notice the change. Toots knew there would be no getting around telling Abby now. Goebel was good, and Abby knew that. If he failed to locate the "mysterious" new owner, and the former owner, Rodwell Archibald Godfrey, known as Rag to his former employees, her daughter would become even more suspicious. Toots knew full well her days were numbered. Soon, she would have to tell Abby her big secret and hope for the best.

Goebel cast a quick glance at Toots. He raised his eyebrows when she shot him a killer look. "Uh, sure. Just let me know when you're ready."

Toots would discuss the problem with Goebel later.

"I will," Abby said, before turning to stare at Toots. "Mother, is there something wrong? Why do I have the sneaking feeling you know something I don't? Did you speak to Chris? Is he married? Did he run off with that stupid actress? Because if he did, you can tell me. I don't really give a good rat's ass what he does anymore. For that matter, he can stay wherever the hell he's been hiding for the past four days. *Idonotcare!*"

Toots smiled. Abby had it *bad*—real bad. "No I truly didn't speak with Chris." *At least that was the truth.*

"Well, don't tell me if you do. I hate him, okay?" Abby pushed her chair away from the table and stomped out to the deck. Chester and Coco shot out the door behind her. Toots was glad, as she wanted a few minutes alone with Goebel.

"I know what you're going to say, and you don't even have to say it, okay? Let's just say if I were to search"—he made air quotes with his large hands—"it might take me a while to locate such a huge corporation. All that corporate red tape."

Toots breathed a sigh of relief. A temporary sigh of relief, but for now, she'd take it.

"Of course. I understand," Toots agreed. Soon very soon, she'd come clean.

Abby stepped back inside, ending any further conversation. Chester and Coco panted at her heels and ran to the refrigerator.

"Okay, I know I promised you both a treat. Give me a sec, all right?" Opening the refrigerator, Abby quickly located Coco's supply of turkey breasts and pinched off small pieces for the couple and dropped them in their doggie dishes. Both dogs hightailed across the room to their bowls. "You two are so spoiled."

Toots waited patiently while Abby took care of the animals' needs. She needed to address the comments Abby had made about Chris.

After Abby rinsed her greasy hands, she sat down across from Toots. "Okay, go ahead, read me the riot act. I know that look on your face."

Goebel chose that moment to speak up. "I think I'm going to take a stroll. I don't get to see moonlight and beaches too often in my neck of the woods. You ladies mind?"

Both shook their heads.

"By all means," Toots said. "Just make sure you take your shoes off. Get the feel of the sand and all."

"Absolutely." Goebel winked at Toots.

She knew he was simply giving her and Abby a bit of privacy. He really was a gentleman. She would put in a few good words for him with Sophie. Not that he needed them, but it certainly couldn't hurt.

As soon as he escaped through the sliding doors, Toots spoke. "Abby, I know you didn't mean all those things you said about Chris. I know you're angry at him, and that's understandable. We both know Chris wouldn't purposely cause either of us to worry. And I know he's not the kind of man that would . . . shack up with one of those silly starlets he represents. He is a man of integrity, just like his father. I know you have strong feelings for him, Abby. If you didn't, you wouldn't have said those things." Toots paused for a few seconds, trying desperately to find the right words to say even though she wasn't one hundred percent clear on what it was she hoped to convey to her daughter.

"Why are you telling me this, Mom? What's your point?" Abby asked, her voice laced with impatience.

"Abby Simpson, I cannot believe you're talking to me this way! I swear you have it bad. That's what I wanted to talk to you about." *It is,* Toots thought.

"I'm sorry, I don't know what came over me. I'm tired, and yes, you're right. I am worried about Chris."

Toots leaned across the table and took Abby's hand in hers. "It's normal to worry about the man you love."

Abby stared at Toots, her face turning ten shades of red. "I'm worried about . . . his safety." She paused as though she were considering what she'd just said.

"Yes, that's it really. I just hope he isn't hurt. That's all. Yes, I care about Chris, but I don't think I am madly in love with him."

Toots chuckled. "Of course you are. I see the way you look at him when you think no one is noticing. You have a glow about you, a special look. That's the look of love. I'm quite familiar with it."

Abby laughed. "Yes, I suppose you are. But Mom, please let's not talk about Chris and me, you know, as a couple. I'm simply concerned for his safety. Let's leave it at that."

Toots knew when to shut up. And it just happened to be one of those times. Abby was right. Chris's safety was their main concern.

Chapter 16

The three women were quiet as they traveled back to the beach house. Sophie hadn't told Ida or Mavis about her vision, but they suspected something had occurred. As they had finished laying out Mr. Frank, Mavis had asked Sophie twice what had happened at the reading for Mrs. Leigh. Sophie told her she didn't want to talk about it at the moment, but would; she just needed a bit of time. They'd accepted her decision without question.

"Sophie, let's listen to the radio. There may be news of Chris," Mavis said in her sugary-sweet voice, which was really starting to grate on Sophie's nerves.

Sophie didn't want anything to taint her vision, no verbal or visual influences. Any media was out of the question. So much for allowing her time to muse over tonight's events. "I guess I can tell you now since waiting won't change the outcome, or at least I don't think so."

"Stop being so damn dramatic, Sophia." Ida used her given name, something she only did when she was in one of her I-am-queen moods.

"Kiss my butt, Ida. I'm not the drama queen here." Sophie made the turnoff to the beach house. Maybe she should wait until they were inside. That way, she would only have to tell her story once. Yes, that was what she would do. Toots could advise her, and Goebel, she couldn't forget him. Damn, she was falling for that big teddy bear of a man and wasn't sure if she liked the idea or not. Men were trouble. She knew that from her experience with Walter. She also knew not all men were drunkards and wife beaters. She smiled. Goebel was truly one of a kind.

Mavis reached for the radio button. Before she could push it in, Sophie placed her hand on top of Mavis's. "I don't want to listen to the news now. What I have to tell you could be influenced by a news report, and I don't want to be sidetracked. Let's wait until we're at the beach house. I promise I will tell you what happened tonight. I just want to wait so I do not have to tell the story twice."

"Oh, of course. I'm sorry! I just thought there might be some news," Mavis singsonged again.

"I hope whatever it is you have to say is worth hearing. Something tells me you're up to no good," Ida sniped.

"Don't start, Ida, okay?" Sophie turned into the driveway and saw that Toot's red T-Bird was there. Goebel was back from his investigation. Her heart warmed just thinking about him.

Shifting into PARK, Sophie removed the keys, and hit the unlock button so Ida and Mavis could exit the car. "I'm not saying another word to you until we're inside and I've had at least two cigarettes and a cup of coffee." Sophie hefted her small frame out of the large Escalade, then clicked the LOCK button as soon as Mavis and Ida had closed their doors.

The women hurried inside, where they found Toots and Abby sitting at the table. Sophie was the first to comment. "Where's Goebel? I thought he was here. Your hot wheels are parked out in the drive." She always referred to Toots's small sports car as a Hot Wheels toy.

"He went for a walk, said he wanted to see the moonlight and feel the sand. He hasn't been gone that long,"

Toots said. "Abby made a fresh pot of coffee. Who's up for some late-night caffeine?"

"Thank you, Toots, but I think I will just have a glass of mineral water. All that caffeine keeps me awake at night." As Mavis walked over to place a kiss on Abby's cheek, she saw Coco and Chester huddled in the corner. She located her water in the refrigerator, then sat in the chair beside Toots.

Ida rinsed her coffee cup, filled it with juice, then joined them. "Sophie is bursting at the seams with news, or so she says. She experienced something tonight but wouldn't tell me or Mavis, insisting we should wait so she would only have to tell her story once. I for one want to know what's so important."

Sophie listened to Ida run her mouth. She filled her cup with the hot brown liquid, grabbed a package of Marlboros, and headed for the deck. "I'm going to puff. Want to join me, Toots?"

"Not now. Abby hates the smell. You go ahead; we'll wait."

Sophie stepped outside, lit up, took a few drags off her smoke, then popped inside a minute later. "Okay, that'll hold me for a while."

"Soph, I wish you and Mom would stop smoking. It's gross, and it stinks." Abby waved her hand in front of her face.

"I will, Abby. Someday." Sophie slid into the chair across from Toots. "But not today. Soon, though, I promise."

"I'm dying to know what happened with Mrs. Leigh's reading. Please, don't keep us in suspense any longer," Toots said.

Sophie nodded, and took a drink of coffee. "Why don't I wait until Goebel returns? I'm sure he'll want to hear this, too?"

As if on cue, the glass doors opened. With his shoes in

one hand and keys dangling in the other, Goebel entered the kitchen. All eyes focused on him. "You gals okay?" Concern etched across his rugged face.

Sophie perked up, her eyes shining with delight. "Yes and no. We need to talk; you arrived just in time. I was telling the girls I didn't want to repeat this story if I didn't have to. You want coffee?" Sophie jumped out of her chair before Goebel could say yes or no.

He laughed. "You're darn right I do."

She brought the pot to the table, along with a cup. "Sit," Sophie ordered. Goebel did as she commanded.

"Now I know why I like this man," she teased. "He follows orders well."

Ida cleared her throat and rolled her eyes. "Wonderful, Sophia. Just wonderful! Let's stop flirting and get on with it. I want to go upstairs. I'm tired. It's been a long day."

"Okay. Ida's right. It has been a long day, and she and Mavis had their hands full this evening." Sophie directed her gaze at Ida. A huge grin spread across her face at the memory of the man at the funeral home. Not that he was dead, but what the girls had to deal with above and beyond the usual. She wasn't going to say anything to Toots or Abby, at least not yet. Chris was top priority.

Mavis's face turned white, Ida's matched her bright pink hair. "Not now, Sophie," Ida ordered. "Just get on with it."

"I agree. Spit it out. We need to stop screwing around. This is important," Toots said, sobering them all up to their current reality. "Tell us what happened."

"I've never experienced anything like this before." Sophie paused. "It scared me. I had to wait a while before I could do the reading. The woman was a bitch. Well, sort of, just a tad on the weird side. She didn't introduce herself, hadn't a clue what manners are." Sophie looked at Ida. "I know what you're going to say.

"As I was about to start placing the tarot cards, I became so dizzy I was sure I would pass out. Obviously, I didn't, but I kid you not . . . I had a vision. I saw a brilliant white light, then an incredibly bright shade of red. It blew me away because this woman was waiting for me to start turning the cards, and I was in the midst of this . . . this experience. I'm not sure how long it lasted, and at first I couldn't figure out what the images were. Frankly, for a minute or two, I thought I was about to lose it, but I didn't. I ran out to the car without much of an explanation. Then I sat there a good long time until I figured out what I had been seeing."

"And?" Ida hissed.

"I'm sure what I saw was a red car covered with a mountain of snow."

Chapter 17

"That fits with the information I just received. One of the reasons I turned around and came back. I had a colleague run a check on Chris's phone records. He was able to locate the last phone call made from that number. The last possible tower that could have recorded a ping was a tower five hours away from here. If the information I have is correct, and I have no reason to believe it isn't, Chris is somewhere just southeast of Lake Tahoe," Goebel informed the others. "Do any of you know if he has a GPS tracking device on his cell phone?"

"I'm sure he does. I just can't believe he's in Lake Tahoe. What would he be doing in that area?" Abby asked, then remembered Chris's friend Steve, who was staying at Chris's condo. "Chris has a friend staying in his condo, and I'm sure he knows where Chris is." Abby took her cell phone out of her pocket. "I'm going to call Chris's house. Maybe Steve will answer and tell me where the heck Chris took off to, though he swore he didn't know when I asked him. I'm not sure I believe him now."

Quickly, she punched in his home phone number, and paced back and forth. Several rings later, Abby was greeted by Chris's overly cheerful voice. "Hey, I'm not here. Sorry, peeps. Call my cell." His answering machine. She clicked the END button on her phone.

"Nothing. I don't even know if Steve's still there. Maybe I need to take another drive over to Chris's condo and question that guy again. I can't believe Chris could leave, let someone stay in his condo, and not tell them where he was going. What do you think, Goebel?"

"It can't hurt."

"Should we call the police, check to see if there have been any accidents in that area? Maybe Chris is in a car somewhere and needs help. Maybe he's stranded." Toots's voice was laced with new worry.

"Sophie, you said you saw something red in your vision, right?" Abby questioned.

"Yes, a very bright red. It had little sparkles in it, almost like there was a gold-colored glitter mixed in with the paint. And the snow, wouldn't that mean something, Goebel? If he's in the Lake Tahoe area, he could be at one of those damned ski resorts. Stuck without phone reception." Sophie was excited. Maybe her vision really did mean something, maybe she and Chris were connected psychically.

Abby yanked her phone out of her pocket. She placed her hand over the mouthpiece. "I'm calling one of my sources at the police department. Give me a minute." She stepped outside on the deck.

Now in full-blown investigator mode, Goebel asked, "Do any of you know if Chris has any friends in the area? Any business he might have had? A reason for being in the Nevada area?"

"Chris has friends all over the country. If he had business to attend, I don't know that he would've told anyone, especially me. He's a grown man. He comes and goes as he pleases," Toots explained. She'd never had a reason to question Chris's business practices, and now she wished she had been a bit more nosy. In a motherly way, of course.

"I think we can work with the cell phone. I should be able to pinpoint his exact location. I just need to make a couple more calls. Cross your fingers he has a GPS locator on his phone."

Goebel removed his cell phone from his pocket. He punched in a number, then walked out to the deck, where Abby was trying to hook up with her police department source.

Toots had a flash of the two of them working together. A pair of private investigators. Both knew the business. With Abby's reporter instinct and Goebel's experience and contacts, they would make a formidable team. A tabloid, a bakery in Charleston, and a private investigation firm. She could follow in Warren Buffett's footsteps and become a pillar of American enterprise. It was something Toots could give serious thought to later.

As soon as Goebel stepped out, Abby came back inside. Toots knew immediately something was wrong from the look on her face. "You heard something about Chris?" Her stomach did a flip-flop, and her heart pounded so hard she thought it would burst in her chest. She inhaled through her nose, then exhaled, slowing her heart rate.

"No. I just remembered that Laura Leigh has a bright red Toyota Prius. The license plate is IMASTAR. Tell me that's not conceit."

Sophie perked up. "I knew my vision was real. I am *not* cracking up. Thank you, Big Man upstairs!" Sophie raised her fist high in the air, then genuflected.

"No one questioned whether your vision was real or not," Toots said. "I've witnessed what you can do, and if you say you had a vision, then you had a vision."

Abby appeared as though she'd had the wind knocked out of her. She slumped on a kitchen chair. "I think Chris and Laura Leigh are holed up together. I think they did go snow skiing. I can't figure out why Chris's car was towed into his mechanic's, but I'm sure he has a good explanation for that. Maybe he was following Laura, and he actually had car trouble. Knowing that little tart owns a red car, the pings from the cell phone towers, then add all of that with Sophie's vision, I don't see how anyone could reach any conclusion other than that Chris and Laura are having a little ski vacation/minirendezvous. I'm sure they're not listening to the news."

"Abby, stop right now! You will drive yourself crazy. Goebel will find him, then we can get to the bottom of this. I know he's in trouble, but I don't think it's anything that will put him behind bars. Let's just be patient," Toots said, even though she was anything but patient herself. She knew the scenario Abby was imagining, and she did not want her hurt in any way, shape, or form.

"It's going on five days, Mother. The media are swooping down on this story like vultures." Abby caught her faux pas. "The national media. Television. *E!, Entertainment Tonight, Inside Edition.*"

"*The Informer* is a national media outlet, too, Abby. Don't you have your top reporters hanging out at Laura's apartment and those two nightclubs she and Chris frequented?"

Mavis decided to join in the conversation. She directed her attention to her goddaughter. "Is there anything I can do? Would you like a cup of herbal tea? It's quite calming, you know."

"Thanks, but I'm good," Abby said to Mavis.

"If you change your mind, just say the word."

"You're so good to me. All of you," Abby said.

Goebel chose that moment to come back in from the deck.

Abby looked at her three godmothers and her mother.

"I don't know what I did to deserve you all, but I'm not going to question it. Now, Goebel, let's put this GPS technology to work."

Goebel put his laptop on the table. His fingertips raced across the keyboard at lightning speed. He looked up for a moment. "If his cell plan has a service locator, I'll be able to find his location right now. Or pretty darn close. Some cell-phone providers have what they refer to as a family locator. Personally, I think it was designed to keep tabs on teenagers, but it's handy when you want to locate someone."

As he turned his attention back to his laptop, his hands flew over the keyboard again. He stopped and watched as a satellite image filled the screen. "Look at this." He pointed to an image of terrain. The image was green, brown, and blue. He tapped the arrow key, and the image cleared, showing an area of mountainous terrain.

Toots leaned over Goebel's shoulder to view the screen. "What does this mean?"

Goebel pointed to a tiny yellow flashing circle. "This tells me Chris's cell phone is GPS-enabled, and working."

"What if his battery died? Would you still be able to track him?" Sophie asked.

"Yes. The tracking device is implanted inside certain phones. Doesn't matter if they're dead, or even turned off. You can track the phone number as long as the phone isn't damaged by water or fire, or destroyed by some other means."

Ida finally spoke. "Then why can't you just drive to the place where the cell phone is?"

"I'm going to contact the local authorities, have them do what we in the business call a safety check. If all this technology works, we'll be able to solve this mystery within a matter of hours."

"You think so?" Abby asked. "We've tried using this a

couple times at the paper. Trying to follow a few A-list celebs. It never worked."

"They probably have their cell numbers scrambled. There's a computer program that does that. I would expect a celebrity who doesn't want to be found would have used such a program," Goebel explained.

"Makes sense," Abby said.

"So what do we do now?" Toots asked Goebel.

"Once I contact the authorities, all we can do is wait to see what they find."

Chapter 18

For the fifth night in a row, Chris slept in front of the fireplace in a sleeping bag. Laura slept on the pullout sofa. No way was she going to lower herself and sleep in a "nasty old sleeping bag"—her exact words.

Because of the severe cold, Chris had closed off the other rooms to preserve what heat they had. He could've clicked on the central heating system and used the generators, but he didn't know how much longer they would be stranded. His goal was to keep them alive. Part of staying alive meant keeping warm.

With several thick blankets under his sleeping bag, the hardwood floors weren't too bad to sleep on. Again, he thanked Johnathan for thinking and planning ahead. Had it not been for his friend's foresight, Chris had no doubt they would have succumbed to the cold temperatures by now.

At this point, his only hope of being located rested with Toots and the call he'd tried to make. She was a smart woman. She wouldn't wait around for him to call again. Toots was a woman of action. As soon as she discovered he wasn't where he should be, she'd do whatever was necessary to find him. The downside: he hadn't told anyone where he was going, hadn't bothered to contact any of his associates in San Francisco to tell them he wouldn't be attending the conference. Hell, when he thought about it, he hadn't even told Steve where he was headed, just that Steve could stay in his condo for a week and to make himself at home.

Chris wondered if Abby realized he wasn't where he was supposed to be. But why would she? He hadn't told her of his plans, either. He was totally screwed unless the weather did a complete about-face. Laura's hybrid vehicle was great on the open road. It sucked at driving up a mountain. He was sure he'd ruined the transmission, but at the time all he could think of was getting Laura somewhere where no one would find her. He could only imagine the fallout if she'd gone ahead with her plans to blow up the studio.

Rolling onto his side, Chris stared long and hard into the fireplace. A log fell from the neatly stacked wood, sending orange, red, and yellow embers dancing up the flue. Small bits of the hickory log fell, shooting sparks toward him, only to die out as soon as they hit the protective screen. Hissing and popping sounds were the only noises in the large cabin. Except the wind. It had been blowing so much he'd gotten used to the sound; it had become a white noise of sorts. When he'd gone out earlier to see if he could get a cell-phone signal, the wind was bone-chillingly cold, biting right through his clothes.

Punching the down pillow back into shape, he reclined into its softness. He pushed his entire body farther into the sleeping bag. Warm, fed, and beyond tired, he closed his eyes and drifted into a dreamless sleep.

A loud pounding jolted him awake. He didn't know how long he'd been asleep. He hadn't bothered looking at the time when he'd called it a night because time just seemed to go on forever out there in the middle of nowhere. The only concept of time was day and night.

Scooting out of the sleeping bag, Chris stuffed his feet in the dress shoes he'd had on when he'd left Hot Wired.

"What the hell is all that noise? I am *trying* to sleep!" Laura called out from the sofa. "This is like living in a frigging cave!"

"Be quiet, Laura. It's just someone knocking on the door." *Maybe Johnathan. Maybe anybody.* He didn't care who it was as long as they took Laura Leigh away. He had a mental image of men in white jackets strapping her into a straightjacket. He smiled. Best thought he'd had in days.

More banging.

"Hang on," Chris shouted as he raced to the door. "I'm coming!"

Icy gusts of air smacked him in the face when he opened the door. Two burly sheriff's deputies, bundled in heavy coats and tall black boots that hit just below the knee, stood on the wraparound deck.

Quickly, Chris stepped aside, pushing the door all the way open. "You guys must be freezing. Come inside."

They stomped their heavy black boots on the mat before coming inside. "Are you Mr. Clay?" the taller of the two asked.

"That would be me," Chris said as soon as he closed the door. "I have a fire. Why don't you guys warm your hands and tell me why you're here?"

Laura sat up on the sofa, her attention focused on the two deputies. "Did that jerk from the studio send for me? I knew it! See, Chris? They can't make that movie without me!" She jumped off the sofa and headed for the stairs. "I'm going to get my clothes on. Don't you two dare leave without me. And Chris, you're fired," she said as she ran up the stairs.

"I have no clue what the young lady is talking about. We're here to check on a"—the deputy flipped through a small black tablet—"Mr. Christopher Clay. Your cell phone pings led us here."

"Yesssss! Toots, right?" Chris said exultantly. "I knew that old gal would shake things up once she saw I'd called. Never underestimate a woman." Images of Abby flashed before his eyes. He smiled. Damn, she was as smart as her mother. Prettier, too, but he'd never say that to Toots.

The deputy with the tablet skimmed through the pages again. "No, it was a man. Goebel, uh, doesn't have a last name. Just Goebel Global. A private detective."

"I'll be damned! They've called in the big guns. This is Toots's doing."

Both deputies stood in front of the fire, removed their gloves, and spread them across the hearth to dry.

"We're here to make sure you're unharmed, that's all. A safety check. Looks like you and the girl are nice and cozy. I guess we can be on our way," the shorter deputy said.

"No, no, no! You cannot leave here without us! We're trapped here. Hell, I don't even *like* that little twit!" Chris's voice was loud enough to reach upstairs.

Pounding feet raced downstairs. Laura Leigh was wearing the skimpy cocktail dress she'd had on five nights ago. "Did I hear you correctly? Did you just refer to me as a *twit? A twit?* You are fired, Chris Clay, do you understand? I will drag your ass through the mud when I get home."

"Is there something going on here that we should know about? Something more than two stranded lovers? If there is, well . . . then"—Deputy Short looked at Deputy Tall—"we'll have to take you both in."

For a second, Chris couldn't form the right words. Only a second. "No, no, *no!* You have it all wrong. First, we are *not* lovers. God, I can't even . . . never mind. I'm her attorney, she's my client—"

"*Was* your client," the twit interrupted.

"I am her *former* attorney. She is my *former* client." Chris watched Laura while he spoke. He did not trust her at all. "We were . . ."

We were what? he thought. *I was trying to prevent my client from committing a major felony. She threatened to blow up World Con Studios.*

As much as he despised the little shit, he couldn't rat her out. "You know, you guys are right. We came up here to have some time alone, to ourselves, if you know what I mean?" Chris looked at both men. Each wore a smile the size of an extra-large donut. *A cruller,* he thought.

"You lying sack of sh—!" Chris placed his hand over her mouth before she could finish. He pulled her close to him, and whispered in her ear, "You want me to tell them you're an arsonist?" He felt the fight leave her. Gently, he removed her from his embrace. Her sky-blue eyes were cloudy, dark with anger.

Tough, he thought.

"We had an argument earlier. She's mad," Chris said to explain her behavior.

"You're damned right I'm mad, you jerk!" Laura raised her hand high in the air, but before she could move her arm in a full swing, Deputy Tall caught her arm. "Domestic violence. You want me to take you in?"

It was all Chris could do to keep a straight face. He wished she had succeeded in hitting him. She thought staying in the cabin was roughing it. Wait until she had to take a pee in front of a jailhouse full of prostitutes, drunks, and dope dealers.

Laura yanked her arm out of the deputy's grasp. "Don't put your slimy hands on me again, or I'll have a sexual harassment charge against you so fast you'll never work again!"

"Laura," Chris said. "Enough. These gentlemen are here

to help us. I know you're upset, but you need to calm down."

She rolled her eyes. "So you're telling me World Con didn't send them?"

Chris wanted to say the studio wouldn't have sent the lowliest security guard in search of her, but stopped. It would only make a bad situation worse. Until he was out of there, safely at home, he would keep his thoughts to himself.

Out of the blue, Deputy Short said, "I would swear I've seen this young lady before."

Deputy Tall replied, "I think I have, too. You think she's one of those call girls we brought in last month?" He looked at his partner.

Chris grabbed Laura so fast it startled her. "Shhh," he whispered in her ear.

"I'm not sure, maybe we ought to take her in and run her fingerprints. Just in case."

That was going a bit too far. Chris knew he'd best speak up before the backwater deputies decided to take matters into their own hands.

"Have either of you seen *Bloody Hollow?*"

Chris saw the recognition as they stared at Laura. He smiled. Maybe the guys had teenagers, had watched the gory movie with them.

"You're *that* actress!" Deputy Tall exclaimed.

"I'll be damned. Carrie Sue would give just about anything for your autograph. She's got posters of you all over her bedroom walls. Just got her a T-shirt for her birthday last week. It's your face, but you got blood running out of your mouth. Her mom didn't think she should wear something like that, said it was sacrilegious," Deputy Short told them, a strange excitement glistening in his eyes.

Laura's demeanor went from smart-ass to sweet actress immediately. "I'll do better than that. If you have a cell phone with a camera, I'll pose with you. I bet your daughter would like that. She could brag to her friends."

"Damn right! I will take you up on your offer." Deputy Short fumbled around in his heavy parka for his personal cell phone. The two deputies took turns taking their picture with Laura. She was all smiles, and they were giddy as two pigs in a mud bath.

"Want me to snap one of the three of you together?" Chris asked.

"If Miss Laura doesn't mind," Deputy Tall said.

"Laura?" Chris asked, even though he knew she was eating up every second of the attention the deputies showered on her.

"Of course not. I would be honored," she said in her fake/nice voice.

Chris took the outdated cell phone, surprised it actually had a camera. "Okay, on the count of three, I want everyone to smile. One, two, three!" He clicked the photo, checked to make sure it wasn't blurry, then took a second shot. "That ought to please all the guys at the sheriff's department."

Chris gave the deputy his phone. The two admired their photo, and he knew before the night was over it would be plastered on Facebook, Twitter, and maybe the front page of the local paper. Laura would love that.

Wanting to get out of there now that all the niceties were over, Chris figured if he didn't remind the pair of deputies why they'd actually come in the first place, it wouldn't surprise him if they'd opt to spend all night taking pictures and listening to Laura tell them about all the actors and actresses she was friends with.

Grinning mischievously, Chris said, "I guess I'd better put out the fire and get things ready to go. I know Laura wants to get back to her fans."

"Yes, I do. I have movies to make and fans to entertain, so, yes, we had better get ready to go." Again, she used her fake/nice voice.

Chris had to admit that she could act. She was too young and too spoiled to realize her childish behavior was going to cut her acting career short. Maybe this would teach her a lesson. Maybe she wouldn't be so quick to throw temper tantrums and threaten the studio that kept her employed. Time would tell. Right now, he just wanted to get off the mountain. And more than anything, he wanted to see Abby.

He *needed* to see Abby because, when he did, he would tell her how he felt. He would tell her he loved her.

Chapter 19

They'd consumed four pots of coffee, and Toots was as wired as the Energizer Bunny. Ida and Mavis said they were going to stay up in case there was news of Chris, and were in the den watching *Mildred Pierce* for the hundredth time. Sophie and Goebel lounged on the deck. Abby was asleep in Toots's bedroom, with Chester and Coco. Toots was alone in the kitchen when her house phone rang.

Scrambling to answer before the machine picked up the call, Toots said, breathlessly, "Hello."

"Is this Theresa Loudenberry?" a male voice asked.

Instant warning. No one, and she meant absolutely no one, called her Theresa. This couldn't be good. "Yes, this is she."

"Please hold," the male voice said.

Toots had visions of medical examiners, morgues, and drawers that were really freezers with lifeless bodies inside. *Please,* she silently prayed, *do not let this be one of those phone calls. No!* She could not bear it if something happened to Chris. He was her son; she didn't care who'd given birth to him. She loved him as much as she loved Abby. Images of funerals, *events,* flashed before her eyes.

"Toots? Can you hear me?"

Jolted out of her macabre thoughts, Toots said, "Chris? Is this really you?" She crossed her fingers.

"You weren't expecting this call, I take it?" A deputy had to make the call, make sure I wasn't calling Germany or Italy." Chris laughed, and it felt good.

"Oh, Chris, I have been so worried about you! We thought you were dead or that something else terrible had happened. Abby has been crying her eyes out. She doesn't think I know that, but she has. Goebel is here. We called him because the media said you did something vile, or rather they implied you did something vile to that silly actress, and I said there was no way. You're a man of integrity—"

"Toots! Stop, slow down. I'm fine. Really. I'm at the sheriff's department in Mammoth Lakes."

All of a sudden Toots felt as light as a feather, carefree, as though the weight of the world had been removed from her shoulders. "Oh, Chris, thank God you're all right. I won't ask anything. As long as you're safe, that's all that matters. When are you coming home?"

"Good question. It's still snowing like crazy. I'm without a vehicle, and the closest airport is in San Francisco. They tell me there's only one flight a day to LA and that it doesn't leave until four in the afternoon. If I can hitch a ride to San Francisco, I'll be home tomorrow. Actually later tonight."

Toots glanced at her watch. It was after three in the morning. "I can send a private jet to pick you up. You'll be home much earlier."

"Thanks, but I can wait. It's been damn near a week, and another day won't matter."

"Chris, it will matter. I take it you haven't watched the news or had Internet access?"

"Not where I was, no. Why? Is there something I should know?"

Toots took a deep breath. Hating to be the bearer of bad news, she spoke quietly, hoping to soften her words. "The media thinks you're involved with Laura Leigh's disappearance." There was no other way to say it.

"What? What disappearance?"

Toots heard the shock in his words. "The police say you're the last person she was seen with."

"Of course I was. The little brat is right here next to me. If I hadn't followed her, she would've either killed herself or someone else. She was smashed. She told me she was going to blow up World Con because she didn't get the role in *Bloody Hollow, Two.* She was supposed to meet her agent; I think he was going to deliver the bad news, but she knew it already. Someone let the cat out of the bag. I called her while I was following her, convinced her to pull over. I had to get her the hell out of Dodge before she acted on her threat. Took her to Johnathan Kline's cabin. My intentions were to drop her off, let her stew for a few days, then, when I returned from my conference in San Francisco, I planned to take her back to Los Angeles, let her face the music."

For the second time in a matter of minutes, Toots felt as if she were floating on air. Maybe she would be like those puffy images of Bing Crosby and Aaron Spelling she'd seen hovering at her bedside two years ago.

"Toots? Are you there?" Chris's voice was laced with concern.

"Yes, yes. I think I should send the jet. The sooner you and Laura Leigh are back in town, the sooner we can put this nightmare behind us."

"I guess you're right. I can't believe this silly spoiled girl has caused so much trouble. It's no wonder World Con won't hire her for the second gig. I'll ask the deputies to drive me to San Francisco. If they won't, then I'll see if I can borrow a car."

"Ask them while I have you on the phone," Toots instructed.

"Hang on." Chris covered the mouthpiece, but Toots could hear him.

When he came back on the line, he said, "They'll drive me, but it will take a few hours. Why don't you have the jet waiting at say, nine in the morning?"

"I'll make it happen," Toots said. "Where will you stay tonight?"

"This is a tourist town. There's all kinds of hotels, according to the deputies who rescued us. By the way, thanks. I knew I could count on you, Toots. I tried for days to call and never could get a signal. When I finally saw those bars, you were the only person I knew who would get the ball rolling. I can't thank you enough. This girl is out of control. It's a miracle I didn't strangle her."

"Chris, whatever you do, don't let anyone hear you say that. Promise me?"

He laughed. "I'll keep those evil thoughts to myself."

"Smart man. I'm going to make your arrangements. Will your cell phone work where you'll be staying?"

"Yes, I'm sure. It's dead though, so give me a couple hours to get settled, get it charged. Call me if you can't arrange for the jet."

"Chris Clay, *can't* is not a word in my vocabulary. You of all people should know that by now," Toots admonished in a teasing way.

"True. Okay, I'm outta here. Oh, one more thing, Toots. When you see Abby, tell her I want to speak with her about something vitally important. Could you do that for me?" Chris's tone was serious.

"Consider it done, dear." Toots clicked off.

Sophie and Goebel came inside, and both were staring at her.

"That was Chris! He's fine, the actress is fine, and he'll be home as soon as I send a jet to fly him back to Los Angeles."

Sophie's eyes sparkled like jewels. "Hot damn! Was I right? Was he stranded in the mountains?"

"Yes, you were right, Soph. At his friend's cabin." Toots grabbed Sophie by the arms and pulled her in a friendly embrace. "You're good, Sophie. I knew you were right all along. Now, let's tell the others."

Ida and Mavis were both asleep in the den. *Mildred Pierce*, aka Joan Crawford, had just told Veda she would kill her when Toots clicked the DVD player off. Sophie clapped her hands together so loudly, Ida and Mavis practically flew out of their chairs.

"What in the world!" Mavis cried out.

"You're going to hell in a handbasket, Sophie Manchester," Ida said. "Don't ever do that again. I'm sure to have a heart attack."

"They're right, Soph. Too noisy for us old broads. But I have fantastic news. I just spoke with Chris. He's fine, the actress is fine, and he'll be home sometime this evening. Isn't that the best news you've heard in forever?" Toots felt like dancing.

"Oh, that is wonderful news!" Mavis exclaimed. "That poor young man. Is he all right? Was he in the wilderness?"

"That is good news. Did he say where he's been for the past five days?" Ida asked.

"He was in a friend's cabin. Apparently he was trying to prevent Laura Leigh from destroying the movie studio. I'm sure he'll tell us all about it when he gets here."

"I can't wait to hear this." Sophie stood next to Goebel,

his arm casually draped around her waist. Toots couldn't be happier for her very best friend. But there was one more person she needed to deliver the good news to.

Abby.

Toots had a message to give her.

"What's going on, Mom? I heard everyone talking." Fear, absolute terror, stark and vivid, glittered in Abby's eyes. "Is there something you're not telling me?"

"Yes. Chris said he had something to tell you, said it was vitally important," Toots explained. "He's coming home tonight."

Suddenly, Abby was blissfully happy, glad to be alive, knowing that the sun would shine tomorrow and the next day and the day after that. She'd worry about the details later. Chris was coming home!

As soon as Toots had told everyone that Chris and Laura had been found, and both were safe, everyone had gone back to bed. Sophie and Goebel had opted to sleep in the den. She had been very specific when she explained to Goebel that he was not allowed in her bedroom, that she wasn't that kind of girl.

Ida had muttered, "Yet," and they'd all had a great laugh.

Chapter 20

KABC was the first to break the news, courtesy of a tip from *The Informer*'s editor in chief. Helen Woods, the reporter Abby trusted, broke through a network game show to share the new information with the public.

"Missing actress Laura Leigh and her attorney, Christopher Clay, are alive and well. There has been much speculation in the past five days as to their whereabouts. It was first reported the couple were seen together at the popular Los Angeles nightclub, Hot Wired. Later, Mr. Clay's Toyota Camry was found and towed in by his mechanic. The vehicle was combed for evidence. Nothing incriminating was found in Mr. Clay's car. A family member hired a private investigator, who immediately jump-started the investigation by checking Mr. Clay's cell phone for a GPS signal. When it was discovered, the Mammoth Lakes Sheriff's Department located Mr. Clay and Laura Leigh in a luxury cabin in the mountains. Sources say the couple were happily ensconced inside during what forecasters have been calling the storm of the century. The couple was unharmed, and no further investigation is expected. The two lovebirds will arrive at Los Angeles International Airport sometime before noon . . ."

Abby clicked the television set off, more than a bit

ticked at Helen Woods for implying Chris and Laura were two lovers purposely hiding from the public. "I shouldn't have told her. Let them do their own investigation. This is a cruddy business to be in, too much competition."

"I never thought I'd hear those words coming from your mouth," Toots said. "Are you going with me to the airport? Chris did say he wanted to talk with you. I think he said his words were 'vitally important.' I wonder what's so important. Aren't you the least bit curious?"

"No, I have to get back to the paper. I can't let Josh run the place forever. Tell Chris I'm glad he's okay." Abby's voice betrayed her emotions.

"Abby, let's wait to hear from Chris. You don't know that he's involved with Laura Leigh, and I know damn well that's what you're thinking. I believe it's just as he said. That news anchor didn't know what she was talking about. I heard the implications in her report and saw the smirk on her face as she reported it. She isn't as straight up as you said."

Toots knew Abby was anguished over Chris, was uncertain what he felt for her. She would bet the contents of her bank accounts that Chris was head over heels in love with Abby. Toots couldn't voice the words because they weren't hers to say. She could only offer her daughter love and a shoulder to cry on if that was what it came down to.

"Yeah, and it's the last time I'll ever share a tip with her."

"Do you think you could manage to get away for a celebratory dinner tonight? We could go to Moonshadows, that new place on the Pacific Coast Highway. The reviews are good, and of course it's on the beach." Toots wanted to celebrate, kick up her heels, shout to the world because her son was alive and well. It was her new mission for the day—to bring Abby and Chris together.

"I don't know, Mom. It depends on the paper, what's going on there."

"Call me if you can make it. I think we'll need to make a reservation."

"Okay. Think Mavis would care if I leave Chester again?" Abby asked her mother, then turned around when she heard Mavis enter the kitchen.

"Chester can stay as long as he likes. Coco is so smitten, I'm sure her little heart will break when he goes home." Mavis gave Abby a hug, then proceeded to make another pot of coffee.

"Not that organic stuff today, okay? It kills me. And Sophie hates it, too." Toots grinned.

Mavis filled the coffeemaker with spring water. "You girls should have told me. To be quite honest, I'm not that fond of it myself. We'll go back to the Maxwell House." She busied herself searching through the cupboards for the coffee as, behind her back, Toots gave Abby a thumbs-up.

"Will you at least stay for breakfast?" Toots asked her daughter. "It's early. I've plenty of time to get to the airport."

"I can stay for breakfast. No fruit, Mavis. My system can't take it," Abby said, smiling.

Toots burst out laughing. "That's what we've been trying to tell her. While very healthy for your body, too much isn't, if you know what I mean."

"I get it, Mom."

Toots laughed again.

A tired but happy-looking Sophie entered the kitchen. "Did I hear the word *coffee?* I think I've slept about twenty minutes. You can't imagine . . . never mind. Where's the coffee?"

"No, no! Don't you dare tell me something, then not tell me anything." Toots cried. "Does that make sense?" she asked Abby.

"Yes to me, no to the rest of the world," Abby replied.

The coffeemaker made its final gurgling sound to indicate the pot was finished. Mavis removed six cups from the cupboard. Following her lead, Sophie removed the half-and-half from the refrigerator, saw the sugar bowl in its normal position—the center of the kitchen table.

Toots, Sophie, Mavis, and Abby gathered around the kitchen table, each sipping her coffee. Goebel and Ida were nowhere to be found.

"Exactly how long have we been sitting here?" Sophie asked out of the blue.

Abby looked at her watch. "Three minutes."

"Why do you want to know that?" Toots asked.

"Duh. Has anyone seen Ida? Goebel was just getting out of the shower when I came into the kitchen."

Sophie let her words hang in midair. Without saying anything, Toots and Abby raced upstairs to Ida's bedroom. Toots banged on the closed door. She waited a few seconds, then repeated her action. "Ida, if you're in there, you'd better get your ass out here, and I mean now!"

A second later the bedroom door opened. With her bright pink hair standing in every direction, dark circles beneath her eyes, Ida looked rough, and that was being kind. "Were you sleeping?" Toots asked.

Ida turned her back on them, went back inside the room, and sat down on her bed. She motioned for them to come in. "Exactly what do you think I've been doing? Eating bonbons?"

Neither Toots nor Abby knew what to say.

"Mavis has the coffee ready. I'm just surprised you're not up," Toots finally said. "I came up to make sure you hadn't kicked the bucket."

"Well, give me fifteen minutes, and I'll be downstairs. I have to shower and do something with this horrid-looking Ringling Bros. and Barnum & Bailey clown hair. And I *will* get you for this, Toots. You just wait. Revenge is sweet. Now, both of you, downstairs," Ida ordered imperiously.

Leaving no room for further discussion, Toots and Abby headed out of the room. "What did you expect to find in her room?" Abby whispered.

"Goebel," Toots said flatly.

"Mother! You should be ashamed of yourself. Why anyone who has eyes can see he adores Sophie, and she is wild about him." Abby shook her head, an ornery grin turning her mouth upward.

"I know, but Ida can be very seductive when she wants to be. I want Sophie to have a chance with Goebel. I like him. A lot."

"You don't trust Goebel to keep his hands to himself?"

Toots stopped before they reached the bottom of the stairs. "Yes, I trust him. It's Ida I don't trust. At least not when a handsome, rugged man like Goebel is in the picture."

"I really think Ida knows Goebel is off-limits, Mom. There are plenty of men out there, and I'm sure Ida is quite aware of that. Don't tell the others what you just told me, or you'll stir up a hornet's nest."

"You're right. Now, let's go make breakfast." Toots had only slept an hour and needed another pot of coffee. The day ahead promised to be full of fun and, just maybe, a surprise or two.

Mother and daughter returned to the kitchen to find Goebel, of all people, turning the oven on, one of Mavis's aprons tied around his newly slimmed-down waist, and a large mixing spoon in one hand.

"You can cook?" Toots asked, her shock evident by the look on her face. She'd been through eight husbands, and not one of them had ever attempted to make a meal. Sophie had truly lucked out.

Goebel chuckled. "Yes, ma'am. You can't remain a

bachelor your whole life and not learn how to cook. New York takeout gets old. I bought a beginner's cookbook, and before you knew it, I could make chateaubriand. Give those folks over at The Food Network a run for their money." He turned his back to her, but continued to talk. "I'm gonna make you gals a batch of Southern biscuits with homemade strawberry preserves."

Toots raised her eyes when she saw Sophie grinning at her. She mouthed, *You are a lucky lady* and Sophie's grin became even bigger. She just shook her head and winked.

"Is there time for this? I have to pick Chris up at the airport."

Goebel laid the mixing spoon down, rinsed his hands, then dried them on his apron. "Actually, I've made arrangements for Chris and Laura to be escorted out of the airport through the general aviation area. An old pal of mine works security at LAX and said he would take care of it. He owes me a favor. With all this publicity, the last thing any one of you needs is to get caught up in all the hoopla. I was gonna tell you, Toots, but you weren't here when I came downstairs. That okay? I hope I didn't overstep my bounds."

Actually, Toots was relieved. She knew that the press would be out in force. The thought of getting mobbed wasn't pleasant, but she wanted to see Chris so badly she would do whatever she needed to do, as any mother would. "I can't thank you enough, Goebel. Of course you haven't overstepped anything. Why, you're practically family. Right, Sophie?"

Behind Goebel's back, Sophie flipped Toots the bird and grinned from ear to ear.

"Right, Soph?" Toots insisted, smiling broadly, ready to burst out laughing at her friend's discomfort.

"Kiss my tush, Toots. And the dogs' tushes, too," Sophie shot back.

Abby cringed, and Mavis had the good grace to quickly turn away. Toots grinned.

"I think we should talk about . . . the strawberry preserves Goebel is making. I thought it took, like days to make that kind of stuff," Abby said, hoping to change the topic of conversation. She looked at Toots and shook her head. "What about it, Goebel, how do you actually make strawberry preserves so quickly?"

Keeping his back to them, Goebel spoke while he worked. "Just mash up a bunch of strawberries, depending on how much jam you want to make. Add some sugar, a little bit of fresh lemon juice, boil it, and let it cool. Since I'm not actually going to jar the stuff up, I don't need sterile jars or pectin. Just plain strawberries and sugar."

"I am impressed, Goebel. And here I thought making jam was an all-day affair." Toots emphasized the last word, unable to resist getting in another dig. Sophie shot her the bird for the second time.

Before Toots could respond, Ida descended the stairs as though she were royalty. "Good morning, Abby. Did you get any rest at all? You look tired. I think you should give yourself the day off. It's not like you'll get fired or anything," Ida stated matter-of-factly.

Toots turned ten shades of white. Sophie's eyes bulged out like a cartoon character's, and Mavis chewed her bottom lip like a piece of gum.

As casually as she could manage, Abby asked, "Is there something going on among the three of you that I should know about? You've all been acting odd ever since I got up."

Toots felt like a deer caught in the headlights. Should she spill the beans? Or run across the kitchen and yank that hot pink hair out of Ida's blabbering head?

Sophie caught Toots's eye and shook her head left to right, which Toots assumed meant Sophie could read her mind and it wasn't the time to open that particular can of worms. Toots nodded back.

"We're just tired. This excitement with Chris and Laura has been too much for us. Right, girls?"

Toots shot Ida the *I-will-get-you-for-this-later* look.

"Your mother is right," Mavis said hastily. "We've all been very tired."

"What are we doing that makes you think we're acting odd?" Sophie asked.

Toots almost screamed, then bit her tongue. Literally.

The oven timer went off. Toots wanted to jump in the air and shout hallelujah. But if she did, Abby would absolutely know something was wrong. Maybe she would even question Toots's sanity. *No,* Toots thought, *now is not the time to mention the fact that I am the moving force behind all those e-mails and FedEx letters.*

"Hot biscuits," Goebel said. "Sit down and let me serve you gorgeous ladies breakfast."

"I'm starving," Toots said. "And I'm so grateful we're not eating fruit and oatmeal for a change."

"Well, shame on you. I will remember that the next time I serve breakfast." Mavis sat down beside Toots. "I'm only having one biscuit. They're bad for you, and the sugar in the jam is, too. Goebel, you know you can't eat this way all the time?" Mavis chastised him. She'd helped him lose almost a hundred pounds and didn't want to see him pile it back on one biscuit at a time.

"I know that, but this is a special day, that's all. It's not every day that a prodigal son, so to speak, returns home." Goebal placed hot biscuits on a platter. "Losing all that weight was the best thing I've ever done for myself. One biscuit isn't enough to pull me back into that old trap. You have nothing to worry about, Mavis."

She sighed. "Thank you. I didn't mean to be rude. It's just so hard to lose and even harder to keep off."

Glad for the change of subject, Toots reached for a biscuit. "We've all come a long way in the past two years. I can't even imagine Mavis being a pound overweight now. She really has helped all of us change our diets."

"Since when? You still eat Froot Loops when we're out of town. You tell everyone you're a vegan, yet you use cream in your coffee and eat cheese like a mouse. I'm sorry, I don't see a big change, Tootsie," Sophie said.

Goebel poured the hot strawberry jam into three small bowls. "You won't need butter, so don't ask."

Abby eyed her mother and godmothers, then spoke. "Why do I feel like I'm back in elementary school? We're all adults. We can eat whatever we want. If it's not healthful, then it's our own asses that are on the line. And Goebel, I would like some butter. The real stuff that Mom keeps hidden in the back of the fridge."

Sophie took the butter out of the Ritz Cracker box on the bottom shelf. "I want some, too. No healthy crap for me."

"I just might persuade you to change your mind, Miss Sophie. I know I have much more energy now. Energy for other things." Goebel wagged his eyebrows up and down. They all laughed.

"Nope, I won't ever change who I am for a man. Never again, noway, nohow. I spent too many years wasting my life doing Walter's bidding. If you don't like what you see, look somewhere else."

Suddenly, the atmosphere in the kitchen became oppressive, as though an angry spirit had permeated their space, trying to drain the life from its occupants. Sophie jerked up, her attention focused on the door that led to the dining room in which she held séances. "The phone is going to ring," she said.

Rolling her eyes, Ida commented dryly, "That's certainly

a big revelation, Sophia." She'd refused a biscuit, and was sipping her coffee like it was poison.

Sophie continued to focus on her feelings. This was something new. Not gut instinct, but something else she couldn't put a name to. A sense of dread filled her. It frightened her. More than the images of the snow and the car. This was . . . frightening, something she had no control over.

"Are you all right? Sophie?" Abby said her name but got no response. "Mom?"

Toots got up, stood behind Sophie, and placed her hands lightly on her shoulders. She leaned close to her and whispered in her ear, "Are you having a vision?"

Before Sophie could answer, as if on cue, the telephone rang.

Chapter 21

"Let me get that," Toots said, walking away from Sophie, who appeared as though she were in a trance of sorts and wasn't reacting to any stimuli.

"Yes, hello." Toots's words were rushed. "What? Yes, this is she speaking. Yes, of course I know her. I've known her forever." Toots paused, listened to the voice on the phone. "Oh my gosh! When? Do whatever you can, is that understood? I will be there as quickly as I can charter a plane. If there is any change, call my cell phone." She recited the number, then placed the phone back in its stand.

"Mother! What . . . Are you okay?"

Toots struggled to keep it together, she had to. "No . . . uh, yes, yes. That was Charleston Memorial. Bernice suffered a massive heart attack two hours ago. Jamie found her when she stopped by the house this morning before going to the bakery."

Everyone in the room was silent, then all eyes went to Sophie.

Toots spoke first. "This is what you were talking about, isn't it? You had a vision, right?"

Sophie came out of her stupor as fast as she'd entered. "No, I just had a very bad feeling wash over me. I didn't see this. Just felt something. And I knew it would be from the telephone ringing." Sophie shot Ida a *told-you-so* look. "What exactly did the doctor say?"

"That was the ER nurse. Jamie is at the hospital with Bernice right now. Her condition is not good." Toots's eyes filled with tears. Damn that Bernice. She'd been hanging around that damned butcher Malcolm Moretti too long. She'd probably gorged on the finest cuts of beef Malcolm offered. Bernice had been a good customer for more years than Toots could remember. And to think . . . no, she would not think. She would not even consider life without Bernice. Not yet. She just wasn't ready.

An idea blossomed, and before it had a chance to disappear, she picked up the phone. She dialed 411. "Yes, I need the number for Cedars-Sinai Medical Center in Los Angeles, the cardiac floor if you will." She was going to do whatever she could for Bernice. Her icon, Evangelista Thackeray had died last year of congestive heart failure. Supposedly, she'd had one of the best cardiologists in the world. If he was good enough for Evangelista Thackeray, then Toots figured he was good enough for Bernice.

"Thank you," She hung up and dialed Cedars-Sinai. "I need to speak to Dr. Bruce Lowery. It's an emergency."

All attention was focused on Toots while she waited for the doctor to take her phone call. She was surprised when the doctor actually took the call. She took it as a good sign, something that was meant to be. She explained who she was and why she was calling. She added that she'd been considering making a large donation to Cedars-Sinai's cardiac wing. To the tune of $5 million. Just as she'd expected, that got the doctor's attention and kept it.

"Can you travel to Charleston, South Carolina, immediately?" Toots asked, once the formalities were over. Time was not on her side.

"Of course, Ms. Loudenberry. I will have to make a few

arrangements with my colleagues, then I'm all yours," Dr. Lowery assured her. "I will call Charleston myself, talk to the head of cardiology, and find out what's going on with your friend."

"I have a jet that should be at the airport anytime now. I can offer you a ride, if you like," Toots said.

"That won't be necessary, but thank you. Cedars-Sinai has a jet for just such emergencies. I'll contact the pilot immediately."

Toots spent the next few minutes giving the doctor Bernice's information. As soon as she finished, she called Dr. Joe Pauley, her longtime physician and a very dear friend. His voice mail picked up. "Joe, this is Toots. Bernice is in the hospital, and I hope like hell that's why you're not answering your phone, but just in case it isn't, can you get to Charleston Memorial ASAP? I'm preparing to leave Los Angeles, but will be available for the next couple hours if you want to call. Otherwise, I will call you the minute our plane touches down." She ended the phone call. Worry, stark and vivid, glittered in her brown eyes.

Abby came around the table and placed her arms around her mother. "I'm so sorry, Mom. What can I do?"

Toots seemed to be considering her daughter's question. Her thoughts were a jumble, and she couldn't focus on either problem. First Chris, and now Bernice.

"Mom?" Abby repeated.

"Yes, I—no there isn't anything anyone can do." To Toots's dismay, her voice broke slightly. "Pray. We can all pray that Bernice survives. Now, I have to call that jet, make sure they can take us back to Charleston."

Again, Toots made a phone call. The company assured her the jet would remain on the ground as soon as it touched down. While she was beyond being happy that Chris and Laura would soon be safely on the ground, there would be no time to have that celebratory dinner at Moonshadows. Soon, though.

But first things first. Bernice was practically family, like the older sister she'd never had. Toots would do whatever was humanly possible to make what was left of her dear friend's life as close to perfect as she could manage. Knowing there would be time for unhappiness later, Toots shifted her shoulders high, raised her chin just a notch higher—her determined look, as she liked to think of it—then cleared her throat. "Who wants to go to Charleston with me?"

Abby was the first to speak up. "I don't think I can, but if you need me to go, I will."

As much as Toots would have liked her daughter's company, there wasn't really anything Abby could do in Charleston. Toots needed her at the helm of *The Informer*. The last thing she wanted was to worry about the management of the paper. Abby was better off staying in Los Angeles.

"You need to stay here and take care of things at the paper—right, Sophie?" Toots wanted her friend's seal of approval now more than ever.

Sophie caught the hint. "Absolutely. Abby needs to stay here and take care of Chester and Coco, and that rag of a paper. You never know when some movie star might check into rehab. Important stuff, Toots."

In other circumstances, Toots would have flicked Sophie the bird. However, she knew what her friend was trying to do, and she appreciated it. Crazy-ass Sophie was trying to keep things as normal as possible by acting like a smart-ass.

"Sophie, you should be ashamed of yourself," Mavis said. "And what about the animals? Does this mean I'll have to leave Coco behind?"

"I'm teasing, Mavis," Sophie said.

"You know it might be a good idea to leave Coco with Chester. I can stay here at the beach house with the pooches. Take them to work, too," Abby said.

"I can go, too, if you need me," Goebel added.

Sophie grinned.

"Yes, I think you should come along, too," Toots said, then turned to Ida. "What about it? Can you and Mavis get away now?"

Ida and Mavis nodded their heads in agreement. "Mr. Frank was our last—"

"*Stiff*?" Sophie threw in.

Toots smiled. Leave it to Sophie to do whatever she could to lighten up the moment. Friends. How precious they were, though there was no way in hell Toots was going to say that now. Maybe later, she'd tell each one just how special they were to her. Or maybe not. Toots knew they were all quite aware of it.

"You have such a vulgar mind. You ought to be ashamed of yourself, especially at a time like this," Ida said. "For the record, I will go and do whatever I can to help out. Bernice won't be able to clean, once she's home from the hospital. I am an expert at it, as you all know. Count me in," she added with a genuine smile.

"And me, too. Someone will need to be there to help Bernice out with her new diet. She'll need lots of tender loving care, and plenty of fruit and fiber. Whole grains are quite good for keeping one's arteries clean. I'll make sure she doesn't clog the new ones," Mavis said. "But I'm not sure about leaving Coco behind."

At the mention of her name, the little pooch growled from her position in the corner. Chester was curled up next to her like the true love he was.

"Never mind. I think these two lovebirds could use some time alone."

"Then what are we waiting for? Every minute counts," Toots said.

Sophie, Ida, Mavis, Goebel and Toots scrambled away like ants at a picnic. Fifteen minutes later, and after a half dozen hugs to and from Abby, they were on their way to Los Angeles International Airport.

Once again, Toots was needed at home.

Chapter 22

Toots had shared a few much-needed minutes alone with Chris when they arrived at LAX, enough to learn what had happened between him and Laura. Nothing. She smiled. Abby had nothing to worry about. Chris explained a few other things to her as well. Yes, it was going to turn out much better than she'd dared to hope for.

Since Toots and her friends spent most of the night awake, waiting for news of Chris, they all slept for most of the flight to Charleston, waking up only when the copilot announced they were half an hour from landing at Mount Pleasant Regional, a small airport that handled private aircraft in the Charleston area.

Toots looked at her watch. It would be early evening, Eastern Standard Time, when she arrived in Charleston, and even later when getting to the hospital. She had called Pete before they took off from Los Angeles, and he'd offered to pick them up at the airport and drive them directly to the hospital. She accepted his offer.

Jamie had used Toots's Range Rover to drive to the hospital, so that left Pete with her Lincoln. Between the two vehicles, they would manage to get to and from the hospital and wherever else was necessary. Dr. Lowery had assured her he would take care of his own transportation when he arrived in Charleston.

Toots had a few reservations about the doctor's almost instantaneous willingness to take Bernice on as a patient, sight unseen. Of course there was the $5 million she'd promised for the cardiac wing. Money spoke quite loudly sometimes, and she was grateful she had plenty to spread around. She would use it any way she could for her friends and family. It all came down to love.

Their arrival in Mount Pleasant was greeted with none of the pomp and circumstance of their recent trip to Sacramento, when Sophie had met with California's first lady. Toots peered out the cabin window and spied Pete waiting with the Lincoln just outside Atlantic Aviation, a small general aviation facility.

The automatic stairs were barely down before Toots sprang out of the small jet onto the tarmac. With only small carry-on baggage, none of them had to worry about waiting for luggage. All except Goebel had plenty of clothes and necessities at Toots's home in Charleston. He'd packed lightly for his trip from New York to California, so it was simply a matter of taking his small luggage from one place to the next.

Toots gave the pilot and copilot each a thousand dollars in cash. She wanted to make sure, when and if she needed their services again, they would remember her. Thankful that she kept a few thousand in cash stuffed in her pajama drawer at all times, she'd found two bank deposit envelopes in her purse, putting enough cash in for the pilots to at least have a nice weekend getaway in the near future.

"I can't thank you guys enough," she said as she placed the envelopes in their hands. "I don't think Ida left any claw marks on the armrests. If she did, let me know, and I'll take care of the repairs," she joked.

"Anytime. You have our card," the pilot said. "Take care, and I hope your friend does well."

Toots nodded, then headed to the small airport terminal. Pete was as antsy as ever.

Not bothering with the usual niceties, Toots asked, "Have you heard anything from the hospital?"

"Dr. Pauley is there now. They did a heart catheterization as soon as they got her stabilized. She's in recovery now. I'm not too sure what happens next. I just know she'll be glad you're here."

"I wouldn't be anywhere else, Pete. Now come on, we're wasting time. Let's get to the hospital. I want to be there when Bernice wakes up."

Without further ado, Pete helped put their carry-ons in the large trunk, then they crammed themselves into the Lincoln. Toots was glad Mavis and Goebel had downsized weight-wise. If not, they would've needed another vehicle.

Less than an hour later, Toots was racing down the halls of Charleston Memorial, following the directions to the cardiac floor given to her by the clerk at the reception desk.

The odors of rubbing alcohol, burnt coffee, and hopelessness permeated the fifth floor, on which they located a small waiting room with a sagging beige sofa, an older model television set suspended from the ceiling, and a table stacked high with heavily thumbed magazines. The room was empty and silent except for the sound of a soda machine humming in the background.

"Stay here while I see Bernice. As soon as I have any news, I'll be back." Toots quickly left Sophie, Ida, Mavis, and Goebel in the waiting room reserved for friends and family members only, or so the handwritten note taped to the door read. She hurried back down the long hall, where she followed a large black-and-white sign that read RECOVERY.

Saying a silent prayer that Bernice would make it through this, Toots was practically jogging down the corridor when she spotted Joe Pauley.

Winded, she called out, "Joe." As soon as he saw her, he said something to a nurse dressed in light green scrubs, then held his arms out to her. Toots went limp in his embrace. She'd been brave for hours and hours, and now it was all she could do to stand up.

"Hey, old girl, this isn't like you." Joe brushed her auburn hair away from her face when she looked up at him. Tears spilled from her eyes.

"No, it's not." She sniffed.

Joe pulled a handkerchief from his shirt pocket, something she rarely saw.

Blotting her eyes and blowing her nose, she went through her shoulders-back, chin-up routine before speaking. "Okay, give it to me straight. No sugarcoating. Is she going to live?" She hated being so forward, but time was important. Bernice's life was at stake.

"I just spoke with Dr. Becker, he's the on-staff cardiologist and a damned good one. Bernice has five clogged arteries, and needs bypass surgery as soon as an operating room is available."

Toots's heart plunged; her stomach felt like a million butterflies were at war with one another. "Oh Joe, this is not good. Bernice isn't going to like this one little bit." Toots's voice was full of sadness. "She hates going to the doctor. She must be scared out of her mind. Can I see her? I need to reassure her, let her know I'm here and that everything is going to be just fine. Because it will be just fine. I hired Evangelista Thackeray's cardiac surgeon to assist or do whatever needs to be done." Toots ran a shaky hand through her hair, gluing the red-orange tendrils to her cheeks from her tears.

"I'd heard, though I don't know why. Dr. Becker is top-notch, Harvard Medical, worked with Robert Jarvik back in his early days."

"And that means?"

"Robert Jarvik, artificial heart."

"Oh, that's impressive. In case Dr. Lowery doesn't work out," Toots said, then thought how silly she must've sounded.

A squeaking sound from the opposite end of the hall caused Toots to turn away from Joe. A tall man wearing light blue scrubs with bright red Crocs waved at them.

"That's Phil Becker," Joe told Toots. "Must have some news."

He's in his mid- to late sixties, she thought as she observed him. Tall and lean, with a thick head of curly brown hair, a masculine jaw revealed a five o'clock shadow. Dark circles rimmed his electric blue eyes. *He looks like a doctor,* she thought, *but he doesn't wear glasses.* That bugged her. What kind of doctor, especially a *heart surgeon,* didn't wear glasses? Didn't they do all sorts of intricate stuff with tiny veins and even tinier needles?

"Joe," Dr. Becker said, holding out his hand.

"Phil, this is Theresa Loudenberry. Bernice is her housekeeper," Joe said by way of introduction.

Toots shook his hand. A shock of electricity shot up her arm. It felt like she'd stuck her fingers in an electrical socket. Quickly pulling her hand away, she watched him. He seemed puzzled. "Ah yes. Joe has been singing your praises for a very long time. It's good to finally meet you." Dr. Becker smiled.

And when he smiled, Toots's heart lurched. *Shit!* Maybe she had heart trouble now. No, she didn't. She had . . . *nothing.* She was there to find out what she and modern medicine could do to extend Bernice's life.

"How is Bernice? Can I see her yet?" Toots asked, her words all rushed together like a two-year-old's.

"She's in recovery now. She was pretty much out of it when I checked on her a few minutes ago. She should be waking up soon, and you can see her then. Anesthesia affects everyone differently."

"Exactly what does that mean?"

"Toots, don't start. I know you like being in control and running the show, but now isn't the time," Joe said, before turning to Phil. "Is there an operating room available yet?"

"That's one of the reasons I'm still here. They're finishing up a transplant in Operating Room C. As soon as it's ready, I want to get Bernice in there, repair those arteries. Her vitals are all good, and she appears to be in good health otherwise," Dr. Becker said, then turned to face Toots. "You want to go downstairs and have a cup of coffee with me?"

Toots placed her hand on her chest. "Are you talking to me? You want me to have *coffee?* And you think Bernice is in *good health?* Son of a—"

"Toots! Enough already! Bernice is in good hands. Calm down. I think we all could use a cup of coffee. It's going to be a long night," Joe said.

Toots didn't know if she should laugh or cry. She was in the middle of yet another crisis, and this *heart surgeon,* who was about to cut open Bernice's heart, wanted to know if she wanted to have coffee with him! What kind of surgeon had *coffee* before performing open-heart surgery?

"Where exactly is Dr. Lowery? I am donating a hefty sum of money to his cardiac unit. You would think he would have had enough time to scrub up, or whatever it is he should be doing." Her hands shook, and she wanted a cigarette so badly she was ready to sneak inside the ladies' room and risk causing the fire alarms to go off. She grabbed her left hand with her right to prevent herself from snatching the Marlboros from her purse.

Joe cupped Toots's elbow and steered her away from the recovery room. "I'll have him paged." He stopped and spoke to a young woman at the nurses' station. Within seconds, Dr. Lowery's name was called over the hospital's paging system.

"Thanks," Toots said. "I guess I am a little flustered. I'd kill for a cigarette right now."

Joe leaned over and whispered into her ear, "Don't let Phil Becker hear you say that. He'll ream you out like a high school kid. He hates smokers."

She glanced over her shoulder. Dr. Becker was right behind her. He smiled when he saw her. "He's right. I hate smokers."

"Then you certainly won't like me. I try to smoke at least two packs a day. Three if I'm bored." A slight smile brightened her face.

"Then I can almost guarantee you'll wind up on my or some other doctor's operating table before too long," Dr. Becker said pleasantly.

If Toots hadn't heard the humor in his voice, she would have told him to kiss off, but he was teasing her. Part of her appreciated his attempt to humor her, and another part of her, the part that worried about poor Bernice, thought him crass and arrogant for even trying to show he had a sense of humor.

"Don't hold your breath," Toots said dryly. At the end of the hall was the waiting room. She stopped just outside the door and turned to Joe. "You're not leaving yet, are you?"

"No, I'm here for the long haul. Bernice is my patient, too. I'll be observing the surgery." He paused as though considering his next words. "I would never try to tell you what to do, but Lowery hasn't answered his page, hasn't made an attempt to let anyone know he is here and ready for surgery. Between you and me, I'd forget about him and let Phil do the surgery."

Toots listened to his advice, watched Dr. Becker step inside the waiting room and introduce himself to the others. She heard him tell Sophie that Bernice was still in the recovery room.

"I want the best for Bernice. Dr. Lowery is the best."

"Says who? Evangelista Thackeray? Hardly. She isn't alive, remember? Who else recommended him?"

Toots had to think. She was sure she'd heard his name mentioned before, just couldn't recall where. "I don't know, Joe. I just know he's the head of cardiology at Cedars-Sinai. Doesn't that speak for itself?"

Joe shook his head. "You do like that Hollywood stuff, I'll give you that. But remember, it's really not your decision to make. As soon as Bernice comes out of the anesthesia, she'll make that choice. It'll save face if anything."

Toots wrinkled her brow in disgust. "I don't care about saving face! You of all people should know that. I just want Bernice to have a chance, that's all."

"Trust me, Toots. She will get the best care possible. We might not have the reputation that Cedars-Sinai has, but we're good. Phil is good. Why don't you let Bernice make the decision? After all, it is her life," Joe cajoled.

Taking a deep breath, Toots nodded. "True, but what am I supposed to tell Dr. Lowery? He did drop everything to fly out here. Not many doctors do that anymore."

"To the tune of five million dollars, I would fly across the country, too. Damn, Toots. Where is all that vaunted common sense of yours?"

In the pit of my stomach, she thought.

Maybe Joe was right. Maybe Dr. Phil Becker was as good as, if not better than, the absent Dr. Lowery. At least he was there, and that alone was one point in his favor.

Anyway, Joe was right. It was not her decision. Why had she assumed Bernice would want some big-shot Hollywood doctor? She didn't know what she'd been thinking. Bernice needed a local doctor, someone in for the long haul.

What had *she been thinking?*

"As much as I hate to admit it, you're right. I was thinking of myself, I guess—the best, top-notch, all that money could buy." Suddenly Toots was ashamed of herself. Money did not buy happiness, nor could it save Bernice's life. Yes, she would see that Bernice had the best medical care, but in all of the tension, Toots had lost her common sense. Dr. Lowery would get his donation. She was a woman of her word, but he didn't have to operate on Bernice to receive it.

Another nurse, one wearing teal green scrubs with teddy bears all over them, came racing to the waiting room. "Dr. Pauley, your patient in recovery is asking for you. She's awake and doesn't seem very happy to be here."

"Thanks, Karen. I'll be right there." Joe entered the waiting room, said hello to everyone, then asked Dr. Becker to step outside. Toots remained in the waiting room, allowing the two professionals a few minutes alone so they could discuss Bernice's case in private. Besides, she didn't need to hear all the medical mumbo jumbo to know that her dear friend was in trouble, big-time. She was frightened enough as it was.

Sophie looked dog tired. Mavis's hair had flattened from the humidity, and Ida still had the hot pink hair. Her eye makeup was smeared, and she really looked like she was on her last mile. Goebel looked a bit rumpled, but his eyes were bright, and he seemed more alert than ever. Those few hours of rest on the plane had made a big difference for him. Toots remembered that he'd been a cop for more than thirty years. He was probably used to grabbing what sleep he could on the run.

"Why don't you all have Pete take you to the house? Jamie is here somewhere, and she can take me home later."

Pete had remained downstairs—told her he didn't want to get in the way. Toots knew better. Good old Pete was afraid of hospitals and doctors. Just like Bernice. She smiled. Southerners did have their share of superstitions.

"I'll stay here with you," Sophie said. "I'm not even tired."

Toots knew Sophie was lying, but she needed her. "Thanks, Soph. I'd like that."

Ida and Mavis looked relieved, but Toots knew they would stay if she had asked them to. And Goebel, too.

"Maybe you could have Pete run to the grocery store? When Bernice gets home, she'll need all that healthy food Mavis and Goebel are crazy about. You could get some fresh vegetables, toss all that red meat she keeps in the freezer." Toots wanted to send them away, but didn't want them to feel as though she didn't need them. She did need them. All of them. Now more than ever. And that's when she thought of Abby.

"My gosh, I haven't called Abby! I promised her I would!" She took her cell phone out of her purse and was about to punch in her daughter's number when Mavis stopped her.

"I called her, told her there was no news. Said I would call her when we knew something definite," Mavis explained.

"Thanks. I don't know where my mind is."

"You're worried about Bernice," Ida said. "You've spent the past week worrying about Chris. You need a break, that's all. Maybe when we know more about Bernice's condition, you and I can find a hairdresser, someone who can fix this"—Ida lifted a hand to her head of hot pink hair—"stuff."

They all smiled.

"I'll do that," Toots said. "Now, Pete is waiting downstairs. I promise that Sophie or I will call as soon as we have news."

After they said their good-byes, Sophie and Toots followed Joe and Dr. Becker to the recovery room. Sophie looked at Dr. Becker, and lifted her eyes in question.

Toots rolled her eyes, and mouthed *Kiss my ass*.

Sophie slid her hand to her shoulder, her middle finger prominently displayed for Toots alone to see.

They both laughed.

It was going to take a sense of humor and a lot of prayers to get through the next few days.

Chapter 23

When Toots saw Bernice, she completely broke down, falling into Sophie's arms. Bernice was surrounded by monitors, beeping machines, and tubes coming out of every visible orifice.

"You bawl bag." Bernice's voice was scratchy, hardly a whisper. She reached for Toots's hand.

Toots stepped closer to Bernice's bedside and let the tears flow, but she had a grin on her face. "Kiss my wrinkled old ass."

Bernice took a shaky breath. "Can't. Take all day. Don't have that much time."

That sobered them all. Joe stepped up to Bernice's bedside, looked at the numbers on her monitors, then cleared his throat. "You remember what happened to you?"

Bernice nodded. "In the kitchen." She lifted a frail hand and placed it across her chest. "Pain." She tapped her chest with her fingertips.

"You had a heart attack. We've looked at your arteries, and I hate to say this since you've been under my care for a long time, but you've got some blockage, and we need to make a few repairs." Joe allowed Bernice a few minutes to soak up what he was telling her.

"Am I gonna die?" she asked.

"We're all gonna die someday, but you're not going to die today," Joe answered her.

Toots wished she shared his confidence. How could he say such a thing to poor Bernice? Give her false hope? But then Toots realized there really wasn't anything else he could say. She knew he didn't want to tell her she might die; what kind of doctor would tell a patient she was going to die right before open-heart surgery? Yes, Toots knew Joe would explain the risks to Bernice, but they would be fast and sweet. The benefits, he'd explain as slowly as possible.

Dr. Becker came to Bernice's bedside, and took her pale hand in his. "I'm the guy that looked inside your arteries. I think we can fix you up, but there are a few things you need to know first. If you have any questions, please feel free to interrupt me at any time, okay?"

Bernice nodded. Toots took her other hand and squeezed. Sophie grabbed Toots's empty hand in hers. They listened while Dr. Becker explained what had happened and what would happen during surgery.

"We just did a cardiac catheterization. That's why you're here in the recovery room. We inserted a small tube through a large blood vessel in your leg, and injected an X-ray dye into your circulatory system. You've got five areas that need immediate attention, but the good news is, even though you had a pretty nasty heart attack, there doesn't appear to be too much actual damage to your heart."

Bernice nodded and squeezed Toots's hand so hard, Toots thought it might break.

"We'll do what we call an on-pump open-heart bypass. You'll be put to sleep under general anesthesia, and we'll begin by harvesting blood vessels that we'll use as the grafts. There is a vein in your leg called the great saphenous vein, and it's what we usually use because we're able to create multiple grafts from it. Once we remove the vein, we'll open your chest area by making an incision along the sternum—your chest bone. I'll cut the sternum, which will allow me to open your chest cavity. Now this might sound scary, but I do this every day, and while this is major surgery, it's very successful. The outlook for a full recovery is very good.

"In the traditional procedure, the heart is stopped with a potassium solution, so I won't have to work on your heart while it's moving. We will have you hooked up to a heart-lung machine, which will do the work of your heart and your lungs. I will take the grafts removed from your leg and reroute blood flow around the blockages. As soon as the grafts are complete, we will get your heart started again in order to provide blood and oxygen throughout your body. I'll close your sternum to its original position, then we'll 'close you up.'

"Barring any complications, we will have you in ICU until the anesthesia wears off. This might scare you; it is what most patients fear more than anything. You'll have a breathing tube while you're sedated. Chest tubes will be sticking out all over you—they always remind me of that old Frankenstein movie." He smiled.

"The tubes are inserted around the surgical area to help remove any blood that might've collected around your heart. As soon as you wake up, the breathing tube will be removed. If you can breathe fine on your own, great. If not, we'll have to hook you back up to the ventilator, and the breathing tube will have to be reinserted. When we get to this point, and I have no reason not to believe otherwise, you'll stay in ICU for twenty-four hours or so, then we'll get you up, maybe in a chair. You can even walk if you feel like it. And then the real fun begins." Dr. Becker was smiling the entire time he explained.

Toots eyed Joe Pauley, who continued to monitor Bernice's vitals. Sophie let go of her hand and practically raced out of the recovery room.

Toots was shocked at her behavior, but shouldn't have been since Sophie had experienced such odd visions the past week. Maybe she'd had a vision of poor Bernice! Had she seen that Bernice wouldn't survive the surgery?

"She probably needs to smoke," Toots said, hoping to explain Sophie's sudden departure.

Toots thought Bernice looked tired and suggested to Dr. Becker and Joe that the three of them leave the recovery room so Bernice could rest.

A slick Hollywood hunk lingered in the hallway just outside the recovery room entrance. With his close-cropped black hair, unnaturally blue eyes, and tanning-bed look, Toots knew without an introduction that this was the famed heart surgeon who'd cared for the great movie star Evangelista Thackeray. Dr. Lowery was wearing a silk Armani suit, a white shirt with French cuffs, and shoes that were surely handmade from the best Italian leather money could buy.

"Dr. Lowery, I'm Theresa Loudenberry; I spoke with you on the phone."

"Ms. Loudenberry, wonderful to meet you. Such generosity, too." Dr. Lowery held out his hand. For reasons she couldn't fathom, Toots did not want to touch this man, this slicked-up doctor who dressed in silk suits before surgery. She kept her hands at her sides.

"Yes, well I . . ." There were no words to name what she felt then. Fortunately, Dr. Becker and Joe introduced themselves.

"Great, just great. Now where is the patient? I'll need to run more tests, do my own evaluation. You did a heart catheterization, correct? I'll want to look at those results, possibly do another. I like to be as thorough as possible. My concern is always the patient."

No one said a word. Both doctors looked at Dr. Lowery as if he had grown another head out of the side of his neck. Even Toots stared at him. Oh shit! She knew if Bernice had heard those remarks she would be ready to cuss someone out. And in this case, that someone would be the famous heart surgeon to whom she'd promised $5 million. Famous or not, she wasn't going to allow him to cut into Bernice's chest and remove a single thing, let alone patch up her heart. Why *had* she called this . . . gigolo?

She almost started laughing right there on the spot. Toots knew her obsession with the once-famous movie star was over. She'd let silly movies and Hollywood rule her life a little too much.

Chapter 24

"Dr. Becker is quite familiar with the patient, and he's local," Joe explained to Dr. Lowery after Dr. Becker and his team took Bernice into surgery.

Toots had made an instant decision based on her gut feeling of what she thought Bernice would want her to do. Dr. Lowrey had been understandably upset, but as soon as Toots told him she would still donate the $5 million to Cedars-Sinai, he seemed almost relieved. "Then if I'm not needed here, I suppose I should see what kind of entertainment Charleston has to offer."

Toots almost choked, but somehow managed to suggest several upscale restaurants in the Charleston area. She also told him that anyone who was anyone must have a praline from The Sweetest Things Bakery. She left out the fact she was a half owner. She would make sure Jamie made a *special* batch of pralines just for him if he was still in town tomorrow. Toots smiled at the thought.

As soon as Dr. Lowery disappeared, Sophie reappeared. "I hope like hell that . . . man isn't doing Bernice's surgery. He's evil, I swear! The second I laid eyes on him, I had the same feeling I had right before you got the phone call telling you about Bernice. Surely he's not the real thing?"

"That's why you ran out of the room?"

"Yes, I was absolutely terrified of the feelings I was having. His vibes, karma whatever you want to call them, are evil. How do you know this man and why did you insist he be the one to take care of Bernice?" Sophie asked.

Toots didn't know those things herself. Only that he'd been Evangelista Thackeray's physician, and she'd been Toots's secret heroine ever since she saw her in *Black Beauty*. Throughout the years, she'd followed her career and her many marriages, something they shared in common.

"I don't know." Toots's adulation of the great actress seemed silly and childish now.

"I think we should hold a séance as soon as we get back to your house."

"So you really didn't run out of the recovery room because you had a bad feeling about Bernice's surgery?" Toots asked, still not one hundred percent convinced.

"I wouldn't lie about something like this. You should know that by now," Sophie said.

"Of course you wouldn't. I don't know why I even said that. Let's go to the cafeteria and have a cup of coffee. Jamie is waiting for us. She sent me a text message earlier. Poor kid has been here all this time, and I've yet to see her. I told Joe to call my cell the second Bernice is out of surgery."

"Great, I want to be here when the old broad wakes up. See if she had one of those near-death experiences people are always talking about."

"Good grief. Do you have to be so damned morbid?"

They waited at the bank of elevators. As soon as the doors swished open, they stepped inside, pushing the C button for the cafeteria.

"I'm not morbid," Sophie said. "Just psychic."

"I do believe you are. I just wish it hadn't taken all these years for you to find out. Just think of all the grief you could've saved me. I sure as hell wouldn't have married that cheapskate, Leland."

They laughed, then the doors opened, preventing any further conversation.

Only a handful of people were in the cafeteria when Toots and Sophie entered. The lights were dim in virtue of the lateness of the hour. A group of nurses seated at a round table in the corner were giggling at some private joke. Two doctors sitting across the room from them appeared to be engrossed in a stack of papers.

Jamie was seated at a table close to the cash register. She saw them and waved, her smile as bright as sunshine. Her once-blond choppy-short hair was a soft warm brown that reached her shoulders. She was much prettier than Toots remembered, pretty enough to give Abby a run for her money.

"I've missed you so much." Jamie stood to give Toots a warm, welcome-home hug. "And you too," she said, hugging Sophie.

"I ordered you both coffee." Jamie removed a plastic food storage bag from her backpack. "And I knew you'd want some of these, so I had Lucy bring a fresh batch over before we closed shop earlier." Jamie placed the bag of pralines in front of her.

"Oh, I have been craving these! Thank you so much." Toots removed a praline from the bag, then offered one to Sophie. "Is Lucy the new girl you hired?" Toots asked between bites.

"Yes. You'll love her. She's a fantastic baker. She's learning to make pralines, too. When Bernice comes home, I'll invite her over. Now tell me exactly what they are doing to Bernice. I cannot tell you how worried I've been. She's like a second mother to me."

"She has five blockages, and they're doing the bypass

surgery right now. Dr. Becker seems to know what he's doing. According to Joe, who I trust with my life, he's the best around. Said he'd trained with the doctor who invented the artificial heart.

"I feel like such a fool asking Dr. Lowery to travel across the country to save my friend, then tell him not to. He asked me what kind of entertainment there was, said he might as well enjoy the trip since he was here. Until I volunteered that I would still donate the promised five million to the cardiac unit at Cedars-Sinai Medical Center, he was not a happy camper at all. But once I said the magic words, everything was wine and roses.

"I thought I was an expert when it came to men. Shows you how little I know."

"I could have told you that," Sophie said.

Jamie laughed, then her tone turned serious. "You two are quite the pair. So does this Dr. Becker think Bernice will . . . you know . . . survive?"

"The doctor said that, other than having had a massive heart attack, she's in pretty good health. He said her heart has sustained very little actual damage. Go figure that one out. Apparently he believes she's strong enough to survive the surgery. He wouldn't do it if she weren't."

"Did he say how long it would take?" Jamie's expression was laced with concern.

"No, but I'm sure it will take the rest of the night if all goes according to plan." Toots reached into the bag and took another praline. "These are so good, I swear I could eat a dozen of them. Mavis has had us on such healthy diets, it's made me sick."

Jamie burst out laughing. "Well, a few at a time are good, but I don't think I could eat a complete diet of nothing but sweets even though I adore baking the stuff."

Toots smiled, then something told her to check out Sophie. She was looking at the clock above the cash register. Her normally olive-colored complexion had turned as white as the walls of the hospital.

"Would it be terribly rude if we went home for a while?" Sophie asked out of the blue.

"Are you all right? Is there something you're not telling me?" Jamie asked.

Recalling how Sophie had acted just before the phone call telling Toots that Bernice had had a heart attack, Toots became very concerned. She liked it much better when Sophie was being her usual smart-ass self rather than this worried, frightened woman she'd just turned into.

"I'm fine. I have a feeling someone wants to make contact with me. Sooner rather than later."

Chapter 25

"Tell me you're kidding," Abby said. "After all the bullshit she caused, to think World Con would even consider hiring her for *Bloody Hollow, Two* is a nightmare, and now you're telling me they've actually re-hired her?"

"I'm as surprised as you are. I guess her disappearing act carried a lot of weight with her fans. When they found out she'd lost the part for the next movie, they picketed the damn studio this morning. The fans say Laura Leigh is the only one who can play the role of Ella Larsen. Apparently the powers that be agreed with her fans. Her agent called me, and I wanted to tell you so *The Informer* can be the first to report this earth-shattering news," Chris explained. He hadn't been home twenty-four hours, and he was already back in the swing of things, as good as new.

Abby liked a man who bounced back from adversity. Liked that he'd thought of sharing the news with her so she could report it in *The Informer*, but was that *it*?

"That's why you called?" The words came out before she could stop them. She remembered what her mother had said when they located Chris. He wanted to speak with her, and it was, she believed her mother's exact words were, "vitally important." Surely he remembered saying this to her mother. But if he didn't, far be it from her to remind him. He had enough explaining to do as it was.

"Yeah"—he chuckled—"that's why I called. Have you heard from your mom? How is Bernice?"

"Mavis called. Poor Bernice. She's having bypass surgery tonight. The doctor didn't want to wait. All that meat she gets from her friend, that butcher, Malcolm something or other. Bet he'll think twice from now on before plying her with all that artery-clogging beef. She'll be vegan before all is said and done. I wish I could be there, but duty calls."

"I'll call your mother in the morning and check in. I'm so damn glad she used her brains when she saw my cell number. Another day with that little twit, and I would've gladly risked hypothermia to get away from her."

Chris sounded like he meant what he said. So maybe he really wasn't involved with the twit.

"Did you actually believe her when she said she would bomb World Con? It's hard to see you falling for something that far-fetched."

"Abby, that girl was so drunk, I wouldn't have put anything past her. As her attorney, I had to do what was best for my client. She was driving, so I followed her. Lucky for her and everyone else on the road that night, I called her cell and convinced her to pull over. I left my car, as you know, and, well, the rest is news for *The Informer.*

"So, to answer your question, I did fall for her lies, assuming they really were lies. With someone as spoiled rotten as she is, no one can figure out what she thinks she is entitled to do. For God's sake, when the deputies showed up, she actually thought the studio had sent them to rescue her even though it had already decided not to cast her in the next *Bloody Hollow* film. Go figure."

Abby was curled up in her mother's king-size bed, with Chester on one side and Coco on the other. Her mother didn't like the dogs on the bed, but Abby didn't want to be by herself in the giant bed—which made her think of sharing it with Chris. She visualized him stretched out beside her, his hair mussed from her hand running through it. Stop, stop, *stop!* Hadn't she learned anything? If Chris's feelings were as serious as hers, he would've said so by now. He was an upstanding kind of guy. Her mother said so, and she herself knew it. So, what was she waiting on? A proposal?

"Abby, if you don't answer me, I'm coming over there," Chris said, louder than normal.

"What? Oh, sorry. The dogs were . . . jumping on the bed. Mom doesn't like the dogs on her bed."

"I'd bet the rent they're both curled up next to you on your mother's great big bed." Chris teased.

Abby chuckled. "You'd win. It's too quiet here. I'm not used to staying here all alone."

"Is that an invitation? My place needs to be cleaned. Steve and Renée didn't bother to pick up after themselves, so if you're asking—"

"I'm not," Abby said quickly before the conversation got out of hand. But wasn't that exactly what she wanted? Things to get out of hand with Chris? Yes and no. Maybe, maybe not.

"Have you had dinner?"

Abby looked at her watch. Still early. "I've munched on fruit. I've been working, hadn't really thought about dinner. Why, did Steve and Renée eat all your mint-chocolate-chip ice cream? If I remember right, Renée could definitely use a little fattening up."

I can't believe I said that!

She could practically *feel* Chris's question.

"I didn't know you'd met Renée."

Abby waited for him to question her further. When he didn't, she figured she might as well spill the beans before

Steve told him about her visit in the wee hours. Obviously he hadn't listened to his voice mail.

"It was either the second or third night you were missing. I drove to your condo. I didn't expect to find anyone there, and I ran into Steve and Renée as I was leaving." Abby was not about to go into details about her snooping. If Steve or Renée wanted to, that was up to them.

"And there I was out chasing that obnoxious brat," Chris finished. "I'm sorry. I feel like a jerk. I had no clue. I'd make the news. I was just trying to prevent Laura from making the news. What a witch!"

Abby laughed. Coco's ears moved, and she emitted a low growl. "Excuse me, Queen."

"Are you alone?"

"Just me and the dogs. Coco growled at me."

"So, you never answered my question. Do you want to have dinner with me tonight? We could go to Pink's if you're up for the ride."

Pink's.

It had been over two years since that night at Pink's when Chris kissed each and every one of her fingers, one at a time. One of the most memorable dates of her life. A few little kisses and a couple of hot dogs and she was toast. What she wouldn't give for another night like that.

So did she want to leave the comfort of her mother's king-size bed, the companionship of her two favorite animals in the world, to accompany Chris Clay to dinner?

Yes, she did. More than anything, but not that night. Not when Chris was headline news. She wanted to wait until the rumors died down. The public thought him romantically linked with Laura Leigh, Abby had her moments, but common sense overruled her jealousy. Chris would not involve himself with a client. She was as sure of that as she was that the sun would rise in the east tomorrow, but there was no way she was going to divulge this to him. Not yet, anyway.

"No, I can't. I'm sorry." How she hated telling him no!

"Okay, maybe another time then," he said, regret clear in his voice. "I might go grocery shopping. I need to get some cleaning supplies and some ice cream. So, you run with the story. You have an 'inside source' if asked. And if you hear anything new on Bernice, call me."

"Thanks, Chris, I will." Abby hung up the phone, then curled up next to Chester. He was a great friend, but he wasn't Chris.

Chapter 26

"I have to admit, I'm a bit nervous. This whole new feeling thing has creeped me out something fierce. But I need to do this, and fast. Something about that Dr. Lowery pushed me over the edge. Whatever the reason, I need to find out. Is everyone ready?" Sophie asked, then turned to Jamie. "Are you sure you want to participate? This might be a little scary for you the first time."

Even though Jamie had witnessed Sophie in action at the bakery, she'd never involved herself in their séances.

"She's right. It's not too late to change your mind." Toots wasn't sure *she* wanted to participate in the hastily planned performance, but Sophie was more serious than ever about doing it before Bernice came out of surgery. If they were lucky, they'd contact a spirit and maybe *it* would have an explanation for Sophie's urgency.

Ida and Mavis placed the candles in the formal dining room. In Charleston, they didn't have the old wooden table or the purple silk sheet Sophie always used, so they had to make do with an old tablecloth that had horses splashed all over a dark green background. Toots had no clue where it had come from. But it was old, and old worked. She kept extra rocks glasses in the hutch in the kitchen.

Mavis shut the heavy drapes and made sure the air-conditioning vents were closed. "Do you have the glasses?"

"Right here," Toots assured her. "Let's hurry it up. Sophie's getting pencil and paper just in case this spirit decides it wants to communicate by scribbling."

The props were finally in place. As soon as Sophie flew downstairs with her pencil and paper, they gathered in the dining room and prepared to receive any otherworldly entity that cared to make its presence known.

"Jamie, there are a few things I always say beforehand. We don't have a lot of time, so I'm going to condense what I normally say. Are you sure you're up for this?" Sophie asked in the voice she always used during the séances. Calm, soothing, nothing like the crass, loud Sophie they all knew.

"Yes. I'm a little nervous, but I'm excited, too. I'm hoping sometime we can try to contact my grandmother," Jamie whispered.

"She might contact us tonight. We won't know until someone does visit us. Let's get started. Remember, we don't have the luxury of time."

The dining room was dark except for the candles placed throughout the room. The golden flames danced despite the lack of any air circulating.

Sophie sat at the head of the table, Toots to her left, Mavis to her right. Ida sat next to Mavis, and Jamie took the seat next to Toots.

"Let's all join hands," Sophie instructed in her soothing voice. She took a deep breath, exhaling slowly.

"We're here tonight to make contact with the other side. If there is a presence in the room and you wish to communicate, slide the glass in the center of the table to the right for yes. Slide the glass to the left for no. We ask that you enter peacefully, without evil intent." Sophie and the others watched the glass.

Nothing.

Taking another deep breath, Sophie closed her eyes. Once again speaking in a soft tone, she tried coaxing the netherworld to the present. "Is there a spirit who is willing to speak through me? I am not frightened. We are not frightened. We want to help you." Sophie squeezed Toots's hand. Toots squeezed back.

"Is there a male spirit, perhaps once married to one of us in the room, who wants to make his presence known?"

Toots shot Sophie a dirty look. She knew who Sophie was referring to.

Ida chose that moment to mumble. "Toots, I guess now that Evie Thackeray is dead, you can finally claim the title of living woman with the most ex-husbands."

"Be quiet, Ida! Now isn't the time," Sophie admonished.

Not caring that they were in the middle of contacting the other side, Toots responded to Ida's taunting. "I've always wondered who awaits me in the afterlife. Am I going to have my own harem of husbands waiting for me?"

"Only if they all end up in hell," Ida stated.

"No, I'm serious. Who is going to be there to greet me, and which one could I end up stuck with for eternity?"

Temporarily giving up on the séance, Sophie chimed in, her crass voice taking the place of the calming one she'd used just minutes before. "Hopefully not the pervert. Which husband was it that used to get off on watching you go to the bathroom?"

"How is it you remember all of this, and I don't?" Toots asked.

Jamie smiled, but remained silent.

"I've always wondered what goes on in the afterlife. I mean, if we were sexual dynamos in life, will we be able to have as much sex as we want, or will we be required to sit around and listen to harp music while everyone tries to keep their white robes clean? I bet Evangelista Thackeray is up there right now trying to figure out which ex-husband she wants for eternity," Ida said.

"Spoken like a true slut," Sophie added.

Not wanting to be left out, Mavis added her two cents' worth. "I wonder if she will look like she did when she died, or like she did forty years ago? I'm guessing that would make a big difference in her ability to pick up a new husband in the afterlife."

"I wonder if we could find that out? I would sure like to know that for myself. If I have to spend eternity looking the same way I do when I die, I'm going to reconsider my views on plastic surgery. Of course, if I'm lucky enough to have Ida do my final face, I guess I won't have to worry about it," Sophie said before turning to Toots.

Before Toots could say anything, Ida said, "I don't think it would be that hard to get an answer. Maybe we should try and find out for ourselves. What about it, Sophie? Would it be a sin against the paranormal to use your abilities in pursuit of our eternal beauty?"

"It probably is, but I don't think there's any harm in finding out. I'm actually a little curious myself. It's just a matter of trying to channel a spirit who is willing to give up some time from their eternal happiness to provide us with beauty tips. We would have to find someone who had lost her beauty and would be able to tell us if she got it back." Sophie was herself again, the serious medium gone.

Toots wondered if it was Sophie's uncanny ability of offering a sort of psychic comic relief.

"I bet Evangelista Thackeray would know the answer to that," Ida said.

Excited, Mavis asked, "Do you think we have a chance of getting in touch with her? I agree with Ida. If anyone would be able to tell us about regaining her looks, she would be the right person to talk with. So what do you think, Sophie, is it possible?"

"Anything is possible."

"Then let's give it a try since I'm dying to find out," Toots said.

"I bet that's the exact same thing Evangelista thought right before she passed, so be careful what you wish for, Toots," Mavis advised.

"Okay, enough with the smart-alecky remarks. We need to get serious and focus if we're going to be able to channel someone specific at will. What do you think is the best way to go about doing this, Sophie?" Ida asked, overly excited at the prospect.

"We're not going to need specific answers, just a simple yes or no, so I imagine there really won't be very much to it. You girls just need to settle down and get serious. Respect the process, or it won't work."

Sophie watched as the candlelight flickered. She suddenly got a feeling of trepidation, as if there was a bigger underlying reason behind this séance than what she and the girls had been thinking. Noticing the sudden change in her demeanor, the group gathered around the table suddenly realized something wasn't right with Sophie. Her fierce, firm, unafraid appearance was gone, replaced with the face of a genuinely frightened woman.

"Is everything okay, Sophie?" Mavis asked. "You don't look good."

"I'm not sure. I've got a feeling there is something more to this than we think, and I'm afraid to find out what it is."

"That's never stopped us before. If anything, it's all the more reason for us to go ahead. There might be someone trying to get through, Sophie." Toots held Sophie's hand tightly, afraid to let go.

Resigned, Sophie perked up. "This might be the perfect time for me to try out the new toy Goebel gave me."

At that point, there was no way Ida could help herself. "Really, Sophie, I don't think that's a good idea. The spirits might get offended once they heard the humming noise coming from between your legs."

"Jeez, Ida, not that type of toy! Get your sluttish mind out of the gutter and act serious. I'm talking about this." From her purse under the table Sophie retrieved a small, square black box about the size of an answering machine, adorned with a row of colored lights, with a speaker in the middle.

"What's that?" Mavis inquired. "I've never seen anything like it."

"It's called a ghost box," Sophie explained, her voice changing as she spoke.

"Exactly what does it do?" Toots asked.

"According to the man who made it, there are different sensors in it that pick up on small changes in the environment around us. Everything from electromagnetic fields to changes in temperature. The processor inside then interprets the changes and calculates a certain word that corresponds to the changes. In essence, a spirit has the ability to manipulate the environment around us, and this device will pick up on the changes and convert them into words so we can hear what the spirit is trying to say. Goebel has a friend who makes them, and he's gotten some great results with them. The hard part is knowing when and where a spirit will be so you'll know when to turn it on. In our case, that's the easy part. We only need to summon a spirit just as we have before, and it will be able to make contact with us through this device."

"Sounds fishy to me, but then again, two years ago, so did the idea of speaking with the dead, so I guess anything is possible," Mavis said.

"Let's give it a shot. At worst, nothing will happen. At best, Evangelista Thackeray herself will show up to answer all our questions. Anyway, we're running out of time," Toots said, glancing at her wristwatch. It had been more than two hours since they left the hospital. She said a prayer that Bernice was holding her own.

"Let's start just like we have in the past. I'll try to channel a spirit's thoughts with the pencil and paper, so if this thing doesn't work, we will not have done this in vain. I'm going to need each of you to clear your mind and focus."

They held hands, channeling their thoughts together in hopes of reaching the spirit of the woman widely acknowledged to have been the world's most beautiful woman for well over half a century. Who, they hoped, could advise them from beyond on the ins and outs of beauty in the hereafter.

"We come here in peace, seeking to contact the spirit of the late Evangelista Thackeray, in the hope that she will be able to pass her knowledge on to us. If you're listening, Evangelista, we would very much like to speak with you."

Nothing. The candles shone steadily, the room was utterly still, and the air was warm and muggy. That wasn't good. Cold air always brought forth a spirit. The room was too warm.

Sophie held the pencil in her left hand above the legal pad. She closed her eyes, then began to chant. "Come to me. I mean you no harm. Come to us. Our hearts are open, ready to receive you." She repeated herself.

Mavis slowly opened her eyes and looked at the legal pad resting underneath Sophie's hand and noticed that there was nothing there. No handwriting, nothing to indicate that Sophie had or would make contact with a spirit.

"I'm starting to sense something. We request the presence of Evangelista Thackeray. If you can hear us, grant us your company and wisdom." Sophie spoke in her medium/psychic voice.

Suddenly, a light from the ghost box started to flicker. Sophie looked at the box, her face going completely void of expression and color.

Looking around, Mavis spied the lights on the box toggle on and off, and before she knew what to think, an electronic voice spoke the word "*Actress.*"

Sophie almost jumped out of her skin. "Are you an actress? Are you Evangelista Thackeray?"

Their eyes opened simultaneously as they heard the word "*Yes*" come from the box.

Sophie drew in another cleansing breath. "Can you answer a question for us?"

"*No.*"

"If you won't speak with us, then why are you here?"

"*Murdered.*"

"Oh my God, not another Thomas," Ida screamed.

"Shhh! Are you saying the word *murdered*? Are you saying that *you* were murdered?

"*No . . . friend.*"

"A friend of yours was murdered?"

"*Yes . . . help.*"

"Who was murdered? Can you tell me the name?

"*King . . . swing.*"

"King swing? Is that your friend's name?"

Mavis spoke, "I think she means the king of swing. It's common knowledge that she was very close to Maximillian Jorgenson."

"Are you trying to tell us that Maximillian Jorgenson was murdered?"

"*Yes.*"

"We really stepped in it this time," Toots said.

Taking advantage of the willing spirit, Sophie asked, "Who killed him? What can we do to help you?"

"*Doctor . . . drugged.*"

"His doctor drugged him because he wanted to murder

him? That doesn't make sense. Why did the doctor want to kill him?"

"*Money.*"

The speaker in the box crackled with static. A chill swept through the room.

"So let me get this straight. We just talked to the spirit of Evangelista Thackeray, and she told us that one of the biggest celebrities of all time was murdered for his money? Is that what you all just heard?" Ida asked.

Jamie finally joined in the conversation. "Do you realize what that . . . that *box* just said? *Ohmygosh!* This is unbelievable!"

"I'm sure he was murdered for his money. That was precisely what I thought when I first learned he'd died," Toots said, directing her attention to Jamie.

"What do we do now? Aren't the police already investigating his doctor for something connected to his death?" Mavis asked.

"Yes, he was charged with negligent homicide. *The Informer* covered the story. Jorgenson's doctor gave him an intravenous drug, something one would get in the hospital, a knockout drug. I can't recall the name.

"I don't know what this has to do with . . . *Bernice*. She doesn't even like Evangelista Thackeray or Maximillian Jorgenson. Sophie, is there a connection, and we're missing it somehow?"

"I don't know. We can try again if you want," Sophie said.

"I don't know. It's getting late. Bernice will be out of surgery. I plan to be there when she's wheeled into the recovery room. I say we all call it a night. I'm going to the hospital. You all stay here, get some sleep," Toots said.

"Are you sure?" Mavis asked. "You said yourself there might be something we're missing."

Toots contemplated Mavis's point. "Sophie, is there a

connection? Do you have one of those special feelings about this? Something we can . . . *work* with?"

So fast that no one could have seen the change unless they were looking her squarely in the face, Sophie went from being herself, the crass woman they loved, to a pale, trembling version of herself. Her eyes doubled in size, and her hands shook.

"Paper." The word came out in a hoarse whisper.

Mavis placed a pencil in Sophie's right hand, sliding the notepad beneath it. Sophie's hand moved furiously across the paper, back and forth, as she continued to write one word, over and over. Then, as fast as she began, she stopped, the pencil dropping from her hand. She fell back against the chair, exhausted, as though she'd just completed a marathon.

Toots, Mavis, Ida, and Jamie stared at her, waiting for an explanation, needing to see what she'd written on the paper.

DBL DBL DBL DBL DBL DBL DBL DBL DBL DBL DBL.

Sophie, shaken and pale, stared at the paper. "I'm clueless."

Toots studied the letters, trying to decipher their meaning. "Yes . . . this is . . ." Her mouth dropped open and she shook her head from side to side. "*DBL.*"

"Toots, what?" Sophie asked.

"DBL. Dr. Bruce Lowery. He's the connection."

Chapter 27

Chris stared at his cell phone as though he expected it to speak to him and explain why Abby had refused a simple dinner request. If she was working, he could understand her reluctance. But she wasn't. She was at the beach house, in bed with two dogs, for crying out loud. *What's with that?* he asked himself.

Exactly where that placed him on her list of priorities was quite clear.

She'd rather spend the evening in bed with her dog and her dog's girlfriend, that little yappy Chihuahua, than with him.

Chris looked around at the condo he called home. *No place like home? What bunk,* he thought. It was so close to his heart that he loaned the place out like an old bicycle he was on the verge of trashing. Hell, he'd had bikes that he'd liked more.

The place wasn't a home. It was where he slept, showered, and ate mint-chocolate-chip ice cream. Where he allowed his friends a place to stay when they were on vacation. He looked around the living room, walked out to the terrace, where, he had to admit, he did have a magnificent view of the Pacific Ocean. But a home would surely make his heart race just at the mention of going there. A home would have evidence of a life, and pictures on the walls. A favorite afghan, made by someone who loved him and he loved in return, tossed carelessly over the back of a much-loved chair. Magazines and books scattered about. Maybe a dirty glass, a plate with cake crumbs left on the countertop.

Nope, he gazed around the condo many people would give their eyeteeth to own. All he saw was a picture-perfect image suitable for a travel magazine hoping to tempt travelers to spend their money somewhere.

Disgusted with his thoughts, Chris became antsy for reasons only he could fathom—meaning Abby Simpson. He plunged through the condo with a mission.

In the master bedroom, he stripped the sheets off the bed and tossed them into a laundry basket he kept in the closet. Inside the master bathroom, he gathered damp towels and washcloths, tossing them in with the sheets. Beneath the bathroom sink was a plastic caddy filled with cleaning supplies. He sprayed bathroom cleaner inside the shower, the bathtub, and the two sinks. With a terry-cloth rag, he buffed and polished until the place sparkled. Grabbing the laundry basket, he headed to the utility room. He stuffed the washing machine with the sheets and towels—figuring what the hell, it's not as if he were at a Laundromat with a bunch of disapproving housewives watching him—and proceeded to pour a generous amount of liquid detergent in the machine. From there he located the broom and a mop. He scrubbed the bathroom floors until he was out of breath.

Then he polished the furniture in all the rooms, ran the vacuum, and, when all was finished, cleaned the sliding glass doors. Three hours later the condo sparkled, ready for that magazine ad.

Chris had made a decision while cleaning the lifeless condo. He was going to put the place on the market first thing in the morning. He wanted a home, and someone to share it with. And the only woman who came to mind when his thoughts went in that direction was Abby.

Now all he had to do was convince her to marry him. It would be tough, given the fact that she seemed to prefer spending the evening with her animals. *But I'm a patient man,* he told himself. And if that didn't work, well, he would call in the big guns.

Toots and the godmothers.

The image made him smile. Those old girls would back him one hundred percent. He'd bet his life on it.

Abby punched the pillow for the third time. She should take the dogs to her place, where she could sleep in her own bed, but it was already too late, and she was just too tired. She was hungry, too—which reminded her of Chris.

Sitting up in bed, turning the light on, she scooted past the two balls of fur without disturbing them. She went downstairs, turning on the lights as she headed to the kitchen. Surely her mother, the queen of junk food, had something to eat besides fresh fruit and vegetables. Dear Mavis. She'd come so far in the past two years. Abby was extremely proud of her godmother for her weight loss and the dedication it took to stick to a diet and exercise plan. Still, one had to indulge now and again. She opened the refrigerator, searching for something sweet. Nothing there, so she searched the freezer.

"Ice cream. Mom always has ice cream." Abby moved a box of frozen green beans, and found a carton of chocolate-chip-cookie-dough ice cream, her favorite.

"Thank you, Mom," Abby said out loud. She grabbed a spoon and headed outside to the deck.

The late-night breeze felt cool against her skin. A tinge of salt scented the air. Abby breathed deeply. She loved the smells, the sounds as the ocean's waves gently bathed the shoreline, leaving behind a bubbly white froth.

Plopping down on her favorite deck chair, with the carton of ice cream in one hand and a spoon in the other, she took several bites of the cold, creamy concoction. She let her mind wander. Thoughts of all the work that awaited her tomorrow didn't cheer her as it normally would.

More than a bit concerned about Bernice, Abby wished she could've made the trip to Charleston, but knew Bernice would understand. She had a major story to write, courtesy of Chris. It should put *The Informer* in the number one slot this week. Unless that rat's ass Laura Leigh had told her story to one of Abby's competitors.

"Damn! Why didn't I think of that?" Abby said to herself. She was definitely slacking off.

Had Chris told Laura to keep the story quiet? Would she even do so if he'd asked her to? Abby needed to know, and she needed to know right away. There was no time to contemplate what the other papers would do. If they had Laura Leigh's story, she had best beat the others to press. The only way she was going to do that was to be one hundred percent certain she was the only tabloid with the story.

Before she had a chance to change her mind, she went inside, put the ice cream away, and ran upstairs for her cell phone. Chester and Coco were still sound asleep, snuggled against each other. *They are so in love,* Abby thought. *If only people could love so freely and without reservation.*

Back downstairs, she sat in her mother's chair, wishing Toots was there to advise her. But Abby was a big girl, and she didn't need to ask her mother's permission to run a story or make the call she was doing everything humanly possible to avoid.

She glanced at the clock. It was late, but who cared?

"Shit, here goes nothing." She dialed Chris's cell-phone number

He answered on the second ring. "This better be good."

"Listen, I hate calling at this hour, but I need to ask you a question; it's kind of important," Abby said.

"Okay, shoot."

He wasn't even going to chastise her about the late hour? Abby smiled. The shit. He was awake, too.

"Are you sure you're giving *The Informer* the scoop? I just had a thought; what if Laura Leigh goes to one of my competitors with her story? And if she does, will it match up with yours?" There! She'd done it.

Laughter bubbled across the phone lines. "Abby Simpson, you should be ashamed of yourself. I can't believe you'd question me. What, you don't think I told the whole truth and nothing but?"

"That's what I want to make sure of," she shot back. "There's no way this will be in another tabloid?"

"You know I can't promise you that, Abby. The tabloids have their sources same as the real papers, do—"

"*Real papers,* Chris? Is that what you think? I don't work for a *real* newspaper?" Abby wanted to choke him for his insensitive remark, but knew it hadn't been intended maliciously.

"Stop, you know exactly what I'm trying to say. Laura Leigh assured me that she wouldn't take her story to the press. That's why I wanted you to be the first to report this. I know you will report exactly what I told you and nothing more. Laura's agent doesn't want her even talking to the press right now. She's already walking on thin ice with World Con. Does that answer your question?"

"Why do you always have to be such a smart-ass, Chris? Why can't you just say, 'Yes, Abby, that's right, Abby, anytime, Abby' instead of making . . . Oh shit, forget it." Abby could only imagine the look on Chris's face.

A broad smile, crinkles at the corner of his eyes. Sandy hair disheveled. Wrinkled jeans. No shoes.

Damn, I've got it bad for him.

"Abby, is there something else? Because if there isn't, it's late, and I am going to bed."

"No, there isn't anything else, Chris. You have a good night, okay?"

"You know what, Abby? I did not have a good night. I spent the entire evening cleaning this boring condo because I didn't have anything better to do. Because you, Abby dear, would rather spend your evening holed up at your mother's beach house with two dogs than have dinner with me. Just so you know."

Abby grinned from ear to ear. *Damn, Chris has it bad, too.* Now the question was, who was going to be the first to give in?

"Okay, I appreciate your telling me. And, Chris, thanks for the story. I'll e-mail you a copy of tomorrow's paper." She clicked off before he had a chance to reply.

Satisfied that *The Informer* had an exclusive on the story, Abby went back upstairs and called it a night.

Sweet dreams, Christopher Clay.

Chapter 28

"If you don't slow down, you're going to kill us," Sophie said. "I don't know why you're in such a hurry all of a sudden. You called the hospital, and that freak isn't anywhere to be found."

Toots eased off the accelerator. Sophie was absolutely right. The last thing she needed was to be involved in a car accident on the way to the hospital. She'd wind up sharing a hospital room with Bernice. "That they know of. He could be lurking in some . . . utility closet for all we know."

"You've watched too many episodes of *Law & Order,*" Sophie remarked. "A man like Lowery sticks out. He isn't going to be able to wander through Charleston Memorial without being noticed by some horny young nurse."

"You could be on your deathbed, and you'd still find a way to get a sexual dig in." Toots smiled for the first time since she'd deciphered the initials Sophie had written on the notepad during her trance.

DBL.

Dr. Bruce Lowery.

"I know. I'm good at that. Remember how I used to spend my days struggling to keep my opinions to myself? I guess it's gonna take a while before I'm whole again. All those years with Walter left their mark. I have to say what I think when I think it."

Toots steered the Range Rover into the parking lot, grateful to find an open space close to the hospital's entrance. She shifted into PARK, removed the keys from the ignition, and grabbed her purse. "You coming with me?"

Sophie hadn't made a move. Still as a stone statue, she held her hand out. "Give me a minute, I'm . . . I've got one of those *feelings* again."

Toots closed the driver's side door and ran around to the passenger side. "Are you all right? Is it Bernice?"

"No, no it's not Bernice . . . it's that damn doctor! He's"—Sophie rubbed her temples—"involved with Maximillian Jorgenson's death! Yes, that's what I've been trying to put together! Mavis was right. Everybody knows that Evangelista Thackeray and Maximillian Jorgenson were very close friends. They did a lot of work together for AIDS causes. I'm sure you've read about it in one of the tabloids."

Toots had. "Yes, there's always something about her or him in them. Being such a fan of hers, you would think I'd have paid more attention to the stories, but if truth be told, I was more interested in her clothes and what kind of jewelry she wore."

Sophie suddenly relaxed like a deflated balloon. She sank into the seat, leaning against the soft leather. She took a deep breath, then grabbed her bag. "Okay, I can do this. Let's see how Bernice is. I think we need to tell Goebel about this . . . *vision*. Maybe he can tell me what to do or call someone on the police force. The man has more connections than a longtime pimp."

Toots helped Sophie out of the car, steering her toward the hospital's entrance. "We can call him as soon as we get an update on Bernice. He said he didn't mind if we woke him up."

"Okay, let's get this over with."

Inside, the hospital was relatively quiet. Swishing doors, rubbery-sounding footsteps, and an occasional outbreak of quiet laughter were the only noises that could be heard as they headed toward the bank of elevators. Toots punched the button for the fifth floor and the steel doors opened, emitting a noise sounding like a gush of sucking air.

Both women were silent as they rode to the surgical floor. When the doors opened again, they were greeted with the sounds of machines blipping, the ventilators' precise inhalations and exhalations keeping bodies alive, oxygen to the brain, blood flowing throughout the circulatory systems of those unfortunate souls who lay comatose on the hard rubber mattresses.

Toots and Sophie walked down the long hall past the waiting room they'd left a few short hours ago. Toots looked at her watch. "It's been five hours. Do you suppose she's still in surgery?"

Sophie took her hand. "These kinds of operations can take hours, Toots, you know that. If there were complications, well, you know . . . All kinds of nonlife threatening events take place in an operating room.

I remember once during my training in obstetrics, we had this poor woman all prepped for surgery—she'd been knocked out, shaved, and sterilized—the whole nine yards, and the damn doctor never showed. An intern did his first Caesarean section, and the doctor was fired. I admit it wasn't life threatening, but it could have been. We had to keep that poor girl sedated too long, and that's dangerous."

"How is it you continue to come up with yet another new story after all these years? Sometimes I think you're fibbing to me, that you make this stuff up just to distract me or make me feel better."

"Did it work?" Sophie asked, when they reached the recovery room.

Toots laughed. "I suppose it did for a minute. You sure can tell some whoppers, Sophie Manchester. I'll give you that."

"Who said I was lying?"

Toots rolled her eyes. "Enough, Soph. Okay?"

A high-pitched squeal came from behind the double doors that read OPERATING ROOM C NO ADMITTANCE. Two nurses in pale pink scrubs wheeled Bernice from the operating room into the recovery room. Both wore bright smiles, which Toots took as a good sign. Two seconds later, Joe and Dr. Becker exited through the double doors. Toots practically ran toward the pair. Both looked tired, ready to call it a night.

"Toots, how did I know you'd be waiting?" Joe said as he motioned for her and Sophie to follow him.

"Because I called and told you I would be here? I thought you were smarter than that."

Laughing, he shook his head. "Come on, let's see your friend."

Bernice was the only patient in the recovery room, surrounded by machines, tubes coming out of her mouth, nose, and chest. When Toots saw her old friend, she burst into tears. She knuckled her eyes, mopping up her tears. "How is she?"

Dr. Becker stood next to the bed. "She is doing fantastic. The harvested vein was as good as it gets. I was able to reroute all five blockages with no problems. And her heart began to pump the second we removed the heart-lung machine. Her oxygen levels are perfect, blood pressure is excellent. If I were to hazard a guess, and this is just a guess, Bernice will be up and around by this time tomorrow."

Toots would have collapsed had it not been for Sophie's support. "I can't thank you enough. I'm so relieved. So what happens next? Does she have to undergo therapy or anything? I need to know because someone will have to drive her to and from. She doesn't drive. Though Jamie could help out when we need her to, right?" Toots looked at Sophie.

"Yes, we're all going to stick around, however long it takes. It's not like we can't do our jobs from anywhere in the world."

"Of course I'll stick around. I didn't mean to imply I wouldn't."

Dr. Becker gave a tired smile. "To answer your question, yes, she'll need physical therapy. I'll want to monitor her, make sure the grafts don't close up. She's going to have some tough times ahead, but I think she'll notice a difference in the way she feels. She's likely to have more energy, her color will be nice and rosy. Things you wouldn't have noticed before you'll notice now. Was Bernice a smoker?"

Toots almost choked. "No, she wasn't. She hated cigarettes."

Toots realized then that her nasty habit had contributed to Bernice's heart disease. Over a twenty-plus-year period, Toots had thought nothing of smoking in Bernice's presence, had made light of it when Bernice complained about her smoking. Secondhand smoke.

"I have some material I want you to read before Bernice leaves the hospital. It might make you stop and think before you light up around her again." Dr. Becker's tone was serious, all traces of his earlier humor gone.

It was serious stuff, Toots knew. She and Malcolm Moretti had both had a hand in contributing to Bernice's heart condition.

Maybe it was time to give some serious thought to giving up her habit. She and Sophie could quit together. It was supposed to be easier to quit with a partner. Support each other and all.

"Take these, read them when you can. Now I am going to call it a day. Bernice is in the trusted hands of one of my colleagues for the night, Dr. Clark. If there are any problems, he'll be able to handle them." Dr. Becker gave Toots a handful of pamphlets.

"Thank you. I mean it. You probably saved her life, and I can't tell you what that means to me." Toots had already held out her hand to shake the good doctor's when she remembered her earlier reaction. Too late, he took her hand in his. Sparks flew up and down the length of her arm, stopping at her fingertips, where they were still tingling when she pulled her hand away.

Dr. Becker looked at her then. Really looked at her. Not like a doctor views a patient, but the way a man looks at a woman. A woman he was attracted to. "I'll look forward to your thoughts." He nodded at the literature he gave her, then turned and walked away.

"Of course." Toots watched him as he pushed the steel doors aside.

All that time, Sophie stood there observing her, a shit-eating grin on her face.

"Are we thinking of a number? Maybe . . . *nine?*"

Toots grabbed Sophie's arm and led her down the hall to the waiting room. Inside, she practically dragged her across the floor to the worn beige sofa.

"Now tell me exactly what that meant? Exactly, Sophie." Toots's eyes flashed with excitement.

"I don't have to tell you anything. That look in your eyes says it all. It's okay to be attracted to Dr. Becker, Toots. He's certainly eyeballing you. Has since the minute he laid those sexy blue eyes on you."

Flustered, Toots brought her hand up to her chest. "That's a crock. I have no interest in a man. I told you, when I buried Leland, that was it for me. Eight times for Sophie. Eight times I walked the walk, and I swore I would never do it again. I would like to believe I'm a woman of my word. So, there."

But it seemed clear Toots was trying to convince herself as much as Sophie that she was immune to the handsome doctor's attention. "Besides, I'm over with that half of my life. I have two businesses to run, two houses to care for, a daughter, you, and now Bernice. Where in the world would I ever find time for a . . . relationship?"

"You'd make the time, Toots, just like me. I'm going to tell you this, and if you laugh, I swear I'll deny it. It kills me every time I see Goebel because I know it's only for a short time. I'm so worried about the moment he leaves, I can hardly take pleasure in the fact that he's here. Tell me, Toots. Do I have it bad or what?"

Chuckling, Toots took her friend's hand in her own. "If anyone deserves to 'have it bad,' it's you, Sophie Manchester. There's nothing to be ashamed of. So you miss Goebel? Do you tell him? Does he ask you to visit him in New York? Has he said, 'Hands off, Sophie, I'm taken'?"

"No, he's content. At least I think he is. I care about the old fool. Is that crazy or what? I'm so damn glad he lost all that weight. Oh, I liked him before he lost the weight, but he's healthier now. His energy is twice what it was when we first met. You know we really should think about giving up the cigs. Maybe we could get those new pills that help you quit. I've seen them advertised on TV."

"I was thinking the same thing when I saw Bernice. I feel partially responsible for her condition. All these years I've huffed and puffed around her. And Abby! What if she's suffered from my bad habit? God, I don't think I could live with myself!"

"Stop it, Toots. You're tired, and you probably need a cigarette," Sophie grumbled. "If you don't, then I do."

Toots nodded and glanced at the stack of papers in her lap. "Here, let's look at this stuff, then I won't have to lie when he asks me if I did."

Toots read from the first pamphlet she opened.

"Exposure to toxins in secondhand smoke can cause asthma, cancer, and other serious problems. Secondhand smoke causes or contributes to various health problems, from cardiovascular disease to cancer. Understand what's in secondhand smoke and consider ways to protect yourself and those you love from secondhand smoke.

"The dangerous particles can linger in the air for hours. Breathing secondhand smoke can irritate your lungs and reduce the amount of oxygen in your blood.

"Secondhand smoke contains thousands of toxic chemicals, including carbon monoxide, formaldehyde, lead, and nickel. Secondhand smoke, also known as environmental tobacco smoke—big surprise there—*includes the smoke that a smoker exhales and the smoke that comes directly from the burning tobacco product*—"

Sophie held her hand out. "That's enough. I know all this. I've read it myself a hundred times. Makes all smokers sound like idiots."

"Okay. So we'll think about giving up our smokes? I know one thing, though. It will be a cold day in hell before I light up in Bernice's presence again."

"Yeah, me too." Sophie sighed. "Are we going to spend the night here, or what?"

"You can go. I want to stay. Like I said, I want to be here when she wakes up. I'm afraid that Dr. Lowery might be lurking around. I should've said something to Joe, had him alert security or something. What if he comes after Bernice?"

"You really need to get a grip. You haven't slept in two nights, and your imagination is working overtime."

"Mine?" Toots said incredulously. "You think *my* imagination is working overtime? You, my friend, need to get real."

"I don't have control over the stuff that I see, at least I haven't learned how to turn it off and on. But I will. I know it can be done. I've read about it. It takes a lot of practice, focusing on the moment. Can you believe we're even talking like this? It blows my mind."

"You need to go home, Sophie. You're tired, I'm tired. I'll just lie here on this old sofa and rest a bit. The nurses will come and get me if there's any news."

Toots placed the stack of papers on the table, then removed her shoes. "Go home before I kick your butt."

Sophie removed her shoes and curled up in a ball on one end of the sofa. "I'm too tired to drive. Here"—she tapped the opposite end of the sagging sofa with her bare foot—"there's plenty of room for two."

Toots curled up at the other end of the sofa. Within seconds, they were sound asleep.

Chapter 29

Abby wanted to make sure she'd reported the story of Laura Leigh's disappearance precisely the way Chris had told it to her. She hadn't even taken her usual liberties with the story to spiff it up. This story would be told with the skill of a consummate professional. Laura Leigh wouldn't approve. Abby simply did not care, but she knew Chris would.

All she really wanted was to make that man happy. She had no clue how to tell him so, when she would, or even if she could. Learning that he wasn't in love with that twitchy-nosed, two-bit, B-grade actress was the best news she'd had yet.

She read through her copy one more time.

MISSING ACTRESS ALIVE AND WELL!!!
Solved! Missing actress Laura Leigh was found alive and well by Mammoth Lakes authorities when they were alerted to a possible location by Mr. Christopher Clay's cell phone GPS.
Laura Leigh was last seen leaving LA's popular nightclub Hot Wired with entertainment attorney Christopher Clay. When Miss Leigh failed to call her family after three days, a missing persons report was

filed. A one-hundred-thousand-dollar reward was offered for any information leading to her whereabouts.

Will Mr. Clay collect the hefty reward?

When he'd discovered his client at the nightclub, she'd just learned she was no longer being considered for the role of Ella Larsen in Bloody Hollow, Two. *After indulging in one too many alcoholic beverages, Miss Leigh stormed out of the club in a rage. Mr. Clay proceeded to follow her. When he saw that she was out of control, a danger to herself and other motorists on the road, he called her on her cell phone and insisted that she pull over. When she did, Mr. Clay joined her in her car and left instructions with his auto repair shop to tow his Camry away until further notice.*

When police learned the location of the vehicle, they went so far as to comb Mr. Clay's car for trace evidence. KABC reported that Mr. Clay was a "person of interest" in Laura Leigh's disappearance.

Mr. Clay stated to a reliable source that Miss Leigh made several threatening remarks, and he feared for the public's safety. The source asked that the actual threats made by Miss Leigh not be disclosed to the public at this time.

Lucky Leigh! Mr. Clay just happened to have keys to a luxury cabin hideaway on Mammoth Mountain. Unlucky Leigh. Unlucky Mr. Clay. He and Miss Leigh became stranded in what meteorologists last week were calling "the storm of the century." Thanks to Mr. Clay's survival skills, the couple was found when Mr. Clay's stepmother, Theresa Loudenberry, followed up on a missed call she had received from her stepson.

Abby admitted to exaggerating Chris's survival skills, but what the heck, she didn't want the world to know he'd had a generator and enough food and water for another few days. She knew he'd like that little bit of embellishment.

She uploaded the same pictures KABC had used in their reports, skimmed through the brief report again, then clicked SEND. It would go through the proper channels immediately. Abby directed that the story be placed below the top fold.

She'd been alerted to another story. Another possible player in the Maximillian Jorgenson tragedy—courtesy of Sophie, and another one of her visions.

Chris heard the ping on his Mac, letting him know he'd received an e-mail.

Abby.

He opened the attached file she'd promised to send. He read the article once, then again. Downright boring. He liked it that way. And he loved that bit about his survival skills.

Yep, he was going to marry the woman. She just didn't know it yet.

Chris had spent the rest of the night snapping pictures inside his condo while it was sparkling clean. He had a pal who was in real estate, and sent him the info, the photos, and the asking price. He knew it wouldn't stay on the market for long, so he scanned a few apartments, deciding they were just more of the same old, same old. He wanted a home, which was the purpose of selling his condo. Maybe he'd look for a little ranch house in Brentwood.

Suddenly, Chris decided there was no time like the present. If he didn't at least tell Abby he loved her, he would never get to marry her. He'd been waiting for that perfect moment, one like they'd had at Pink's two years ago. He had to tell Abby that very minute how he felt about her.

He grabbed his cell phone from the table and punched in her number.

She answered on the first ring. "What?"

"Did I ever tell you your telephone etiquette sucks?"

"*What?*" Abby said again.

"You need to learn how to answer the phone properly."

"You called me just to tell me that? Chris Clay, have you been nipping at the bottle?"

He cracked up laughing. "Nipping, Abby? What's that? A new Hollywood term for drunks?"

She couldn't help but laugh. "No, Chris, it's not. Now tell me why are you calling me at this ungodly hour? I have to be at work in a few hours. Unlike some people I know."

"Didn't you just call me half an hour ago? What's changed, Abby? The dogs not keeping you warm enough?"

"Chris, the next time I see you, I swear I'm going to smack you right upside the head. What in the hell has gotten into you?"

"You, Abby. You've gotten into me. And that's why I called. I couldn't wait another minute to tell you that I love you." There, the cat was out of the bag.

"Did you hear what I just said, Abby? . . . Abby?"

"I heard you, Chris. I heard you." She was breathless.

"And? Aren't you going to tell me what a jerk I am? Call me a few choice names? Smack me right upside the head?"

She was stunned, surprised, and over the moon. Totally over the moon. He'd said the three words she'd been waiting to hear from him for longer than she cared to admit. She was *over the moon*. Big-time. Very, very big-time.

"No, Chris, I don't want to do any of those things to

you. What I want is for you to get your butt in that boring Toyota Camry you drive and come out here so I can tell you I love you back to your face." Abby was practically flying.

"I'm on my way, sweet girl, I'm on my way."

Chapter 30

"Wake up, sleepyheads. Someone wants to see you," Dr. Becker said in a very loud voice.

Toots jumped so fast it startled her. Groggily, she looked around the room. It took a couple seconds before she realized where she was. The hospital waiting room.

Bernice.

Toots sat up, and grabbed her shoes. "Is she awake?"

He nodded. "And asking for you and your friend . . . sort of. Said something to the tune of 'tell her to get in here before I have to come and kick her wrinkled old ass'. Of course, I knew you'd want to know."

"How was she able to speak with a ventilator?"

"She motioned for a pad of paper. The staff is amazed at her progress. Once we get her settled in a room, I'll take her off the ventilator."

"Wonderful," Toots said.

She poked Sophie, who was snoring softly. "Wake up. Bernice is asking for us."

To Dr. Becker, she said, "Do you ever sleep?"

It dawned on her she was wearing the same outfit she'd had on all day yesterday. She'd slept in it, and knew she appeared unkempt. Her makeup, at least what was left of it, had to be smeared all over her face. Her mouth felt like she'd gargled with toilet water. "I'm a mess. I'll hit the ladies' room and be right there."

"To answer your question, I slept in the doctors' lounge, just in case Dr. Clark needed me."

Toots smiled. "That's considerate of you, Dr. Becker. I like considerate doctors. Excuse me," she added as she started to make her way to the door. In her disheveled state, she didn't want to remain in the presence of the handsome doctor a second longer than she had to. *I must look like puke warmed over. Damn.* I'm *starting to think like Ida.*

She raced out of the waiting room and down the long hallway to the ladies' room. She tended to immediate business first, then looked at herself in the mirror. "Good grief. If I had even the slightest chance with Dr. Becker, it's sure as hell gone now. I look like a wild woman."

"I knew you were interested in him," Sophie said from inside another stall.

Toots about jumped out of her skin for the second time. "Damn, you're gonna give me a heart attack one of these days. What did you do, follow me?"

"Yep. I had to pee." The toilet flushed, and Sophie came out of the stall. As usual, she looked like she'd just stepped out of a bandbox.

"How come you don't look half as shitty as I do?" Toots asked.

"I brushed my hair."

"Oh."

"Hurry up, Bernice wants to see you. Oh, I almost forgot. Dr. Becker mentioned Dr. Lowery was here this morning looking for you."

Toots whirled around. "What? Why is he still here?"

"Probably wants that five-million-dollar check before you change your mind."

Leave it to Sophie to cut to the heart of the matter. "Well, I've decided I'm not giving it to him. I won't be taken advantage of like that slimy doctor tried with Ida. What is it with doctors these days? What happened to the good old-fashioned caring doctors? All they want now is money."

"I don't think Becker wants your money. He wants you, Toots, and don't you dare say another word. Let's get the hell out of here before someone starts to suspect we're lesbians."

"You're disgusting, did I ever tell you that?" Toots splashed her face with cold water, rinsed her mouth out, and brushed her hair, pulling it back in a loose ponytail. She added a touch of lipstick and pinched her cheeks. She was too pale.

"More than once."

"Do you realize we haven't smoked the entire time we've been here?" Toots asked, as they traveled back down the long hall to the recovery room.

"Don't remind me. It was the first thing I thought of when I woke up. That and coffee," Sophie said.

They entered the recovery room, where Bernice was wide-awake. Toots stood by her bedside, tearing up again. What the hell was wrong with her? She didn't want to smoke, she was bawling like a baby all the time, and she might be interested in another man. This was not a good thing. Especially the man part.

"Bernice, oh you sweet old thing. What did you do?" Toots leaned over the bed, careful not to tangle herself in all the tubes and wires coming out of Bernice's body.

Bernice rolled her eyes, ever the smart-ass.

"Okay, I know what happened. What I want you to know is that we're all here, even Goebel. We're going to nurse you back to health. Mavis is going to plan a heart-healthy diet for you so you can treat those new arteries with tender loving care. And no more visits to that damn butcher shop, either."

Bernice reached for Toots's hand. One by one, she pulled her fingers back until the only one left was her middle finger. Then Bernice turned Toots's own hand to face her.

They all burst out laughing.

"I think she's trying to tell you to go f—"

"Sophie!" Toots hissed.

"Oh. Well. I meant she is trying to tell you to get screwed. Right, Bernice?"

"Naughty, naughty. Shame on all of you," Dr. Becker said. "In here less than a minute, and you're already getting my patient riled." He looked at her monitor and checked the tubes around her surgical site. "Looking good, Miss Bernice. Lookin' good."

Poor Bernice. She tried to smile with all the paraphernalia down her throat and up her nose, but couldn't manage to bring it off.

"Okay, ladies, I imagine you two want to go for a nasty smoke and a cup of coffee. We're going to get Bernice squared away. And she's going to sleep most of the day, which is my advice to the two of you. You've seen her, she's fine. Now skedaddle."

"Bernice, we'll be back this afternoon. Dr. Becker, you have all my numbers just in case she needs me?"

"Oh, I have your number all right," he teased.

"What's that supposed to mean?" Toots asked.

"Whatever you want it to mean. Oh, before I forget. Dr. Lowery was here earlier looking for you."

Toots cringed at the mention of his name. "If he comes around asking for me again, call security. This man could be serious trouble, just so you know."

"What kind of trouble? Something I should be concerned about?"

"Yes, but I won't go into the details yet. We're having him . . . never mind. Just take my word that he isn't all he claims to be," Toots said, then leaned over the tubes and machines to kiss Bernice. "I'll see you later, old gal."

"Later, Bernice," Sophie said.

They walked out of the room, then stopped when they reached the bank of elevators. Toots pushed the button to the main lobby. Steel doors opened and closed.

As soon as they exited the elevators, they located a coffee vending machine. Toots bought two large cups with extra cream and sugar. Once they were outside, Sophie reached for her ever-present pack of Marlboros. "I am dying for a damn cigarette. I don't give a shit what your boyfriend says. I need to puff. You gonna join me?"

"I'll have a drag off yours, but not in the car. And he's not my boyfriend," Toots added.

"Yet."

Sophie lit up, Toots took a few puffs, downed her coffee, then crawled into the Range Rover. She hadn't been that tired in a very, very long time. Too tired to argue with Sophie.

They were quiet on the drive back to Toots's Charleston home, both lost in their own worlds.

Toots felt the same familiar excitement again as she pulled through the wrought-iron gates. Giant live oak trees dripping with Spanish moss draped the path to the old Southern mansion. The beauty of her gardens never failed to amaze her. She had to remember to give Pete yet another raise. The man was brilliant.

"This is my home, Sophie. No matter where I may travel, my heart is always here in Charleston."

"I understand. I love this place, too. I've been thinking about buying a place of my own. And not in Los Angeles or New York. Here in South Carolina. What would you think of having me for a neighbor?"

"I think you have to do whatever makes you happy, Soph. If being my neighbor is what works, then I'll be the first one to offer my decorating skills. I've missed that, you know."

"I know you have. Toots, have you decided if you're going to tell Abby about *The Informer?* It's been two years. She's going to hate us all when she finds out that we've been lying to her. I hope she only hates you, Toots, and not the rest of us." Sophie cackled. "Just teasing. Seriously, don't you think it's time we all 'fessed up?"

Toots agreed. It was time, but not today. "When Bernice is home, and we're all back to normal, whatever normal is these days, I'll tell her. I promise."

She parked the Range Rover behind the house. They entered through the kitchen, where they were greeted by Jamie carrying two large mugs of coffee. "How is she?"

"She flipped Toots the bird," Sophie said. "But used Toots's hand. It was funny as hell."

Jamie clapped her hands. "Now that sounds like my Bernice."

Goebel grabbed Sophie in a hug before she could put her coffee cup down. She barely managed to keep from spilling coffee all over the place. "Careful, big guy, or you'll be wearing this."

Sophie put her cup on the counter and gave Goebel a real hug. Freshly showered, he smelled like Dial Soap and Prell Shampoo. Damn, but if he didn't keep getting better and better.

"Sophie has something to tell you, Goebel. Serious stuff, right, Soph?" Toots said as she carried her cup of coffee over to the table. "Where are Mavis and Ida?" she asked Jamie.

"They're still upstairs. Mavis came down earlier, poured

two cups of coffee, and took them with her. She said something about Ida getting a gig on television."

"*What?*" Toots shouted, then caught herself. "I'm sorry. You said Ida is going to be on TV? Did I hear that right?"

Ida chose the perfect moment to make her grand entrance, pink hair and all. Mavis followed, a sheepish grin spread across her face.

"How is Bernice?" they asked at the same time.

"Ornery. Dr. Becker says she's doing better than most. They're keeping her in ICU for the day to monitor her. He told me right before we left that he'd probably take the ventilator off today. I know Bernice will be glad. She'll be able to talk then.

"I'm worn-out, so tell me your news before I have to strangle it out of you," Toots said to Ida.

"Well, if you're going to be an uppity old hag about it, I am not going to tell you." Ida smiled when she said it.

"Ida, I will kick your ass. Spill it," Sophie said. She and Goebel sat at the table next to Toots.

"Okay, but it's not a sure thing yet. I've been checking into a line of cosmetics for . . . seasoned women. I hired a team of chemists to work on this a few months ago. I've kept it to myself because I didn't want to tell anyone until I was sure they could make a product worth using, a line of products that would work, not cost a fortune. And this is the big surprise. The Home Shopping Club heard of my venture through the entrepreneur grapevine. They've invited me to market my line of cosmetics as soon as they're available."

"Ohmygod, a real frigging Estée Lauder. Damn, Ida. How were you able to keep this under wraps? Your mouth usually has hinges on it," Sophie teased.

"This is fantastic, Ida! Congratulations. I am very proud of you. You know we've all been to hell and back a time or two, and just look at us now. Four seasoned women, at the prime of our lives, each with a new passion and profession. We've come a long way, baby!" Toots had tears well up in her eyes for the second time that day.

"I'm going to call the cosmetic line Seasoned. What do you think?" Ida gushed with pride at her accomplishment.

"I think it's fabulous," Mavis said. "We're all a bit seasoned, like old cast-iron skillets."

Toots, Sophie, and Ida glared at Mavis as though she'd taken temporary leave of her sanity.

"An iron skillet? Surely you can come up with a better analogy than an iron skillet! For crying out loud, Mavis, you were an English teacher!" Sophie huffed, apparently not liking being compared to an old seasoned cast-iron skillet.

"Oh, you know what I meant."

"I think we all get your drift. I love the name. Seasoned. Ida, you've become quite the entrepreneur. I for one will be the first caller as soon as you're on the show. I used to watch that channel all the time. When I lost a husband and couldn't sleep, I shopped. I have so many unopened boxes in storage. Someday, I'm going to go through all that stuff and donate it to charity, but now, ladies, I simply have to call it a day. I want to rest before I have to go back to the hospital. Who knows what Bernice will be up to?"

Toots swallowed the last of her coffee, rinsed her cup, and placed it on the top rack of the dishwasher. Upstairs, she took a quick shower, then crawled between the cool sheets. Her last thought before drifting off to sleep was, *I don't even want a cigarette.*

Epilogue

Two weeks later

Bernice sat at the kitchen table, delighted at the changes she'd made already. With Mavis and Goebel's help, she'd lost twelve pounds, her sugar cravings were all but gone, and she was going to the rehabilitation center every day for her physical therapy. Yes, she was sore, and yes, she wished she'd taken better care of herself, but it was what it was. She was doing everything in her power to make the best of the situation.

"You'll love this new herbal tea. It's full of antioxidants, plus it actually tastes good," Jamie said as she served Bernice her breakfast. She'd let Lucy open the bakery today just so she could spend some quality time with her ladies.

The entire gang, as they'd recently started referring to themselves, gathered around the table for breakfast. All had agreed to let Mavis and Jamie prepare a healthy breakfast. Jamie wanted to start offering a healthy choice at The Sweetest Things, and today they were all going to act as guinea pigs.

"You all have to try one of everything," Mavis insisted as she placed a large platter of breakfast meats in the center of the table. "Promise?"

"Yeah, we promise. Now let's get on with it," Sophie said in her usual crass manner. She hadn't been allowed her normal dose of caffeine, and it showed. "It's one thing to do without coffee, but Toots and I are down to three cigarettes a day. Toots wants to hook up with Dr. Becker. That's why she's quitting."

"Kiss my ass, Sophie. You know that's not true!" Toots flipped her the bird.

Sophie shot her one back.

"Talking about hooking up, have you heard anything from Abby about what's with her and Chris?" Sophie asked Toots.

"No, I have not. And, to answer your next question, No, I am not going to ask her. If there's anything to tell us, one way or the other, she'll do so when she thinks it's time. And don't you dare push her about this. She was feeling bad enough about the situation when Chris was missing. So there, Miss Psychic America."

"It's okay, sweet thing. You're gonna like this stuff." Goebel patted Sophie's hand.

"Sweet thing?" Toots said. "I, for one, would never refer to Sophie as 'sweet thing.' "

"Good, because I don't want to ever hear you calling me that either? Is that clear?"

"Jamie, let's hurry up so we can dose Soph with a pot of caffeine. She's anything but sweet." Toots wanted a real cup of coffee, too, but they'd all promised to try herbal tea first.

"Patience, Toots, patience. Good things come to those who wait. I'm the perfect example," Jamie said.

And she was. She'd turned The Sweetest Things into one of the hottest bakeries in Charleston. People stood in line for hours for a batch of her pralines. Toots was so proud of her. She'd continued to live in the guesthouse with Toots's blessing. She and Bernice were like two peas in a pod. Jamie was the daughter Bernice always wanted, and Bernice filled the void that Jamie's grandmother's passing had left.

"What is this?" Ida wrinkled her nose in distaste. "It's . . . off-color."

"We're not telling you until you try it. That was the deal. Now let me fill your plates." Mavis was in her glory. Healthy living had truly become a way of life for her, which was ironic when you thought about it. She'd created a small dynasty with her line of clothing, Good Mourning—clothes you could wear *after the event.*

"Come on, ladies, let's quit yakking and get to work. I, for one, am hungry," Goebel said.

Mavis forked a slice of the off-color meat onto their plates. All but Goebel hesitated before biting into the strip of unknown meat product. They seemed surprised when they realized they weren't eating flavored rubber.

"This is really good. I'm surprised." Ida reached for another slice.

"It's soy bacon," Jamie said. "Not bad, huh?"

For the next hour, they tried all the delectables Jamie and Mavis plied them with. Though Sophie wasn't too thrilled with the gluten-free blueberry muffins, Ida loved them. Toots was impressed with the arrays of meat that weren't actually meat, but tasted like meat. Bernice liked it all, as did Goebel.

"So, there's something out there for everybody. Do we agree on that?" Jamie asked as she cleared the dishes.

"Yes, we do, but I for one will never give up real coffee. That herbal tea is nice, but I need that extra jolt of caffeine," Sophie said for the umpteenth time.

The phone rang. None of them seemed to care, and let the answering machine pick up. When Toots heard Abby's voice on the answering machine, she hurried over to take the call before she hung up. "Abby, you still there?"

"Mom, thank God you're there. You're never going to believe what just happened."

"Well, from the sound of your voice, I'd say it's exciting."

"That crackpot doctor you wanted to hook Bernice up with has just been arrested for murder!"

"Ohmygod, are you serious? Never mind, of course you're serious. What and who and why?" Toots placed her hand over the phone and repeated what Abby had just relayed to her.

They had told Bernice about the doctor, the séance, and the ghost box. She'd told them all she thought they were full of it, but was glad Dr. Becker had been around. She then accused Toots of trying to have her killed. They'd all laughed at the time, but now it was no laughing matter.

"It's who, what, when, where, why, and how. You'd never make it in the newspaper business, Mom."

"Abby, before you tell me about Dr. Lowery, there's something I've been meaning to tell you. I've wanted to for a very, very long time, but suddenly I find the time is right. You just said I would never make it in the newspaper business, right?"

Abby laughed. "Yes. So?"

Toots looked at Abby's godmothers, Bernice, and Goebel. If Abby rejected her, she would need them, need a shoulder to cry on, someone to tell her she wasn't the most wicked mother alive. They would be there, she knew that. She just hoped she wouldn't need them for that particular reason.

"Remember when your old boss sold the paper and ran off with the money?"

"How could I forget? Of course I remember. He hasn't been found to this day. Actually, I was going to talk to Goebel about him. I'd like to find him and tell him exactly

what I think of him. So, what's that have to do with anything?"

"It was me, Abby." There! After two long years, she'd
finally come clean, told Abby the truth, come out of the
closet.

"What was you, Mom? You're talking in circles."

Toots guessed she was really going to have to spell it out
for Abby. Taking a deep breath and offering up a quick
prayer, Toots lowered her voice, then spoke into the
phone. "It's me Abby. I'm the face behind *The Informer.*"

Silence.

More silence.

"Abby? Are you there?"

Still more silence.

"Say that again, Mom, because I'm sure I didn't hear
you," Abby said slowly.

"I said I'm the face behind *The Informer.* It's me, Abby.
I bought the paper so you could have a job. When I heard
what that traitor did, I had to do something. I knew you
didn't want to go back to work at the *Los Angeles Times,*
and you didn't want to move back to Charleston, so I did
what any decent mother would do." Toots looked at the
group gathered around the table. All of them, even Goebel,
gave her a thumbs-up.

Encouraged, she went on. "I knew if you found out I
bought the paper, you'd quit, and end up with a job you
didn't like. I had to do this, Abby."

"Wow." Abby's voice was barely a whisper.

"Abby, talk to me. Tell me you don't hate me. Tell me
you understand," Toots pleaded with her daughter.

"Mom, it's okay. Truly. I'm just shocked. Hell I'm
floored, but not in a bad way. I can't believe I didn't find
out. All this time, and you never once let on. Do the three
Gs know? Shit, of course they know, what I am thinking.
They know, right?"

"Of course. They've known since day one. It's part of the reason they came with me to California."

"It is?"

"Yes. We thought we might have to work there. I really don't know what I thought except I didn't want you to be unhappy. That was my main motivation. Can you forgive me?"

Tears were rolling down Toots's face. If her relationship with Abby was seriously damaged, she would totally lose it.

"Mom, come on! I'm not three years old! I can't believe you'd go to such lengths. Oh, what am I saying. Of course you would go to whatever length necessary to see that I was happy. Oh, Mom, I'm not angry at all. I'm honored that you would do something so phenomenally, fabulously, off the wall just to make me happy. There isn't another mother in the world who would do something so gigantically crazy. Why should I be angry? I'm humbled and bowled over, but angry? No way."

Toots had been worried for nothing. Abby truly was her father's daughter.

"Abby Simpson, you're the absolute best daughter a mother could ever ask for. Have I told you that lately?"

"Tell me again," Abby said.

"You're the absolute best daughter a mother could ever ask for."

"Thanks, Mom. I know you did it because you love me, truly."

"You've got that right, Abby," Toots said, her eyes filling with tears.

"So you still want to know the who, what, when, where and why?" Abby asked her.

"I'm all ears," Toots said.

"It seems Dr. Lowery and Maximillian Jorgenson's personal physician had something in common. They both had a thing for the same woman, who just happens to be dead. She was found in her apartment by a neighbor last night. Seems the good Dr. Lowery's fingerprints were all over the place."

"Oh my God! Sophie did it again!" Toots said.

"What did I do this time? Please, tell me. I want to know," Sophie asked.

"Abby, can you hold on? I've got to tell the others."

"Sure."

"Dr. Bruce Lowery, our own *DBL,* has just been arrested for murder, Sophie. That's what you did, old girl. You used your God-given talent to identify a killer. Again," Toots said.

Sophie was all smiles. Without waiting for him to make the first move, Sophie wrapped her arms around Goebel. "You want to see what color my toothbrush is?"

Goebel actually blushed. "I thought you'd never ask."

"Wait, not yet. Don't go anywhere, Sophie. Abby, I'm going to put the phone down, but I want you to listen, imagine that you're here, okay?"

"Okay, I'm there," Abby said.

"I think this calls for the old high-school handshake." Toots positioned the phone so Abby wouldn't miss a sound.

Without another word, Toots placed a hand on the table. Sophie laid hers on top, followed by Mavis, then Ida. Then without being asked but knowing it was the right moment, Bernice placed her hand on the top of the pile.

"On the count of three . . . one . . . two . . . three . . . When you're good, you're good!"

Goebel's Quick Strawberry Jam

INGREDIENTS

2 to 3 pounds fresh strawberries, hulled
4½ cups of white sugar
¼ cup of lemon juice

DIRECTIONS

In a wide bowl, crush strawberries in batches until you have 4 cups of mashed berries. In a heavy-bottomed saucepan, mix together the strawberries, sugar, and lemon juice. Stir over low heat until the sugar is dissolved. Increase heat to high and bring the mixture to a full rolling boil. Boil, stirring often, until the mixture reaches 220 degrees F (105 degrees C). Transfer to four hot, sterile jars, leaving ¼ to ½ inch head space, and seal. Process in a water bath. If the jam is going to be eaten right away, don't bother with processing and just refrigerate.

052106201

CHASE BRANCH LIBRARY
17731 W. SEVEN MILE RD.
DETROIT, MI 48235
578-8002